Davey Jones's Locker

The Navy Cadets

C.R. Cummings

Also By
CHRISTOPHER CUMMINGS

The Boy and the Battleship

The Green Idol of Kanaka Creek

Ross River Fever

Train to Kuranda

The Mudskipper Cup

*Davey Jones's Locker

Below Bartle Frere

Airship Over Atherton

Cockatoo

The Cadet Corporal

Stannary Hills

Coasts of Cape York

Kylie and the Kelly Gang

Behind Mt. Baldy

The Cadet Sergeant Major

Cooktown Christmas

Secret in the Clouds

The Word of God

The Cadet Under-Officer

Barbara and the Smiley People

Davey Jones's Locker

The Navy Cadets

C.R. Cummings

DoctorZed
Publishing
www.doctorzed.com

This 2nd edition published 2015 by DoctorZed Publishing

DoctorZed Publishing books may be ordered through booksellers or by contacting:

DoctorZed Publishing
10 Vista Ave, Skye, South Australia 5072
www.doctorzed.com

ISBN: 978-0-9943329-6-7 (sc)
ISBN: 978-0-9872061-2-1 (e)

National Library of Australia Cataloguing-in-Publication entry

Creator: Cummings, C. R., author.
Title: Davey Jones's Locker : the navy cadets/ Christopher Cummings.
Edition: 2nd edition
ISBN: 9780994332967 (paperback)
Series: Cummings, C. R. The Navy Cadets
Subjects: Adventure stories, Australian.
        Navy cadets—Queensland — Fiction.
Dewey Number: A823.3

Cover design © Scott Zarcinas

Printed in Australia
DoctorZed Publishing rev. date: 11/11/2015

Dedication

This book is respectfully dedicated to my late father
Captain Herbert (Bert) William Cummings
Master Mariner
1912- 1993

With particular thanks to LT(ANC) Geoff Brown CO of TS 'Coral Sea', Townsville Australian Navy Cadets who provided me with inspiration and assistance in the preparation of this book.

Thanks also to the very professional and friendly instructors of 'Diving Dreams', Townsville, for their excellent training and encouragement.

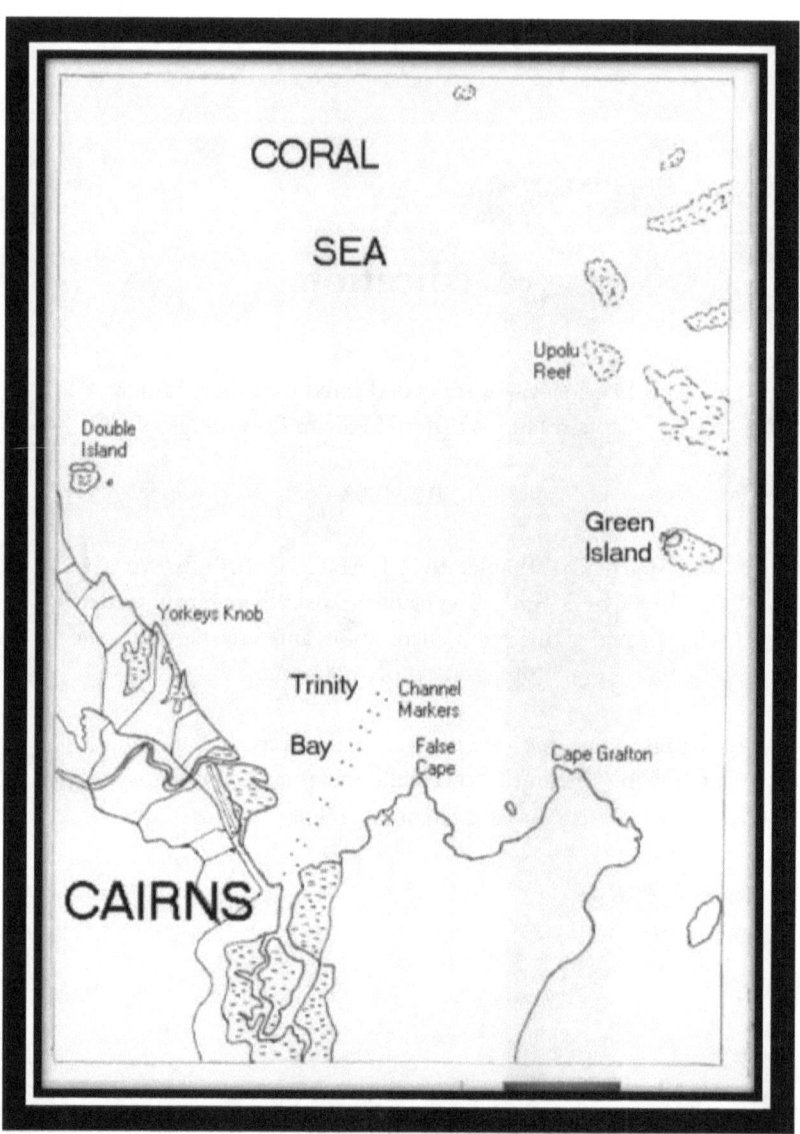

Map 1: The Coral Sea

Chapter 1

Andrew

Andrew strove to master rising panic as he peered through his face mask into the murky green water. The rasping sound of his own breathing coming through the 'second stage' regulator and air pipes of his SCUBA equipment didn't help either. It sounded very loud and seemed to be quite inadequate for what he needed to stay alive. His rational mind told him not to be silly, that he was only a few metres below the surface, but that was little help. It wasn't just the awful feeling of being crushed and trapped that was causing his heart rate to shoot up, but the imagined fears of what might lurk in the water.

The list of what might be lurking was long and cataloguing it was the wrong mental approach for peace of mind. Andrew knew that but had trouble controlling his thoughts. He was well aware that he was swimming in the Coral Sea which was home to all sorts of aquatic 'nasties': sharks, crocodiles, deadly jelly fish, sea snakes, poisonous octopuses, stone fish.....

What made these fears particularly strong was the memory of the shark attack on one of his friends only three weeks earlier. It had happened just after one of the sailing races. Max Pulford, a boy from the same school, had dived overboard and been fooling around in the water when a shark had taken off his leg below the knee. Another friend, Graham Kirk, had rescued him. Andrew had helped carry Max ashore and the sight of the blood soaked bandages wrapped around the stump was an image that made him nauseous to think about and which filled him with fear.

'Stop thinking about it you idiot,' he chided himself, but he found it very hard to resist the urge to keep looking over his shoulder to where the water faded into gloomy green depths. Where Andrew was swimming was only a bit over his head if he stood on the bottom. Actually it was a fairly boring bit of seabed, mostly sand, with the odd rock and hardly any fish. The most interesting thing he had seen was an old rubber car tyre.

In spite of his efforts to push the fear out it kept coming back and Andrew had to battle with himself. 'Stay calm! Breathe normally! Stop worrying,' he told himself. A glance upward showed him the rippling effect of the gentle waves that were lapping into the bay. They were just large enough to cause movement in the water. This was stirring up the fine silt, making the water cloudy and lowering visibility to about ten metres.

Andrew knew that the whole idea of taking the diving course was probably a mistake, one that he had allowed himself to be talked into. He admitted to himself that he had agreed rather than let others think he was scared. But it was not only his own self-discipline that held him under water. There was the even stronger desire not to let Muriel think he was a coward. Muriel was the new love of his life. She was the same age, 14, but went to a different school, so he had not met her until a few weeks earlier when she had joined the Navy Cadets.

Andrew was a navy cadet and very proud of it. He had been a cadet for over a year now and was rated as a Seaman. He had strong hopes of being promoted to Able Seaman, having done the promotion training and exams during the recent June camp. This was strengthened by his ambition to be a naval officer, as both his father and grandfather had been.

It was through navy cadets that Andrew came to be swimming along in Bosuns Bay, just past Giangurra on the eastern side of Trinity Inlet near Cairns. Two of the adult staff, Sub Lt Sheldon and Petty Officer Walker, were both keen SCUBA divers and were qualified dive instructors. A weekend expedition had been organized to build on the basic training lessons carried out in the swimming pool. Bosuns Bay had been chosen because it was the closest coral reef to Cairns, although it wasn't particularly clear water and it was a sad little reef really- more rocks and mud than the pretty coral of the tourist brochures.

But now Andrew was having forcibly brought home to him something he had known but tried to ignore- he was scared of swimming underwater. It was a real shock as he had always considered himself to be brave. 'I should have known,' he told himself, remembering several other experiences, such as rescuing Martin Schipholl from the weeds and lilies of Ross River the previous January. In that incident he had almost been drowned in the murky water. A later experience of searching for a boy who had slipped under while trying to swim the river added to this sense of horror. The boy had drowned and the incident had made Andrew very aware of his own mortality.

The particular dive they were now doing was listed in the manual as 'Open Water Dive Number 1'. This had so far involved a 200 metre open water swim (which Andrew had managed but which left him puffed and feeling weak), cramp removal practice, and a 25 metre tired diver tow. All of those had been on the surface and had made Andrew very conscious of how useful the snorkel was, even in such small waves, and of what a vital piece of equipment the BCD (buoyancy control device) was.

Now the class was under water doing a very gentle swim along the bottom after having completed a controlled descent to a depth of 12 metres. That had not sounded much during the theory lessons in the classroom but the reality of swimming hundreds of metres out from the shore and then sinking down into the murky green water had taken some courage on Andrew's part. The group were swimming at a leisurely pace back towards the shore, their depth decreasing slowly as they followed the gently shelving seabed.

What was really nagging at Andrew's courage was the knowledge that soon he would have to face the challenge of deliberately flooding his face mask and then clearing it under water. Even in the swimming pool in waist deep water he had found that a challenge, causing fluster and near panic. The thought of having to do it on the seabed was enough to raise his anxiety level so that his heart rate and breathing were all much faster than normal. The situation was made worse by him feeling that he was not able to suck in enough air through the regulator. He knew that the instructor had stressed the need to breathe normally and not too deeply. But just knowing that he was under water and dependent on the gadget to keep him alive made Andrew stressed. The thought of swimming up to the surface while he still could was very appealing!

With an effort of will Andrew made himself stay under, all the while glancing anxiously around for a glimpse of the flitting shadow which might warn him that fangs or teeth were about to rip him apart. It was only the closeness of his companions that helped keep the fear to a manageable level- and the thought of what Muriel might think.

He found out what she did think within minutes of surfacing. The group splashed up into the shallows near the beach, pulling down their face masks, or taking them off altogether. As Andrew removed his and flicked water off his face his eyes met Muriel's. She had swum over beside him and now sat in the shallows close to him.

"Oh Andrew, that was fun!" she cried.

Andrew managed a smile and actually did feel glad, though it mostly relief that they had finished the dive. Still marvelling at the wonderful chance that had brought Muriel into his life, he pulled off his swim fins and stood up. Muriel did the same. As she began wading ashore she turned her head and their eyes met. For a fraction longer than normal Andrew held her gaze. A smile was his reward before she looked away and began chattering about how good the dive had been.

'She is beautiful!' Andrew thought, taking in her sparkling hazel eyes, lovely smooth, tanned skin and dark hair. 'I would love her to be my girl-friend. I wonder if I have a chance?' He had never had a 'proper' girlfriend so wasn't quite sure how to go about this. Anxious lest he make a mistake and scare her off he kept the conversation on diving and tried to sound casual.

Up under the trees lining the back of the beach was a tarpaulin. On this lay a row of air bottles and plastic carry boxes. After placing his facemask and fins in one box and his weight belt in another Andrew offered to help Muriel remove her SCUBA equipment. To his relief she smiled and said yes so he stood behind her and took the weight while she undid the straps on her BCD. He then lowered the set to the ground. Muriel thanked him, then turned to him. "I'll help you," she offered. As Andrew's 'dive buddy' was actually Blake, and hers was Shona, he was more than happy. Muriel took the weight and he undid the clips, then turned and grasped the handle on the BCD and lowered the set to the ground. Once again their eyes met. 'I definitely have a chance,' he decided.

While he dismantled the gear, screwed valves closed, expelled air and water from his BCD and tidied up, Andrew found his gaze continually drawn to Muriel. As she peeled off her wet suit he found he just had to look. She was, he noted, quite slim but still nicely shaped. Her bathing costume was a dark green, one-piece lycra which hugged her body in a tantalising way. The material moulded itself to every contour of her body and he was very aware of the outline of her nipples, made erect by the cold water. The sight of the lovely soft swelling of her bosom caused his mouth to go dry with desire.

To his adolescent eyes her breasts were perfection, even though they were only quite small, being a pointy shape rather than the more rounded variety which the only other girl he had any real experience of, Letitia Schipholl, had been wont to display. Not that he had much experience at all, and certainly not with Muriel. Until the previous Friday night he had not even been aware she existed.

Muriel was so attractive that Andrew began to get aroused. That was both enjoyable and potentially embarrassing as he began peeling off is wet suit as he wore only his bathers underneath. It also bothered him as he believed in true love and was vaguely disturbed to find that lust was lurking in his own thoughts. With an effort he concentrated on packing up and then went to dry himself with his towel. But his eyes kept being drawn back to Muriel as though by a magnetic force. Not wanting her to notice this made him keep looking away.

It was the presence of Andrew's big sister Carmen that most inhibited him. She turned from loading her gear into the van and saw him looking. That caused Andrew to blush and look away, hoping she had not really noticed. To add to his discomfiture his friend Arthur Blake, a navy cadet Seaman like himself, came and stood beside him.

Blake raised an eyebrow. "You doing a line for Muriel, or is she doing a line for you?" he asked.

Andrew blushed again. "Neither. She's just friendly," he replied, peeved that his secret admiration had been noticed by others, and angry at himself for lacking the courage to admit the truth.

Blake grinned and winked as he helped Andrew hoist his SCUBA tank into the back of the ute. "Well it looks like it," he commented, adding in a murmur, "Good luck to you. She looks like a real goer."

"Bite your bum! It's not like that," Andrew hissed back defensively, but he blushed fiercely as he said it

Blake laughed and said, "Isn't it?"

"What about Shona then?" Andrew counter-attacked. Blake had confessed to him the day before that the only reason he was taking on the diving course was because of the pretty, black-haired Shona Wellings.

The dart went home and Blake glanced around to where Shona was talking to PO Walker. "Not doing as well as you seem to be," he admitted.

While they talked the boys towelled themselves dry. Then Andrew pulled on an old shirt and pair of shorts. Muriel slipped a loose cotton shift over her bathers then walked past, indicating the nearby house. "Come on, time for lunch," she called.

Sub Lt Sheldon looked up from the gear he was checking. "You sure your grandparents won't mind?" he asked.

Muriel nodded. "Positive! They don't get many visitors over here," she replied. "It is too far from town for causal visits."

The thought of meeting Muriel's parents and grandparents caused Andrew's heart to flutter with anxiety, although they did not know he liked her ('Or do I love her?' he wondered). He followed her out onto the driveway and moved up beside her.

As they walked up the driveway Andrew took in the details of the house. He was already familiar with the outside layout from seeing it for much of the morning. The house was built on a fairly steep hillside above the small bay. It was a big house with a steep concrete retaining wall on the side where the driveway led down past it to the beach. Wide doors led in from the driveway to under the house, suggesting a cellar, or downstairs area.

Leading up from the beach beside the driveway was a solid, concrete-walled boatshed. This was set well above the high-tide mark and two pairs of rusty steel rails led up under the two large wooden doors. These were obviously for launching boats. Equally obvious, from the rust, sand and drift wood piled across the lower end of the tracks, no boats had been launched for a long time. Paint was flaking off the white timber doors and the boatshed had an air of neglect.

A set of concrete steps led up between the side of the boathouse and the driveway to a flat area. This turned out to be a very pleasant garden, built on a terrace about twenty metres square and surrounded by flowering shrubs and trees. The scent of frangipani filled the air, adding a spicy hint of exotic romance. On the far side of the lawn was another concrete retaining wall. A door and several windows were set in the wall, almost obscured by the garden shrubbery.

The group passed across the lawn to a second set of steps, which led up to a covered patio at the rear of the house. The house was a lovely old 'Colonial' bungalow style, with wide verandas all around and many open doors and windows.

Seated around tables on the back patio were four adults. Two were clearly Muriel's grandparents, marked out by their grey hair and age. The other two were middle-aged; a man and a woman. Andrew looked at them curiously, and not without a twinge of apprehension.

'These are Muriel's parents,' Andrew thought, curious to see the family resemblance, and a little disappointed to note that Muriel's mother had quite a stout body. A comment by his dad about looking at the mother before deciding to marry a girl crossed Andrew's mind- not that he had any thoughts of marriage at his age. It was just pure romance that was setting him all a-tingle.

Andrew's gaze shifted to Muriel's grandparents. He was able to stand back and study them while the adults were introduced. Muriel's grandfather was a solid, square faced man with deep brown eyes, set wide apart. His face had a flattish appearance and his hair was grizzled and grey.

"Joshua Murchison," the old man said as he shook Sub Lt Sheldon's hand. He then gestured to Muriel's grandmother. "My wife Violet."

Andrew shifted his attention to her and was surprised to note that she was a tiny little woman with a slim build. Then he was looking at Muriel's father, Basil Murchison. He was obviously his father's son, the same wide eyes and flattish face, which Andrew now noted was also a characteristic of Muriel's face, not that it marred her attractiveness. Muriel's mother was introduced as being Ivy.

Then it was Andrew's turn to meet them and shake hands He found himself tongue tied and could only mumble his name. Thankfully he stepped back to let Blake and Carmen move forward.

The group were expected and were settled into chairs with the Murchisons. Andrew made sure he was seated beside Muriel but did not make any overt displays of friendship or affection. Grandma Murchison and Mrs Murchison went off with Muriel to bring out cold drinks: cordial and fruit juice. Andrew found he was feeling very shy and anxious and could only mutter and point when Muriel's mother asked him what he would like. He sat back and sipped at a fruit punch.

The adults began talking about what they did for a living. Andrew learned that Muriel's father was an accountant, which seemed to look right somehow. While the cadet staff talked to the adults Andrew settled and looked around. He found it very pleasant on the patio. A cool breeze was wafting in around the end of the building. Beyond that was a rocky ridge covered with dry savannah woodland and grass trees. On the other side of the house, beyond the driveway and just visible through the trees, was the roof of another house.

The view from the patio was enough to hold Andrew's attention for several minutes. Just visible below was the beach and the little bay with its rocky headlands. The headlands were grey granite covered with mottled black lichen. The water looked fairly clear and he could clearly see the bottom for some distance out, even to being able to see the dark shadows which denoted the small fringing reef they had been diving on, and outlying rocks.

Beyond that the sea shaded off into green, then to a dark blue, speckled with a shimmering pattern of sunlight on the waves. Far off, at least a dozen kilometres away, was the other side of Trinity Inlet. The city of Cairns, where Andrew and the other cadets lived, was out of sight to his left, hidden by the trees on the next ridge. The dark blue shapes of the coastal mountains north of Cairns were clearly visible, although hazy in the distance. The distinct shapes of Yorkeys Knob, Earl Hill, Buchans Point and Double Island were all easily identified.

To Andrew's right the faint glimmer of a flat, white disc was just visible. It was, he knew, one of the sand cays out on the Great Barrier Reef. He searched his memory to try to sort out which one it was. 'Upolo Cay or Michaelmas Cay,' he thought, and was mildly nettled that he could not remember which it was.

A passing 'Big Cat' ferry on its way out to Green Island, somewhere off to his right but hidden by the hillside, held his attention for some time. Then a motor launch came into view closer in and heading for Cairns.

Sub Lt Sheldon was speaking to Old Mr Murchison. "Are you still working sir?" he asked. Andrew shifted his attention back to the conversation.

Old Mr Murchison shook his head. "No, thank heavens. I'm comfortably retired and can get on with my reading."

"What did you do sir?" Sub Lt Sheldon enquired politely.

"I was a gold miner mostly," Old Mr Murchison replied.

Muriel then cut in. "And a diver. You were a diver for a long time weren't you Grandad?"

Old Mr Murchison gave her a smile but looked mildly annoyed. "Yes, but that was a long time ago."

"When was that sir?" PO Walker asked.

"Oh before the Second World War and during it," Old Mr Murchison replied, "When I was young and fit."

"Were you in that war sir?" Sub Lt Sheldon asked. It was over sixty years since that great event but it still roused Andrew's attention.

Grandfather Murchison made a face but nodded. "Yes, I was in the navy."

Andrew leaned forward. "What ship were you on sir?" he asked. He was particularly interested because his own grandfather had been in the navy during the war.

Old Mr Murchison glanced at him and seemed to scowl momentarily. Andrew feared he had intruded onto a delicate subject but the old man then replied, "On the cruiser HMAS *Hobart* till 1941, then I was promoted to Petty Officer and transferred to the boom defence vessel *Kowrowa*."

Muriel again interrupted. "Grandad was in Sydney when the Japanese midget submarines attacked. He was one of the divers who helped salvage one of the wrecks, weren't you Grandad?"

"Yes," Old Mr Murchison nodded.

Andrew was very interested now. He had read about the Japanese midget submarine attack on Sydney in 1942 and had even seen one of the recovered subs at the War Memorial in Canberra.

Sub Lt Sheldon leaned forward. "That must have been very interesting. I imagine diving was very different in those days from what it is now?"

"Yes, much tougher I reckon," Old Mr Murchison grunted, but he did not elaborate.

Muriel said, "Grandad has lots of photos from then. Would you like to see them? Is that alright Grandad?"

For a second Andrew thought that Old Mr Murchison was going to say no, as he frowned, but then he smiled at Muriel. She hurried off into the house and the conversation went on, Sub Lt Sheldon and PO Walker asking about the submarines, and then about other events in Old Mr Murchison's career. By listening Andrew learned that Old Mr Murchison had spent the last few years of the war doing salvage work, mostly around New Guinea. That interested him as his own grandfather had been involved in similar work.

'I wonder if they knew each other?' he thought. He was about to ask when Muriel returned, carrying a large, black covered photo album. This was placed on the coffee table in front of them and Muriel knelt to turn the pages. Old Mr Murchison took a pair of glasses out of his shirt pocket and put them carefully on, then leaned forward to squint at the pictures. Andrew was fascinated to note the black pages and tiny photos, now yellowing with age.

The group crowded round to look. Andrew found it hard to imagine that the lean, fit young man in the photos was the grey-haired old man seated opposite him but was still intensely interested. There were dozens of photos of ships, some famous, like the cruiser HMAS *Australia*, or the British Battleship HMS *King George* V, many small and unknown to him: launches, boom defence vessels, tugs and similar small work craft.

There were quite a number of photos of Old Mr Murchison in his diving gear. The diving gear was the old-fashioned type with brass helmet, a rubberised canvas suit and huge lead boots, all festooned with lifelines and air hoses. In several photos Old Mr Murchison was seated or standing with the helmet off. In others he was climbing up or down ladders with his helmet on.

Some of the photos had handwritten captions, now faded but just legible. One said: 'Recovering bodies from crashed RAAF Beaufighter- Oro Bay- New Guinea- 1943'.

'That would be horrible!' Andrew thought, but he knew that divers were often called on to carry out such gruesome tasks.

Muriel kept turning the pages. There were a lot of wrecks and small craft on beaches around Bougainville in 1945. Then there was a large studio photo of Old Mr Murchison in his dress whites. Andrew stared at the row of medal ribbons and was impressed.

Muriel pointed to the photo. "Gee, you were handsome Grandad!" she cried.

The old man flushed with pleasure. "What do you mean were? I still am," he replied.

They all laughed at this and Muriel turned to give the old man a hug. Andrew was amazed at the transformation of the craggy, lined face. It softened and his eyes twinkled, then watered. He patted Muriel's back, then suggested she get on with it so they could have lunch.

Muriel turned back to the photo album. Most of the photos were larger now, post-card size, and the dates were after World War 2: 1946, 1947. Old Mr Murchison had stayed in the navy after the war, being a regular naval man, and had retired after 12 years in 1953. Andrew noted that he was a Chief Petty Officer by then and that caused him not to ask about his own grandfather and father as both had been officers. Andrew had never known his own grandfather as he had been lost at sea, but he had seen photos of him, his own family having several similar photo albums.

Thus it was with some surprise that he found himself staring at a photo which he had seen in his own family album. His pulse quickened and he leaned forward, stopping Muriel from turning the page.

"What is it?" Muriel asked.

"This photo," Andrew indicated, pointing to one which showed five men: two white divers and three black Torres Strait Islanders, on the deck of a small sailing ship. The handwritten caption read: 'Lugger PEARL REEF - diving for trochas shell off Cape Grenville- 12 Sep 1956'

"What about it?" Muriel asked.

Andrew leaned forward to check, then nodded. It was definitely the same photo. "That man there," he said, pointing to one of the two white men in diver's suits. "He is my grandfather."

Old Mr Murchison let out a gasp. "What's that? What did you say?" he cried.

Andrew looked up in surprise, afraid he had startled or offended the old man. "We have a copy of this photo at home. This man here is my grandfather."

"Are you sure? What.... what did you say your name was?" Old Mr Murchison asked, gripping Andrew by the wrist and staring hard at him.

"Andrew Collins," Andrew replied, feeling quite frightened by the intensity of the old man's reaction. "My grandfather was Herbert Collins."

Old Mr Murchison peered intently at him. Andrew stared back, his heart beginning to beat with anxiety. To his dismay he noted the old man's eyes widen and his face go pale.

"No! No! It.. it can't be true.. I...." Old Mr Murchison gasped. Then he fainted and slid back into his seat.

Chapter 2

Faded Memories

Andrew stared at Old Mr Murchison's pale, waxy face in dismay, worried that he had caused the old man to have a heart attack. "Is he alright?" he asked.

Muriel moved to hold the old man's head and Carmen helped her keep him in the chair. Grandma Murchison stood up and went pale, making Andrew wonder if she was also going to have some sort of attack. PO Walker then took charge and shoved the boys aside to kneel and feel the old man's pulse.

"I think he has just fainted," he said. "His heart seems to be beating strongly."

That was a relief. Andrew looked around at the faces of Muriel's mother and father and felt an irrational feeling of guilt. This flared into anger when Muriel turned on him.

"Oh Andrew!" she cried. "Look what you've done!"

The accusation was so unexpected and seemed to Andrew to be so unjust that he snapped back, "I didn't do anything! He was just looking at the old photograph."

For a moment he and Muriel stared hard at each other. Andrew was at a loss for words but now did feel guilty. He was saved from the necessity of a reply by Old Mr Murchison uttering a loud groan and opening his eyes. Mrs Murchison and Grandma Murchison both moved in to help sit him up. As Mr Murchison arrived with a glass of water Andrew stepped back, to join Blake and Shona on the edge of the group.

Helped by Mr Murchison and PO Walker Old Mr Murchison was lifted to his feet and assisted to walk into the house through the nearby double doors. Only when the group, including Grandma Murchison and Mrs Murchison, had gone from view did the remaining people speak. An anxious babble broke out as they discussed the old man's collapse.

"He just fainted," Sub Lt Sheldon offered.

Shona frowned. "But why?" she asked.

Carmen answered. "Andrew showed him this photo," she said. She turned to Andrew, even as he experienced another wave of guilt. "Is this really our grandad?" she asked.

Andrew nodded and pointed to the diver on the left in the photo. "I'm sure it is. We have a copy of this in that old photo album that dad has. See, you can make out the name of the lugger on this lifebuoy behind them."

Carmen bent to study the photo. "*Pearl Reef*," she read. She nodded. "I seem to remember dad telling us that grandad was a pearl diver for a while."

The others also moved to study the photo and Andrew found himself looking into Muriel's eyes. She looked upset but also puzzled. He said, "I'm sorry Muriel, I didn't mean to cause any harm. I was just curious."

Muriel shrugged. "If it really is your grandad then I suppose your curiosity was justified."

Mr Murchison and PO Walker came back out, followed a few minutes later by Grandma Murchison and Mrs Murchison.

"He is alright now," Grandma Murchison said. "He is resting. I wanted to phone the ambulance but he assures me that it was just the shock of seeing young Collins here that caused him to have a bad turn."

Andrew felt deeply embarrassed. "I'm sorry Mrs Murchison," he replied.

"That's alright. Not your fault. You weren't to know."

Carmen cut in. "Know what Mrs Murchison?"

Grandma Murchison looked at her, "That Joshua and Bert Collins worked together."

"I'm Carmen Collins Mrs Murchison. Herbert Collins was our grandfather." She gestured to include Andrew.

Andrew was puzzled. "But even if they did work together, why should seeing me cause Mr Murchison to.... to faint?"

"You don't know?" Grandma Murchison asked.

They both shook their heads. Grandma Murchison shook her head sadly, then said, "Because they were both working on the same ship, as partners, when your grandfather died."

Andrew knew that his grandfather had died at sea but had never really been interested enough to enquire into the details. Now he was seized by a desire to know. "How Mrs Murchison? What happened?"

Grandma Murchison settled herself in her chair and took a sip of fruit juice before answering. "It was very sad," she said, staring off over the balcony towards the ocean. For a minute she was silent then she went on. "It was a long time ago- nearly fifty years. Joshua had just retired from the navy when Basil here was born. Joshua teamed up with Bert Collins. They had met during the war. Between them they managed to put up the money to buy a pearl lugger, a little sailing schooner thing, called the 'Pearl Reef'. It wasn't much but they had great hopes."

Grandma Murchison paused and gave a wry smile. "They were going to make their fortune with pearl shell. It was much in demand then, but that was before the days of plastic buttons and cultured pearls of course. But I wasn't very happy as it took a lot of our money and we had four young sons to look after."

"Buttons?" Blake interjected.

"Yes buttons. They used pearl shell to make them for fashionable attire. Divers went down and picked the pearl shells off the seabed and sent it up in baskets. The shells were then cut open and the meat scooped out. The shells were then cleaned and stacked for sale. Of course they always hoped they would find a pearl and make a lot of money."

"Did they?" Carmen asked.

Grandma Murchison gave a dry laugh and shook her head. "No. I think they only found a few tiny pearls. Anyway it all ended when a cyclone sank the lugger. That was in nineteen fifty six. They were wrecked on the beach at Bathurst Bay and were lucky to survive."

"But you said grandad died at sea," Andrew said.

"No, not then," Grandma Murchison replied. "They went and used the insurance money and raised a loan to form a diving and salvage company. They bought two boats. One was a worn out old harbour tug named the *Wallaman Falls*. The other was some sort of little workboat named the *Deeral*. They fitted them for diving and salvage. There should be a picture of the tug somewhere there." She indicated the photo album.

Andrew nodded "Yes, the *Wallaman Falls*. We have several photos of it at home. What happened Mrs Murchison?"

"Blasted boat!" Grandma Murchison said, shaking her head in annoyance. "Here I was with four children, young Basil only three years old, and your father has to throw all our money away in a wild scheme to try to salvage some gold."

"Gold?" Mr Murchison echoed.

"Yes, gold. A coastal steamer named the *Merinda* had struck a rock or a reef or something during a storm and she was supposed to be carrying a load of gold from Cooktown. Josh and Bert worked out where they thought she might be and went sailing off to try to find her."

"When did this ship, the *Merinda*, sink Mrs Murchison?" Andrew asked.

"Only a few days before," Grandma Murchison replied.

Andrew frowned. "So how come they did not know where she was?" he questioned.

"She went down in a storm at night and there were only a couple of survivors, and they had only a rough idea of where the ship sank," Grandma Murchison replied. "I think there were six or seven men in her crew, plus five or six passengers. It was very sad as some of them were young girls on their way to boarding school."

"Did they find the gold Mrs Murchison?" Carmen asked.

Grandma Murchison shook her head. "No. All they got was more bad luck. Their boat struck a reef at night in bad weather and sank. All the others on board were drowned. Grandad only survived by sheer good fortune. He drifted in a lifebuoy for four days before he was washed ashore. He landed on Hayman Island, that's down in the Whitsundays I think, and crawled to the tourist resort."

Shona nodded. "I've been there," she added.

Grandma Murchison went on, "Anyway it was such a cruel blow that Joshua never went back to sea again. I don't think he ever went diving again either."

Muriel looked puzzled. "What did he do instead Gran?" she asked.

"It was terrible hard for a few years," Grandma Murchison replied. "Joshua worked as a storeman, then as a surveyor's offsider. Finally he took a job with a tin mining company for a few years. During that time Joshua became interested in prospecting. He went tin scratching in his spare time, and wandered around looking for garnets and opals and such like. Found some nice ones too. There are some in that brooch of mine you like so much dearie." She looked at Muriel, who nodded happily.

Grandma Murchison went on, "Then Josh went off up Cape York Peninsula with an old crony from the war days, crocodile shooting and fossicking. They found a bit of gold and Josh got the gold bug bad. From then on he would go away for weeks at a time up into the Cape and usually came back with enough gold to pay our bills."

"That must have been hard on you Gran," Muriel said.

"It was dearie, but people thought it normal for husbands to go away for long periods in those days."

"Not my husband," Muriel said firmly.

"Then don't get married," Grandma Murchison replied. "Till death us do part is what you swear to; and 'for better or for worse'; so you choose well and stick by your promises."

"Yes Gran," Muriel replied, looking slightly annoyed at the lecture. Andrew felt sorry for her but agreed with Grandma Murchison- a promise is for ever.

"So when did you come to live here Mrs Murchison?" Carmen asked.

"Oh about twenty years ago- nineteen eighty four it was," Grandma Murchison replied.

"It's a lovely house, and a wonderful view," Carmen added.

"Yes it is," Grandma Murchison replied.

Blake gestured with his hand. "Must have cost a bit," he added, looking around at the spacious patio and quality furniture.

"We were lucky," Grandma Murchison agreed. "Joshua made some investments that returned a good profit so we were comfortably well off. So when the boys had all left home we moved here."

"It's a long way from town," Shona commented, "don't you get bored?"

Grandma Murchison shrilled with laughter. "Heavens no dearie. At our age you don't need the shops and theatres to keep you entertained. Anyway, we have TV and radio."

Muriel nodded. "It's only about half an hours drive to Edmonton," she added.

"It's a nice spot," Andrew agreed.

Mrs Murchison now cut in. "We had better have lunch if you young people want to do any more swimming this afternoon. It is nearly one O'clock."

Sub Lt Sheldon glanced at his watch. "Oh heavens yes!" he agreed.

The party moved to where a long table was loaded with covered plates and bowls. These were uncovered to reveal cold meat, salad, fruit, bread and biscuits. Andrew suddenly felt very hungry and was only too glad to 'tuck in' as he was bid. For the next half hour he sat and ate, happy just to be beside Muriel.

After eating lunch Sub Lt Sheldon said that they were all to lie down for a rest. Muriel objected strongly. "Oh sir! We are fourteen, not four! We aren't kindergarten kids."

"Too bad," Sub Lt Sheldon replied. "You should never swim just after eating, and diving is harder work than you realize. Half an hour's rest will do you good. Besides, PO Walker here certainly needs his beauty sleep."

At that PO Walker snorted indignantly then burst out laughing. He said, "I certainly need my 'kindy', so let's all have a little nap, and no arguing."

Muriel and Blake both grumbled but had to give in. Andrew was glad as it postponed the moment of having to go back under water again. He took the opportunity to go to the toilet and had another big drink, cordial this time: Mango and Orange.

He then helped clear the lunch plates and carry them to the kitchen. Carmen helped and cried with delight at the kitchen, which was large and airy and overlooked the patio and sea from the back windows. "It is certainly a lovely house," she said.

Andrew usually didn't notice such things but had to agree. The walk along the tiled corridor to the toilet was sheer pleasure in his bare feet and the toilet and adjoining bathroom were both spotlessly clean and smelt of pine and lavender.

By then the others had made their way downstairs. Andrew and Carmen thanked Grandma Murchison and followed them. Back down at the beach they made their way over to where the others were spreading towels and blankets in the shade of the paperbarks and cottonwood trees which lined the foreshore. Muriel was already lying down and gave Andrew a smile as he unfolded his towel.

'Will I lie next to her?' he wondered, 'or is that too obvious?' For a moment he pondered this, before walking over to her. 'Faint heart never won fair lady,' he quoted to himself, 'and anyway, the others all know I like her.'

As he spread his towel and lay down he looked around. Carmen was making herself comfortable beside him and the two Instructors lay nearby. "Where are Blake and Shona?" he asked.

Muriel giggled. "They went off around the other side of those rocks."

"Why?" Andrew asked, then blushed at the thought of how silly the question must have sounded.

"What do you think?" Muriel whispered with another giggle. As Andrew stretched out beside her she looked into his eyes and set his heart pounding and thoughts racing. 'Is she trying to give me a message?' he wondered. But he did not dare ask. Instead he lay back and closed his eyes.

He had not wanted to lie down but now that he had he was glad. Tiredness seemed to sweep through him and he deliberately relaxed his muscles and tried not to think about Muriel lying beside him. This proved impossible and she wriggled to try to get comfortable. Once her knee touched his. To Andrew it was like an electric shock and caused his heart rate to shoot up.

'Was that accidental?' he wondered. He risked a glance but saw that her eyes were closed. Not having gained any clue Andrew moved slightly further away and rolled on his side. 'I don't want her to think I am hassling her,' he told himself.

For perhaps ten minutes he lay resting, his mind exploring options to help him speak to Muriel. She then provided it by rolling over and resting her arm on his back. This got his mind racing and he became even more hopeful.

To his surprise she began to tickle his ear with a piece of grass. Not sure what was happening he sat up and turned to look at her. Her face crinkled into a mischievous grin.

"Stop it," he whispered. "I'm trying to rest."

"Don't you want me here?" Muriel whispered back.

"Of course I do, but there are others here," Andrew replied. By 'others' he particularly meant Carmen. Having his big sister present was a real cause of anxiety. 'If I try anything she will frown disapproval or tease, or tell Mum,' he thought.

Carmen made her presence even more noticeable by saying, "Stop whispering you two. I'm trying to sleep."

Muriel giggled aloud and this drew a muttered grumble from PO Walker. She lapsed into silence and snuggled against him, her bare arm just touching his. This caused Andrew to get even more aroused and he was glad he was dressed in the baggy old shorts and shirt and was able to lie so that it wasn't noticeable. He badly wanted to be alone with her and to kiss her but contented himself with taking the daring step of touching her arm with his finger tips.

That caused Muriel to murmur with pleasure and to snuggle even closer. Andrew lay on his back and stared at the leaves moving gently in the breeze. 'I might be in luck,' he thought hopefully. After a while he closed his eyes and gave himself up to the sensual pleasure of feeling Muriel's bare skin and the soft caress of the afternoon sea breeze.

Chapter 3

Underwater

Andrew was more tired than he realized and slipped into a deep sleep. He was roused from this by PO Walker calling out. As he opened 'gummy' eyes Andrew realised that Muriel was snuggled right against him with her head on his pillow. She was so close he could detect her very pleasant scent and see the details of her skin: the pores, the tiny hairs. It made him sigh with longing and sent his hopes up.

'Has she just done that by accident in her sleep?' he wondered as he tried to move without disturbing her. He decided she must have. 'She wouldn't be that forward,' he reasoned. But he wasn't sure. What he was worried about was that the two cadet Instructors could see them. It wasn't a cadet activity so the usual strict rules on 'fraternisation' did not apply, but Andrew did not want to give them the wrong impression. He sat up, moving to one side as he did.

Muriel opened her eyes and blinked sleepily up at him, then stretched. "Oh I needed that," she said, "and I had such a good dream."

Andrew had too, but he did not want to ruin his chances by being too pushy. Instead he stood up and rubbed his eyes. Carmen met his eye and winked and that caused him to blush furiously. 'I hope she didn't see,' he thought. He had no wish to be teased by his sister.

PO Walker stood at the side door of the van while drinking water from a plastic bottle. He turned and called out, "Where are Blake and Shona?"

"Don't know P.O.," Andrew replied. "I think they may have gone for a walk."

"Well go and find them. We are supposed to be diving, not snogging," PO Walker called back.

"Yes P.O.," Andrew replied. He hurried off along the beach to the left.

"Hang on, I'll come with you," Muriel called. She hurried after him.

Andrew wanted her to but didn't want to make that too obvious so he nodded and kept on walking, skirting an outcrop of rocks at a slow stroll.

As Muriel caught him up Andrew spotted Blake and Shona. They were walking along the beach towards them and were holding hands and conversing happily. That was exactly what Andrew wanted to do with Muriel and he experienced a spurt of genuine jealousy. 'Lucky Blake,' he thought, wondering how his friend had managed to make so much progress.

What made it hurt even more was the obvious way the pair were engrossed in each other. Shona's face was alive and her eyes seemed to sparkle. When Blake said something to her she laughed and clung to his arm. 'How do I get Muriel to do that with me?' Andrew wondered.

At that moment Blake saw them. He grinned and Shona waved. "What's happening?" Blake asked.

Andrew pointed behind him and said, "The instructors sent us to get you. It's time for our next dive."

Andrew turned and led the way back around the rocks. As he did Muriel caught his eye and smiled. He was so surprised he stubbed his toe, then tried to pretend it hadn't happened as he didn't want to look a fool. Hiding the tears in his eyes he led the way.

Back at the vehicles the two adults were laying out SCUBA tanks and equipment. Carmen was helping. The teenagers were told to suit up. Now all romantic ideas were driven out of Andrew's mind by anxiety about the test he was about to face. Feeling decidedly scared he hurried to prepare for the dive. Wet suits were tugged on and then air cylinders secured to BCDs. Andrew's anxiety was now a help as it made him concentrate on the equipment and the drills. He turned on his air and checked the pressure, then helped Muriel to hoist on and secure her tank. After sorting out her air hoses he checked that her air was turned on and then made sure the tank was secure, plus all the straps. She then helped him on with his gear and did the same checks. They then both checked their regulators and alternate air sources and did a quick practice of breathing from each other's alternate.

Next they walked down the beach and helped push the safety boat out into knee deep water. Sub Lt Sheldon climbed in. The outboard motor was started and the boat puttered out into the little bay, its bow lifting gently to the small waves. The group, now joined by PO Walker, Blake and Shona, waded into waist deep water carrying their fins and face masks. Here Muriel stood beside Andrew and adjusted the straps on the tanks, then tested the valve before sitting to pull on her flippers.

As she did she whispered, "Shona and Blake must really like each other."

"I think they do," Andrew replied. For a second his eyes met Muriel's and his mind raced. 'I wonder if I have a chance?' he thought.

Feeling puzzled and anxious he turned his attention to the diving. He spat into his face mask and rinsed it, then pulled it on and adjusted the fit. Satisfied, he placed his snorkel in his mouth and slid forward to begin swimming, his mind now dominated by the fears of underwater swimming. The water was only a metre deep at that point so he swam with half his face mask above water and half below. The split picture intrigued him and it was something he enjoyed doing. He liked to check on the sky and on where the safety boat was at the same time as seeing below the surface.

He also kept glancing around to see if there were any triangular fins slicing through the waves towards him. He knew it was most unlikely he would ever spot any shark in time as they mostly swam underwater and he tried to tell himself that shark attacks on divers were very rare. But the rational mind could not completely conquer the fears and he kept glancing around in spite of himself.

Several small, striped fish suddenly flitted into his vision, causing his heart to miss a beat. A moment later they vanished in a flash as Blake came swimming past. His flippers churned up the surface and the silt on the bottom and obscured Andrew's view. He moved aside and found Muriel swimming up alongside on his left. Shona and Carmen were splashing along beyond her.

PO Walker stopped them when the water was too deep to touch bottom. He instructed them to keep swimming but to practice a snorkel/regulator exchange. By this time Andrew's heart was beating fast with anxiety but he knew he had to try or be shamed so he swapped the snorkel for the regulator. Andrew allowed himself a minute or so to get used to breathing through the regulator. As always he felt anxiety tightening his chest and he had the feeling that he was struggling to breathe, that the valve was not giving him enough air, even though he knew it was a demand valve and would give him as much as he needed, and at the pressure of the surrounding water.

To calm himself he deliberately kept his face in the water looking down at the sandy bottom. He also enjoyed the view. But it could drive out that nagging fear that soon he would have to dive and then would come the ordeal of deliberately flooding that face mask!

PO Walker led them out until they reached the safety boat, which had anchored in water about ten metres deep. Here they hung onto a large, orange polystyrene float with handles on it. A blue and white diver's flag fluttered above the float. To Andrew, looking fearfully around, they seemed to be a long way from the shore- right out in deep, spooky, dark green waves.

PO Walker detailed what he wanted them to do: "We will dive and wait on the bottom in a line," he explained. "I will then get you one at a time to do a regulator recovery and clearance. Then you will do a partial mask flood and clear it. When everyone has done that you will do a stationary alternate air source use. Finally we will ascend. All understand? Good. Now, let's have a practice of recovering your regulator on the surface."

They did that. Andrew had no problem and was confident he could do it, but the mask flood began to loom ever larger in his mind. Secretly he wished something would happen to delay or prevent the dive. But nothing did and with a sick feeling of near panic he saw PO Walker give the signal to dive. Reluctantly, but on cue, Andrew lifted the release valve and began letting air out of his BCD. In spite of his fear he even managed to return Carmen's smile before slipping under.

To his annoyance Andrew found he could not seem to go right under. He bobbed about with his face half submerged. Annoyed, he pressed the release valve again and this time went down- too fast. Almost at once he felt the squeeze of pressure and had to quickly blow air into his BCD to stop the descent then pinch his nose and blow to try to equalize the pressure in his ears. This worked and he was able to get his descent under control. Having the anchor line of the raft to cling to helped as well, keeping him from becoming disoriented. Only after he had his breathing and pressure under control did he look around, noting Carmen near the bottom, Muriel sinking steadily below him and Blake and Shona still above him.

Releasing air from his BCD in tiny amounts got Andrew sinking again. The sandy bottom seemed to rise to meet him and he settled on the points of his fins, then tucked them behind him and sank down on his knees beside Muriel. PO Walker swam down in front of them and indicated that they should move sideways to make room for Blake and Shona. Having successfully reached the bottom Andrew felt better. He even looked up and noted with some satisfaction that both Blake and Shona seemed to be hav- ing trouble coming down. In Shona's case it was obviously an equalization thing and Blake appeared to be staying with her. PO Walker rose to help and slowly coaxed Shona down.

Andrew now tried to calm himself even more, telling himself to relax. Despite that his anxiety remained high and he kept glancing around into the green murk and shadows. Even just breathing was a challenge and he had to continually fight down the desire to pull the regulator out of his mouth and swim to the surface.

'I hope they can't see I am scared,' he thought, noting that Shona was looking quite wide-eyed and worried.

Then the testing began. PO Walker moved slowly along the line, kneeling in front of each diver and watching while they carried out the test of skill. Carmen was first in line and Andrew watched her take out her regulator and toss it away from her without any apparent concern. Then she calmly swung her arm back, recovered the regulator and put it back in her mouth. As she vented to clear it Andrew's eyes followed the rising bubbles.

'I can easily reach the surface if I have to,' he told himself, again trying to calm the fluttering nerves while Muriel did the test.

Then it was his turn. As PO Walker signalled Andrew kept telling himself what to do. To his own surprise he did it all quite easily, only being ashamed that PO Walker had to remind him, by signalling, to keep his mouth open and not to hold his breath. Nodding with embarrassment Andrew emitted a gentle flow of bubbles while he recovered the regulator. After that it was easy and he quickly purged the regulator and resumed breathing.

'Phew! One done,' he thought. But the anxiety kept rising because that mask flood was next!

Andrew disliked this exercise very much. He had done it several times in the swimming pool and knew it was important for safety, but here in the ocean it all seemed quite different. While he waited he was unable to stop himself glancing to his left to where the seabed sloped away into deeper water; a murky green and purple that could contain anything. He tried to comfort himself by estimating the visibility at about 15 metres.

'I might just spot a shark before it attacks and be able to fend it off,' he thought. 'Besides, there are six of us. It might go for one of the others.' That reminded him of the sardonic joke that said: swim with a friend, it reduces the chance of shark attack by 50%.

Then the test he dreaded began. With mounting apprehension Andrew watched Carmen partially flood her mask, then blow to clear it. Then it was Muriel's turn and she did it with apparent ease. 'Oh no!' he thought, aware that his heart was racing and that he was gulping breaths much faster than he should. Through a mist of rising apprehension he saw PO Walker give Muriel a congratulatory clap, then move himself sideways to face him. In a state close to panic Andrew saw PO Walker signalling to carry out the partial mask flood.

'I must do it!' he told himself. His rational mind told him he could easily swim to the surface if he had to but that wasn't much help. Knowing that PO Walker was one of his cadet instructors was more helpful. 'I don't want him to think I am a coward,' Andrew told himself. Driven by that thought he took a deep breath and put his hands up to the top of the mask. Even then it took a deliberate act of will power to break the seal and allow water in. He hated it. As the water squirted in he shut his eyes and held his breath. The salt stung his eyes and some water went up his nose, making him splutter and sneeze. On the edge of panic, but trying to appear calm and unruffled, Andrew opened his eyes and saw that the water now half-filled his mask. Breathing as steadily as he could manage he tilted his head back, pressed his fingers to the top of the mask, and blew strongly through his nose.

He was only partly successful in expelling all the water and had to try a second time, leaning back, holding the top of the face mask to press it against his forehead while blowing hard. This time he managed to expel most of it. Through eyes that were watering he saw PO Walker give him a clap and he sighed with relief.

'Now act as though it was all just a boring chore,' he told himself, aware that Muriel would be watching. He turned to her and grinned, then pointed to her pressure gauge and did a check, thus taking both their minds off his efforts. Then he nodded and turned to watch Blake flood his mask. Blake did it without any apparent effort, causing Andrew mild jealousy. Shona on the other hand made a real drama of it, blowing half a dozen times to clear the water out. She appeared to be on the edge of panic but PO Walker calmed her and she managed it at last.

Through all of this Andrew was still trying to get himself under control, blinking and telling himself to calm down. He knew he was alright but the sound of water snuffling in his breathing equipment was no comfort either. As soon as he could Andrew looked around fearfully, to check that no monster of the deep had come sliding up while he could not see. None had but he remained anxious.

The test of using another diver's alternate air source was much less of a problem. Andrew was confident he could swim up. Just in case, he fingered the valve that inflated his BCD, telling himself that, if worst came to worst, he could just inflate and go up. He even toyed with the quick release on his weight belt. However when the test came he did it easily. Apart from getting a couple of signals in the wrong order he was able to exchange his regulator for Muriel's alternate. That put them very close together and he looked, as instructed, straight into her eyes. 'Is she laughing at me?' he wondered. Her eyes certainly seemed to be twinkling.

During all this they had remained kneeling on the bottom, held down by their weight belts. Even so he and Muriel had bumped against each other a lot. Most of the time her knee was touching his and he suspected she was doing it deliberately. However it had no effect in stimulating him. He was too scared for that and really just wanted to get the exercise over and get out of the water.

Thus he was very relieved when PO Walker signalled to surface. They did this in pairs, practising an ascent using their buddy's alternate air source. In this case it was Muriel using his. They rose easily and broke apart at the surface. Andrew quickly inflated his BCD and then lay back with a huge sigh of relief. Only after a few minutes did he remember to look around for sharks.

The dive had lasted nearly half an hour and Andrew found it a real relief when Sub Lt Sheldon indicated they should swim ashore. In the shallows they removed fins and face masks, Andrew being chided for pushing his up onto his forehead.

"That is the sign of a diver in trouble," Sub Lt Sheldon reminded. Blushing at his mistake Andrew hastily pulled the face mask right off.

They then walked up the beach. Andrew found this a real effort, weighed down as he was by weight belt and SCUBA gear. Glances at his companions showed they were all finding it a strain as well, which was some comfort. He was surprised at how tired and weak he felt, as he considered himself to be fit.

Once under the trees they helped each other off with tanks and BCDs and then loaded all the diving equipment into the van and ute. Wet suits were peeled off and they then picked up their clothes and followed Muriel up to the house. This time they went in through the garage door. Inside was not only space to park two cars (a gleaming silver 'Mercedes', and a lovely maroon 'Jaguar'- 'his and hers', Muriel explained), but also for a laundry, workshop and downstairs bathroom and toilet. A passageway led off under the house to other rooms.

"We can all have a shower to wash off the salt," Muriel said.

"What? All together?" quipped Blake.

"Oh poo to you!" Muriel said with a laugh. "You and Shona can if you like."

That got Andrew's imagination racing. He had a vivid flashback to the previous January when he had been joined in the shower by Letitia after he had tried to find the drowned boy. It was the first time in his life he had been alone with a naked girl and it had been a glimpse of heaven which gave him hot memories. For a few seconds he remembered sliding his hands over Letitia's lovely smooth skin, and of fondling her ample breasts while she had held him. They had come so close to having sex that Andrew trembled with emotion every time he thought about it. He was sure that only the interruption by others had stopped them and that troubled him badly. This was because he liked to think he had good self-control. It was also one of his beliefs that sex was a very special and intimate thing that should only be done with a person during a state of mutual love. He did not want to openly admit that he was of the opinion that sex should only be between people who were married but he knew that idea lurked deep in his sense of morality.

Thus it troubled, yet excited him, when he found his thoughts straying to contemplate having a shower with Muriel, of his hands sliding over those lovely breasts, of her....

'Stop it!' he told himself, aware that he was torturing himself, and was worried lest he expose himself to be a weakling and a hypocrite. To push these thoughts out of his mind he stood and talked boats with PO Walker while the others took turns at having a shower.

Carmen got a bit anxious about how long Shona was taking and asked Muriel, "Won't we use up all the water?"

Andrew pictured the relatively dry bush on the surrounding hillside and also wondered.

Muriel shook her head. "No, there is a little dam up the creek," she replied. "We swim in it sometimes. There is plenty of water."

Andrew wasn't sure which creek, as he could not remember seeing one, but he was reassured and quite happily took his turn in the shower. As he stripped off to rinse himself he had more thoughts of Letitia, Muriel and of sex. He examined himself and was satisfied he was quite normal but the thoughts and touch got him stiffening up so he hurried his shower, quickly dried and dressed in dry clothes, then went up to the patio via an internal stair well.

On arrival on the patio Andrew found Carmen talking to Old Mr Murchison. Andrew seated himself and at once inquired of the old man how he was. On being assured he felt fine- 'as fit as a flea'- Andrew said, "I'm sorry for upsetting you sir."

Old Mr Murchison smiled and shook his head. "That's alright boy. You weren't to know. It was a long time ago. Tell me, how old are you?"

"Fourteen sir," Andrew replied.

Old Mr Murchison nodded and pursed his lips, then said, "I'd say you will be the spitting image of your grandad when you are a bit older. Now that I know who you are I can really see the resemblance."

"It must have been a bit of a shock," Andrew replied.

"Yes, a sort of 'ghost from the past' thing," Old Mr Murchison replied. "So tell me about your family. I haven't seen any of them for twenty years at least."

Andrew and Carmen proceeded to describe how their father, Cuthbert Collins, ran a tourist business, while their mother owned a small but very trendy 'boutique'. It was while trying to explain the family history that

Andrew realised just how little he actually did know about his own family background. He resolved to remedy that by talking to his parents as soon as he got home.

However such thoughts were thrust from his mind by the more immediate problem of what to say to Muriel as they said farewell. She and her family were staying over at the house so he would not see her until the following Saturday at cadets. 'Unless I can organise something for Friday night,' he thought.

As they all said goodbyes and made their way down to the lawn Andrew paused and met Muriel's eye. He was sure now he was really in love and he badly wanted to see her again. "Can we meet again?" he asked.

"I'd love to," Muriel replied. "What did you have in mind?"

"Oh....er... maybe the movies on Friday night or something?" Andrew suggested.

Muriel made a face. "Maybe, but only in a group. Mum and dad think I am too young to be going on dates yet."

"With Blake and Shona then?" Andrew replied.

"Yeah, OK. Phone me tomorrow night at home and we will discuss it," Muriel said.

Andrew wanted badly to kiss her but restrained himself. Instead he smiled and then hurried down the steps to the driveway. As the van drove up past the house he saw her waving from the terrace and waved back, his spirits soaring. 'She wants to see me again!' he thought happily. All the way home he sat in a haze of romantic euphoria, day dreaming of wonderful things they might do together. To give him hope were the thoughts that she would be at cadets the following Saturday afternoon, and that there was another dive trip planned for the next Sunday.

Only when he and Carmen were dropped off at home did Andrew remember the old photos and think to ask his mother. She nodded and said there were several old albums around, and to ask his father. Andrew did this at once. His father had just got up from his Sunday afternoon snooze and was a bit grumpy but became interested when Andrew described the photos at Old Mr Murchison's.

Mr Collins led the way downstairs to the storeroom. On the door being opened Andrew's hopes nose-dived at once. The room was a jumble of boxes, bags and assorted junk. Mr Collins snorted with annoyance and gestured in. "Now, there is a job long overdue! Instead of sailing around the bloody bay you might clean up the house."

"Yes Dad," Andrew replied, his hopes sinking even further. "Would you know where the photo albums are?"

"No, but they are in an old brown leather suitcase I think. So, if you really want to find them, get to work, but only after you have done your homework."

"Yes Dad," Andrew added with a sigh. His father insisted he show him his completed homework before school every day and he knew there would be no escape from this. Reluctantly he made his way back upstairs.

Thus it was four hours later, at 9pm that Andrew returned to the store-room. For a while he stood in the doorway, all but overwhelmed by the magnitude of the task. 'This is hopeless!' he thought, but even as he began to turn away, his stubborn streak took over and he stopped. 'There must be a smart way to do this,' he mused.

So he began to systematically clear a path in through the room so that he was able to see what was stacked on either side. The displaced articles were taken out to the workshop area, to be re-stowed later.

An hour later his mother called him from upstairs, "Time for bed Andrew. Give it up and come up for your Cocoa. You've had a long week-end and you don't want to be tired for school."

"Yes Mum," Andrew called back without conviction. He backed out along the 'gully' he had cleared in the junk and reached for the light switch. Then, just as his finger closed on it, he saw the brown leather suitcase.

Chapter 4

Family Album

Andrew seized the brown suitcase and dragged it out of the storeroom. From upstairs his mother called again and he muttered with irritation. His problem was to open the suitcase. It had old snap catches that were stiff and took some working on. At last they flicked open and he was able to lay the suitcase on its base. With some difficulty he prised up the lid. Inside were numerous books, papers and folders.

As he leafed through these, wrinkling his nose in disgust at the musty smell and scuttling of numerous silverfish, Carmen came down the back stairs and called to him, "Come on Andrew. Your cocoa's getting cold- and Mum's getting annoyed."

Feeling frustrated Andrew closed the lid and went grumpily upstairs. He drank his cocoa and cleaned his teeth, then said goodnight to the others and took himself to bed. Here he lay and thought about the events of the day. At the top of his consciousness was Muriel. To his mild annoyance his daydreams about her were tinged with images of sex. Through his mind flitted memories of her in her swimsuit, then of Letitia- in the shower with him, and nude on the beach at Endeavour Island during the family holiday in April. That got him all jealous and aroused.

More memories came to heighten his arousal: Letitia sunbathing nude; Letitia and the Naked Painter having sex on the beach in the moon-light. That one really hurt. Andrew became both very aroused and anx-ious. Worry about Letitia harming herself by such activities, and his own self-knowledge of desire and jealousy all combined to make him quite emotional. The uncomfortable thought that, if he was given the chance, he might succumb to temptation made him feel confused and hypocritical.

It was a mixed-up and unhappy boy that slipped into sleep- a restless sleep disturbed by dreams. The dream that stuck in Andrew's mind when he woke, feeling tired and strained, was about diving. He had swum out with the others to where the safety boat waited and they had gone diving.

Down in the dark water, which was so deep he could not even see the bottom, he lost touch with Carmen and the others. In his anxiety he turned to look at Muriel to check she was there. She was but he was stunned to see her eyes blazing with anger. Suddenly she reached out and snatched off his face mask. Panic had welled up and he had been sure he was drowning and had swum quickly to the surface, ignoring the threat of decompression sickness. But on reaching the surface he was dismayed to find that the safety boat was nowhere to be seen. On looking around he had found that he was much further offshore than he had realized. Nor were any of the others in sight. Then the waves and current had increased and he had found himself being swept out to sea. Dark shadows had begun to flit around under the water but he had been too scared to put his head under to see if they were sharks. Sweating with panic he had woken up.

'Oh I wish I had never said I would go diving!' he thought, shaking his head and feeling drained. How to get out of any further dives without loss of dignity occupied his thoughts as he showered and dressed. He knew there were three more to complete the diving course- and each one of them required fully flooding the face mask under water!

Thus he thought no more about the old photos until he returned home after school that afternoon. Even then he forgot about it until his father came home from work. He came and stood over Andrew's desk, on which was spread his homework.

"You might have put that suitcase back when you finished with it," he said.

"Suitcase?" Andrew echoed foolishly. "Oh yes!"

He hurried down stairs and set to work sorting the contents. Most of the papers in the case appeared to be old accounts, invoices and bills but there were also numerous old letters and postcards. Andrew picked one up that had a hand- tinted photo on the cover. "Brampton Island- Playground in the Sun," he read aloud.

The photo albums were there, two of them. There was also a large brown envelope full of loose photos. They were all 'black and white'. The very first one was a stern view of a schooner or lugger tied up at a wharf. After studying the background Andrew muttered, "Taken in Cairns, but what ship, and when?"

Turning the photo over revealed part of the answer. '*Manahaki* ready for lay-up', read the ink handwriting on the back.

At that moment Carmen and her friend Jennifer Jervis joined them. Jennifer was a trim blonde who went to the same school as Muriel. She was English and her father was a Royal Navy Lieutenant Commander on exchange with the RAN. Andrew was a bit wary of him, so was shy with his daughter, even though he thought her very pretty.

Carmen leaned over to look. "What are they?" she asked.

"Grandad's old photos," Andrew answered, holding up one that showed the tug *Wallaman Falls* running at speed on Trinity Inlet.

He passed her the photo. Soon all three were seated on the concrete floor looking at photo after photo. To Andrew's annoyance many of the photos had no writing on them to say who, where or when. Even so he found them fascinating. So engrossed did the three become that they did not notice the passing of time.

It was Andrew's mother who reminded them. "What are you children looking at?" she asked.

"Old photos of Grandad's, Mum," Andrew answered.

Mrs Collins peered at them and then nodded. "Very interesting. Now, Jennifer, it is nearly six O'clock. You had better get home. And you children need to tidy all this up and then have a wash ready for tea."

This was done. Andrew packed the suitcase away but kept the photo albums and packet of photos. These were taken upstairs. After tea, and after the TV news, he spread them out on the dining room table. Carmen joined him and then both parents. Andrew found a head-and-shoulders photo of a man in an old-fashioned diving suit but without the helmet. The man was standing on the deck of a small sailing vessel and the people in the background looked to be Melanesians. Andrew glanced at the back, found no writing and grimaced, then said, "Who is that Dad?"

His father shrugged. "He looks like my dad, but I'm not sure," he replied.

Andrew was even more irritated by that. "These photos are really interesting but it is frustrating when they don't say who it is or where it is."

"Your Gran might know," his father said.

Andrew hesitated before asking the question that was on his mind. "Dad, can you tell us more about Grandad?" he finally asked.

His father looked uncomfortable. After thinking for a moment he replied, "Well... yes... I can. But I am ashamed to admit I don't know too much. I was only three when he died you see and Mum, your Gran I mean, wasn't too keen to talk about him. Over the years it sort of stayed that way. I was reluctant to ask and you know how it is, the longer you leave something, the harder it gets."

"Do you mind if I try to find out some more about him," Andrew asked, anxious that he not cause further embarrassment.

His father laughed. "No. Go ahead. I don't think there are any skeletons in the family closet."

That image, and the concept of family scandals, caused Andrew to blush. To change the subject he picked up another photo. This showed the ramp of a navy Landing Barge on a beach. Standing on the ramp were two naval officers in white uniforms. Behind them, clustered on the bows and around the nose of a truck parked in the barge's well deck, were a dozen men in a variety of clothes: mostly khaki shorts and shirts with their sleeves rolled up, or with no shirts at all.

"That is your Grandad on the ramp," Andrew's father said. "He was a lieutenant in the navy then. I think it was at one of those amphibious landings in New Guinea during World War Two."

That made Andrew feel very ignorant. He was vaguely aware that there had been fighting on and around New Guinea during the Second World War but he did not know any details. A glance at the back of the photo was no help. 'Unloading trucks,' was all it said.

"No date. No place. No names. How annoying!" he muttered.

They looked through other photos. There was one of a wooden tourist launch. Andrew recognized Castle Hill, the main landmark in Townsville, in the background. 'MV *Malita'* was all that was written on it.

There were others showing several groups of people on a beach or under palms on Brampton Island. "Where is that?" Andrew asked.

"Not sure. One of those tourist resorts in the Whitsundays I think," his father replied.

"Further south, closer to Mackay," his mother put in. "I went there once for a trip. Lovely place."

They sorted the photos into groups. Some were obvious: Herbert Collins in uniform as a naval officer, on various navy ships, standing on the deck of some small ship, standing in a full helmet diving rig on a ladder over the side of a lugger, baby photos, a wedding photo, several ships and barges in unknown harbours. It was simultaneously both fascinating and frustrating.

"Ask Gran," his mother advised.

"I don't want to upset her or make her embarrassed," Andrew answered.

His mother shrugged. "I don't think you will, not too much. It was a long time ago after all. Besides, I think you have a right to know."

Andrew was still reluctant. Seeing this his mother said, "I will arrange it. After school tomorrow. I will invite her over for afternoon tea and explain why. That way she will be able to prepare herself."

So it was arranged. Tuesday afternoon found Andrew, Carmen, their parents and Gran (Mrs Collins Senior), all seated around the dining room table, the tea cups pushed aside and the photos laid out. Andrew was still anxious so he said, "I hope you don't mind Gran. It is just that I.. we.. felt we wanted to know. If it is going to upset you then don't."

Gran smiled at him and shook her head. "Oh, it's alright. I was just a bit annoyed with him- the silly man- going off treasure hunting and then dying so that I had to bring up three kids on my own. Very hard going it was, and there weren't all the Social Security payments in those days. We were very poor and had a lot of trouble making ends meet I can tell you. But I loved him. He was a good man."

They were silent for a moment, waiting while Gran wandered back over the years in her memory. As Andrew watched he saw her face soften and she smiled several times. Then she picked up a baby photo. "This is him, when he was six months old. He was born in 1919, just after the Great War. His dad was a regular naval officer, Lieutenant Commander, Royal Navy, but after the war the British cut the size of their navy a lot and he was one of the ones dismissed. He came out to Australia to try his hand at business."

She picked up a photo that showed a very stern looking man with a large spade-shaped beard. He was wearing an old-style naval officer's full-dress uniform. On the back it was noted 'Lt Cdr Egbert Collins, HMS *Sword*', but no date. Andrew had known that both his great grandad and grandad had been naval officers and seeing the photo made him very proud.

Next Gran picked up a photo of three boys sitting on a rug on the lawn. They wore shorts with a bib and shoulder straps. Gran pointed to each in turn, "Norbert, Egbert and Albert," she said. "There was a sister too. Ah! Here she is- Matilda."

Andrew stared hard at the faces of these relatives of long ago with fasci- nated interest. The word 'ancestors' crossed his mind but he wasn't sure if it was appropriate. Carmen took the photo and began writing the details on the back. Next were photos of various houses, mostly old-style 'Colonial' bungalows or high-set 'Old Queenslanders'. Gran named the places and Carmen carefully wrote the details onto the back of each photo.

"As you can see, they were quite well off," Gran commented, pointing to a photo which showed a garden setting with a large house in the back- ground.

Next she picked up the one of the MV *Malita* at Townsville. Now she did smile. "That is where your grandfather and I met," she explained. "He was on his first job, as a deckhand; and I was on my first job too. I was the girl who served behind the refreshment counter." She smiled again and then added, "I've never been able to see a packet of 'Jaffas' or 'Fantales' since without thinking of him."

Carmen leaned over and hugged her. "Oh Gran! How romantic!" she gushed.

Gran nodded and patted her hand, then picked up one of the photos of Brampton Island. "This is where we met next. He was still a deckhand on a tourist launch but was working on his Mate's Ticket. I had a job as a 'domestic' at the little tourist resort. It was a lovely place, and a wonderful time to be alive. Nineteen thirty seven that was. He was eighteen and I was seventeen."

Once again Carmen sighed and smiled. Andrew quickly worked out the dates and deduced that it was only two years before World War 2 began. The next photo was smudgy little one of a small coastal steamship. There was no name and Gran could not remember it. "It was a sugar lighter," she said. "I can remember that much. It was used to carry bagged sugar from the little ports like Mourilyan and Lucinda to Cairns or Townsville, where it was transferred to big ocean-going vessels. There were none of the bulk sugar terminals in those days. It was all loaded by hand in those bags. Bert was the Mate."

Several very small photos, now faded to a yellowish brown, showed small sailing 'luggers' and groups of black men sorting sea shells. "That was just before the war broke out," Gran said. "The second war I mean. Bert had earned a Coastal Master's Ticket and was captain of a lugger at Thursday Island. I can't remember its name but it would be written somewhere. That is when he began diving."

"Diving?" Andrew queried.

"Yes, the silly man. Looking for pearls. He had one of those horrible canvas diving suits with the huge lead boots and that great big copper helmet. I was so scared when he told me, but he just laughed. I was so sure he would get caught in a giant clam or the air hose would be cut or something but he said it was really interesting and not nearly as dangerous as I imagined. But there were horrible accidents."

"What sort of accidents Gran?" Carmen asked.

"Oh, divers getting dropped by accident too quickly into water that was too deep and getting all squashed up inside their helmets by the water pressure, that sort of thing," Gran replied.

Carmen looked horrified. "Oh Gran! That is ghastly," she said. Andrew could only feel anxious as he tried to imagine what it must have been like in an old-fashioned diving suit.

Gran went on, "I was ever so glad when he got a job as mate on a big coastal steamship."

The next photo was of Bert in naval uniform, as a Sub Lieutenant RANVR and was dated 1940. It was followed by several on a big ship, "A British transport named the *Islander*," Gran explained.

There followed the first one of Bert in a diving suit. "Because he had done some diving the navy sent him on a special diving course. He told me he volunteered for it, the silly man! Then he was sent on a salvage vessel named the *Ringarooma* or something to Darwin. That was in 1942, to help clear the harbour of wrecks after the big Japanese air raids."

Andrew had at least read about that and could nod and appear intelligent. He was even more interested to see a photo of a big ship lying on its side with a low coastline of coconut palms across the water. '*Anshun* at Gili Gili, Milne Bay' read the caption.

"I've heard of Milne Bay," he said. "There was a battle there wasn't there?"

At that Gran shook her head sadly and snorted. "Huh! You young people! You don't know anything. Battle alright! It was the one that saved Australia from the Japs. It was the first big land battle in which the Japanese army was ever defeated, and it was us Aussies who did it."

"And Grandad was there?" Carmen asked.

"No, he arrived just after it. But he was in action helping salvage ships damaged by enemy aircraft further north. He got a decoration for bravery. I've got the medal and citation at home somewhere."

That was news to Andrew and he badly wanted to see those. He asked if he could and Gran nodded, "If I can find them dearie. They've been packed away for a very long time."

Next was a photo taken at Lae in 1944, with landing barges. One was a group photo of some divers and their assistants and on seeing it Andrew pointed and bent closer. "That is the one we saw the other day. That man there is Old Mr Murchison."

At that Gran snorted angrily. "Oh him! Humpf!"

Sensing he was a sensitive subject Andrew did not mention he had just met Old Mr Murchison. Instead he turned the page of the album. This revealed a large wedding photo. "Our wedding day," Gran said, smiling. Andrew's mother beamed and Carmen cried with delight

"Oh Gran! You were a beautiful bride!"

"And so will you be dearie," Gran replied, again patting Carmen's hand lovingly.

"When was that Gran?" Andrew asked.

"Nineteen forty seven, just after Bert returned from the navy," Gran answered.

"You waited ten years!" Carmen cried in dismay.

Gran nodded. "Yes. That's how things were then. We did think of getting married during the war but decided it was not fair to any children we might have, so we waited till it was over."

The next photo was of a small coaster called the M V *Bloomfield*. "Carrying timber from Bloomfield and Daintree down to Johnston's Sawmill at Stratford," Gran explained. "Bert was the skipper. He liked that run but I think he spent too much time in the hotels in Cooktown."

She tapped another photo showing two men in 1950's tropical business clothes: Panama hats, long-sleeved shirts with ties, long trousers, polished leather shoes. "That is Johnston, and the man with him is Bert," she said.

Andrew wasn't interested in the business details but was amused to see his own father's baby photo. He knew his father's full name was Cuthbert and that he was secretly ashamed of it, thinking it was silly sort of name. Like his father before him he was usually called Bert. There were other baby photos. Gran named them and provided dates. "This is your Aunty Bev," she said.

"We know Gran," Carmen said. "We stayed with her and Uncle Mel in January."

"Of course you did dearie. How silly of me to forget. And this one is Evaline. She married an American so I never see her."

Both Andrew and Carmen bent closer to look. Carmen shook her head and said, "She is really beautiful Gran." Andrew could only agree. Gran snorted and said, with a twinkle in her eye, "Your good looks come from your mother's side of the family."

"Oh, they do not!" Andrew's father cried indignantly. "You were the beauty Mum."

At that Gran smiled and patted his arm. She then looked back to the album and turned the next page. The next picture was a pearling lugger. "The *Pearl Reef*," Gran said. "That's when he and Murchison went off trying to make their fortunes. Nearly sent us broke that boat."

Two pictures side by side showed the crew of the lugger and the two divers. To Andrew's surprise the crew of the lugger were all black men-Torres Strait Islanders. 'Francis Sailboat' said a pencilled note on the back.

The next photo was the one Andrew had seen at Old Mr Murchison's. It was also on the *Pearl Reef* but showed all five men at once. As he remembered how Old Mr Murchison had reacted Andrew looked up and met Carmen's eyes, but all he said was, "That is the photo we saw the other day."

An excellent full length photo of Bert in his diver's suit and holding the big brass helmet was next. Gran looked at it and shook her head. "Oh silly man! I don't know how he could do that, going down in that ocean among all those octopusses and giant clams and whatall."

Carmen laughed. "Oh Gran, it's not that bad! We went diving the other day and it was fun."

Andrew didn't agree but remained silent. In his mind he agreed with Gran, particularly about the 'whatall'. 'I wish I hadn't allowed myself to be talked into it!' he thought.

There was then another picture of the tug *Wallaman Falls*, this time executing a sharp turn in Trinity Inlet. Two more photos followed, showing some sort of barge being towed. Another picture was of a large cargo ship apparently stuck on a sandbar. "Their first salvage job," Gran explained. There were a dozen small photos of rope and anchor arrangements for towing or hauling, then one taken on a wharf in Smiths Creek. In the foreground were Bert and another man looking at a large cylindrical object. In the background were two Torres Strait Islanders standing on the deck of a small ship, ready to hoist the object up with a derrick.

That was the last photo. After that there were just blank black pages. Gran bit her lip and looked at them, then closed the album. "That was the last one ever taken. That is him and Murchison about to head off to look for the *Merinda*."

There was silence. Andrew saw that Gran's lower lip was quivering and he regretted asking her to explain the photos. Then a tear trickled down Gran's cheek and Andrew bit his lip. Carmen leaned forward and hugged her.

Chapter 5

Hopes and Fears

That night Andrew had another diving nightmare. This time he dreamt he was down on the bottom of the sea in an old-fashioned diving suit. Something was wrong but he did not know what it was. It cost him an enormous effort to peer through the tiny glass portholes in the big brass helmet but all he could see were gloomy blue shadows. His fears grew, exacerbated by the rasping sound of his own breathing and the hiss of escaping air. Then he realized he could not move his right foot. By making a huge effort he was able to bend his body enough to look down. To his horror he saw that his right boot was firmly gripped by the jaws of a giant clam. In a desperate effort to get free he tugged at the rope to tell the men on the lugger to pull him up. They tried and tried but to no avail. By then Andrew was perspiring freely and on the edge of panic. Then he heard a peculiar hissing and gurgling noise and saw that his rubber air hose had come off and was drifting away. Before he could grab the hose it was out of reach.

'Cover the inlet!' his terrified mind cried, but his groping hands could not seem to find this. Water began to spurt and swirl into the helmet, stinging his eyes. In desperation he tried to block the flow- to no avail. He struggled frantically but the water rose above his mouth and nose, choking him.

Andrew woke up, bathed in sweat and with his blankets wrapped tightly around him. "Oh! Thank God!" he muttered, as he realized it was only a nightmare. For the next hour he lay awake, trying to will himself to think nice thoughts, about Muriel, or even about Letitia- but with limited success. The horror of the deep was upon him.

With it was the nagging fear that he still had those three dives to do, and no reasonable excuse to chicken out. 'How will I ever face them?' he wondered miserably.

Somehow he drifted off into a restless sleep, to wake feeling tired and drained. He took himself off to school, feeling deeply troubled. 'Am I a coward?' he wondered miserably. In an effort to drive all thoughts of diving out of his mind he concentrated on his school work and on being social with his friends.

But despite his efforts he found his mind continually returning to diving. During the lunch break he took himself to the library and did some reading up on the Second World War in the Pacific. It was an eye-opener to him, especially learning about the ferocious naval battles in the Coral Sea and among the Solomon Islands. That huge fleets of warships, even mighty Battleships, had clashed in vicious, close-range night battles off Guadalcanal really stirred his imagination.

The 'Internet' gave more information, then led him straight back to diving. Before he thought about it not being a good idea he had clicked on a site titled 'Sunken Glory of Ironbottom Sound'. It was about divers exploring the wrecks of some of the warships sunk in that infamous strip of water. Seeing the barnacle and coral encrusted wrecks in colour both fascinated and alarmed him.

There was an article about an American transport, the *President Coolidge*, which had struck a mine in 1942 off the entrance to Luganville Harbour, Vanuatu. The wreck was in quite shallow water but just looking at the pictures made Andrew feel uneasy. Some of the photos showed divers right inside the huge ship: looking at the gauges in the engine room, and down in the hold.

'I could never do that,' he thought, deeply aware that there was a dark corner of his being that he did not even want to face. The fear of being trapped underwater lurked right on the surface of his conscious personality. 'At least my diving course has nothing like that,' he mused, his course being a basic 'Open Water' diving course.

Even though he wanted to drive the fears out and his rational mind told him to stop thinking about diving he found himself drawn to such information. It was as though he felt he had to face it, if only to prove to himself that he was not a coward. He also had to admit that the stories held a dreadful fascination.

In the City Library he found an old book titled 'Ordeal by Water', a World War 2 biography by Peter Keeble on Marine Salvage in the Red Sea and Mediterranean. It was full of interesting and grim facts about the dangers of diving back in those days of primitive equipment and limited knowledge. The very idea of crawling around inside a wreck in the dark, groping with his hands to locate dead bodies, repair damage and render booby traps safe was enough to make Andrew shudder. It certainly increased enormously his admiration for his grandfather.

'How did he do it?' he wondered.

Another concern to Andrew was his friend Graham Kirk. Graham was in 9B. The previous year the two had been quite good friends and Graham had joined the Navy Cadets as soon as he turned 13. What made Andrew think of that was hearing Peter Bronsky say to Graham, "Happy Birthday!"

On learning that it was Graham's 14th birthday Andrew asked casually, "Are you having a party this year Graham?"

The response was a shake of the head and a look of such misery that Andrew thought for a moment that Graham was going to burst into tears. As the party the year before had been a big event that got him even more worried. Andrew remembered how Graham had a burning ambition to be a naval officer but had discovered that his eyes were not good enough. Graham had dropped out of Navy Cadets. The shattering of his dreams had sent Graham into a suicidal depression. Andrew had thought he was over that but now, looking at him, he wondered and worried. Unsure how to help, he left him to the company of his new friends: Peter, Stephen and Roger.

The bright spot in Andrew's life was Muriel. She was not allowed to go to the movies ('Too young for dates' her parents insisted) but he was able to talk to her on the telephone every evening. These phone calls got longer and longer until, on Thursday night, his father put his foot down and told him to cut it short and to keep the chats to fifteen minutes 'So other people can use the phone'.

They did not meet until Saturday afternoon. Usually the Navy Cadets met every Friday evening but that week the parade was a half day for sailing. As usual Andrew rode his bike to cadets with Carmen and Blake. All wore their 'short white' uniform but carried backpacks with 'pirate rig' (old clothes) for wearing while sailing. All the way Andrew found his heart all a-flutter with anxiety and anticipation, hoping that Muriel would still like him.

She did. Her genuine smile of welcome and bright, cheerful conversation immediately convinced him of that. Andrew's spirits soared. 'She is so pretty!' he thought. From then on he used all his efforts to be nice to her and to try to impress her. The only dampener was when she asked if he was looking forward to their diving trip the next day.

Even just thinking about it made Andrew's heart turn over with a lurch. 'It will mean flooding my face mask again,' he thought. The dive after that was even more daunting. That would involve completely removing the mask under water, then replacing and clearing it. Just thinking about it made Andrew feel sick in the stomach but he managed to make himself sound calm and enthusiastic.

To help take is mind off diving he concentrated his thoughts on sailing. Immediately after parade and roll call the cadets split into four person boat crews and set to work rigging their 'Corsairs'. These worked best with a crew of three but there were more cadets than boats so the extra crew member was added to each. Andrew's boat was captained by his 'Divisional' leader, Cadet Midshipman Bob Armstrong, a big, burly lad who Andrew really admired. The other members of the crew were Andrew, Muriel and Percy Parsons.

Having just spent two months of sailing almost every second day during the sailing competition with the army cadets (Read 'Mudskipper Cup') Andrew could have rigged the boat blindfolded. Thus theirs was the first boat on the water, followed closely by Carmen's, crewed by an all-girl crew which included Shona, Jennifer and Tina Babcock. As soon as the safety boat was in the water and radios tested sails were hauled taut and the sailing practice commenced.

The afternoon was merely a simple training activity to familiarise recruits and Seamen with steering so for Andrew it was just a pleasant outing. He sat in the centre of the boat and held the jib sheet while Muriel took the tiller. That gave him plenty of time to think and look around. As the sailboat slipped quickly down the Inlet past the main city wharves he was vividly reminded of the photos in the old album. The taste of salt spray and the smell of the sea, mixed with a waft of diesel fumes from a passing launch, instantly brought to his mind the image of the tug *Wallaman Falls*.

'This is where that photo of her turning at speed was taken,' he decided, looking across the Inlet to the line of mountains that sheltered the port on the eastern side. That made him think of diving but he firmly resolved to not think about it and again concentrated on sailing.

In this he was only party successful, mainly because their course led them close along the eastern shore of the harbour. This took them past the beach at Giangurra and then across the end of the headlands at Bosuns Bay. Muriel wanted to go right into the small bay so that she could wave to her grandparents but Midshipman Armstrong vetoed this.

"The tide is on the ebb," he pointed out, "And there are too many rocks for my liking."

"This is where we went SCUBA diving last weekend," Muriel explained, "And that is my Gran's."

That just brought back memories of being scared underwater, and of causing embarrassment to Muriel's Grandparents. 'That photo certainly caused Old Mr Murchison to have a bad turn,' Andrew mused. Once again he tried to change the thoughts in his mind by thinking about Muriel.

At every opportunity, when it would not appear he was doing so, he studied her and hoped. That helped but so did the requirement for some tricky tacking to avoid a shoal of semi-submerged rocks off the next point.

Andrew then refocussed his thoughts on admiring Muriel, noting her clear, tanned skin, firm jaw, bright eyes and short brown hair being whipped around her ears by the wind. 'She is really pretty,' he thought. 'I mustn't upset or annoy her.' He began to consider how he could move their friendship forward.

The voyage took them right out to False Cape. Andrew had been past there before when sailing and stared up with new interest at the old World War 2 coast defence gun positions in the scrub. His reading gave him a new appreciation of their place. 'I must visit them for a closer look,' he thought, his gaze travelling up the long ridge studded with trees and bushes and noting several man-made structures as it did.

Only when they were level with the end of the cape and encountering the larger waves sweeping in from beyond Cape Grafton did they turn back. As they did Muriel pointed out to sea. "I can see Green Island," she cried.

Andrew shielded his eyes and looked. As the sailboat rose on the crest of the next wave he clearly saw the flat, grey-green shape that marked the coral island. It was a sight he had often seen before, but this time it caused his stomach to turn over again.

Muriel made it worse by saying to Cadet Midshipman Armstrong, "We are going diving there tomorrow. It will be great fun, don't you think Andrew?"

Andrew could only nod and grin, then despise himself for being a weakling and a coward. He was ashamed of being scared of going underwater, and also depressed at not having the moral courage to tell the truth. 'Only three more SCUBA dives,' he consoled himself. 'Then I will never have to do it again.' Knowing that the water off Green Island was usually crystal clear and not all that deep helped him to calm his growing anxiety.

His apprehension grew as the afternoon and evening wore on. It even overshadowed the pleasure at being with Muriel and of knowing he would be with her most of the following day. It made him tense and snappy and she twice frowned at him, causing him to silently curse himself for being a weakling and a fool.

That night he had another nightmare. This one began well enough; with him sailing on the deck of a large yacht. Somehow the yacht shrank to a Corsair, then to a tiny, single-sail 'Sabot'. By then the vessel had sailed rapidly out of a harbour past mangroves and into deeper water where the waves became increasingly large. Then the Sabot became a sailboard and Andrew was drenched by spray and cold. By then he was scared and trying to turn back to the shore, which now looked to be a dismayingly long way off. In the same frustrating way the sailboard slipped under and he found himself in the water. As a strong current swept him on out to sea and into larger and larger waves he began to panic. Somehow he found himself under water and looking frantically in all directions for a huge shark that had materialized.

He woke up feeling tired and anxious, a sick feeling in his stomach. As he lay there he considered saying he was sick as an excuse not to go diving but when Carmen came to the door of his bedroom, all cheerful and raring to go, he could not summon the courage to lie. Instead he smiled back and dragged himself out of bed, dreading the day.

By 9:00 am he and Carmen were on a large 'Quickcat' ferry heading out from the Cairns wharves. With them were Sub Lt Sheldon, PO Walker, Muriel, Blake, Shona and Luke Karaku, a Torres Strait Islander. Both Andrew and Carmen had been to Green Island several times before over the years, as had Muriel, but neither Blake nor Shona had been. Andrew tried to take his mind off the coming ordeal by focusing on nautical things like how the big, powered catamaran handled the waves and by talking to Muriel. Even so he became increasingly tense as the flat outline of the island appeared over the horizon, then seemed to slide inexorably closer.

Muriel stood at the front rail laughing and relishing the occasional showers of spray. Her eyes danced with the joy of living and she cried happily, "It's a perfect day!"

It was. It was North Queensland winter at its best- real 'Tourist weather'. The sun shone. The sea sparkled. The wind was just cool enough to make Andrew wish he had a pullover on. The dozens of tourists all wore casual 'tropical' clothes, as did the friends. Among the tourists were many very attractive female 'backpackers'. Some of these wore very skimpy bikinis or short, revealing clothing that got Andrew both interested and then ashamed.

For a while the waves were quite large but Andrew was a good sailor and merely enjoyed them. He was also interested to watch a large bulk carrier making its way north along the 'inshore route' inside the Barrier Reef. By the time it had 'sunk' to hull-down in the distance the launch was nearly at Green Island. As the launch nosed in through an opening in the reef Andrew stared hard at the shallow water on either side. As always he was astounded at how clear the water was. The transition from the deep blue water in the channel to the pale green, almost clear water over the coral sand he found amazing.

At 10:00 the Quickcat edged in to tie up at the long concrete finger pier that jutted out for 500 metres from the island. Green Island itself was just a low, flat sandy cay; covered with trees and buildings. A narrow strip of white sandy beach showed between the trees and the water. The group disembarked with the other passengers and then walked in along the pier. As they did Andrew kept looking over the side at the brown patches of coral that showed clearly on the sandy bottom.

'It looks nice and clear,' he told himself, trying to build up his confidence.

At the end of the jetty they were met by a man who had their equipment. This was being hired for the day and there was a half hour of trying things on for fit. Having endured a pair of fins that did not fit properly during the pool training Andrew made sure he had ones that did. It had been astonishing to him quickly the rubbing had developed into quite sharp agony!

The first swim was to be with a snorkel instead of SCUBA. That suited Andrew. He had been snorkelling before and could cope with that, as long as they stayed in shallow water near the shore. Even so he was so anxious he barely had time to appreciate Muriel's female form as she pulled her wet suit on over her bathers. Then they were walking down the beach, fins in hand. As they waded in beside the end of the pier Andrew could not stop himself from continually looking out towards the encircling dark blue water, his mind trying to suppress thoughts of sharks and other creatures.

'At least it isn't the 'Stinger Season',' he thought. During the period from October to May each year deadly jellyfish sometimes infested the coastal waters, making swimming in the sea a hazardous activity.

The water still felt cold- at least to a person acclimatized to the tropics. Andrew was glad to lower himself in out of the wind. After spitting in his facemask and then rinsing it he adjusted it for a good fit. Then, with an answering smile to Muriel, he slid forward in the water. Side by side they swam out into deeper water. The bottom shelved very gradually so that even a hundred metres from the beach it was still only about 5 metres deep. There was very little marine life and the few outcrops of coral were unimpressive. Andrew saw a few tiny grey fish, then a larger one, then a few tiny blue and black striped ones before finally spotting a really pretty coral sunfish. For a few seconds he admired its bright yellow stripes before the movement of another snorkeller sent it flitting away among the coral rocks.

The proximity of dozens of other snorkellers was both a comfort and a source of irritation to Andrew. Apart from their own group the tourist launches had brought many others, including several large groups of Japanese. Because of his fear of sharks Andrew kept glancing out towards the deeper water and also tried to make sure that other swimmers were between him and the open ocean. He deliberately lingered in the shallower water until Muriel swam on. Then he felt compelled to follow.

The actual snorkelling he enjoyed. To try to prove to himself that he wasn't really scared he deliberately made himself dive down to the bottom and then practice snorting his snorkel clear when he returned to the surface. The only part of that he did not enjoy was the rattling, sucking sound of the water drops which remained in the tube after he had blown most of the water out.

They snorkelled for half an hour, swimming out almost to the end of the pier and then back in again. As they swam slowly back on the other side of the pier Andrew felt his nervousness increase. The next dive was upon him!

Chapter 6

Tested

Even as the group waded into the shallows and then walked up the beach Andrew was tested. Muriel chattered on happily about how enjoyable the snorkelling had been. Beyond her was Shona, who partially unzipped the front of her wet suit. This exposed her cleavage and Andrew had to make himself look away so that he would not stare. The wet suit was squashing Shona's boobs up so that they bulged quite noticeably.

'I don't want Muriel to think I am like that,' he thought. But he found he could not stop himself glancing frequently towards Shona and that got him annoyed at his own weakness.

Setting up their SCUBA equipment helped him take his mind off that. The gear was laid out on a tarpaulin under a tree at the top of the beach. Andrew swung on his weight belt and did it up, then secured his air tank to his BCD and checked the pressure, very aware that the instructors were watching. Next he hoisted Muriel's tank and BCD up and held it while she did up her straps. He then checked they were secure. She did the same for him and they then stood facing each other and tested their air sources.

Carmen then insisted they have some photos taken. She got Andrew to take one of her and then she took one of him. That gave Andrew the idea of getting a photo of Muriel and he suggested Carmen take photos of the others as well. Carmen gave him a knowing look but nodded and asked if anyone else wanted a photo. Both Blake and Shona readily agreed and asked for both individual shots and one of them together. By then Andrew was worrying that Muriel might say no. To his relief she finally said yes and then posed shyly while Carmen took the snap.

As soon as Carmen had put her camera back in her bag Sub Lt Sheldon led them down the beach and into the water. He had a polystyrene float about 1m X 2m with lines attached and a blue and white diver's flag on it. This was towed out by him as the group waded in. Once it was deep enough they sat or crouched and pulled on fins, then spat in face masks and rinsed them.

As Andrew adjusted the fit of his face mask he was aware that he was gulping air from anxiety and he tried to calm himself. 'It is only for a minute,' he told himself, trying to push the face mask test to the back of his mind.

Sub Lt Sheldon explained the sequence of tests and the navigation for the dive. PO Walker set off towing the raft while he did this. The dive was simple enough; first a 50m surface swim using the compass; then a free descent to no more than 9 metres; and lastly the mask flood and clear. After surfacing they would be tested at removing equipment in the water.

"We will have a bit of a swim around under water before we do the test," Sub Lt Sheldon said. "The whole dive will be for about half an hour. OK, snorkels in and start finning!"

There was nothing for it but to do as he said. There was no way Andrew was game enough to admit he was scared! He fitted his snorkel and slid forward beside Muriel. For the next ten minutes he concentrated on swimming along using the underwater compass. The whole group swam out for about 200 metres, this time going well clear of the pier and other groups. By the time they reached the point where the float had been anchored Andrew was both puffed and very anxious. The bottom looked a long way down. Worse still they were now out on the fringe of the reef and the deep water looked to be only another fifty or 100 metres.

To Andrew that dark blue, with its rippling waves and touches of purple and flecks of white, was a terrible place that he did not want to go to. That was where the big fish lived- and the even bigger things with teeth. It was no good the books and instructors telling him that shark attacks on divers were very rare. His rational mind was overridden by his deepest fears and by the memory of Max's bloody stump.

'It's a long way back to the beach,' he observed unhappily. From that far out the island seemed to have shrunk to only half its size.

None of the others seemed to be worried at all and they floated around the raft with smiles on their faces and chatted happily as they bobbed on the small waves. One by one Sub Lt Sheldon took them to do a navigation swim. The others waited. As he floated there, suspended comfortably by his BCD, Andrew had to continually hold mounting fear at bay. His dominant concern was of just letting his legs dangle down below him. To him they were just bait tempting any shark to rush in and grab. Into his mind kept flashing images of Max's leg and ghastly thoughts of the ripping of flesh and blood vessels and the grinding of muscle, gristle and bone as the shark's teeth had torn the lower leg off. The fear was so strong Andrew had to continually fight the urge to curl his legs up, though he frequently did. The other fear was the mask flood test. With every second it got closer and he became more tense.

The navigation was easy. Andrew enjoyed that and was anxious to demonstrate his skill and understanding. It was just the need to swim across several deep gutters in the coral that got him worrying. All the time he was aware of that gloom from the deeper water further out.

Then the real testing began. Once every person had done their navigation Sub Lt Sheldon again briefed them and then signalled to dive. Resisting a panic attack Andrew swapped his snorkel for his regulator, adjusted his facemask and began to let air out of his BCD, all the while watching Muriel as she did the same. Very slowly he sank below the surface of the water and then below the depth which the waves affected. Pressure equalization was no problem and he was able to control his descent.

Looking down he saw a nice area of clear sand between clumps of coral and was able to descend onto it, quite close to where the lead anchor weight of the float lay. Muriel settled beside him and he could see her eyes smiling. He gave her an OK sign and settled to rest on his knees. Above him Shona and Blake were again both having difficulties in descending. Carmen and Luke just settled and joined the line. While they waited Andrew looked around, noting numerous small fish, many of which were brilliantly banded with purple, black and blue.

When Shona and Blake had joined them the two instructors settled, PO Walker behind. Sub Lt Sheldon then swam slowly along, checking that each diver was alright. Despite his fear Andrew gave him a confident OK sign. Sub Lt Sheldon then got them all to do a fin pivot. That involved getting their buoyancy just right so that, when lying face downwards, they would pivot up to 45 degrees on the tips of their fins when they drew in a breath, then sink back to horizontal as they breathed out. Andrew actually enjoyed that but he was still feeling very anxious. He was acutely aware they were 9 metres down- his depth gauge told him that- and he was also still fretting about what might suddenly appear from the gloom.

Just breathing normally became a bit of a test for him. His mouth began to dry out and he was very conscious of the noises of the breathing equipment and of the fact that it was what was stopping him from drowning. Several times he tilted his head back to watch the bubbles he exhaled as they made their way upwards.

'The surface is just up there,' he told himself as he looked at the moving pattern of sunlight and shadow from the waves. He again comforted himself by think he could just swim up there if he had to. But even so, in his anxiety, he trouble breathing. Several times he had to resist the urge to hold his breath. Of more concern was the feeling that he might vomit.

'If I do I must take my regulator out and just float up without trying to breathe in,' he reminded himself. 'And keep on emitting bubbles.'

It was all very stressful! And now the worst part of the test began- the mask flood. This time it was a complete mask flood. His heart hammering with anxiety Andrew watched as Luke flooded his mask and cleared it. He did it quickly and with minimum fuss. So did Carmen, much to Andrew's relief as he wanted her to be good at diving and to enjoy it. Muriel also made it look easy. Then Sub Lt Sheldon moved along in front of Andrew and signalled for him to do the test.

For a few seconds Andrew hesitated. By a deliberate act of will he put his hands up to the top of his mask and went to break the seal. Fear then froze him and his breathing became uneven and he felt the bile rise into his throat, gagging him. 'Stay calm!' he told himself. 'It's only water! You can swim underwater in the pool without any face mask at all. You do that all the time!'

Still he could not bring himself to do it. 'Come on, you coward!' he chided, hotly aware that the others were all watching. 'Muriel is watching. You don't want her to think you are gutless!'

Taking a deep breath he pulled at the top of his face mask. Salt water squirted in and he had to struggle not to panic. With an effort he kept the seal broken until he felt sure the mask was fully flooded. To check he forced his eyes open to look. Yes, the mask was full. Through a blur he could see Sub Lt Sheldon waiting. 'Breathe normally,' he warned himself, very aware he was gasping and almost choking. With an effort of will he slowed his breathing. Then he placed his finger tips onto the top of the mask, tilted his head back and blew through his nose.

It worked, but not completely. Annoyed and scared he blew several more times until he could see properly. Another two snorts left only an irritating residue in the bottom of the mask. Blinking and panting with relief Andrew faced Sub Lt Sheldon, who swam over to him and then shook his hand and clapped. As he had not done that for the others Andrew became anxious lest the others realized he was scared of the mask clearing.

'I did it!' he thought. 'Only once more and it is over.' During the fourth and final Open Water dive they had to completely remove the mask and then replace it. That now loomed as a real test. While Shona and Blake were tested Andrew knelt on the bottom and watched, deliberately calming his breathing. He even remembered to check air pressure with Muriel. As he did he tried to act calm and as though nothing had happened.

He was surprised to note that his remaining air had fallen to only 80 and he signalled that to Sub Lt Sheldon. Most of the others signalled 100, telling Andrew that he was breathing too often and too deeply. Once again he tried to steady himself. It was with genuine relief that he saw the signal to surface. That was a pleasure to do and he allowed himself to float slowly up, keeping with the others in a steady ascent.

Once on the surface Sub Lt Sheldon had each in turn take off their BCD and tank, then sit on it before putting it back on, all while bobbing in the small waves. Andrew had no problems with that. Nor did he encounter difficulty with the test of removing his weight belt (without dropping it - or any of the lead weights) and putting it back on again while out in the water. He was just glad to be up on the surface in God's good air. His main impression, apart from feeling relieved, was the taste of the salt in the seawater.

Then it was back to the beach. Andrew wanted to get away from that deep water as quickly as he could but found he was both tired and puffed. The swim back was something of a test on its own. Wading in the shallows and lugging the gear up the beach was a real effort, which surprised him. 'I'm not as fit as I thought,' he mused.

While they took their gear off Andrew looked happily around, blinking with pleasure in the bright sunshine. Feeling quite elated he sniffed at the sea air and licked salt from his lips. 'I did it!' he told himself. He grinned at the others and went on de-suiting. Fins, face mask and weight belt were placed in a carry box. Then he took his air tank and placed it with the others lying on the tarpaulin. He then helped Muriel and Carmen with theirs. Next he unzipped and tugged off his wet suit. As he did the breeze chilled him and he shivered. The urgent need to go to the toilet distracted him.

So did Shona's bikini top. It had small cups which seemed to barely hold her breasts in. As she bent forward to do things to her diving gear it looked to Andrew that they would fall right out and several times he glimpsed part of her nipples. It got his heart beating faster and he licked his lips with guilty lust, before making himself look away.

By then Andrew was both very thirsty and hungry but Sub Lt Sheldon would not let them go. "First you must work out your Dive Tables," he insisted. This was part of the test so they sat and set to work with pencil and paper on prepared work sheets. For ten minutes Andrew struggled with the mathematics of Residual Nitrogen, Actual Bottom Times and Total Bottom Times. He found reading the double-sided dive tables easy but still felt he did not fully understand. To his satisfaction Sub Lt Sheldon marked his answer correct.

They then had to fill out their dive logs and both Sub Lt Sheldon and PO Walker signed these. Sub Lt Sheldon then said, "You need a break before you do another dive. Next time we are going down to eighteen metres. So, to allow your residual nitrogen to dissipate to a safe level we will have an hour and a half break. Have lunch now and then walk around the island. Be back here by two O'clock."

Andrew shivered. 'Two hours, then one last test,' he told himself. He shivered again and wrapped the towel more tightly around his shoulders. Beside him Muriel wrapped her towel around her waist and sat down with a drink of cordial and a sandwich. Andrew thought she looked very pretty, even with her hair all tousled and damp. Seeing him looking at her caused her to smile back. That got his hopes up. 'I might be able to win her heart,' he thought.

For twenty minutes the group sat and happily ate and drank. Then they began to disperse. Andrew took himself off to find a toilet. On his return he found only Carmen and Muriel. "Where are the others?" he asked.

"Gone sightseeing," Muriel replied.

Andrew nodded, then plucked up the courage to ask, "I'm going to walk around the island. Would you like to come?"

Muriel smiled and said yes, sending his hopes even higher. To try to make out it was nothing special Andrew turned to Carmen, who was lying reading a book, and asked, "You coming Sis?"

Carmen looked at them and shook her head. "No thanks. Make sure you are back on time."

Andrew slipped on a shirt and hat, then waited while Muriel applied some more sun lotion. The smell of that, mingled with the sea smells and aromas from the island all combined to make Andrew feel good. As the pair began walking counter-clockwise around the beach he breathed deeply and looked happily around. To him everything was just about perfect: the sunlight sparkling on the sea, the palm trees waving in the gentle breeze, the gritty feel of the coral sand between his toes. He pretended to study the distant coastal mountains but actually looked at Muriel, admiring her lithe, athletic form with its graceful feminine curves.

In his happiness Andrew felt almost overwhelmed by the sheer 'tropicalness' and beauty of the place. The lush green of the palms and other vegetation was balanced by the bright, white coral sand. This shaded into the clear water, which gave way to pale greens and browns as the water grew deeper or gave way to corals. The line of white surf which rimmed the outer edge of the reef then gave a bright contrast to the darker blue of the deep sea. Even the clouds looked bright and clean, as though they had been washed and hung up to dry.

Andrew and Muriel strolled slowly along, picking up sea shells and commenting on the view. There were a few other people lying on the beach or under the trees to begin with but after a few hundred metres they had the place to themselves. 'Oh! I wish Muriel was my girlfriend,' Andrew thought. 'We might hold hands and have a kiss then.'

After walking another couple of hundred paces they were on the far side of the island. This was the windward side and was much cooler. The view was also quite different. Now the grey-green mountains were off to the right and the view ahead was out over a few hundred metres of shallow coral reef to a line of breakers and then to the deep water of the ocean. The deep water was a dark blue and the waves appeared to be much larger than before. In the far distance Andrew noted the upper works of a big ship that was heading north inside the main reef.

For something to say he pointed to this. Muriel replied, "Where?" and leaned over so that her bare upper arm touched his as she squinted along his pointing arm. The touch seemed to electrify Andrew and his whole body reacted. His heart hammered faster and he gulped air as though he was doing the mask flood test. Turning to her he said, "I think you are a really nice person."

Muriel looked at him and their eyes met. "I think you are too," she answered.

For a moment Andrew was tongue-tied but then he swallowed and stammered, "I.. I.. I'd like to be your friend."

For a few seconds her eyes searched his face. Then she nodded and smiled. "I'd like that too," she answered.

Andrew could not believe his ears. His heart seemed to leap and sing. Without realizing what he was doing he reached out and gently took her hand. She squeezed his and let him keep hold as they resumed walking. Her hand felt warm but slightly gritty from the dry salt and sun oil. Andrew licked his salty lips and sighed softly with relief and happiness. He did not push his luck by trying anything more and was happy just to walk along holding her hand and talking.

They seemed to have a hundred things to tell each other and before they really wanted to be they were around on the sheltered side of the island again. Almost at once Andrew was tested again. As they rounded the gentle curve of the shoreline he saw three people frolicking in the shallow water just off the beach. He took no particular notice until he and Muriel were only about fifty paces away. Only then did he realize that the three were naked. All three came walking up out of the water, laughing and talking quickly in some foreign language.

Seeing the three nudes: two women and a man, immediately sent Andrew into a turmoil of embarrassment and anxiety. One of the women was very buxom. Her large breasts swung and wobbled as she walked and the sight was enough to send Andrew's mouth dry. The man was fit and had an all-over tan and his penis was long and uncircumcised.

'Oh dear! I don't want Muriel to see this,' Andrew thought, not wishing her to be affronted. He was also embarrassed at seeing the naked man's penis waggling as he walked. But what to do? To turn around and walk away would make the incident even more obvious. He decided to act 'cool' and to ignore them. Out of the corner of his eye he glanced at Muriel, trying to judge her reactions. By then the three tourists had walked up the beach in front of them and had picked up towels and begun to dry themselves. They glanced at Muriel and Andrew but then ignored them, apparently unconcerned at being seen nude.

Burning with embarrassment Andrew kept his eyes averted as he and Muriel walked past. Once they were out of earshot he said, "Sorry about that."

Muriel shrugged. "Just some tourists," she replied. "Swedish or Danish I think."

"I didn't want you to be offended," Andrew explained.

"I'm not, so stop worrying," Muriel replied.

That put Andrew into an even bigger turmoil: if Muriel didn't mind that sort of thing would she ever do it with him? Surging fantasies of lust began to battle with his values about decency and how to behave. It left him all mixed up and despising himself for having such weak and lustful thoughts. Memories of nudity on Endeavour Island added to his discomfort, causing him to become very aroused and battling to control it.

There were more little tests like this to come. First they walked past two more nudes, a man and a woman. They were lying face down on towels so, apart from their bare backsides and the bulge of the woman's breasts, there wasn't much to see. Andrew just pretended not to be interested.

Next they passed several sunbathing female tourists who were topless. Some of these lay on their back and one girl was sitting up oiling her skin with sun lotion. She glanced at Andrew and just kept on with rubbing the oil on her left arm. His desire shot up and he could not help noting, and admiring, her nicely tanned, pointy breasts as they trembled to her movements.

To Andrew's surprise Muriel said, "She's got a nice body."

His response was to grunt and pretend he had not looked. However his mind was a riot of speculation. Would Muriel do something like that? 'Do I want her to?' he wondered. To his own disgust he knew he did.

By then the pier had come back into view. The beach from here on was thick with tourists but they were all dressed. Seeing a boat bobbing close to the end of the pier got Andrew's heart rate going again. 'Time for the final test,' he thought, his anxiety level shooting up and driving all thoughts of sex from his mind.

Chapter 7

Final Test?

This time the group swam right out to the edge of the reef. That was a real test for Andrew. As the dark blue water got closer he became more and more scared. When they finally reached the edge of the deep water he was almost on the edge of panic and was having to struggle with himself to hide it from the others. He grabbed the float and clung to it with his legs curled up underneath and panted for breath.

Seeing a floatplane come in to land a few hundred metres away did little to help. That brought to the front of his consciousness vivid flashbacks of the plane crash he had survived the previous year. It had been a day trip to Green Island and a day just like this. The plane had come down in the sea and flipped over. Somehow Andrew had got out, helped by Graham Kirk. They had then pulled the unconscious pilot from the sinking wreck and then saved their crippled friend Ken. Ken had been in a wheelchair. For the next 15 hours they had struggled to stay alive, being borne northwards by the current. The fact that an obvious current was even now tugging at Andrew did nothing to ease his fears because the current was flowing away from Green Island and the fringing reef and out into the deeper water.

'Poor Graham,' Andrew mused. It had been just after he had learned that his eyes were no good and it had taken a lot of persuading by him and Ken to stop him just giving up and letting himself drown. The memories of drifting in big waves many kilometres from land in very deep water had caused almost paralysing fear in Andrew. Only the need to keep the injured pilot afloat had kept him from giving way to sheer terror. The night had been worse; hour after hour of draining fear. To be rescued by the navy patrol boat next morning had been the most wonderful relief.

'If this current takes me away I will have to suffer all that again,' Andrew thought, looking fearfully down current and across the waves of the deep water. The arrival of a small inflatable boat with an outboard motor driven by PO Walker was some comfort, but not much.

Then it was time for the final test. Almost hyperventilating with fear Andrew made himself descend with the others. As he went under he focused on the anchor rope running down from the float. But fear made him keep looking around. He saw that the reef ended in a number of isolated clumps with white sand between. Then the sand sloped steeply downwards into deeper water, the dreaded murky blue that shaded off into a dark wall in which all his fears were hiding.

It was a relief to settle on the sandy bottom with a ring of coral outcrops around. There were gaps several metres wide between the outcrops but they gave some illusion of protection. Andrew now focused on easing his pressure and in attaining negative buoyancy so that he remained kneeling on the sand without effort. A check of his depth gauge told him that Sub Lt Sheldon had spoken correctly- 18 metres. That surprised Andrew as it had not seemed to be any particular effort to sink that deep. He looked up and thought it did not appear to be noticeably further to the surface. Both the float and safety boat were clearly visible.

Carmen settled beside him on his left and then Muriel on his right. Shona and Blake made their way down and then the two instructors. Once all were ready the testing began. The first test was pure fun. They had to make themselves hover. By getting their buoyancy just right they could float gently up and down just by breathing in and out. Andrew found it easy and enjoyed the sensation of hovering. 'Levitating' he called it. It just felt good to do.

It even pushed the fear of the mask removal test out of Andrew's mind for a while. The navigation by compass test also helped. This was easy for Andrew and he found he could even spend some of his thoughts on admiring the brilliantly coloured fish as he finned across the reef with Sub Lt Sheldon beside him. Only the awareness of that dark blue gloominess off to one side affected him. Turning onto the back-bearing and returning the 50 metres to the others was no challenge either.

But then he had to kneel and wait for the others to be tested at navigation. While he did the anxiety began to build up again. Andrew tried to battle with that by looking around at the coral and marine life. He also kept glancing anxiously out into the blue murk for the first flicker of grey that might indicate a shark. In fact he became absorbed watching a shoal of brilliantly coloured fish swimming around the kneeling divers.

Looking at the others and smiling at Muriel also helped, as did concentrating on checking air pressure and depth gauge. Andrew found he could clearly see all the details on the others. With fascinated pleasure he watched Muriel's hair swaying in the current. The sparkle of sunlight reflected through tiny air bubbles which clung to parts of her equipment enchanted him. He watched her breathing and the swirls of ascending bubbles. That got him watching his own and listening to the gush and roar of his own breathing. Consciously he slowed and steadied his breath.

And then it was time. With beating heart Andrew watched as Sub Lt Sheldon indicated that Luke should remove his face mask. Luke did so, making it appear very easy. Then Carmen did the same. At each second Andrew felt more anxious, mainly because he did not want to panic. Then it was his turn. 'Get it over with quickly,' he told himself.

Taking a deep breath he reached up and firmly pulled the mask off, holding it as he had been taught. 'Breathe normally,' he reminded himself. Opening his eyes he blinked and realized he could see reasonably well. He was also reassured that no water had gone up his nose and that he was able to keep breathing with good steady breaths. That reassured him and he knew he could swim without the mask if he had to.

'Ok, mask back on,' he told himself.

It was easy. A few seconds later he was busy blowing air through his nose to clear the water out. That worked too and he was able to blink the salt-water clear and look out at a nodding Sub Lt Sheldon. 'Done it!' Andrew thought with elation.

Then he worried lest Muriel have trouble. Anxiously he turned to watch and was relieved to see that she did it with apparent ease, her face look-ing calm the whole time. For a few seconds their eyes met and Andrew managed an 'OK' sign and a smile. Then, to hide his embarrassment and confusion he looked away, pretending to be interested in the marine life.

To his own surprise he found it both fascinating and beautiful. 'Just like on TV,' he thought, remembering all the nature programs he had seen. This impression was reinforced when Sub Lt Sheldon swam along checking their remaining air, then signalled for them to follow him in pairs. As he led off Andrew began to fin after him, Muriel keeping pace beside him.

To Andrew's dismay Sub Lt Sheldon swam out through one of the gaps in the coral to the outside of the reef. Then he turned left and swam along, keeping just clear of the wall of coral growths. Close below them the sand sloped steeply off into the blue gloom. Just thinking about what might lurk out there got Andrew's anxiety level up again but he also found his atten-tion continually drawn back to the amazing coral formations and incredibly colourful and varied marine life living among it.

After a few minutes Sub Lt Sheldon turned left and led them into a deep 'gully' a few metres wide. This wound its way back into the reef and Andrew relaxed and began to enjoy the swim, his head continually turning to look at things, and to check that the others were following.

Only then did it dawn on him. 'We are just sightseeing,' he thought. 'We have finished our course. I have done it! I have qualified! I won't ever have to take my face mask off underwater again!'

Relief flooded through him and he felt a sense of euphoria and sheer pleasure. For the next few minutes he just swam happily along admiring the beauties of the reef. Then his anxiety ebbed even more when Sub Lt Sheldon led them back through a cluster of coral outcrops to where the anchor line ran up to the float and boat. When he signalled to surface Andrew wanted to shout with joy.

On reaching the surface he did take out his regulator and grin. Muriel grinned back and all the others seemed to be chattering happily. But then Andrew remembered that they were still right on the edge of the reef and of that deep water. He inflated his BCD so that he floated easily and as he rose on each wave he looked towards the island, feeling worried about how small and far away it looked.

It was a relief when they began the swim ashore. To Andrew it seemed to take forever and he was niggled by the others continually stopping to look at things along the way. The group swam on the surface using snorkels as they were butting into the small waves and heading up against the current. That taxed Andrew's fitness as well but he forced himself to keep swimming, not wanting to have Muriel think he was weak.

And now thoughts of Muriel began to dominate. 'How can I ask her for a date?' he wondered. Remembering the earlier problem of her parents thinking she was too young to be going out he considered what options there were. 'A group to the movies or ten pin bowling or something,' he decided. But how to ask her?

That now loomed as an even harder test than taking off the face mask underwater!

After what seemed like a marathon swim the group reached the shallows beside the pier and then stopped to remove fins. By then Andrew felt so tired he was almost staggering but he gritted his teeth and plodded gamely up the beach, the weight of his gear feeling like a crushing load. It took him a real effort to pretend he was fine while he helped Muriel remove her air tank and BCD. Then she did the same for him and he sighed with relief. The weight belt came off next and then everything was dismantled and packed in the boxes.

Last of all the wet suits were peeled off. That got Andrew's mind going again as the girls swimsuits were again revealed. To his eyes Muriel looked just perfect and he bit his lip and began looking for an opportunity to ask her. But what to say? And how to say it? It all seemed very difficult and he became all anxious again.

What he wanted was a chance to get Muriel on her own so that the others might not see his failure. However no such chance seemed to arise. She went off to the toilet with the other girls and after Andrew had done the same and they met up again at the shop it was time to walk back out along the pier to the ferry.

In a concealed fever of anxiety Andrew strolled along beside Muriel, chatting to her and agreeing easily enough that the dive had been great and that it was wonderful to be a qualified diver. It was, but his focus was now on her. In his own mind Andrew had firmly resolved never to go diving again. He was also torn up by the desire to hold her hand again but felt paralysed with anxiety, scared lest she think him too pushy or too possessive. So he walked beside her, his hand tingling from the intensity of his thoughts.

On the ferry things were a bit easier. The group gathered on the upper deck in the shade and Andrew made sure he was seated beside Muriel. As the ferry manoeuvred away from the pier and turned to make its way out through the narrow channel in the reef Andrew's attention was taken up by the ship handling and by looking down into the water. Then he was spurred by a sharp stab of jealousy when he saw Blake put his arm around Shona. She snuggled against him and it was obvious that Blake's arms were firmly up under Shona's bosom.

Andrew so badly wanted to do that with Muriel that his mouth went dry and he felt quite sick in the stomach with worry. 'How do I go about it?' he worried. He could not even bring himself to touch Muriel. When her knee accidentally touched his he almost jumped and hastily moved his own leg away, his heart rate shooting up. Then he wondered if that was not the tactic to try. 'If she moves away then I will know she doesn't want that and I can stop,' he reasoned.

But easier thought about than put into action!

Somehow it happened anyway. A larger than usual wave caused her to lean firmly against him. To keep her balance she put her hand on his thigh and he grabbed her upper arm.

"Sorry," she said, her eyes meeting his.

"My pleasure," he murmured back.

To his surprise she leaned against him and said, "You are really sweet!"

Before he thought about it Andrew returned her smile and took her hand in his. Even as he wondered if he had made a mistake she smiled and snuggled against him. To Andrew it was as though the sun had come up again. His heart beat faster, the sun shone brighter, the water droplets from the sea spray sparkled, the foam of the waves and wake looked unbelievably white.

For the next hour Andrew was in heaven. The only thing bothering him was the reaction of his body. Muriel's touch caused him to become very aroused and he found himself torn by the pleasure of the sensation and the moral concern that it was lust, not the true love he wanted it to be. There were also the amused looks by his sister to niggle at him. It was obvious that Carmen did not really object but Andrew knew it was giving her ammunition for the next brother-versus-sister battle that might erupt at home.

Carmen reinforced this by taking out her camera and snapping another photo. That secretly pleased Andrew and he determined to obtain a copy at the first opportunity.

All too soon the voyage ended. Andrew watched the familiar landmarks come into view and then slide astern: Cape Grafton, False Cape, Koombal, Bosuns Bay, Giangurra, then Bessie Point. When the dark smudge of the mangroves lining the eastern side of the Inlet slid into view he knew that the end was close. As the ferry slowed and turned to berth Muriel sat up and disengaged her hand. She did this with such obvious reluctance that Andrew's hopes went even higher.

"When can I see you again?" he asked. He knew she lived out at White Rock and that was a long way for him to ride his bike after school.

"I don't know. What did you have in mind?" Muriel asked.

"I was hoping we could go out, like to the movies or something. I know your parents think you are too young but I thought if we could organize it as a group thing they might let you," he suggested.

"That's a good idea," Muriel agreed. "When?"

"What about one night during the week?"

Muriel shook her head. "No chance. It will have to be next weekend."

That was a disappointment but what Andrew had expected. "Ok. Will you ask your parents?"

"Yes. But first I will get a few friends to agree to make up the group," Muriel replied.

"Can I call you on the phone?"

Muriel made a face. "Y..e.s, but I think you had better let me phone you. That way it won't be so obvious."

Andrew had to leave it at that, all hanging up in the air and nothing tied down. Regretfully but bubbling with hopes he stood up and followed Muriel down the gangway, his bag held across his front to hide his aroused condition.

The sight of his mother waiting to pick them up quickly cured that physical state but it returned several times during the evening. At home Andrew had to sit and tell his parents all about the diving. To his own private shame he made himself sound enthusiastic but every time he thought of that deep water or of having to take the mask off he shuddered and vowed he would avoid such experiences in future.

Carmen then put him on the spot by saying to their parents, "We can do the Advanced Open Water Diving Course now. That will be really good. "

"What does that involve?" their father asked.

"Oh, deep diving, down to thirty metres; and a study of marine life; and a night dive."

"Night dive!" their mother cried. "Oh, I don't know if I like that idea."

Andrew certainly didn't. The very idea seemed to him to be like a nightmare and he doubted if he had the courage to face such an event. All he could do was give a sickly grin and hope it never happened. The fact that both parents seemed less than enthusiastic about the idea gave him hope.

Carmen kept on though. "Oh Mum! It isn't that bad. They do it all the time. And there is a wreck dive too, if we want it."

"Wreck? What wreck? That sounds dangerous," their father said.

"I think it is a bit risky," Carmen agreed. "But that is what the training is for. I think they dive on a wreck somewhere down near Townsville."

"Townsville!" their mother said. "This all sounds like it is getting a bit too expensive. I think you might have to wait till you are older and have saved a bit more money."

That was music to Andrew's ears. He had no desire to crawl around inside sunken ships with all the risk of getting trapped or attacked by some horrible thing like a moray eel. He took himself off to his room to lie down and think about Muriel.

"How can I win with her?" he asked himself as he lay on his bed. Romantic images of actually kissing and of her wanting to be with him floated in his consciousness. It mingled with memories of the walk around the island and the ferry trip home and it was a very happy and hopeful boy who dropped off to sleep that night.

Chapter 8

Romantic Hopes

Monday meant school. It also introduced a new interest. This happened during History. Andrew's History teacher, Mr Conkey, handed each student an assignment sheet.

"You must select a topic yourself to research," Mr Conkey said. "As it says on the form the subject must be about some aspect of North Queensland history."

Andrew liked Mr Conkey, who was a chubby and cheerful man in his late forties. He was also a captain in the army cadets and OC of the school's army cadet unit. That increased Andrew's respect and also sometimes led to a bit of good-natured chaffing between teacher and student. After reading through the sheet and noting the main requirements: minimum of 1000 words, must have maps, illustrations optional, must use more than one reference and include a Reference to Sources, he pondered what topic to choose. The class had just studied the Sea Explorers: The Dutchmen, Cook, Flinders and so on, and were now starting on European Settlement: First Fleet, convicts, etc.

'I could choose an explorer,' he thought, 'or maybe do something on the goldrushes. I wonder if I can do something about ships, perhaps the navy in the Second World War?'

He put this question to Mr Conkey. The teacher thought for a moment, then shook his head. "We study the World Wars in Year Ten. I think you should save that till then."

Andrew felt disappointed but nodded. That still left plenty of subjects. Luke Karaku, the only Melanesian in the class, helped by asking if he could write about Pearl Divers.

Mr Conkey nodded. "That would be a very good topic. There was a lot of that in the early days and it led to some fascinating stories."

Graham Kirk then put his hand up. "Sir, could I write about the history of coastal shipping, or about one of the ports?"

As Graham's father actually owned and operated two coasters, a ship and a landing barge, that was logical. Mr Conkey agreed. "You could certainly do that. Remember there used to be a very important coastal trade, even to the south. That was before the railways were built. They even had big passenger liners that serviced all the ports up the coast from Sydney and Brisbane."

"Didn't some of them get sunk in cyclones sir?" Graham asked.

Mr Conkey nodded. "Yes they did. The biggest was an eight thousand ton steamer named the S S *Yongala*. It was sunk near Townsville back in Nineteen Eleven or thereabouts. And there was a smaller one named the *Merinda* that went down somewhere off Bowen in the Nineteen Fifties. There have been hundreds of shipwrecks off the east coast of Queensland."

'*Merinda*!' Andrew thought in surprise. Hearing the name gave him quite a jolt. 'That is the ship Grandad was looking for when he was drowned.' He thought about it for a few more minutes and as he did the idea grew until he knew he just had to find out as much as he could. He put his hand up.

"Sir, could I write my assignment on the *Merinda*?"

"Yes. But you might find it a bit hard to get information," Mr Conkey replied. "You might find it easier to try another topic."

Andrew shook his head. "I would like to try sir."

"Alright. I will see what I can do to help you get some information," Mr Conkey replied.

Further discussion was ended by the bell, sending them on to their next lesson. The topic did not come up again till the next day when Mr Conkey took the whole class to the library to start researching. Once there Mr Conkey recommended that Andrew read a book by Hector Holthouse titled 'Cyclone'. There was a copy on the shelves so Andrew booked it out. While looking for it he also discovered another called, 'Ships in the Coral', by the same author. There several other books which touched on the sea trade of the region but between them all they only provided a single sentence: 'The coastal steamer *Merinda*, carrying a crew of 14 and ten passengers, vanished somewhere off Bowen on the night of 24 January 1958 during a cyclone.'

That was frustrating and piqued Andrew's curiosity even more. 'There must be more facts available than that,' he thought. But where, and who to ask?

The first person he asked was Mr Conkey, who suggested the internet. Andrew tried that but was disappointed. If there was information no one had yet transferred it to the computer in a usable form. He went back and told Mr Conkey of his lack of success. Mr Conkey suggested writing to the Oxley Library in Brisbane, and also to the State Archives to see if there was a government report. "There is always an official enquiry after any maritime disaster or accident," he explained. "Or maybe you should rethink which topic to do your assignment on?" he added.

That just stiffened Andrew's resolve. Now he was determined to find out more. 'I will ask Gran and see if she can remember anything else,' he decided.

After school Andrew pedalled home and had afternoon tea. He then telephoned his Gran to see if she was home. She was, and was more than happy for him to visit. As Andrew was getting his bike from under the house Carmen came home.

"Where are you going Little Brother?" she asked.

"To Gran's. I want to ask her if she knows any more about the wreck of the *Merinda*," Andrew replied. He explained his History assignment.

"Do you mind if I come?" Carmen asked.

"No. Let's go. I want to be home before Mum and Dad," Andrew replied.

"Suits me. I have to work tonight," Carmen replied. She had just started part-time work at a supermarket as a 'checkout chick'. This gave her nine or ten hours work each week on three evenings.

So brother and sister pedalled over to Till Street. Gran had afternoon tea set out ready. Seeing the fresh baked pumpkin scones and cream biscuits made Andrew feel quite guilty. 'Gran doesn't mind having visitors,' he thought. 'She is lonely and looks forward to them.' To ease his guilty feelings he resolved to try to visit more often.

After two cups of tea and several scones Gran looked at him and said, "Well? What do you want to know this time?"

"Aw, Gran! I didn't mean to make it sound like that," Andrew said. "I just wanted to know more about Grandad and the ship he went looking for. But if it bothers you then don't worry about it."

"Of course it bothers me!" Gran replied. "It is the sort of thing you never forget, but life goes on, and at my age you've seen it all, so it doesn't matter if I get a bit weepy. It is good that you want to know about your Grandad."

"Thanks Gran," Andrew answered, blushing with embarrassment. He finished another scone, then said, "I have to write a History assignment and I chose to do it on the wreck of the *Merinda*. But I can't find any books on it and hoped you might have some information."

Gran snorted. "Blasted ships! Well, I think there are a few old papers here somewhere but what they are about I am not sure. But if you want to talk to someone who knows a lot more than me then go and have a chat to old Michael McGackey. He worked on her as a cook I think; and he was a cook on a couple of ships that Bert was on as well."

"Where do I find him Gran?" Andrew asked.

"Oh, the 'Tropic Seas' Retirement Home I think. I will ask," Gran answered. "I will just look for those papers. You children eat some more scones while I do."

Gran left them for about twenty minutes, then returned with a small pile of papers. One was a faded newspaper. "This talks about the wreck," she says. "It has an interview with one of the survivors."

"Survivors?" Andrew asked in surprise. "I didn't think there were any."

Gran shook her head. "No, three or four of the crew survived. That was how Bert knew where to go looking."

Andrew and Carmen bent over the musty, yellowed page and read. It had a smudgy and blurred photo of the *Merinda*. That gave Andrew his first clear idea of what the ship looked like: superstructure taking up the aft half of the hull with cargo hold and focsle forward. A single black funnel, two lifeboats, two masts and an open bridge above the wheelhouse. 'Built at Denny's on the Clyde in 1912,' read part of the explanation.

Three men had survived: a deckhand, a stoker and a passenger named Hoolihan. The deckhand, Frederick Longton, said that the ship struck a reef during a storm at night and had its bottom ripped out. 'She sank like a stone,' he said. 'We only survived because we were on deck and were able to grab a raft as it floated past.'

There was a photo of the raft. To Andrew it looked like one of the 'Carly Float' type he had seen in photos of World War 2 ships- a float with ropes looped around the outside and a netting bottom. 'The float on the beach at Bowen, held by Mr Rowbotham', read the caption.

The survivors had drifted for four days in mountainous seas before washing ashore near Abbot Point, a few kilometres north of Bowen. When asked where the ship had gone down all the deckhand could say was: 'Next morning I got a glimpse of Holbourne Island a few miles to the north.' When pressed to confirm this he had commented that he was not sure. He had not been on duty for nearly 8 hours. 'In fact, I was just going up to take over on the wheel at 4am,' he said. 'That was why I was awake and dressed. If I'd been asleep I would have gone down with the ship she sank so fast,' he added.

The deckhand added that when he had been on duty as the quarter-master at the wheel the previous afternoon he had noted the pencil line on the chart indicating the ship's planned course ran quite close to Holbourne Island. 'That was normal,' he explained. 'The main shipping route goes near it, keeping well clear of Nares Rock (The rock on which the SS *Gothenberg* was wrecked in 1875 with the loss of 102 lives) and I have seen Holbourne Island a dozen times on previous voyages.'

On reading about the wreck of the *Gothenberg* Andrew was amazed. "There seem to have been a lot of wrecks in that area," he commented.

Gran nodded. "I think there have been. A dangerous piece of water. Now, here is the one about the loss of the *Deeral*." She handed him a newspaper cutting.

One glance made Andrew's chest tighten with emotion and anxiety. There were two blurry photos but he had already seen the original of one. It showed two white men and two black men standing on the deck of a small ship in Cairns Inlet. The other was of a small motor vessel.

THREE LOCAL MEN PERISH AT SEA read the headline. TREASURE HUNT TURNS INTO TRAGEDY was the sub-heading. Andrew met Carmen's eye and bit his lip. The photo was the one in the album at home and showed Bert Collins and Joshua Murchison. The two black men were not named in the caption. However they were named in the first paragraph.

'The sea has claimed the lives of three local men who had spent their working lives on it. Last Wednesday the 56 foot motor launch *Deeral* struck a reef off the Whitsunday Islands in bad weather and sank. Mr Joshua Murchison, one of the partners who owned the boat, was the only survivor. The other partner, local salvage expert and diver Mr Bert Collins, went down with the vessel. Also lost at sea in this second maritime tragedy in two weeks were two crewmen, Francis Sailboat and Solomon Tapau.'

Andrew glanced at the photos again, then read on. 'The men set off in an attempt to locate the wreck of the SS *Merinda* which sank off Bowen two weeks ago. It was rumoured that they were hoping to find the wreck and salvage a large quantity of gold that was part of the *Merinda's* cargo.'

'According to Mr Murchison the *Deeral* sailed from Cairns on 3rd February. She was off Townsville by sundown the next day. On the afternoon of the third day they reached Holbourne Island and began a systematic search. For the next week the men searched every reef in the vicinity, including the inner edge of the Great Barrier Reef. During the afternoon of 12th February the weather deteriorated. The *Deeral* was turned for Bowen but the wind shifted and the waves became so high that they had no choice but to run before the weather.'

'By nightfall the weather was so bad they had to heave-to and turn into it. For the next two days they could do no more than ride the storm. By the second night they were not sure of their position but Mr Murchison believed they were well to the east of Holbourne Island, having been on that heading for many hours. While attempting to gain shelter in the lee of a coral reef during the night *Deeral* struck an isolated outcrop of coral. The unfortunate little vessel was holed and rolled over almost at once.'

Andrew paused for a few seconds, his mind filled with horrifying images of men struggling in darkness and foam, of being pounded on sharp coral. He read on:

'Mr Murchison was flung into the raging sea and says he almost immediately lost sight of the boat, which he thinks was still afloat but upside down and being driven by the waves on into deeper water. He says that something stuck his face and he grabbed at it, finding it was a lifebuoy. But for that providential stroke of luck Mr Murchison says he felt sure he would also have perished.'

'For the next three days Mr Murchison clung to the lifebuoy until, almost crazed by thirst, he was washed ashore on the seaward side of Hayman Island. Throughout this ordeal he says he was several times circled by sharks and gave himself up for lost. "Prayer saved me," he said.'

On reading that Andrew had a series of vivid flashbacks to his own ordeal the previous year and shuddered. 'Poor bugger. I know just how he felt,' he thought. He again bent to study the paper.

The second photo now held his attention. It was a blurry image of the *Deeral.* The text told him it was a steel work boat with a diesel engine. The photo showed that it had a single mast with a derrick and a small wheelhouse and cabin aft.

"Can we borrow these Gran? I will photocopy them and bring them back," Andrew asked.

"Of course dearie. They've just sat in a box all these years," Gran replied.

Carmen now said, "We had better go. I have to get to work by six."

Gran held up another box. "Just wait a few minutes. I also found these." She lifted out a small cloth bundle, from which came the chink of metal. The bundle was gently laid on the table and carefully unwrapped. When he saw what the cloth contained Andrew gasped in delight.

"Grandad's medals!"

Gran nodded. Both children bent to study the medals with great interest. Andrew marvelled at how shiny they still were after all the years. Carmen commented on how pretty the ribbons were. That got Andrew biting his lip. He knew that the medal ribbons indicated the meaning of the medals but was quite unable to recognize a single one.

"What are they for Gran, do you know?" he asked.

"Oh dear! That's a hard one," Gran replied, holding a hand to the side of her face. She picked up one of the medals and turned it over. "Ah yes! Here, it tells you."

Andrew bent closer and read: Pacific Star. On the other side his grandfather's name had been engraved. They were able to read the other three:

the 1939-45 Star, the 1939-45 Defence Medal, and the Australian Service Medal (1939-1945).

"Gran, do you know what this little copper leaf badge on this one means?" Andrew asked, pointing to a metal clasp on one of the medal ribbons.

"That means Bert was mentioned in dispatches; that his name went to the king in a report," Gran answered. "The citation saying what he actually did is somewhere here."

That really excited Andrew's interest and pride. 'Grandad was a hero in the war!' he thought happily. "It would be great if you could find it Gran," he answered.

Carmen looked at her watch and let out a little gasp. "Oh, look at the time! Thanks Gran. We really must fly. We will see you again soon."

As they went out the front door of the low set timber house Andrew turned and said, "Could you please arrange for us to talk to this Mr McCackle bloke Gran?"

Gran smiled. "Mr McGackey," she corrected. "Yes, I will. Thank you for calling children."

Brother and sister jumped on their bikes and pedalled hard. As the rode along they discussed the new information and Andrew's thoughts dwelt on the fact that his Grandad had been a brave man. That made him a bit unsure of himself. 'I'm not very brave, at least not underwater, and Grandad was a diver in wartime. Maybe I am a coward?' he worried.

It was only after they arrived home that Andrew's thoughts shifted to another worry: Muriel had not phoned the night before. 'Maybe she has changed her mind?' he fretted.

The worry grew into gnawing anxiety as the evening wore on. Teatime, TV news, homework; all slid by with no call. Carmen returned from work at 9pm and still the phone had not rung. Andrew's hopes kept sliding down and he became moody and grumpy.

Suddenly the phone rang. But before Andrew could reach it his mother picked it up and answered. "Hello, Mrs Collins. Who is speaking please? Who? Oh yes, Andrew. Here he is."

She turned and gave Andrew a smile which made him blush. "Muriel," she said as she handed him the phone.

'Muriel!' Andrew thought, his romantic hopes shooting up.

Chapter 9

Pressure

Andrew was thrilled. 'Muriel! She has rung me!' He had to swallow to clear his throat before answering, "Hello Muriel. How are you?"

"Fine," Muriel replied. "Did you have a good day?"

"Yes," Andrew answered. Now that she had called he found his mind blank and could not think of anything sensible to say. His hopes kept rising though.

Muriel said, "I tried ringing after school but you weren't home."

"Carmen and I went to see our Gran," Andrew explained. "She had some really interesting stuff on the sinking of the *Deeral*," he added.

"The what?"

"The *Deeral*, the ship Grandad and your Grandad were on when... when.. when my Grandad was lost at sea.. when they were looking for that ship-wreck, the *Merinda*," Andrew explained.

"Oh yes," Muriel replied. She did not sound very interested.

"I'm going to do a History assignment on the *Merinda*," Andrew said.

"That should be interesting," Muriel again replied in that flat tone.

Goaded by a feeling of mounting worry Andrew asked, "Have you asked your parents about the movies yet?"

"No, not yet," Muriel replied. "I will though. I think it is a great idea. Jenny Jervis and Shona and Tina all said they wanted to go."

That was good news to Andrew so he asked what movie Muriel might want to see. That led to a fifteen minute discussion on the relative merits of the movies that were currently showing at various cinemas. Muriel then began speaking to someone else and said, "Sorry Andrew, but my dad says I have to finish my homework. I will have to go. I've got an English essay due. It should have been done over the weekend but diving got in the way."

"Well, that is over anyway," Andrew commented.

"It was great fun wasn't it?" Muriel replied, her voice now vibrant with enthusiasm.

Not wanting to be a liar Andrew made non-committal noises. Muriel then further increased the pressure by saying, "I really want to do the Advanced Open Water Course now."

"Will your parents allow you?" Andrew replied, hoping very much that they wouldn't.

"Yes. Dad says that if a shark eats me it serves me right. I really want to do the night dive. That will be a real test of courage."

"Yes, it will be," Andrew agreed. Just thinking about it made him go cold with fear. "Can you afford it?" he asked, still hoping the idea would go away.

"I have to do work for Mum, but yes," Muriel replied. "Will you come with me if we do it?"

That really put Andrew on the spot. "I don't know if I will be allowed," he answered.

"Ask please. I really want to do it and it will be no fun with strangers," Muriel answered.

"I will," Andrew replied, almost sweating with anxiety at the thought.

"Thanks. I will try to ring again tomorrow at the same time," Muriel said.

"Thanks, bye."

"Bye."

Andrew hung up and went to his room with very mixed feelings. To be with Muriel was what he urgently desired; but at the price of diving in the ocean again? And at night? Remembering the accounts he had read of the World War 2 divers swimming in enemy harbours in the dark made him shudder and he doubted if he was brave enough to do it. But how to get out of it without losing his self-respect? 'And Muriel will think I am a coward,' he thought. A horrible feeling of being trapped made him feel very anxious.

That night he had another diving nightmare. This time he was deep underwater in murky green water. His mind kept telling him to surface before he ran out of air and before it got dark but he could not find Carmen, who was his diving buddy. Becoming more and more frantic by the second he swam around the coral outcrops and around the weed and coral encrusted remains of an old wreck. Fearing she might have become trapped in the wreck Andrew swam to it and looked in, then summoned up the courage to enter. Before he knew it all the light was gone and he found himself in absolute blackness and unable to work out which way was up or where the opening he had entered by was. Panic welled up, causing him to sob and gasp. Suddenly a light shone in his face and he saw a hand reach out.

'Saved!' he croaked, only to have the hand suddenly snatch off his face mask. As the salt water stung his eyes and flooded up his nose he dimly saw the light fade.

He woke up shaking and gasping for breath. His bedclothes were twisted around his chest and neck and his pyjamas were soaked in perspiration.

"Oh bloody hell!" he muttered weakly. "Only a nightmare. Oh God! How will I ever be able to go diving again?"

Sleep would not return and it was an unhappy boy who lay awake brooding as the first grey streaks of dawn appeared in the sky.

Feeling depressed and tired Andrew made his way to school. He had found it an effort to pretend to his parents and to Carmen that he was well and happy but on his own the gloom and doubts seemed to return with redoubled force.

The thing that took his mind off his own woes that day was worry about his friend Graham Kirk. During Period 1 Andrew sat daydreaming of sailing (with Muriel) and staring out the window, wishing he was out there, free. The arrival of a police car at the front of the school attracted his attention. He became even more interested when he saw Graham climb out and walk in to the school with a policeman.

'Strewth! Poor old Graham! He looks pretty miserable. I hope he isn't in trouble. I wonder what happened?' Andrew thought.

However he had no chance to ask Graham between periods so at morning break he went looking for him. Thus he was witness to another incident involving Graham. Andrew checked the place where Graham usually sat with his mates of the 'Hiking Team' but he was not with them so Andrew headed towards the tuck shop with Blake. Half way across the side of the quadrangle he saw Graham get into a fight.

Blake drew his attention to it by nudging him and pointing across the grass quadrangle. "Look Andrew. Kirk is arguing with that bully Larsen."

Andrew, like all the Year 9s, knew who Larsen was, and was glad he had not yet attracted his attentions. Larsen was a big, red-haired Year 11 boy with a reputation for tormenting younger kids. Near the two arguing boys stood a curvy blonde, a Year 9 girl in Graham's class named Ailsa. She was looking anxious and seemed to be trying to calm them.

Larsen suddenly swung a punch at Graham; a vicious uppercut which he just managed to dodge. In response Graham stepped in and punched Larsen hard in the stomach, causing him to double up. A right cross to Larsen's jaw sent the bully sprawling on the sand.

Blake clapped his hands. "Oh bloody good hit!" he cried.

Andrew had to admit he was pleased. Larsen had been the bane of their life all year and it was certainly satisfying seeing him getting some of his own back. But there was anxiety too. Larsen was bigger and obviously stronger- and now he was very angry, having been humiliated in front of his girl friend and cronies. He scrambled to his feet and rushed at Graham, fists flailing.

Andrew began hurrying towards the fight, along with a hundred other students. He wasn't sure what he would do when he arrived but felt a need to help his friend.

A ring of shouting, chanting students quickly formed around the combatants, blocking both Andrew's vision and path. He glimpsed fists flailing and saw both boys manage to get solid blows home. Graham hit Larsen on the jaw again, sending him staggering back. Then, as he drew back to deliver another punch his arm was grabbed by Mr Page, the Senior Geography teacher. Mr Conkey arrived from the other direction and restrained Larsen.

There was then no way Andrew could help. All he could do was stand in the crowd and watch as the two were marched off to the office.

"What was that all about?" Andrew asked Angus MacDougal, a boy in Graham's class.

"Oh, Kirky was silly enough to make a pass at Ailsa, but she is Larsen's girlfriend and he took objection to that," Angus explained. "Silly bugger!" he added.

It wasn't until Period 7 after lunch, during Chemistry, that Andrew met up with Graham. He at once went over and asked him how he was, noting a big bruise on the side of his face, a split lip and a puffed up nose, plus various minor bruises. "You look like you've been in the wars," he commented. "What happened?"

"Had a fight with Larsen," Graham grunted.

"I saw that. You did a great job, got him a couple of beauties!" Andrew replied enthusiastically. Then he went on. "Er.. um .. It's none of my business but I saw you arrive in a cop car this morning."

Graham nodded. "Yeah. I wasn't in trouble. I had a fight with gang of hoons who were harassing some little sheilas from St Monicas."

Graham then related the incident but the story was cut short by the arrival of the hugely fat and very bossy teacher, Miss McLeod. Andrew did not get another chance to talk to Graham and, when he looked for him after school he saw no sign of him. He did linger for a few minutes to watch the school's army cadet company start its weekly training parade, mainly to compare their drill to the navy cadet's way of doing things.

Next he went to the library to photocopy the newspaper clippings of Gran's and some of the old photos. Then he rode home and sat to do his homework. This included drafting letters to various libraries and the State Archives.

When Carmen came home she informed him that she had organized with Gran for them to visit Mr McGackey the next afternoon. That suited Andrew as he had plenty to do. His homework done he lay down to read. This time he read an account of the Italian 'Frogmen' who had bravely penetrated Alexandria harbour in December 1941 and badly damaged two British Battleships, HMS *Valiant* and HMS *Queen Elizabeth*. The men used two-man torpedoes and it all made Andrew wonder if he could ever swim underwater at night. It was a terrifying prospect.

To his consternation he was almost immediately put under more pressure by Carmen saying she wanted to do the Advanced Open Water Diving Course. "Will you come with us?" she asked.

"Us?" Andrew asked.

"Muriel has asked me to sign on with her," Carmen replied, giving Andrew a sly look that made him blush.

"Mum and Dad won't let us surely?" Andrew answered. "They will think it is too dangerous."

But they didn't immediately say no, much to Andrew's consternation. With that he fell back on cost. Even that was discounted as they said they would think about it. That got Andrew secretly hoping they would say no, but left him in a state of growing anxiety.

Muriel rang again that evening and she increased the pressure by adding that Carmen had agreed to do the diving with her. Poor Andrew just could not pluck up the courage to admit he was terrified! Instead he changed the subject to the movies on Saturday night. Muriel's answer was that she would be driven to and from the cinema by her mother, along with her girl friends. "We will just have to meet inside," she said.

That was a lot better than nothing so Andrew went to ask his mother if he could go. She wanted to know who he was going with and that made him say Blake and Luke.

"How are you getting there?" his mother next asked.

"Don't know," Andrew replied, kicking himself for not having his plan thought through.

"I will drive you then," his mother replied.

That left Andrew with no option but to ask Blake if he would come. As soon as he saw him at school he went over and asked, "Can you come to the movies on Saturday night?"

To his relief Blake could and he agreed to ask Shona. "I might get lucky," he added.

Images of himself with Letitia in January flooded Andrew's mind making him feel both aroused and jealous, then guilty. 'Would I do 'it' if the opportunity arose?' he wondered. To his own regret he suspected he would, but was sure it would not be with Muriel. 'She is much too nice and too special,' he thought.

After school he hurried home and dropped of his schoolbag. Then he and Carmen rode their bikes over to the Retirement Village. Andrew felt very self-conscious going in there, for once aware of his age. The people at the office directed them to a lounge room where they found Gran and a wrinkled old man with skin as brown as a walnut. His head was bald and shiny and his hands were all curled up but there was a bright twinkle in his eye.

Gran introduced them to Mr McGackey, one time cook and deckhand on various ships. Mr McGackey stared hard at Andrew, looking him slowly up and down. Then he nodded. "Aye, ye be the spittin' image of Bert Collins when he were a boy, I reckon," he said.

"You knew him then?" Andrew asked.

"Aye, knew him very well. It was only pure chance that I were not with him on that last voyage when he was lost at sea," Mr McGackey answered.

"Why is that?" Carmen asked.

"Well, I were workin' on the *Deeral* as deckhand, cook and general jack-of-all-trades when he and Murchison decided to use her to go lookin' fer the pot of gold at the end of *Merinda's* rainbow. I would'a bin on her but just that same day they got a call to haul a big barge off a sandbar at Mourilyan. That meant usin' the *Wallaman Falls*. She was a tug yer know."

Andrew nodded. "Yes, we know. We've seen photos."

Mr McGackey went on, "Well, as luck would have it, Percy Westcott hurt his hand the day before. He were the regular deckhand on the tug yer see. Anyhow, seein' that they needed a deckhand straight away I were transferred to the *Wallaman Falls*, seein' as how I knew the ropes on her, so to speak."

Brother and sister nodded politely while Mr McGackey nodded to himself and stared off into space for a few moments. Then he went on, "Luckiest thing I ever did. Otherwise I would have gone down with the *Deeral*, like as not, particularly seein' as I can't swim." He chuckled, then said, "Caused a bit of an argument it did, between Bert Collins and Murchison. Bert wanted me along but Murchison insisted I go to the tug. In my place they hired two T.I. boys. Good lads they were too, and used to divin', which was Murchison's argument."

Carmen looked puzzled. "I'm sorry. I don't understand."

Mr McGackey looked thoughtful for a moment, then explained. "Your Grandad, Bert Collins, he was usually the skipper of the *Deeral,* with me as her other crewman. Too small for more than that, not even an engineer yer see," he said. There was another pause, then he went on. "That Murchison, he was just a diver. Didn't have no tickets yer see, I mean certificates to be a mate or a master. Allan Penwold were the master of the tug, and a right, good man. So I weren't on the poor little *Deeral* when she made her last voyage."

Carmen frowned, then asked, "You sound as though you don't like Mr Murchison?"

"No, I didn't," Mr McGackey replied. "I thought he was a bit too tight, a real penny-pincher, yet greedy with it. Sorry, but he put me wrong a few times and I didn't trust him. But then, ye say don't. Is the man still alive?"

Andrew listened to that with some embarrassment. He answered. "Yes, he is. He lives in a house over at Bosuns Bay."

"Well I never!" Mr McGackey commented. "Ah well, they say the Devil looks after his own. Fancy that, him still alive after all that!"

There was an uncomfortable silence. Andrew broke it by asking, "The *Deeral,* what was she? I've seen a photo but not a very good one. Could you tell us about her?"

"Certainly," Mr McGackey agreed. "She were a good little ship that, a fifty six footer, made of galvanized steel. She were built on the Clyde as a workboat for the British Army during World War Two. She had a six cylinder G.M. diesel engine what rated at one hundred and fifty horse power. That pushed her along at about six or seven knots. Not much to her though. Only five foot of freeboard fully laden and just three compartments. Seaworthy enough in normal conditions though. But... well, we were always a bit wary of her."

"Why was that?" Carmen asked.

"Her number," Mr McGackey answered. "Her army hull number was AV 1313." There was a pause and Mr McGackey looked slightly embarrassed. Then he explained, "Well, sailormen of my generation, we was a bit more superstitious than yer modern folk. Bad enough having one thirteen, but two! Well, some said it would all end in tears, and it did. To cap it off they sailed on a Friday. Bert didn't want to but I heard Murchison arguing with him. 'If we wait some one else might beat us to the wreck,' he said. So they sailed, and look where greed got them eh?"

"Was the ship in good condition?" Andrew asked.

"Oh fair enough. For all that they tried to keep costs down she was maintained alright. Bert seen to that, despite Murchison's moaning about expenses."

Carmen frowned. "I thought they were friends as well as partners. Was there some sort of disagreement?" she asked.

"There was a bit of tension," Mr McGackey replied. "They had been friends but I think the business put a strain on that."

"Can you tell us anything about what happened?" Andrew asked.

"No more'n you will have read in the papers," Mr McGackey answered.

"Would you know where she sank?" Andrew asked.

Mr McGackey shook his head. "Nah! Don't think anyone really knows. Somewhere out from the Whitsundays I heard."

"What did the A. V. stand for?" Carmen queried.

"Army Vessel," Mr McGackey replied.

Andrew was surprised. "Army? I thought the navy ran the ships?"

"Maybe now, but not then. Both our army and the British Army had their own boats, to move their own stuff wivout havin' ter wait for the navy to agree yer see."

Carmen nodded. "The army still has boats. They operate the small landing craft. You've seen them Andrew, those L.C.M 8s we saw in Ross River last January."

Andrew had a vivid flashback to paddling in a canoe down the lower reaches of Ross River with the voluptuous Letitia sitting in front of him. She had been so much outside his experience he still found it hard to come to terms with her blatant sexuality and nudity. It made him ashamed and yet aroused just thinking about her. He nodded and asked more questions about the *Deeral*. Mr McGackey couldn't tell them much more and his thoughts wandered off the topic to reminiscing about other trips on other ships with their grandfather. That was interesting to Andrew and he was glad he was making the effort to learn more about his own family. Already he was much prouder of his grandad.

After afternoon tea and thanking both their Gran and Mr McGackey brother and sister rode home. When he got there Andrew at once wrote down in a notebook all the facts he could remember from the interview, then sat and considered what else he might like to know. That sent him to the computer and he looked up shipbuilding companies on the internet and browsed for a while.

Muriel did not phone that night, making Andrew feel quite anxious. He was worried that she might have met someone else, or might have decided she did not like him. This worry kept him tense all day at school on Friday.

His thoughts were now focused on that night's Navy Cadet parade and he was edgy and irritable until he and Carmen were dropped off at the depot at 6:45 that evening.

At once the tension evaporated. The first person Andrew met was Muriel. She had been waiting near the gate and was all smiles. "How was your day?" she asked, quite oblivious to his nervous state.

After that cadets was wholly enjoyable. The first parade was fine and then the lessons were interesting: coiling and heaving lines, flag signals, and ship identification. During the canteen break the details for the Saturday night movies were agreed on. Andrew wasn't all that thrilled that Tina Babcock and Jennifer Jervis were going to be there, along with Blake and Shona, but he accepted it as the price he had to pay.

All evening he kept flicking surreptitious glances at Muriel, admiring her beauty and longing to hold her hand, to kiss her. But then, immediately after the dismissal parade, Sub Lt Sheldon drove all such thoughts from his mind and placed him right back under pressure by asking if he still wanted to do the Advanced Diving Course.

After swallowing and wondering how to get out of it without admitting he was scared Andrew replied, "Oh, I'm not sure if my parents will allow it." The knowledge that when he had signed on for the Open Water Dive Course, he had indicated that he was also planning to do the Advanced Course made Andrew squirm inside. But that had been before he knew what diving was like; what his real reactions might be. Now he just wanted to get out of it.

Sub Lt Sheldon nodded then said, "We can ask your mother when she comes to pick you up."

To that Andrew could only hope she would say no. Muriel then added to the pressure by saying, "Oh come on Andrew! You said you would, and I want you there."

At that moment Carmen appeared with their mother. Sub Lt Sheldon smiled a welcome and said, "I will ask now."

Chapter 10

Hoping for More

Mrs Collins raised an eyebrow and looked at Sub Lt Sheldon. "What do I have to decide on?"

Carmen answered that. "Whether we can go on the Advanced Open Water Diving Course," she said.

At that Mrs Collins frowned. "Oh, I don't know. Your father and I have talked about this and we are not happy. Not only is it very expensive but it sounds quite dangerous."

"Oh Mrs Collins, it's not!" Muriel cried. "Please say they can. They can pay you back by mowing the lawn and washing the dishes for the next ten years."

Mrs Collins smiled. "They do that already. I'm sorry, we haven't been introduced."

Andrew blushed at his bad manners and stammered an introduction. His mother smiled and said, "Muriel. Yes. Andrew has told me about you. Are you allowed to go Muriel?"

"Yes I am," Muriel answered. "My parents say that if a shark eats me then it serves me right. Oh please Mrs Collins! I don't want to be on the course with a bunch of strangers."

Mrs Collins bit her lip and looked to Sub Lt Sheldon. "What exactly is involved?" she asked. "I have to be sure that what they plan to do is safe. There is something about a wreck isn't there?"

"Yes Mrs Collins, there is. They will be leaving on Friday in two weeks if they come with us. We are driving to Townsville and going out that night on a launch to the Barrier Reef. Next day we will do four dives. First is a revision dive. Next they do a navigation dive. Then, after another safety rest, they are to do a dive to study and report on marine life. That involves recording and photographing. They are all quite safe activities within a hundred metres of the boat."

"Yes, go on."

"That night there is a night dive. Now, I know that sounds dangerous but we do it in a group and with lights and a lot of safety precautions and with experienced instructors," Sub Lt Sheldon explained.

At the thought of that Andrew's anxiety level shot up and he fervently hoped that his mother would say no. To his consternation she nodded and said, "I've heard about that. There are supposed to be some pretty spectacular sights that only appear at night I gather."

"That's right. And we have the surface spotlighted so they can easily find the boat at any time," Sub Lt Sheldon added.

"It is the idea of them diving on a wreck I don't like," Mrs Collins said.

Sub Lt Sheldon nodded. "I can agree with that. Wreck diving can be very dangerous. Without proper training it can easily lead to potentially fatal situations. That is why we are planning this one to be as safe as we can. Usually we dive in thirty metres on a large wreck called the S. S. *Yongala*."

Mrs Collins looked thoughtful. "I don't like the sound of that. Is this *Yongala* wreck among rocks or coral outcrops?"

Sub Lt Sheldon shook his head. "No. It is on a flat, sandy bottom miles from the nearest reef. It is in the open sea out of sight of land."

At that Mrs Collins bit her lip. "Oh I don't know. I don't like the sound of that either. I would much prefer it to be in shallow water in some place where there are no currents or big waves or anything."

Sub Lt Sheldon nodded. "I see what you mean. There are a couple of wrecks down that way that are close to shore. There is the old sailing ship called the *Moltke*. She is only a hundred metres off shore at Magnetic Island, in Geoffrey Bay. There are a couple of others too. In fact some of my friends are diving on a newly discovered wreck this weekend. It is close to shore and might be suitable."

At that Carmen asked, "Oh sir! What's the name of this wreck?"

Sub Lt Sheldon shook his head. "Don't know. Some local fishermen only reported it recently. They say it is a small vessel but at present the location is a bit vague. The Townsville diving club are going to try to locate and mark it this weekend."

The sailing ship wreck sounded more interesting to Andrew so he asked about it. To his disappointment he was informed by Sub Lt Sheldon, who had dived on it, that there wasn't much left, "and certainly no ghostly masts and yardarms still standing in the water."

Sub Lt Sheldon then turned to Mrs Collins. "Sorry to press the issue Mrs Collins but we need to make a booking. It is only two weeks away. If we can find a nice safe little wreck in sheltered and shallow water can they do the course?"

At that Mrs Collins wavered. "Oh alright. I will see if their father will agree. How soon do you need to know?"

"Next Friday night for sure," Sub Lt Sheldon answered.

"Please Mum!" Carmen pleaded. "If we don't do it now then it might be months. We have a cadet camp coming up and then the holidays."

"What's this about a camp?" Mrs Collins asked. "I thought you had your annual camp in June?"

"We did. This is a specialist training camp," Carmen answered.

"Where is it this time? Will it cost much?" Mrs Collins queried.

"Mackay," Carmen answered, evading the issue of cost.

"Yes, alright. Now come on you children. Time you were home and in bed," Mrs Collins replied.

As he walked away with his mother and sister Andrew kept glancing back at Muriel. She was smiling and called, "See you tomorrow night." That sent his hopes soaring and kept him from thinking about diving all the way home.

That night, when in bed, Andrew fantasized about being a hero to impress Muriel. He conjured up dreams of being a naval officer commanding a patrol boat. A radio message sends them to the aid of a cruise ship attacked by pirates; Asian pirates- Chinese or Filipino- hard, ruthless men with black balaclavas and sub machine guns. The fighting is fierce and desperate. He gets aboard the liner- but no- the pirates have fled with hostages. Muriel is one of the hostages. The patrol boat pursues. The pirate boat has guns and they fire at the patrol boat. But it can't shoot back in case they hit the hostages.

Andrew was a bit stumped by that but then decided that a navy helicopter was available so, after dark, they swoop on the pirates and he slides down a rope onto the deck. Savage hand-to-hand fighting erupts. He saves Muriel. But then- he paused and bit his lip. Somehow she didn't seem to be the sort of person who needed saving. 'She might resent me thinking that way about her. She is just as likely to be saving me,' he decided.

At least he got through the night without any nightmare, or at least none he could remember. Saturday morning found him tingling with hope and excitement. His body kept getting aroused, which annoyed him a little as he wanted to think he was in love with Muriel, that it wasn't just lust. But he had to admit that she was a very attractive girl and that he was hoping for just a bit. 'Only what a decent girl would allow though,' he rationalized.

The day was spent doing chores: mowing the lawn, cleaning the storeroom, changing the water in the aquarium, checking the sails on their skiff.

By lunchtime it seemed to Andrew that the evening would never come and he became impatient and fretful. Having spare time was no help either. An attempt to lie on his bed and read was a dismal failure and he had no interest in computer games or TV. Instead he set to work again and cleaned out the skiff and polished the hull. It was an old wooden boat owned by their father and the shiny, lacquered plywood was, as always, a joy for Andrew to touch and shine.

Finally the day ended and the routine of the evening took over. After tea Andrew showered and dressed in his going-out casual clothes. Carmen noted this and gave him several sly grins which he did his best to ignore. His story about going to the movies with Blake she plainly did not believe.

Andrew's mother drove him to the cinema and dropped him off. To his relief Blake was there but there was no sign of Muriel or the other girls. After waving his mother goodbye Andrew was left wondering what to do next: stand and wait, or go and buy two tickets? A check of the prices made him hesitate. They were just expensive enough to stretch his already strained finances.

'What if Muriel doesn't turn up?' he fretted.

For a while the two boys stood and waited. While they did the thought that he might be going to be 'stood up' caused Andrew waves of anxiety and anticipatory humiliation. As the minutes ticked by he became more and more anxious. To add to his concern the movie started and still there was no sign of the girls. Even so he did not want to let on to Blake that he was worried or that anything unusual might be happening so he stood in the foyer and chatted in as casual and light-hearted a voice as he could manage.

While they were standing there Graham Kirk and Stephen Bell arrived. They chatted for a few minutes then went inside. A few minutes later four girls from their school arrived: Louise, Amanda, Karen and Annette. All four were in Year 9 and Andrew knew them but they were obviously in a group so, apart from casual smiles and greetings, he said nothing. The girls went inside. More minutes of embarrassing waiting ticked by.

Then Andrew caught Blake making surreptitious checks of his watch and it dawned on him that maybe he was having the same worries. That helped a bit but it still hurt. Finally he mustered his courage and said, "It looks like the girls aren't coming. Are we going in?"

Blake shrugged and tried to smile but Andrew glimpsed the pain in his eyes. "Suppose so, now that we are here," Blake answered.

The two boys strolled over to the ticket office. Blake went first. Andrew dug out his money and was counting it ready when a girl's voice called out, "There he is!"

It was Shona. With her was a girl Andrew had never seen. His own hopes shot up, then plummeted. Blake at once perked up and became all smiles and jokes. The friend was introduced: Cassie, and they once more moved to the ticket window. By this time Andrew was feeling humiliated and embarrassed. He did not want to admit that he was waiting for another girl, but loyalty made him stand-offish with Cassie.

Shona obviously thought that he would make a good partner for her friend and made several strong hints to that effect. These had the effect of making Andrew consider not going in at all. 'If I do and Muriel gets to hear about it, even if this Cassie chick and I don't become friends, it could cause trouble,' he reasoned. He began casting around for a face-saving excuse to back out.

But by then he was at the window and his courage failed him. He placed his money on the counter and opened his mouth to ask for one ticket. As he tried to speak the shriek of girlish giggles made him look towards the entrance. Through the door scurried Muriel, Tina and Jennifer.

"Hurry up, the movie has started," Jennifer was saying. Then she saw Andrew and the others and added, "Oh! Oh here they are, still waiting."

In an instant Andrew's eyes registered the girl's appearance: Muriel in a pair of white slacks and a loose, white cotton top that buttoned down the front; Tina in jeans and a floral cotton blouse that bulged and wobbled as she hurried along; and Jennifer in a tight-fitting pale blue dress that really accentuated her trim curves. Tina gave him a smile but it was one that did not quite reach her eyes and that caused Andrew a tiny spasm of guilt as he suspected that Tina was wishing they were going together. Several times in the past she had hinted at this and he had been tempted.

To Andrew's intense relief Muriel hurried over and stood close beside him. "Oh thank you for waiting Andrew. I'm sorry we are late. Mum's car had a flat battery and she had to call the RACQ." As she said this she cast several searching glances at Cassie. That made Andrew very glad that he had not weakened and given in to temptation. He made no attempt to introduce her, leaving that to Shona. As she did he turned away and purchased two tickets.

As soon as he had them he took Muriel's arm and steered her towards the entrance to the theatre. Only after a dozen steps did he realize what he had done but by then Muriel had put her hand down to grip his and he understood that he had acted rightly in the circumstances. As they were ushered into the darkened theatre Muriel gave his hand a squeeze and his hopes went even higher.

The group seated themselves in a row near the back. Muriel went on the left hand end with Andrew beside her. Next came Tina, then Jennifer and Cassie. Blake sat next to her with Shona on his right next to the aisle. For a few minutes all sat and tried to focus on the movie. Andrew knew the outline of the story but had difficulty concentrating. Most of his thoughts were on Muriel, who sat pressed against his left arm, her hand still holding his.

Then began one of those agonizing tests of adolescent social skills. Andrew badly wanted to cuddle Muriel, to feel her body against his, to kiss her. But he was terrified of making the wrong move and thereby ruining his chances! So he sat there in a cold sweat of worry, wondering if Muriel really wanted to concentrate on the film or whether, like him, it was just an excuse to allow them to get together. From listening to his friends and their older brothers he had some idea of the tactics that he might employ, but that only got him even more tense. To make a move- or not to?

To further inhibit him was the close proximity of the other girls. Andrew was very aware of Tina's presence, her well-filled blouse being very much in his peripheral vision. Indeed Tina's large bosom always had an unsettling attraction for him and again he felt the social pressure. He was very aware that the girls would note every single move he made and there was the embarrassing probability that they might even compare notes later, to rate his performance against other boys. That was a very unsettling thought!

So was his physical arousal. Muriel's touch had caused him to become very erect and that got him all confused and anxious about his motives and desires. Heated memories of Letitia added to his excited state.

The dilemma of teenage movie theatre tactics was then abruptly forgotten as a piercing scream suddenly caused them all to jump. The first movie was an old horror story about a psychopathic murderer who crept into houses to kill women with a huge knife. The movie had reached a scene in which a girl was having a shower (unfortunately only showing her bare back!). The maniac crept into her house and then into the bathroom. By then Andrew was on the edge of his seat. Just as the madman reached forward to slash the girl's throat the scream sounded.

It came from close behind Andrew and he jumped in fright. Muriel also shrieked, as did most of the girls in the cinema. Muriel gripped Andrew tightly as they turned to look. Across the darkened theatre flashed the beam of a powerful torch. It lit up Louise and Stephen. Stephen was sitting behind Louise and had obviously grabbed her by the throat.

Louise turned and shouted angrily, "Stephen Bell, you are a bastard!"

A large male usher arrived, the torch he held now focused on Stephen. "What's going on? Is everything alright?" he asked. A female usher with a torch hurried down the next aisle to join him.

"No it is not!" Louise cried. She quickly explained how Stephen had grabbed her by the throat. Next to her was a sobbing Annette.

"It was only a joke," Stephen replied defensively, blinking through his glasses in the bright light.

The male usher shook his head and angrily pointed to the door. "I don't care. Out!"

"Aw! Fair go!" Stephen replied.

"Out I said!" the man thundered.

Stephen stood up and made his way along the row. As he did the torch beam settled on an embarrassed looking Graham. "What about you?" the usher asked. "Were you involved?"

"No," Graham replied, but he stood up and made his way along the row after Stephen.

"Bloody Stephen!" Andrew muttered. "Trust him."

"Do you know them?" Muriel asked.

Andrew realized she was still clinging tightly to him and he silently thanked Stephen, then nodded. "Yes. They are in Year Nine at my school. They are in some of my classes."

"That poor girl! She must have nearly died of a heart attack," Muriel said, twisting around and craning to watch as Graham went through the back curtains.

Andrew had to chuckle at that but shushing noises from people around them made him stop talking. He settled back to watch the movie. Muriel relaxed but kept leaning firmly against him, keeping his hopes high.

For perhaps half an hour Andrew sat there almost paralyzed with anxiety (He did not want to admit it as fear). So still did he sit that his muscles began to cramp. To add to his worries he knew he was perspiring, despite the air conditioning. 'I hope I don't smell,' he fretted.

After fidgeting for a bit he leaned forward and risked a quick glance along to his right to see how Blake was getting on. What he saw was both enlightening and challenging. Blake had his right arm around Shona's shoulders and his hand appeared to be hanging down so far that it looked to be touching her right breast! That got Andrew even more anxious. He had heard that that was one way to 'test the water' but could not imagine himself doing it- except that he burned with hypocritical shame at scorching memories of fondling Letitia's very full breasts!

For another ten minutes Andrew sat there, knowing that he was possibly damned if he didn't and maybe damned if he did! He was acutely aware of every little movement made by Muriel, of her breathing, of the warm feel of her hand, of his own hot desire. Finally he steeled himself to try his luck. 'May as well,' he reasoned. 'If I don't and she thinks I am cold or a coward then I lose anyway.'

Thus, hoping that Muriel would give him warning signs if he looked like doing the wrong thing, he gently eased his hand free of hers. She turned to look at him and her eyes shone in the flickering light, large, liquid eyes that seemed to be full of promise. Seeing her quizzical eyebrow he deliberately raised his left arm and placed it behind her shoulders. To his enormous relief she smiled and snuggled closer to him.

For a few minutes Andrew sat in silent happiness, allowing his anxious heart to slow down again. Then he began to very gently stroke her shoulder and upper arm with the fingers of his left hand. That brought him another smile and she snuggled even closer, pressing her right breast firmly against his body.

Next Muriel leant her head on his shoulder. The gentle tickle of her hair on his cheek and neck was a revelation of tantalizing promise and made him both happy and anxious. Very tenderly he turned and kissed the top of her head. That drew a murmur of appreciation and she looked up at him. Andrew saw that her eyes looked liquid and misty and that somehow her face was softer, more appealing, her lips slightly parted. With hammering heart he bent down to kiss her. She came to him and there lips met. This time Andrew was better prepared and he was able to kiss her properly.

For several minutes their lips remained locked together. Then he drew away and hugged her to him, his right arm going to her left shoulder. As he looked over her shoulder Andrew knew he was experiencing sheer delight. A feeling of wonder flooded him and he knew he was in love. Panting slightly from his rapid heart rate he kissed her again.

This was even better. She responded eagerly and this time the tip of her tongue began to probe and explore between his lips and against his teeth. His confidence growing by the minute Andrew kissed her ardently, his own tongue now exploring her mouth. She sighed and pressed harder against him, encouraging him to continue. Andrew knew he was now drinking her saliva, and she his, but somehow it did not seem disgusting. Instead he kept kissing, relishing the intimate contact and the scents and flavours that went with it.

After what seemed like hours they drew apart and again hugged. Only as he glanced to check what the others were doing did Andrew realize that his right forearm was pressing against Muriel's bosom. As she made no move to remove it he left it there, preparatory to the next move. A glance along the line revealed that Blake and Shona were kissing passionately. Shona had her arms around his neck and Blake now had his left arm tightly around her front, holding her against him.

'Now, how do I shift so that Muriel will put her arms around my neck?' Andrew puzzled. He decided he had to shift so sat up and moved to half turn towards her. She looked at him and smiled, then did exactly what he wanted. The feel of those silken arms against the skin of his neck made Andrew even more excited. He hugged her tightly to him, his right arm sliding around her side and back to do so. For several more minutes they kissed, she as apparently eagerly as he. Then, when they eased apart and she settled back, the bottom of her breast came to rest on the top of his arm.

Andrew was acutely aware of this, his heart hammering even harder as his body stiffened in response to the touch. The breast was soft, yet firm. To Andrew that touch held all the promise of ecstasy and his hopes rose even higher. That she must have been aware of it emboldened him to contemplate the next step, the actual touching, or caressing.

'But not here,' he reasoned, noting that Tina was able to watch every move if she looked. Another glance showed Blake and Shona locked in another embrace and kissing as though their lives depended on it. 'But how to get Muriel on her own?'

For lack of a better plan Andrew kissed Muriel again. During it he gently but firmly pressed upwards with his arm. That drew no resistance or reproach so he was even more encouraged. When they drew apart again he opened his mouth to whisper a suggestion to go outside. However this was not uttered as he noted with dismay that the movie was ending.

Where had the time gone! Andrew was astonished, and also worried. The usual problem of not wanting the others to see his aroused condition got him squirming to try to hide it as the lights came on. Then he was standing, luckily at the back of the line. As he did he kept hold of Muriel's hand and she snuggled against him, making him even happier.

As they walked side by side up the aisle Andrew was further thrilled to have Muriel keep holding his hand. When she kept holding it out in the full glare of the foyer lights he knew it was a very public declaration of her acceptance of him. The other girls clearly noted this and smiled indulgently; except Tina who looked a bit withdrawn. Blake and Shona hurried outside and Andrew urged Muriel towards the door, wanting a few more minutes of passion and hoping for privacy.

They did not get it. Out on the footpath it was well lit and he could not summon the courage to lead her away from the others. Instead they stood and talked. Even so Andrew was happy and Muriel snuggled against him, keeping his body aflame with desire.

"Can we meet again?" he croaked.

"Yes please," Muriel answered, sending his spirits soaring even higher.

"When? Where?" Andrew asked.

That drew a wry smile from Muriel. "Not this weekend, I'm sorry. Mum says that I have to get all my school assignments done if I am to go on the diving weekend."

The thought of that gave Andrew a momentary spasm of anxiety but he thrust that aside, thinking that it wouldn't be so bad, and not wanting Muriel to guess he was a coward. "What about one night during the week?"

She shook her head. "No chance. I will be able to phone, that's all."

"What about next weekend?" Andrew asked, becoming more and more desperate and anxious.

"Yes. If I have done all my work," Muriel replied. Then she said, "What about a sleepover?"

That was a wonderful idea to Andrew. He smiled and nodded. "Where, your place or mine?"

"I was thinking of Gran's," Muriel replied.

"At Bosuns Bay?" Andrew asked. He liked that idea even better. 'There should be plenty of places and opportunities there for us to get away on our own for a while,' he thought.

Muriel nodded. "Yes. We often stay there on weekends. We could ask the others to join us."

Andrew wasn't quite as keen on that, until he thought about it for a moment. 'If there are only the two of us then our absence will be really obvious,' he thought. 'But if there is a group we will be less noticeable.' He asked, "Who did you have in mind?"

"Shona and Blake, and maybe Carmen, and Tina and Jennifer."

Andrew wasn't keen on his sister being there but did not know how to say so. Instead he commented, "That's a lot of girls. I will feel a bit out-numbered."

"Then bring a friend to give you moral support," Muriel replied with a teasing grin.

"Will your grandparents mind having such a crowd?" he asked, while wondering what other boys he could ask.

"They will love it," Muriel assured him. "And there is plenty of room, if you don't mind sleeping on a mattress on the floor."

"To be with you I will happily sleep on the tiles," Andrew answered, then realized what he had said and what it implied.

Muriel blushed and giggled. "Don't you be naughty!" she chided, but without any heat, encouraging him even more. Suddenly she let go and stepped away from him. "Uh oh! Here's my mum. I will phone you and let you know what we organize."

Andrew wanted to kiss her goodnight, as Blake was doing to Shona, but under the interested gaze of Mrs Murchison he could not bring himself to do that, as he not sure if it would get Muriel into trouble or not. The girls all giggled and chattered happily as they said goodnight, then climbed into the car. A minute later they were gone, leaving the two boys standing there.

Blake grinned at Andrew, then smirked and said, "That was pretty good. I think I am going to win with Shona. How are you getting on with Muriel? Do you reckon you will get on?"

Andrew grinned back and nodded but did not answer. His male pride demanded he act that way but in his heart he knew his idea of winning with Muriel was to gain her love and affection, not a sexual conquest. 'If we are truly in love then other things might happen naturally,' he reasoned. To keep the conversation going he put the idea of the sleepover to Blake. He was enthusiastic and nodded eagerly.

"Great idea! We could have a real party," he agreed.

Then Andrew's mother arrived and he was able to say goodnight. By then his heated body had cooled and relaxed but he was put on a spot when his mother asked what the movie was like. Luckily he was able to describe the incident when Stephen had grabbed Louise and that diverted the conversation. His mother wasn't amused but did not pursue the topic of the movie.

At home Andrew again related the story of Stephen and Louise for Carmen's benefit while they had supper. Carmen made a wry face and said, "Poor Louise. That Stephen can be very silly sometimes."

Andrew agreed but still chuckled. It was actually Graham he felt sorry for. 'He should choose his friends more carefully,' he mused as he cleaned his teeth. Then it was into bed and a replay of the night's events. Reliving every moment quickly got Andrew hot and excited and he drifted off to sleep hoping there would be another chance to be with Muriel. 'And this time alone!'

Chapter 11

Tingling Anticipation

All Sunday Andrew felt as though he was being charged by electricity. His poor young body seemed to be quite outside the control of his mind. With embarrassing frequency he found himself having erections, even when he wasn't thinking about Muriel. To avoid embarrassment he stayed away from his mother and sister as much as possible. Much of the time he played computer games but eventually 'Carriers at War' and 'Up Periscope!' palled.

Out of boredom Andrew lay on his bed after lunch and began reading Hector Holthouse's book: *Cyclone*. That was a revelation to him. He had never experienced a real cyclone, only been on the edges of a few, but he knew enough to have a healthy respect for the gigantic tropical storms. As there were usually four or five a year in the Coral Sea each summer he was aware that one could affect his life, but he hoped the eventuality would not arise.

What particularly struck him was the number of ships, big ships some of them, that had been sunk by cyclones. That got him paying particular attention to the account of the sinking of the *S. S. Yongala*. He was still hoping that something would happen so that he did not have to do the advanced diving course but equally he was half-consciously trying to mentally prepare himself for the ordeal. The concept of winds blowing at 120 kilometres per hour, or even stronger, he could not grasp. All of his daydreams allowed him to heroically save his ship (and the fair maiden aboard).

Waves that were so big that they could cause a 3,000 ton steel steamship to founder he had only ever seen on movies or videos. That left him with the uncomfortable thought that maybe, if he actually had to face such things, he might be found wanting, might crumple from pure fear.

Another diving nightmare that night did not help. It made him feel relieved when the sun came up and he was able to push the ugly fears into the back of his mind. Then it was off to school. Once there he enquired of Graham exactly what had happened at the movies. Graham was short tempered and did not want to talk about it and only said it had not been a very enjoyable weekend.

The diversion from what had developed into an uncomfortable conversation was provided by Anthony Simmons. He strolled over and grinned at them. "Have you heard about that mad bugger Willy Williams?" he asked the group.

"The Mad Professor in Year Eight?" queried Peter Bronsky.

"That's the guy," Anthony agreed.

"What did he do?" Graham asked.

"Blew himself up with a rocket," Anthony explained. He then gave a colourful account of how Willy had made his own 'space rocket' out of aluminium tubing, stuffed it with home-made solid propellent, then tried a test firing. Apparently the rocket had not gone 'woosh!' up into the sky but instead had gone 'bang!'

"Is he alright?" Andrew asked.

"In hospital," Anthony replied. "Blew up some old farmer too," he added.

"How did he do that?" Graham asked.

"Apparently he and his mates took the rocket out into the country to some farm near Kuranda. They set the rocket up and lit the fuze, then got under cover. But then this old codger came wandering along, heard the noise of the fuze burning and went over to investigate. Just as he got there the thing blew up."

Most of the boys laughed at the description but Andrew was appalled, and puzzled. "So how did Willy get hurt if he was back under cover?" he asked.

"Ran forward to try to warn the old bloke," Anthony explained.

At that Andrew's estimation of Willy, who he thought was a noisy little show-off, went up considerably. The incident was discussed at length, during which Graham slipped away. Andrew watched him go with some anxiety, wondering how he could help his friend. No opportunity arose during the day, even though they were both in the same classes for Maths A, Physics and Maths B. Maths B was last period for the day and both Graham and Stephen were among those kept in by Mr Ritter to finish their homework.

'Poor old Graham. He's not having a very good time,' Andrew thought as he walked down the stairs away from the classroom. As things like Maths were simplicity itself to him he could only half understand Graham's problems. With a shrug he thrust his friend's difficulties from his thoughts and instead concentrated on Muriel. That got him all a-tingle again and he hoped she had been able to get permission for the sleepover.

At home he did his homework. Part of this was working on his history assignment on the *Merinda*. Not having any more information yet he could only edit and re-write and plan. 'I need a good map,' he decided. A search of the house did not uncover any suitable one so he decided to go to Lieut Commander Hazard's chandlery the following afternoon to buy one.

That night Muriel phoned. To Andrew's delight she said that the sleepover was approved by both her parents and by her grandparents. That got Andrew plotting. "Will your mum and dad be there?" he asked.

"Some of the time," Muriel answered. "At night anyway. Why, what does that matter?" Muriel asked in a teasing tone.

The husky timbre of her voice vibrated through Andrew like and electric charge and he became instantly aroused. He could only mumble that they might not like him. Muriel laughed and said, "Are you thinking of doing something they might not approve of?"

Andrew instantly blushed. "No.. er.. no," he denied.

Again Muriel laughed. "Spoilsport!" she said.

That really got Andrew's mind racing with speculation. 'Is she wanting me to try something?' he wondered. That got him both very aroused and very anxious. To keep the conversation moving he asked about the administrative details.

Muriel then asked, "Have you asked Carmen?"

"No, not yet," Andrew replied, feeling distinctly uncomfortable.

"Ask her please," Muriel requested.

"Ok," Andrew reluctantly agreed.

So he did. It took an effort but at last he went into her room and put the idea to her. Carmen was delighted. "Great idea! I was wondering what to do next weekend. Have you asked Mum yet?"

Andrew shook his head. "No, not yet."

"We will do it now," Carmen said. She stood up and walked through to the lounge, where their mother was busy sewing while watching TV.

Andrew followed, now anxious lest his mother say no. To his relief she agreed. "But only if all your homework and assignments are done," she added. Then she asked, "How will you get there? Are they picking you up, or do I have to drive you?"

"We could sail over Mum," Carmen suggested.

Mrs Collins looked thoughtful, then nodded. "Alright, but no sailing out to sea or anything."

"No Mum," Carmen agreed. "Thanks Mum." She hurried away, saying over her shoulder, "I will phone Muriel right away and let her know."

That was fine by Andrew. He just shrugged. When his sister took control he knew from experience it was easier to just go with the flow. Feeling happier he went back to his own room. That night in bed he again fantasized about Muriel, picturing daydreams of rescuing her. To his annoyance he kept getting images of Endeavour Island, and of a nude Letitia. It took a real mental effort to push her image out and replace it with that of Muriel. The memories got him all horny and he went to bed tingling with arousal.

Tuesday at school was similar to the day before. Andrew heard via the gossip mill that Stephen and Graham were both in trouble for a silly prank the previous afternoon. After being kept in they had tried to sneak out through the sliding divider to the next room. Stephen had been caught and Graham had got away, except that his absence had then been noted. He was now at the office in trouble. All Andrew could do was shake his head and wonder how he could help.

The day was a repeat of the previous one. Andrew spent time in the library and on the internet searching for more information on the wreck of the *Merinda*. He found almost none but did get a lot on the *Yongala*. It amazed him to see the advertisements by diving companies and it dawned on him that the wreck was a world famous dive site. Even so he was still scared of diving to see it.

When he read that it was in open water and that diving on it was very weather dependant he cheered up. 'If the waves are 2 metres or more then it is unsafe,' he read. "With a bit of luck the wind will get up," he muttered. That got him worrying about the other wreck that Sub Lt Sheldon had mentioned and he hoped that it would turn out to be unsuitable.

Last period was again Maths B with Mr Ritter and once again those that had no done their homework were kept in. As Andrew stood up to leave he saw Graham and Stephen still seated. Graham had a look of misery in his eyes but Stephen just looked annoyed. 'Poor old Graham. He should have done his homework,' Andrew thought. Still puzzling over a strategy to help his friend he left the room.

This time he did not go home but made his way down town to Lt Cdr Hazard's shop. This was a chandlery and Andrew always found it a fascinating place to visit. The sheer variety of nautical objects, allied to the medley of smells, kept him interested. The CO was quite a different person in his normal civilian guise and cheerfully asked Andrew what he wanted and showed him around. A copy of the chart of the coast and Great Barrier Reef between the Palm Islands and the Whitsunday Islands was quickly extracted from a huge map cabinet.

It was expensive but even so Andrew hesitated over buying the one for the next section of coast south past the Whitsunday Islands to Mackay. "According to the reports I have read the *Merinda* went down somewhere near the join of these two charts," he explained.

Lt Cdr Hazard chuckled and said, "That's how life always is, at the corners of four charts, with a headwind, and raining. Well, let me know if you want this other one."

"Thanks sir," Andrew replied. He paid for the chart and then hurried home to study it in detail. As always he was amazed at just how cluttered the Coral Sea was. There were hundreds of reefs, many not part of the long chain of reefs inaccurately labelled 'The Great Barrier Reef'. As he scanned the chart his eye caught an odd purple symbol and the words 'Historic Wreck (see Note)'. That caught his interest and he quickly scanned the note in the margin. To his disappointment it was merely a legal warning that all historic wrecks were protected by law.

Then the name of a nearby reef caught his eye. Morinda Sh. it read. 'Morinda? Is that a miss-spelling of *Merinda*?' he wondered. That got him speculating that the historic wreck might be the *Merinda*. Then he shook his head. 'I thought nobody knew where it was.' Then his gaze picked up the name Cape Bowling Green to the west of the historic wreck. 'No, not the *Merinda*. Must be the *Yongala*.'

That sent him to his books and after rereading an account of the discovery of the wreck of the *Yongala* in 1947 by the minesweeper HMAS *Lachlan* he measured the distance of the historic wreck from the coast and decided it had to be the *Yongala*.

Andrew's gaze them followed the coast south to Cape Upstart. He had heard of it but had no idea what it was like. On the chart it did not look very big but he dimly appreciated that was a scale problem. The numbers indicating quite high mountains on the cape gave him pause for thought. 'Hope I never see the place,' he mused.

Next he read another account of the sinking of SS *Gothenburg* in 1875. This account made the statement that the *Gothenburg* had run onto a reef called Old Reef. That puzzled Andrew because the other accounts he had read all stated that the ship struck 'a shallow reef near Nares Rock'. The book also showed a sketch map which placed Old Reef and another named Stanley Reef due east of Cape Bowling Green and nowhere near Bowen or Nares Rock. Intrigued by the discrepancy Andrew unrolled his new chart and located Old Reef on the map, then Nares Rock. He saw that they were at least 50 km apart. As the two descriptions were otherwise almost identical, word for word, he was left wondering exactly where the *Gothenburg* had come to grief.

Further reading of the salvage attempts by divers, with grisly descriptions of drowned people, caused him to shudder with revulsion. That got him worrying about how he might cope when faced with the challenge of diving on a real wreck. In particular the thought of deep diving, particularly at night, made him go cold with fear, much to his own disgust.

That night he had another diving nightmare but could only remember the vaguest outline of it when he woke. As he went about his morning routine it dawned on him that the sleepover was now approved and that in only three more days he would again be with Muriel. 'And for the whole weekend!' he thought happily, tingling with excitement and anticipation.

At school that day the work was, as usual, easy and not all that interesting. The only notable incident was again provided by Graham. Andrew learned that he and Stephen had again been caught trying to escape from detention (This time by climbing out of the classroom window. They had been caught by Mr Fitzgerald, the much-feared Deputy Principal). There was also gossip about Graham being picked up by the police when drunk, and of him writing graffiti on the toilet wall that morning.

The incident was in Maths A. The teacher, a bad-tempered, middle-aged man named Burgomeister (Buggermaster to the student body), seemed to make a point of picking on Graham. Sarcastically he said to Graham, "Ah! Master Kirk, who is sick. Show me the homework Mr Fitzgerald said you were to do. You too Bell."

On hearing that Andrew stopped working and looked back. He saw Graham shake his head and admit that he had not done it. Mr Burgomeister proceeded to lecture Graham, telling him what a failure he would be unless he 'pulled his socks up.' He ended by saying, "You are on the road to nowhere, you stupid boy!"

'That isn't right,' Andrew thought. 'He has no right to insult Graham like that.' Even so he hoped Graham would not react. To Andrew's distress he did. This led to a shouting match which stung Graham to react. He stood up and clenched his fists. Thinking to avert a real disaster Andrew stood up.

As Andrew took a step towards them Stephen stepped into the aisle ahead of him, inadvertently blocking his path. By then Mr Burgomeister was pointing to the door and screaming angrily at Graham, "You threaten me! Office! Get to the office!"

Stephen then did what Andrew had been thinking of doing. He grabbed Graham's arm and pulled him away from the teacher, propelling him towards the door. Andrew halted and watched, then met Mr Burgomeister's hostile glare and retreated to his seat. By then Graham had fled sobbing onto the veranda with Stephen still holding him.

The incident upset Andrew more than he wanted to admit but he was still unable to think of a sensible plan to help, beyond trying to be friendly. 'Graham should have stayed in the Navy Cadets,' he thought. 'At least there he would have had a bit of focus and might feel like he belonged.' That was how Andrew viewed Navy Cadets and he was deeply glad of it.

He did not see Graham until last period as he was in 'time out' during the lunch break. During Maths B Graham appeared but he sat next to Stephen. Andrew had no chance to speak to him. He planned to talk to him after the lesson but that did not eventuate either as both Stephen and Graham were kept in again for not doing their homework. Feeling quite sad Andrew made his way downstairs. Here he stood for a few minutes and watched the school's army cadet unit forming up for parade. Satisfied that the Navy Cadets did better drill he turned and walked thoughtfully to the bike racks.

That night he and Muriel had another long telephone conversation. Just listening to her voice got him aroused and tingling, the excitement barely dampened by the knowing looks given to him from time to time by Carmen and his mother. It was his mother who finally told him he had better hang up and get to bed.

In bed Andrew again fantasized about romantic adventures. After practising kissing his pillow he hugged it and lay there in the darkness calculating. 'Only about forty hours and we will be together.' It was a wonderful thought and again got him tingling with anticipation.

At school on Thursday Andrew had no opportunity to find out what had happened to Graham until after morning tea. During Chemistry he was able to ask Peter Bronsky if he knew.

To Andrew's surprise Peter grinned and said, "Graham has been made join the army cadets."

"Made? Can the school do that?" Andrew asked, both pleased and surprised.

Peter shook his head. "No. It was an agreement between the principal, Mr Conkey, Graham and his parents. His other choice was to be expelled. I think it is a really good idea."

"So do I," agreed Andrew. "Graham really needs something at the moment."

Peter nodded. "Let's hope it works. I really enjoy being in the army cadets."

"Army cadets!" Andrew scoffed good-naturedly.

At that moment the teacher, Mr Feldt, a likeable old chap with short grey hair, called over to them, "You two stop gossiping and get on with that experiment."

Andrew and Peter settled to work and did not get another chance to discuss Graham. But the news made Andrew feel much happier. 'I hope it helps him,' he thought. Then he shifted his own thoughts back to Muriel.

That night she again phoned him and she sounded very keen to see him. 'I hope so!' he thought, his body reacting to his desires and her voice. That sent Andrew to bed in a high state of arousal which he increased by fantasizing. Then he experienced a surge of guilt a having sexual thoughts about Muriel, and for the disloyal ones (mostly of Letitia, but some of the naked Sheena's Gang) which kept creeping in.

During Friday at school Andrew spoke briefly to Graham during Physics. Waiting till Miss Tate was busy explaining something to a student on the other side of the room he leaned across and said, "Peter tells me you have joined the army cadets."

Graham nodded and grunted but did not seem keen to talk about it. Sensitive to this Andrew nodded as well and said, "That's good. You should enjoy that. All your bushwalking will have been good experience."

Once again Graham nodded. He seemed to relax a bit. Then the teacher, Miss Tate, turned in their direction and came over to see how much work they had done. Andrew had almost finished but Graham was in trouble for having barely started.

Andrew did not see Graham at lunchtime as he was still on 'time out'. But by then Andrew's focus had shifted to that night. 'I will see Muriel in a few hours,' he thought happily, but anxiously. Now that their meeting grew closer anxiety crept in lest she had changed her mind. Even so just thinking about those heavenly kisses got Andrew all excited and the hours seemed to drag.

By the time he and Carmen arrived at Navy Cadets that evening Andrew was so nervous he was biting his nails and squirming in his seat. As he turned away from the car after saying goodnight to his mother Andrew looked anxiously around. Almost at once he saw Muriel and immediately his doubts were set at rest. She was walking quickly towards him, waving and smiling. An answering grin lit up Andrew's face and he had to suppress an urge to run over to her.

That set the tone for the evening. Even on parade he kept glancing around at her. Each time their eyes met she gave a little secret smile and her eyes seemed to sparkle and dance. Andrew tingled and trembled and felt a continual urge to be with her. The chance came after parade. He was sent to the storeroom to get some ropes for knot tying. While he was collecting them Muriel came in.

"Hello," Andrew croaked. "What are you looking for?"

"Signal flags," Muriel replied.

"Over here," Andrew answered, pointing to a locker at the end of the room. As Muriel walked towards it their eyes locked and a charge of electricity seemed to spark between them. Without conscious thought he stepped across and put his arms out. Muriel cast one quick glance over her shoulder, then stepped into his embrace. Her eyes lit up and she seemed to glow. No words were spoken but their lips came together.

After a minute of passionate kissing they drew apart, still holding each other. By then Andrew's heart was hammering and he had to swallow to moisten his dry throat. "Oh that was wonderful!" he croaked. "I've been wanting that all week."

"Me too," Muriel answered, smiling and sending his pulse rate even higher.

Once again they came together in a heated bout of kissing.

Chapter 12

Sleepover

Andrew could not believe his luck. He hugged Muriel to him and kissed her passionately, all the while stroking her back and sides. She responded, pressing against him and probing his mouth with her tongue. Surges of fierce desire swept through Andrew and he began to get an erection. That bothered him a bit as he could feel it pressing against Muriel and he did not want her to get the wrong idea.

Suddenly a female voice- Shona's- penetrated his consciousness. "Hey! Stop that you two. Not here. Save it for later."

Andrew jerked back and looked around, a wave of shame adding to his heat. Muriel just laughed and said, "Go away Shona. You are just jealous."

Shona grinned but shook her head. "You'd better behave; the 'Buffer' is just outside."

At the mention of the Chief Bosun's Mate Andrew experienced a spasm of fear, followed almost immediately by one of guilt. He was ashamed of his own weakness as he knew that 'fraternizing' was forbidden at cadets. There was also the anxiety that he could be disciplined. 'I might not get promoted. I could even be tossed out of cadets for such misbehaviour!' he thought. Those thoughts got him stepping well away from Muriel.

She wasn't quite as worried or as keen to stop but pouted and then shrugged. "Later then," she said.

At that moment Cadet Warrant Officer Chris Pike, the buffer, stepped into the storeroom. He looked around and then snapped, "Hurry up you people! Get the stores you need and get to your lessons. Where is the storeman?"

"Don't know Buffer," Andrew replied, scooping up a bundle of neatly coiled ropes. As quickly as he could he left the storeroom, leaving Muriel asking the buffer where the signal flags were.

For the rest of the training parade Andrew was in a state of arousal and hopeful excitement. Every time he saw Muriel he looked at her and was cheered by her giving him an answering smile. Once she even winked and he felt his heart skip with promise. Several people noticed and there was a bit of chaffing and teasing and twice he was reprimanded by instructors for inattention.

During 'Sunset' (the dismissal parade) Lt Cdr Hazard addressed them and reminded them that there was a camp planned for the first week of the September school holidays. The camp was to be in Mackay. They were to nominate for specialist courses and to get permission from their families to attend. He then went on, "Now we have a very pleasant duty to perform."

That got Andrew's attention and he looked with interest as Lt Cdr Hazard held up a sheet of paper. Lt Cdr Hazard then said, "This is a list of names of cadets whose promotions have been approved by the North Queensland Flotilla HQ."

Hope stirred in Andrew and he tensed with anticipation. Lt Cdr Hazard then said, "The following cadets fall out and form a line in front of me."

Andrew's was one of the names read out. He was promoted to Able Seaman. Puffing with pleasure and pride he marched out and stood in line. Lt Cdr Hazard then came along, assisted by CPO Walker, who had a packet of rank badges and a camera. Each cadet was congratulated, handed their new rank badges and then photographed in that pose. The cadets were then told to rejoin their divisions on the parade.

Next the instructors handed out 'Instructions' and Permission Forms for the Specialist Training camp. Lt Cdr Hazard then cheered Andrew even more by adding, "As you will see when you read the Instruction it is planned that we will be travelling to camp aboard the navy Landing Ship HMAS *Tobruk*. Now, that is not a promise. Things may change and the plan might fall through. The *Tobruk* might be redeployed for some operational reason at short notice. But at the moment we are booked to go aboard."

'Sunset' was then piped and the colours lowered, during which Andrew stood rigidly at attention. The cadets were then given, "Ship's companeeee... Dis... miss!"

Andrew turned to the right and marched off the 'quarter deck'. As he did Muriel joined him and they grinned at each other. "Are you still coming over this weekend?" she asked.

"You bet! Just wait a minute while I put my name down for one of the training courses," Andrew replied. He was very keen to get more qualifications and to get promoted in the cadets.

"I'll come with you," Muriel said. So the pair joined the queue outside the Training Officer's cabin. On the noticeboard outside was a list of the courses being offered. Andrew ran his eyes down the list: Seamanship,

Catering, Stores, Signals, Medical and Gunnery. So far Andrew had been merely a Recruit and a Seaman and had not qualified in any particular branch. Now he tried to decide what specialization he would follow. He knew that such a choice would also be required when he joined the Navy, 'If I get in'.

Seamanship really appealed to him and he hesitated over that, but the idea of gunnery also had appeal. He rejected signals because he wasn't at all sure he would be any good at it, not that he doubted its importance. Nor was he interested in medical, stores or catering. Into his mind leapt images from old 'newsreels' and historical videos of battleships firing their mighty guns. His rational mind told him that was silly. He knew perfectly well that modern naval warfare was conducted by missiles rather than guns; was more electronics than gunpowder. Even so he decided that gunnery was the one for him. He noted that the course available was for Quartermaster Gunners.

'That is the one for me,' he decided.

When Andrew reached the head of the line Sub Lt Sheldon, who sat behind the desk, asked him what his choice was. Andrew told him and he wrote it down without comment. Then he looked up and said, "I need to speak to you and the other divers about the diving course next weekend before you go. Please ask them to wait. And you are incorrectly dressed. You should be wearing Able Seaman rank slides."

"Aye, aye sir," Andrew replied. He saluted, about turned and marched away to make room for Muriel. Outside he quickly took the new AB ranks slides from his pocket and looked at them. Gently, almost reverently, he felt the gold embroidered reef knot on its black epaulet. A thrill of pleasure ran through him but he tried to act cool and unaffected. 'Casually' he slipped the rank slides on to his shoulder straps and then waited for Muriel.

"What course did you put down for?" he asked when she came out.

"Medical," Muriel replied. "I'm thinking of doing nursing when I leave school."

While they discussed the specialist courses Shona, Blake and Carmen joined them. There were congratulations all round as Carmen had been promoted to Leading Seaman and the others to AB. After handshakes they began discussing the arrangements for the weekend. As they talked Andrew's mother arrived. With her was Muriel's mum. Seeing her made Andrew feel all self-conscious and he blushed as he said hello, memories of that stolen kiss making him feel very guilty- and very pleased.

The mothers then had to be told about the promotions and there were more congratulations and hug for Andrew (Which embarrassed him in front of his friends!) and Carmen. The mothers then joined in the discussion about the weekend. Timings, transport, food and what to take were all discussed. The details were all agreed on before Sub Lt Sheldon joined them.

"Well?" he asked. "Who is allowed to go diving?"

Muriel answered at once. "I am."

Sub Lt Sheldon looked at Muriel's mother. She nodded and said, "At this stage yes. Unless something comes up."

Blake also said yes but Shona shook her head. "My Mum can't afford it," she explained.

Luke also said no. "My Mom, she don't want me divin' on any old wrecks. She think it too dangerous."

Sub Lt Sheldon then looked at Andrew's mother. "Mrs Collins?"

Andrew's mother looked very thoughtful. "Well, I still don't like it. It is this wreck diving that I am particularly worried about. I am not happy about them diving way out in the open ocean on this wreck, the *Yongala.*"

Carmen at once spoke up. "Oh Mum! Please! It will be alright."

Sub Lt Sheldon added, "What if they dive on one of the wrecks in shallow water close inshore? There are several close to Magnetic Island as I said. They are only down ten metres or so."

"Won't that disappoint the other people on this course?" Mrs Collins asked. "As I understand it there are other people involved."

"Yes, there should be, possibly half a dozen," Sub Lt Sheldon agreed. He then went on, "It may not. Often there is a basic course being run at the same time, and if the weather gets up then it is not safe to dive on the *Yongala.* In that case we dive on a more sheltered site. In fact the Townsville club are doing an exploratory dive on a new wreck this weekend. It might turn out to be just what we want. They haven't said exactly where it is yet as they want to keep the site secret till they are sure it is suitable and safe."

That got Andrew's curiosity aroused. "What sort of wreck is it sir?" he asked.

"My friends were a bit guarded," Sub Lt Sheldon replied. "It is only a small steel ship and is in quite shallow water. They say it might be the wreck of a trawler or something like that."

That didn't sound too hopeful to Andrew, who had immediately begun to speculate that the wreck might be the *Merinda.* "Do they know its name Sir?" he asked.

Sub Lt Sheldon shook his head. "No. They are diving on it this weekend and will try to identify it. I will phone them on Sunday evening to get the details. So, who do I make bookings for?"

This time Andrew's mother nodded. "Yes, alright. But only if they do the wreck dive in shallow water and on one of these small wrecks."

On hearing that Andrew felt his stomach churn with fear but he could only give what he was sure was a sickly grin in answer to Carmen's delighted cries and Muriel's happy smile. 'Maybe it will be cancelled by bad weather,' he thought, now clutching at straws and knowing it. Inside he despised himself for being a coward and a weakling, but he could not bring himself to admit to Muriel that he was scared.

Sub Lt Sheldon agreed that they would only dive on one of the safer wrecks, then Andrew's mother said, "Well, come on children. Time for bed."

Being called a child in front of Muriel was embarrassing but Andrew was so taken up with her that he could only grin. "Goodnight," he said, trying to add meaning with his eyes.

"See you tomorrow," Muriel whispered back, her sultry voice fuelling Andrew's hopes.

Reluctantly the two parted. Andrew kept glancing across at Muriel as they walked out to their respective cars. 'I wish we were staying together tonight,' he thought, then blushed at the lust and wickedness of his own thoughts.

These stayed with him to give him heated fantasies at home before he dropped off to sleep, then to trouble his rest. Dreams of Muriel were intertwined with nightmares about diving. One moment he would be wrapped in her arms in a passionate embrace, the next he would be trapped under water and gripped by the tentacles of a giant octopus that had slid out of the murky interior of a wreck to grab him. The slimy creature then began to suck so hard that he felt his body was being torn apart.

The dreams left him tired but excited when he woke. Then, as realization that he was soon going to be with Muriel dawned, Andrew's spirits lifted and he sprang out of bed full of life and happiness. But it was not to be, yet. First there were the household chores. Andrew had to do his share and this kept him busy for the next three hours: mowing, washing the dog, weeding a garden, trimming some crotons, and helping his mother hang out the washing. Only after lunch was he able to get ready.

Mrs Collins drove Carmen and Andrew down to the Yacht Club, towing their catamaran behind the family car. Waiting for them there were Shona and Blake. Jennifer was to travel with Muriel in her mother's car. After the usual motherly warnings to be careful and to avoid getting sunburnt and so on Mrs Collins helped them launch the cat, then left them to it. The cat was quickly rigged, the gear stowed and secured, then the voyage begun.

It was a lovely North Queensland 'winter' day, not a cloud in the sky and just cold enough to want a jacket of some sort. The waters of the Inlet were calm and there was barely enough wind. As it was the catamaran just slipped quietly along with a pleasant rippling sound, their speed just above a walking pace.

The slow progress got Andrew all impatient but knowing that he was now an able seaman made him content. He was cheered by soon having their objective in sight and growing steadily closer. The houses at Giangurra and Bosuns Bay were lit up by the afternoon sun and looked very attractive, set as they were among the trees above the shore. Navigation presented no difficulty and it was only the relative lack of wind that caused Andrew to fret.

The catamaran rounded the rocky point of Bosuns Bay just after 3:00 pm. Carmen had the tiller and she conned the cat into the bay in two easy tacks, ending on the beach right near where the rusty rails of the slipway led down out of the old boathouse.

By then Muriel and Jennifer had run down, waving and calling out greetings. Muriel wore tight white shorts and a green T-shirt. The white shorts set off her shapely, tanned legs to perfection. Seeing that, plus Muriel's bright and welcoming smile, got Andrew's spirits up and he became quite excited.

Muriel pointed up to the house as they stepped ashore. "You are just in time for afternoon tea. Grab your gear and come on up."

"What about the boat?" Carmen asked.

"Just drag it up the beach," Muriel answered.

They grouped around the catamaran and, on Carmen's command, lifted and carried the catamaran well up past the high tide line. The anchor rope was secured to one of the large trees which overhung the beach at that point and then the sails lowered and furled. Only when Carmen was satisfied that the cat was secured properly and all ship-shape did she allow them to leave. After the luggage was unloaded the friends set off up the short driveway in a group.

Muriel led the way past the side of the boathouse and then up the concrete steps beside it to the terraced garden. As they went up the steps Andrew followed her and was granted tantalising close-ups of her thighs and bum. It embarrassed him and he pretended not to be looking but found it hard not to. It also had the effect of starting to make him become aroused. The immediate consequence was feeling guilty and ashamed when he found himself saying hello to Muriel's mother and grandmother on the patio at the top of the next set of steps.

Andrew had been hoping to have a chance to talk to Old Mr Murchison about the sinking of the *Deeral* so was mildly disappointed not to see the old man. As he seated himself in one of the cane chairs facing out to sea he asked politely if he was well.

Grandma Murchison nodded and answered. "Yes dearie. He's just having his afternoon nap. You will meet him at tea time."

Afternoon tea was delicious: freshly baked pumpkin scones, hot and spread with melting butter; cordial and fruit juice, biscuits and nuts. Andrew was content to sit quietly and listen, while frequently glancing at Muriel and admiring her beauty. She responded by granting him numerous smiles, sending his hopes even higher.

"What do we do now?" Carmen asked as the afternoon tea things were gathered and carried into the kitchen.

"Games," Muriel answered. She pointed out onto the terraced back garden. "Shuttlecock to begin with."

Andrew gestured inside. "I'll just go to the toilet first."

"I need to go too," Muriel replied. They both stood up. Andrew noted knowing smirks on the faces of Blake and Shona and that made him blush. Muriel led Andrew along the passageway into the house. On one side was a kitchen and dining room. On the right were a bathroom and toilet. The pair stopped in the alcove. "You go first," Muriel said.

As she did Andrew met her eyes. He had stopped close behind her and now found her proximity exciting. He smiled and she smiled back and then glanced back along the passageway. Both moved towards each other. Andrew leaned forward to kiss her even as his arms went to her waist. Hers slid around his neck and their lips met. Muriel kissed with such intensity that Andrew felt quite stunned and overwhelmed. She squirmed and her breathing through her nose was loud in his ear.

When they drew apart Andrew felt quite breathless and could only gasp and stare into her eyes in wonder. Her eyes sparkled and she smiled in a way that made his heart turn over with hope and lust. "I've been wanting that all week," she said.

They kissed again but quickly stopped and drew apart when footsteps sounded in the passageway. It was Carmen. She gave them a wry smile and said, "Hurry up you two. We want to start."

Feeling somewhat embarrassed Andrew hurried into the toilet. Muriel was waiting with Carmen so he did not linger. After he came out he made his way back out to the patio. By then the others were down on the back lawn setting up a net between two posts. Shuttlecock was not a game that particularly appealed to Andrew but he was willing to play almost any game if Muriel wanted him to. So for the next half hour he was an enthusiastic, if not particularly skilful, player.

Wiping sweat from her face Carmen asked, "What about a drink and then playing something else?"

"Good idea," Muriel agreed. "We will play Hide-and-seek."

That sounded like a very good idea to Andrew as it offered the possibility of being alone with Muriel. She obviously thought so too as she kept giving him impish glances and giggling. Cold cordial was drunk and then Muriel laid down the rules.

"No hiding in the upstairs. Grandad isn't well and we must not disturb him. No going off into the bush. You can hide anywhere in the garden and this side of the creek, anywhere downstairs and in the boatshed. I am in, so start running. One.. two... three."

Andrew followed the general rush down the steps beside the boatshed. At the bottom he hesitated. A glance at the bushes and rocks lining the creek on the other side of the driveway tempted him but then he decided that the boatshed was a better option. There was a door right beside him at the bottom of the steps so he turned the handle. To his relief it was unlocked. Equally obviously it had not been opened recently as it was hard to open, the door squeaking on rusty hinges.

Inside it was almost completely dark except for a strip of sunlight coming in under the front doors. Andrew stepped inside and carefully pushed the door closed, then stood with his back to it to allow his eyes time to adjust to the dark. As they did he made out the dark bulk of a boat sitting in a cradle on the slipway. On shelves along the sides were stacked all sorts of oddments: coils of rope, oars, boxes, tools, bundles of canvas.

The boat held Andrew's attention. It was a motor cabin cruiser but of an old-fashioned design. The hull was varnished marine plywood and the small cabin some sort of polished dark wood. The propellers were green with verdigris and there were a few streaks of rust at the stern glands. It had obviously been a luxury boat in its day, but equally obviously had not been in the water for a long time. With a slight sense of regret Andrew gently stroked the smooth, varnished plywood and shook his head on seeing where a timber strake had begun to split.

"What a great boat," Andrew muttered, climbing under the stern to study the hull form. Then he stood and looked around for a place to hide. Along the landward end of the shed were more shelves and stacks of old plywood tea chests. These were dry and cracked with age and were stuffed to overflowing with assorted nautical items: sails, lanterns, ropes, turnbuckles, paddles and so forth. More oars were hung from the wall, along with various spars and booms. Rotten rope was coiled and hung up all along the far wall and there was an untidy litter of tools and off-cuts of timber among the greasy dust of the floor.

Among the objects festooning the far wall Andrew noticed an old-fashioned lifebuoy. It was of the circular variety and had once been painted red and white. A rope was looped around the outside for people to cling to and it was by one of these loops that it was hung on the wall. Intrigued Andrew moved towards it, wishing to read the name of the vessel it came from, the smudgy letters being just visible through layers of mildew, dust and cobwebs.

However, as he reached forward to wipe away the closest cobwebs the side door was suddenly pulled open and he remembered he was supposed to be playing hide-and-seek, not exploring. Thinking that the boat on its cradle might hide him he crouched down- but to no avail.

Muriel's voice came to him, "I see you!" She laughed and made her way in past the stern of the launch. "I thought I might find you in here," she said.

"Am I that predictable?" Andrew asked. He felt slightly peeved at her saying that.

Again Muriel laughed. "All men are," she murmured, stepping closer and fixing his eyes with hers. Sensing what she wanted Andrew stepped closer and put out his arms. A moment later they were in a passionate embrace. To Andrew it was wonderful. He gripped her to him and kissed, enjoying the feel of her against him, the sweet scents, the taste, the sheer stimulating pleasure of her body against his.

One result was that he became very aroused. As he pressed against her he began to worry lest she think it was all he wanted. No wanting to offend or give the wrong message he tried to ease back but she gripped him even tighter and gently writhed her body against his. That had the effect like a volcanic eruption in the top of his head. His senses swam and his heart hammered as he became even more excited.

His hands slid up and down her back and he relished the feel of them moving over the curve of her hips and buttocks. After several more kisses his mind began to speculate on whether she would mind if he touched her breasts. It was now something he urgently desired to do. He could feel them pressing against his chest and when he and she drew apart he could see them moving up and down inside her T-shirt as she breathed.

By then both were panting and hot and Andrew nerved himself to make an attempt. But fear all but paralyzed him. 'If she doesn't approve I will be in trouble,' he reasoned. Fear held his attempt to a few tentative strokes of her sides.

Then, just as he steeled himself to make the attempt, another shadow partially blocked the doorway. Andrew snatched back his hand as though it was red hot as the person who had entered made their way across the top end of the boatshed. 'I hope it isn't her mother!' Andrew thought. Then an even more worrying thought came to him:- what if it is her dad!

Chapter 13

By Moonlight

A ndrew released Muriel, and she him, just as a head poked around the bow of the launch. To Andrew's relief it was Jennifer. "Stop that you two!" she called, her face alight with laughter. "We are playing hide-and-seek, not catch-and-kiss!"

Muriel giggled and called back, "It can be, if you want that."

Jennifer shook her head. "Nah! There isn't a boy here that I fancy, not one that isn't already taken anyway," she replied.

Andrew felt Muriel stiffen and supposed that she had drawn the same conclusion as him; that he was worth chasing. 'Surely she doesn't mean me,' he thought. 'She must mean Blake.' He had always admired Jennifer for her beauty and grace but had never dared to think of trying to win her affection. Now he feared that she had made Muriel jealous.

Muriel sounded annoyed. "You are supposed to be hiding and I am in. So start running," she snapped back at Jennifer.

Jennifer stopped smiling at the tone of voice used to her and nodded, then turned and hurried away. Muriel started after her, then gestured to Andrew. "Come on Andrew, follow."

"Yes, just a minute," Andrew replied. His eye had again caught the old lifebuoy and his curiosity was aroused. He stepped towards it.

Muriel frowned and called again. "Never mind that old rubbish. The house is full of it. Let's catch Jennifer and the others."

Despite that Andrew leaned closer and brushed more cobwebs aside. As he did his eyes made out the faint letter 'C'. That quickened his interest. Ignoring Muriel's calls he gently traced the other letters, noting as he did that the lifebuoy was covered in rotten fabric, some sort of thick canvas. Through the holes in the painted cloth he could make out that the lifebuoy was made of cork. That was interesting to him as modern lifebuoys were either polystyrene or plastic. The painted cloth was stiff but now very brittle and when he tried to lift the lifebuoy off its hook it began to tear. Very carefully he replaced it on the hook and bent closer.

As his eyes made out the lettering his interest grew. 'Yes!' he thought happily. On the two white sections of the cloth were painted the words

DEERAL
CAIRNS

'This must be the lifebuoy Old Mr Murchison survived in,' he thought. It was then borne upon his consciousness that Muriel was sounding cross so he turned and started towards the door, thinking that he must ask the old man when he got the chance.

That ambition was quickly forgotten though as chasing after Muriel was more important. Just watching her lithe form running with athletic grace was enough to divert his thoughts and his admiration grew. 'She is really beautiful!' he marvelled.

As they ran he now saw the creek that she had referred to and it amazed him that he had not noticed earlier. From the other side of the road beside the door of the boathouse the ground sloped gently off into scrubby, dry bush to where thicker, darker vegetation indicated a watercourse. Now Andrew saw that the creek line was about fifty metres from the house but that it angled closer to it further up the slope. As no obvious stream mouth was visible on the beach he was still puzzled but, on arriving there, he saw that no water was actually flowing across the beach. A bar of sand blocked it and overhanging branches effectively concealed the stream bed beyond it.

Jennifer had attempted to hide behind some large rocks near the other side of the stream but in running along the beach had left a clear set of fresh footprints. Muriel pointed to them and laughed, then said, "I don't think Our Man Friday made these."

She then ran long the tracks to the rock. As Andrew followed he had vivid flashbacks to being on Endeavour Island in April. The images of nudity, sex and the violence of the crooks all caused him uncomfortable thoughts. Seeing Jennifer's laughing face helped banish these. For a minute the friends stood and talked, then Muriel looked around and set off back to where the catamaran lay on the top of the beach.

"Gotcha!" she shrieked. Carmen's face appeared and she was all smiles as well as both Muriel and Andrew had run past within a couple of paces and had not seen her.

Once again Muriel looked around. "Now only Shona and Blake to find," she said.

"They will be together," Andrew commented.

"Then we had better hurry to save them from doing things they shouldn't oughta," Jennifer added.

Just thinking about some of those 'shouldn't oughta' things got Andrew all hot and anxious and he knew he was a hypocrite as he wanted to do them himself, had even tried to only a few minutes earlier. 'Maybe we will get a chance later?' he hoped.

The friends found them both hiding in the garage and 'downstairs' storeroom where their gear had been dumped. They were not kissing but both looked happy.

"What do we do now?" Carmen asked.

"We should organize your beds for tonight," Muriel answered. She pointed around the downstairs area. "You will be sleeping down here and can use that toilet and shower."

This was the shower Andrew and the others had used during the diving weekend so he was familiar with it. Next to it was the double garage but in front of the parked cars was a large 'downstairs' area. On the 'downhill' side were a store room, toilet, shower, laundry (with a connecting door through to the back lawn) then the concrete steps leading up to the far side of the patio. On the uphill side were several rooms leading off a central passageway. The group now made their way past the cars to these. The biggest room, on the right, was a workshop. On the other side was some sort of office with an old table covered with a litter of papers and boxes.

Muriel pointed into it and said, "The boys are sleeping in here."

Andrew glanced in and wasn't impressed. The floor was dusty and there were cupboards and what appeared to be a large map cabinet against the walls. A single window opened out just above ground level but gave very little light through its grimy panes.

Jennifer wasn't impressed either. "Yuk!" she cried. "This looks spooky. I hope there aren't rats and cockroaches."

"Where do we sleep?" Carmen asked.

"In the garage near the steps," Muriel indicated. Then she pointed up the steps, "Or, if you don't like that, then you can bunk on the patio."

"Patio I think," Carmen replied, looking around the garage with distaste.

"Where are you sleeping?" Andrew asked Muriel. Then he blushed fiercely when the others looked at him and smirked.

Shona giggled. "Why do you want to know?" she teased.

"Just wondered," Andrew mumbled, blushing fiercely.

Muriel smiled at that and explained that she was in a room upstairs with her mother and that her little brother and father had the other spare bedroom. "Now let's get everyone set up and get ready for tea. It is five now and Grandma always eats at six."

From a storeroom at the uphill end of the downstairs two old foam rubber mattresses were extracted. These were for Blake and Andrew. The table was moved into the far corner of the room. Andrew took a broom to the room they were to sleep in and quickly cleared the worst of the dirt, raising quite a cloud of dust as he did. The mattresses were then placed side by side by Muriel.

"Not that close together," Blake protested. "We don't like each other that much. We aren't like that!"

Muriel laughed but Shona positively shrieked. Blake glowered at her. "You'll get yours!" he mock threatened.

"Promise?" Shona teased.

Blake gave an evil grin and went to try to grab her. Shona shrieked again and fled behind Carmen, then out the door and up the stairs. Andrew watched jealously, wishing he had the courage to chase Muriel so openly. But he felt he didn't know her that well and did not want to annoy or embarrass her. Instead he gave her a grin. What he really wanted to do was make some arrangement to meet secretly later.

Blake returned and went on with making up his bed. Muriel called to Carmen and Jennifer to follow her and led them upstairs as well. Andrew also set about making up his bed. Having done that he collected his towel, toiletries and a change of clothes from his bag, then made his way to the shower. Showering he found arousing because he kept thinking of Muriel and of Letitia, the erotic memories causing him to become very aroused. Only Blake calling out caused him to quickly finish washing, dry himself and dress.

After dressing in clean clothes Andrew went outside and sat on his bed to dry his feet and to comb his hair. Meanwhile Blake replaced him in the shower. Andrew then went to the toilet. By the time he came out Blake was finished in the shower and was testing his bed, lying back and joking. After fluffing up his pillow Andrew did likewise. Settling back he joked with Blake while looking around. Beside him was a cupboard. Out of idle curiosity he reached up and opened it. Seeing nothing but old clothes hanging inside he closed it, then pointed to the cabinet next to Blake. The cabinet was wide and low, with a dozen narrow drawers, each the width of the cabinet.

"What's in that? Is it a map case?" he asked.

Blake shrugged and then reached across to one of the small handles. Tugging at it he pulled the drawer out half a metre. By arching his back and craning his neck he was able to look. "Old charts," he answered.

That got Andrew's interest. He rolled over and stood up, then walked across to look. To do so he had to step on Blake's bed, a procedure that Blake objected to. But he was right- they were old sea charts. Andrew saw that the top one was of the east coast of Cape York Peninsula and the Coral Sea. The names told him it was right up near the Torres Strait.

"Raine Island," he read. "I must go there one day."

"Where's that?" Blake asked, kneeling to look.

"Near where the *Pandora* hit a reef and sank," Andrew answered, pointing to where the words 'Pandora Entrance' were labelled in an opening in the Great Barrier Reef. He lifted the corner of that chart to look at the next, noting that all were discoloured with age. The next chart was of the coast off Cairns and the one below that of the Mackay to Broad Sound area. The next one down was of the Whitsunday Islands and the one after that of the Coral Sea from Townville to east of Bowen. Noting several pencil lines and mathematical calculations Andrew leaned closer.

At that moment Muriel's voice came from the door. "Come up and have tea you boys."

For several seconds Andrew hesitated, fascinated by the pencil lines and bearings on the old chart. 'This is the area where the *Merinda* and *Deeral* sank,' he mused, noting that the chart covered only part of the area on the one he had purchased. It was on a scale that showed a smaller area but in much greater detail.

"Andrew!" insisted Muriel. "You can look at them anytime, now come on."

Reluctantly Andrew let the charts drop back into place and then slid the drawer back in. As he did Blake made his way out of the room, leaving him alone with Muriel. Recognizing the opportunity Andrew at once forgot old charts and instead stepped over to her. "Will we be able to see each other tonight?" he asked, feeling greatly daring.

Muriel lowered her eyes, fluttered her eyelashes and dimpled her lips into a mischievous grin. "I don't know what you mean," she simpered. Then she burst out giggling when he tried to explain. "Of course, if you want to," she laughed.

"When?" Andrew asked, taking her hands and stepping closer.

"After everyone else is asleep," Muriel replied. "At midnight, down on the beach."

Hearing that sent Andrew into a state of high hopes and he put is arms around her and pulled her closer. She smiled and responded and they came together in a passionate embrace. For several minutes they clung together, kissing and caressing. Within moments Andrew was strongly aroused and he firmly, but gently ran his hands over Muriel's back and hips, relishing the soft smoothness and wondering if he dare try more.

The patter of stealthy footsteps reached his ears just as he nerved himself to try. Over the sound of Muriel's breathing he heard Shona whisper, "I'll bet they are!"

Just in time Andrew took Muriel's arms from around his neck and stepped back. Heads poked around the doorpost and Shona's and Jennifer's grinning faces appeared. Shona cried, "Told you so!"

Andrew flamed with embarrassment, felt both angry and foolish, then annoyed as there was no sensible reason why he shouldn't want to kiss his girlfriend. But the mood was destroyed and he did not want the other girl's to see his aroused condition. While trying to pretend that nothing had happened Andrew followed Muriel out and up the stairs behind the other two. By then his body had returned to normal and another anxiety had crept in- meeting Old Mr Murchison.

The memory of how shocked the old man had appeared, and of his collapse, made Andrew worry. As he came up the internal stairs to the patio Andrew now saw that Old Mr Murchison was seated at the large table, along with Grandma Murchison and Muriel's parents and little brother. Carmen and Blake sat at a smaller circular table.

Muriel walked straight over to her grandfather and bent to kiss him, then gestured to Andrew. "Hi Grandad! Feeling better? This is Andrew. You met him a few weeks ago, remember?"

Old Mr Murchison looked irritated and nodded but then turned to meet Andrew's gaze. When Andrew anxiously held out his hand the old man took it and gave it a brief shake. "Of course I remember," he replied. "I'm not senile yet, yer know. Hello young Collins."

"Hello sir. Sorry for upsetting you last time."

"Not your fault boy. Just one of those things. I never thought to meet anyone from your family. Was quite unexpected," Old Mr Murchison explained. Then he harrumpfed and looked away, taking up his tea cup.

Andrew still felt uncomfortable and embarrassed but took the opportunity to move away. Muriel's mother then asked him what he would like to eat and his attention was taken up with selecting from cold meats, salad and fruit. Having loaded his plate Andrew moved to sit between Muriel and Carmen over to one side.

The meal was a fairly silent affair, partly because Muriel's father was listening to the news on a radio. The food was good and plentiful and Andrew particularly liked the fruit cup cordial. Even more he liked watching Muriel as the last glow of the setting sun lit up her face. From time to time she looked at him and smiled, making him feel very special and very happy. While chewing another mouthful he looked out over the terrace and boatshed to the bay and beyond. The last rays of the sun were catching a launch making its way back to Cairns and it was all wonderful to him.

Andrew wanted to ask Old Mr Murchison about the lifebuoy but was reluctant to broach the subject. Then Muriel's mother began bustling around cleaning up and the opportunity was lost. Old Mr Murchison was helped inside and the girls roped into cleaning up. Blake and Andrew were sent into a very comfortable lounge to watch TV.

Later, when the girls joined them, they watched more TV, then played 'Monopoly' for an hour. All the while Andrew wanted to get away with Muriel but her parents both sat in the room, him reading a newspaper and her knitting and chatting to Grandma Murchison. Andrew enjoyed the games but, to his own surprise, discovered he was quite tired.

Thus, when supper was served and then bed suggested, he felt more than ready. This introduced a new worry- how to make sure he did not fall asleep and miss his assignation with Muriel! It was only 10:30 when the boys made their way downstairs to get ready for bed.

Grandma Murchison came down with them to see that they were settled in alright. "Leave the toilet light on dearies," she instructed. "Then you won't bump into anything in the dark."

After Grandma Murchison had gone Blake padded out of the room. Andrew sat up and asked, "Where are you going?"

"Just to check on the girls," Blake replied. He padded off in his pyjamas.

Andrew was wearing his and felt quite self-conscious but got up and followed him. By the time he was half way up the stairs he could hear giggling and the girls calling out. Blake stood at the top and was busy teasing the girls. Between the wall of the lounge room and the balustrade of the stairwell were three mattresses, laid side by side. On these lay Carmen, Jennifer and Shona. All three were in their pyjamas- Shona's being the only slightly risque ones.

While they talked and joked Muriel appeared at the back door, also in her night attire- some sort of cotton shift which left Andrew speculating on what, if anything, she wore under it.

"You boys go away," she said. "Let the girls sleep."

"We are just saying goodnight and checking that they are safe," Blake replied with a grin at Shona.

"Not safe from you!" Muriel replied.

At that moment Muriel's mother came out of the back door. "No talk like that please," she said. Then she looked at them all. "Bed time. And

I don't want any 'hank-panky' from you children. Your parents expect you to be on your best behaviour."

"Yes Shona," Jennifer added, "No sneaking off to meet Blake after we go to sleep."

Shona pouted and looked hurt. Muriel's mother pursed her lips. "Yes, that goes for all of you. No sneaking off behind my back. You hear me Muriel?"

"Yes Mum," Muriel answered in a sulky voice, her eyes flicking towards Andrew.

Muriel's mother intercepted the glance and looked at Andrew. "Promise you won't misbehave Andrew," she said.

That put Andrew right on the spot and he blushed, swallowed and nodded. "Yes Mrs Murchison."

"Good, now go to bed children."

Andrew blushed again, irritated at being called a child. As he watched Muriel's mother go back inside he felt his hopes crash. 'Drat! Now I won't be able to kiss Muriel in the moonlight,' he thought. And it was moonlight. Outside the full moon was lighting up the bush and the back lawn. It reflected off the waves in a shimmering dapple effect and made everything appear silvery and magical.

"Good night then," he said, trying to keep his disappointment out of his voice.

Muriel made a face then walked over to the patio railing as he turned to make his way back down the stairs. "It's a lovely night," she said, just loudly enough for the others to hear. Then, more softly, "See you later then, at midnight."

Andrew was deeply shocked. "We can't," he said. "We just promised your Mum that we wouldn't."

To his dismay and disappointment Muriel just shrugged. "She won't know," she whispered.

That really put Andrew on a spot. In his own mind he had made a promise and he now sensed that he was going to have to choose between his own integrity and keeping Muriel happy. The old saying 'Hell hath no fury like a woman scorned' crossed his mind and made him deeply anxious. There was also deep and growing disappointment and puzzlement. 'How could Muriel do that?' he wondered. 'How could she plan to team up with a man who she knows cannot be trusted?'

But he knew that an answer was needed. There was no obvious way he could avoid the situation as she was standing close and looking at him, obviously waiting for a reply. A bitterness welled up in Andrew as he faced the cruel choice, but with it came regret as he already knew what he would decide. "Sorry. I gave my word. I can't do it," he croaked.

"Oh tosh!" hissed Muriel angrily, plainly stung by his refusal. "Don't you love me?"

"I do," Andrew answered, but even as he did he wondered, knowing that something fundamental to their relationship had just been destroyed.

"Then, if you love me, you will meet me tonight," Muriel challenged.

Andrew's mind raced, seeking a suitable reply that would put off any break or confrontation. He thought, with some anger, 'And if you love me, you won't put me to that test,' but he just shook his head and said, "Sorry. I promised your Mum and I am sticking to it."

"You're scared!" Muriel jibed hotly.

That hurt but made Andrew even more determined. 'I've got to live with myself,' he thought. 'If I start cheating and lying now my self respect will go down the drain.' Again he shook his head. Sadly he said, "Sorry, no. Goodnight."

Feeling distinctly miserable he turned and made his way down the steps. He half expected Muriel to argue, even to embarrass him in front of the others, but she just snorted and turned away. 'I think I've cooked my goose now,' he thought, but he still felt he had done the right thing. Feeling almost ready to burst into tears he flung himself on his bed and turned to face the wall.

Blake followed a few minutes later. By then Andrew was feeling distinctly peeved. As Blake came in he turned the room light off and then made his way to his bed. To avoid talking and thereby revealing his unhappiness Andrew remained on his side and pretended to sleep. He had been so hopeful and worked up- and now he was just frustrated and unhappy. Brooding on this kept him awake and he lay for hours, worrying whether he could recover the situation, wondering if he wanted to. Severe doubts about whether he and Muriel were actually suited swirled round and round in his unhappy mind.

Chapter 14

Regrets

Andrew was roused by murmuring noises. Into his sleep-fuddled consciousness came a girl's giggle, then husky whispering. With a groan of reluctance Andrew rolled over and opened his eyes. He saw at once that it was daylight and that Shona was bending over Blake, lying half on him while they kissed. A sharp stab of deep regret lanced through Andrew as he remembered his actions of the previous night. Mixed in with the regret, was regret at not having given in to temptation- and jealousy that Blake was getting what he wanted, what his newly roused boy's body urgently desired.

The sounds he made caused the other two to stop kissing. Shona turned her head and then giggled again. "Breakfast time," she said. "Up you get."

"That's what I want," Blake quipped, raising his head to look towards Andrew, while still gripping Shona to him.

"What?" Shona asked, turning back to kiss him on the nose, "To have breakfast?"

"No. To get up," Blake replied. It took a moment for the double meaning to sink in but then Shona went red and cried, "Oh don't be rude!" but she said it with no heat in her voice and did not struggle to get away.

It embarrassed Andrew though. He squirmed to a sitting position and wondered if he would ever get to kiss Muriel again. To cover his aroused state and his confusion he groped for his towel, then staggered out to the toilet and shower. The cold water helped wake him up but by then his mind had roamed over all the things he thought he had done wrong and left him gloomily wondering what his fate might be.

Carmen calling down the stairs to hurry up for breakfast did little to help. By the time Andrew had changed into shirt and shorts and made his way to the steps he felt so sick in the stomach from apprehension he had no appetite. It took an effort to make himself walk up to the patio, fearing to learn his fate.

The other girls were all there. Carmen and Jennifer both greeted him cheerfully but Andrew was only interested in Muriel. He saw at once that she was not happy and that she looked tired. As he walked towards them she turned and met his eyes, then said, "Hello," but with no particular liking. Andrew was aware that he must have hurt her feelings and made her feel rejected but he didn't know what to say, or how to say it, to make up. He also vaguely resented the whole situation.

Carmen cast swift glances from one to the other but then asked, "Where are Blake and Shona?"

"Still downstairs," Andrew replied.

"I'll get them," Jennifer said. She stood and hurried to the steps and down them. By then Andrew had seated himself. Muriel met his eyes and he thought he saw regret in them too. "What would you like to eat?" she asked, indicating the spread of cereal, fruit, toast and jams.

Deciding not to say anything much at the moment Andrew indicated 'Weetbix' with butter and honey. As he spread the butter he heard loud laughter from downstairs and shrill denials from Shona. Rather than get involved Andrew looked around. He saw that it as a brilliant sunny day, the light sparkling of the water. Down in the garden were Grandma Murchison and Muriel's little brother but of the other adults there was no sign. His watch told him it was already eight thirty so that did not surprise him, it being Sunday morning.

Shona and a grinning Blake appeared behind Jennifer. "Kissing," Jennifer said impishly.

It was very obvious to Andrew that both Blake and Shona were very happy. They sat and held hands and kept touching each other in a way that made him both jealous and frustrated. That it was also annoying Muriel was clear to him.

"What are we doing today?" Jennifer asked.

Muriel shrugged then said, "Exploring maybe? Or we can swim or play games."

Exploring was voted on but that could not begin until all had eaten, brushed their teeth, put on footwear and collected hats. It was nearly 9:30 before they set off. Muriel told her mother they were just going up the creek for a while and Andrew heard her mother caution her to watch out for snakes. That made him a bit anxious but as they were in a group he soon forgot.

The group made its way out the front door and onto the driveway. Twenty metres in front was the main road and just to the right of the driveway entrance was a low concrete bridge, just visible through the crotons.

Muriel led the way across the driveway and down a short foot track to the creek bed. "We never go across the main road," she explained. "We always go under the bridge."

Hearing that brought vividly to Andrew's mind a scene from one of his favourite books: 'Swallowdale' by Arthur Ransome. The children in that were always pretending they were explorers in some hostile territory; avoiding 'Indians' or 'savage natives'. As he was always daydreaming similar stories Andrew thought it a good idea. Forgetting his unhappiness for a moment he conjured up a story of being with a landing party of marines sneaking ashore to rescue.... to rescue ?... well, it had to be damsels in distress... Muriel preferably.

By then they were making their way under the small bridge at a crouch, the large area of water-smoothed granite making it easy going. The 'creek' turned out to be a mere trickle, not even half a metre wide and mostly only a few centimetres deep. There were nice little rock pools though and they stopped at several to look for fish or other life. Apart from a few water spiders they saw nothing.

The creek bed was only about 5 metres wide, lined with boulders and with frequent rock ledges and small waterfalls. It was lined with a fairly dense growth of vegetation and quite a few ferns. As the trees met overhead it was shady but Andrew could see out onto the hillside on both sides. These were covered in dry eucalyptus 'bush'. Gum trees, mostly spindly ironbarks, and a thin covering of grass, with occasional clumps of weeds and ferns. Beside the creek ran a faint foot trail and a water pipe.

As they clambered from rock to rock up an ever-steepening slope Andrew could not help admiring the girl's legs and shapely forms. In particular his eyes were continually drawn to Muriel, who wore short white shorts and a loose top that left her middle bare. To his eyes she looked very attractive and desirable. His mind shifted from daydreams about pirates or battling 18th Century Frenchmen to more immediate fantasies and thoughts about how to try to make up with her.

His opportunity came sooner than he anticipated. Only a couple of minutes later Blake, who was leading, suddenly sprang aside. "Snake!" he shouted.

At that Muriel, who had been about to step across a small pool from one rock to another, tried to pull back. In doing so she teetered on the same boulder as Andrew. Her hand shot out and grabbed his arm, then her other hand sought his. He steadied her, all the while looking anxiously around for the snake. He saw it then, a small yellow-bellied black. The snake was only about half a metre long and quickly slid off out of sight under some rocks.

Until it was gone Muriel clung to Andrew. Then, still holding on to him, she turned and said, "Thanks."

At that Andrew was moved to whisper, "Sorry about last night. I really like you, you know."

For a second he thought she was going to get angry, but then her eyes softened and she gave a smile, at the same time squeezing his hands. "That's alright."

Feeling very relieved and much more hopeful Andrew continued on up the creek behind her. The going was too rough for them to walk side by side to hold hands but he felt confident she would let him. However that confidence received a bit of a dent when they arrived at the dam. This was a low concrete wall about 3 metres high which spanned the creek. It was just rough concrete coated with black lichen and a slick off moss. On the upstream side was a delightful pool five metres wide and ten long, of clear, fresh water.

"Gran's water supply," Muriel explained.

"It looks lovely," Carmen cried.

Blake wiped sweat off his face and said, "It would make a great swimming pool."

Even though it was 'winter' it was now quite hot. Being on the leeward side of the mountain and in a re-entrant, there was no breeze to speak of and the sun was shining down from a cloudless sky. Andrew was also sweating and saw that the others were perspiring as well.

Muriel said, "We often swim in it, especially in summer when it isn't safe to swim in the sea because of stingers."

"We should have brought our bathers," Carmen commented.

At that Muriel giggled and said, "We don't need bathers. Nobody will see us. We often go skinny dipping here."

That comment was something of a revelation to Andrew and his imagination at once exploded into heated fantasies of Muriel swimming naked in the pool. It was also something of a challenge. He saw at once that everyone was thinking about it, Shona going red and giggling, Jennifer looking coy, Blake grinning and Carmen frowning. It was the presence of his sister that was most inhibiting to Andrew. He loved her dearly and was always careful never to offend her. Otherwise the thought of such a dare held great appeal.

Then Muriel turned to him and directly challenged him. "Are you game to come for a swim Andrew?" she asked.

That really put Andrew on an uncomfortable spot. He blushed and felt simultaneously aroused and anxious. "I'd love to, but I don't want to offend anyone," he mumbled.

"You won't!" Muriel replied scornfully. "You haven't got anything this lot haven't seen before."

Andrew blushed furiously and met Carmen's eyes. She was pursing her lips and not looking happy. "No," he replied. "It isn't right."

"Oh scaredy cat! Now Shona will be disappointed," Muriel retorted.

"Oh poo to you!" Shona cried, but she giggled and Blake gave her a leering grin.

Andrew looked into Muriel's eyes and thought he detected a glint of more than just challenge. 'Is she getting her own back?' he wondered. He was sure she was testing him and that stirred both irritation and resentment. Again he shook his head and this time was supported by Carmen.

"We don't want to swim in your Gran's water supply in winter time," Carmen said. "It won't flush itself well enough. Let's go back to the house and get our bathers, then go for a swim in the sea."

Muriel curled her lip but shrugged. "OK, if you aren't game." With that she turned and began walking back down the hill, this time following the foot path.

Andrew burned with both anger and embarrassment. That last fling had stung and he resented it. He met Carmen's eye and she looked sympathetic. Jennifer looked excited but embarrassed and both Blake and Shona looked mildly disappointed. Andrew was sure that Blake and Shona would have gone in and he found his mind filled with fantasies of Jennifer nude and of Muriel. They hurt too and it was a mixed up and unhappy boy that set off down the trail after Muriel.

The others followed and twenty minutes later they arrived back at the house. Contrary to what she had said earlier Muriel just walked straight across the main road and down the driveway. By then Andrew was feeling hurt and uncomfortable and even more sure he was losing with Muriel. He was also wondering if they were even suited for each other. But that hurt because he felt sure he was in love!

Back at the house they had cold cordial and some cream biscuits. Then they changed into bathers. Even that was a worry to Andrew. By now his overheated mind had him so aroused that he was quite unable to stop himself from getting an erection. All he could do was try to hide it by leaving his shirt hanging out and by draping his beach towel over his shoulder. On top of that Andrew was not keen on going swimming in the sea. He disliked it at the best of times and had no wish to be placed under that sort of stress. Knowing that his fears were mostly irrational did little to help. They were genuine fears and he did not feel like hiding them from the others just for pleasure.

But he went swimming anyway, despising himself for being too much of a coward to admit his fears, or to just stay on shore. The tide was well out and they had to wade for fifty metres even to get to knee deep water. That was more than enough for Andrew but the others went deeper. Then he was tested some more by the horseplay. Blake spent a lot of time chasing Shona, to catch and duck her. During several of the resulting water fights Andrew noted that Blake had taken the opportunity to grasp Shona by her bosom, a process she did not seem to resent but one which made Andrew feel jealous and frustrated.

The most that he managed was to grip Muriel by her legs and trip her up. She later put her arm around his neck and stayed clinging to him. From that he deduced he had been at least partially forgiven and he started to relax and enjoy himself. Later he took her hand as they strolled ashore and she smiled and let him keep hold of it.

She led him to the mouth of the creek and Andrew saw why he had never noticed it before. The fresh water coming down the hillside did not reach the beach but soaked into the sand and there was no obvious watercourse at all beyond the fringe of overhanging branches. What Andrew did notice was a pattern of tracks in the sand made by a very large snake and that got him looking anxiously around. None was visible so he shrugged and went to join Blake in making a sandcastle among some small rocks.

The waves were tiny, only ten or twenty centimetres high, and the tide slowly coming in so they had some entertainment in trying to dam it and to make a harbour. In the process Andrew quite forgot his age and reverted to daydreaming and happily playing. The girls lost interest and went to lie on their towels.

After a while Andrew and Blake also joined the girls. By then the girls had stopped sunbathing and were lying in the shade. Andrew took a chance and spread his towel next to Muriel. To his relief she smiled at him and began to chat happily as he lay down. That cheered him even more and he lay there feeling better, content with her closeness and the sight of her lovely, curvy body.

After a while Jennifer got up and strolled off to the right, picking up seashells and pumice stone off the beach. Blake and Shona strolled off the other way, hand in hand. Andrew relaxed and drifted off to sleep. As he slept he was vaguely aware that Muriel was snuggled next to him, was actually touching him. That was very pleasant and helped him to doze off, drifting into dream-filled slumber. The dreams involved naked girls swimming and Andrew became very aroused and very hopeful.

"Wake up you sleeping beauties," came a lady's voice.

Andrew opened sleep-gummed eyes and saw that it was Muriel's mother. She was bending over and shaking them. To his concern and delight he discovered that Muriel was snuggled right against him, her head on his shoulder. Worse still, she had her right arm resting across the front of his bathers and he became embarrassingly aware that he was very aroused.

'Has she done that by accident in her sleep?' he wondered, at the same time hoping that her mother had not noticed. He quickly sat up, removing Muriel's arm as he did. "Yes Mrs Murchison, what is it?"

"Lunch time Andrew," Muriel's mother replied. She shook Muriel firmly. "Come on Moppet, wake up!"

Muriel opened her eyes and blinked sleepily up at Andrew. Then she smiled and stretched. "Oooh! I needed that, and I had such a good dream," she said.

Andrew had too but he did not want to draw attention to his aroused condition by saying so. Instead he sat and rubbed his eyes. Carmen was standing nearby flicking sand off her towel and he met her eyes. To add to his confusion she winked and grinned.

Muriel's mother looked around. "Where are the others?"

"Jennifer was looking for shells," Carmen said. "She went that way. I think Blake and Shona went the other way."

"Well find them please, then come up and have lunch," Muriel's mother said.

"I'll get Jen," Carmen said, walking off along the beach.

Andrew stood up, keeping his back to Muriel and her mother so that they would not see he was aroused. To his relief Muriel's mother turned and began walking back up towards the house. Muriel stood and hurried after Andrew. "Wait Andrew. I will come with you," she said.

When she caught up she took his hand. This both surprised and pleased him and he felt much happier. The pair strolled hand in hand west around the boulders near the mouth of the creek. As they did Andrew fretted about how he might adjust his bathers without her noticing.

No opportunity arose. Instead Andrew found himself staring at Blake and Shona. They were lying on their towels under the shade of a large tree. Both were wearing only their bathers- or at least part of their bathers as Shona had her top rolled right down to her waist. Blake was lying half on her, his right knee over her right leg. His right hand was firmly gripping Shona's left breast. They were kissing and did not realize that they were being watched until Muriel cried out.

"Oooh! Caught youse at it! Stop that, you naughty pair," she cried. Then she giggled.

That giggle was a revelation to Andrew. He had begun to blush fiercely and had wanted to shield Muriel from the sight but now his mind raced into a riot of speculation. She obviously wasn't offended. 'Maybe that is what she wants?' he wondered. It certainly hadn't been his idea of a loving relationship at their age but it got him thinking hard.

Shona looked up in alarm and Blake gave a guilty start and released Shona's breast as though it had suddenly become red hot. That allowed Andrew a good look. Shona flamed with embarrassment and turned away, but that granted Andrew an even better view from the right rear which placed her breast in delightful profile. 'Very nice,' he thought. 'Lucky Blake!'

As Blake scrambled to cover himself and to pull on a shirt and Shona struggled to pull up her top Muriel said, "Take it easy you two. We aren't going to tell anyone."

That got Andrew's mind racing with more speculation. 'She doesn't mind! Maybe she will let me do that?'

That Muriel was neither offended nor upset was reinforced by her going over to talk to Shona to reassure her. Blake stood up and held his towel in front of him. "What is it?" he asked.

"Just lunch," Andrew answered.

"Yeah, OK," Blake answered. He was plainly embarrassed and worried.

To ease the situation Andrew turned and strolled away, looking out to sea and pretending great interest in a passing launch. Muriel joined him, rushing over and taking hold of his right arm. She snuggled against his arm and giggled, then said, "Oh poor Old Shona! She is so embarrassed. Serves her right. She should have been more careful. You won't say anything will you?"

"No," Andrew promised. He was now enjoying the feel of Muriel against him but had his own problem of his body reacting. It was a relief to reach his towel and to have an excuse to let go of her while he flicked sand off it and used it to cover himself.

At that moment Carmen came walking back with Jennifer. They apparently saw nothing unusual and when Blake and Shona joined them no comment was made by anyone about the incident. It was obvious to Andrew that Shona was highly embarrassed and that Blake was upset but he was more interested in the fact that Muriel had been amused and not offended.

'Maybe I have a chance?' he thought. But when? And how? As they strolled hand in hand up towards the house his mind began turning to the afternoon and to possible future dates.

Chapter 15

Unexpected Opposition

Feeling very aroused and unsure Andrew walked back up to the house holding Muriel's hand. The group made its way in through the garage door and the boys were left to get changed while the girls went upstairs. Andrew found that even something as simple as having a shower to wash off the salt, and then dressing, got him all aroused and excited. Memories of Muriel's touch mingled with images of Letitia and Shona. He became very erect and nothing he could do would make it go down. All he could do was leave his shirt hanging out and hope that nobody would notice.

Burning with embarrassment Andrew made his way up the internal stairs to the patio, leaving Blake in the shower. At the top of the stairs he paused, noting that all the adults were already seated and eating but only Jennifer had yet joined them. The other girls could be heard giggling inside the house. Trying to act cool and unconcerned Andrew strolled forward and seated himself at the end of the table.

To his relief none of the adults seemed to even glance at him until he was seated. Then Grandma Murchison said, "Help your self young fella."

Andrew did, selecting cold ham and chicken to go with bread and butter. As he spread the butter Carmen and Jennifer came out and seated themselves. Muriel's father smiled at them and then asked, "What have you kids been up to this morning?"

"Oh, a bit of exploring and a swim," Carmen answered.

"Exploring eh? Find anything interesting?"

Carmen answered, "Oh, only the dam up the creek where your water comes from."

Mr Murchison nodded and swallowed a bite. "Good spot for a swim in the wet season," he said. "I thought you meant looking around the house."

"Oh we did that yesterday," Carmen replied. "It's a lovely house, and very interesting."

Mr Murchison went 'huh', then nodded. "Certainly plenty of old junk around the place," he commented.

Carmen spread some butter then said, "I love the old motor launch. Do you ever use it still?"

Mr Murchison shook his head. "Hasn't been on the water for years, not since the bitumen road was put through. It was only used to go to town and now it is easier to drive."

"Pity," Carmen said. "It is a lovely old boat, all that varnish and polished wood."

Andrew had been listening with interest while he placed slices of ham on his sandwich. Now he asked, "Does the boat have a name?"

Mr Murchison shook his head. "No, not really. We always just called her 'Runabout'."

Andrew nodded. "It is just that I saw a lifebuoy hanging up next to it and it had the name *Deeral* painted on it. I thought it might have been called that."

Mr Murchison shook his head and looked at Old Mr Murchison. "That is the lifebuoy that saved your life isn't it Dad?"

Old Mr Murchison pursed his lips and seemed to scowl, then nodded. "Yes," he grunted.

Andrew took this as his cue. "Would you mind telling me about that?" he asked.

Old Mr Murchison turned his head to look hard at him. For an instant Andrew thought he was glaring at him. Then the old man emphatically shook his head. "No!" he cried. "I'd rather forget it. A terrible time, and I don't want to talk about it."

This was said with such vehemence that Andrew was shocked. Embarrassed he said, "I'm sorry. I didn't realize. I just wanted to know more about my Grandad."

"And I don't want to talk about it!" blazed Old Mr Murchison. To Andrew's dismay he saw that the old man was shivering and he feared he might be causing him another collapse.

There was an awkward silence and Andrew met Carmen's eyes. She gave a faint shake of her head and he burned with embarrassment. Then Muriel's mother called to the other girls to hurry up and join them. Blake came up the stairs and the conversations began again. For ten minutes they ate and the talk was about school or the weather.

Then Grandma Murchison asked Muriel if she was coming over the following weekend. Muriel shook her head. "No Grandma. I am going diving. I am going to do my Advanced Open Water Diving Course," she said.

At that Muriel's mother looked up sharply. "Well, we haven't agreed yet, young lady. You might be. It depends."

"Oh please Mum! Andrew and Carmen are both going," Muriel pleaded, looking at Andrew.

Carmen answered. "We might be. Mum and Dad haven't agreed yet either. They are waiting for Sub Lt Sheldon to give them a report of some wreck down near Townsville."

"Wreck?" Grandma Murchison asked. "Do you mean a sunken ship?"

"Yes Grandma. Diving on wrecks is part of the course," Muriel explained. "We get taught how to safely explore them."

At that Old Mr Murchison sat up. "Damned silly! Wrecks are dangerous places. You could get trapped and drown. I don't think you should go. In fact, I don't approve of this diving nonsense at all." Having said that he trembled. His hand shook so much that his teacup rattled on its saucer and he had to place it on the table

"Oh Grandpa, you used to be a diver," Muriel replied.

"Yes, and look what good it did me!" Old Mr Murchison cried. "I don't think you should go diving, and certainly not on wrecks. I won't sleep at night worrying about you."

"Oh Grandpa, we will be alright," Muriel replied.

Old Mr Murchison looked angrily at her parents. He was still visibly shaking. "I don't think you should allow it. It is too dangerous."

"Oh Grandpa! Oh Mum, Dad! Please!" Muriel cried.

Muriel's mother pursed her lips and looked anxiously at Old Mr Murchison. "We will discuss it later. Now, does anyone want some of this cheesecake?"

Andrew was upset at the thought that Muriel might not be allowed to go diving but again he saw Carmen give a slight shake to her head so he wisely said nothing. After the meal he got Muriel aside and told her he really wanted her to go.

Muriel nodded, being almost in tears. "I want to go too. I will work on Mum and Dad at home. I will be alright."

"Your Grandpa is very anti the idea," Andrew commented.

"Yes. I've never seen him so angry. He has never said anything against it before. But then he hasn't been well recently. Grandma says he is not sleeping well and has lots of bad dreams," she explained.

They left it at that and the friends began preparing for the trip home. Carmen acted as spokesperson and thanked Grandma Murchison. The old lady beamed and said, "Anytime dearie. It is wonderful to hear young people having a good time. You are welcome to come again."

"Thank you Mrs Murchison," Andrew added. He really wanted to spend another weekend there. The friends then packed up. This got Andrew all sad and anxious as he was worried he hadn't done very well that weekend. When they walked down to the catamaran with their gear Muriel and Jennifer walked with them. After the gear was loaded and secured the cat was lifted and slid into the shallows.

By then Andrew was very anxious. He badly wanted to say a proper goodbye to Muriel and wanted to ask her about next weekend but felt very embarrassed in front of the others. Finally the pair stood in knee deep water beside the catamaran while the others climbed aboard. Nerving himself to ignore the others Andrew looked into her eyes and reached out to take her hand.

"Thanks for a lovely weekend," he said.

She stepped closer and Andrew saw her eyes were full of sparkle and tears. His own felt suspiciously damp. Steeling himself for the embarrassment he put his hands on her hips and gently drew her towards him. She did not resist but moved her lips to meet his. They kissed tenderly and then drew apart.

"See you next weekend," Andrew said.

"I hope so," Muriel whispered.

By now Andrew's heart was hammering and he felt very much in love and very happy. "I will phone," he said.

"Please," Muriel replied. They came together again and this kiss was longer and more passionate. It was ended by Blake making smart comments. Reluctantly Andrew drew apart from Muriel. He pushed the catamaran into deeper water and clambered aboard. By then Carmen had the tiller and Blake had the mainsheet hauled taut. The cat's sails picked up the gentle breeze and slid it out into deeper water. Andrew sat and waved to Muriel, his heart bursting with hope.

Blake teased him but he ignored that. He sat and watched Muriel until the cat rounded the headland. Muriel stood in the shallows waving until then. All the way back up the Inlet Andrew was in a state close to euphoria. Ideas of true love caused his heart to expand and for him to feel intensely alive and happy.

The mood survived unrigging the cat back at the Yacht Club. It even lingered during the drive home. It was 3:15 by the time they had to cat on its trailer and 3:45 before they arrived home. Then there were chores to do. The catamaran had to be washed and stored and then the gear washed and hung up to dry. By then it was tea time and after that came homework. Andrew had no time to call Muriel, or to daydream.

That night, in his bed, Andrew experienced fierce waves of passion. Much of it was lust, which bothered him a good deal but he tried to rationalize it as being normal. He fell asleep fantasizing about rescuing Muriel while diving: from her being entangled in the rigging of a wreck and with a huge shark circling. But even that caused Andrew twinges of anxiety and when he dreamt the same thing later he woke in a cold sweat.

Monday morning was back to school. That brought its own distractions and entertainment. Almost the first thing Andrew encountered was Blake and a couple of his friends teasing a Year 8 boy. Andrew sat down next to Blake and asked, "Who's that?"

"Willy Williams, the Mad Scientist," Blake answered with a laugh. Then he called out loudly, "Hey Willy! Willy's wocket it not go woosh?"

Willy scowled, then grinned. Another boy added his share by yelling, "Willy's wocket it go bang!"

Andrew now learned that Willy had just returned to school after a week in hospital. A closer look at Willy's face revealed a dozen tiny pink scars where pieces of the rocket casing had been blasted into his flesh like shrapnel. That was all very amusing but of more concern was overhearing Graham Kirk being teased at morning break. The incident happened in the tuck shop queue. The person doing the teasing was a Year 10 boy named Derek.

He called, "G'day Kirky. Heard ya was out campin' with the officers on the weekend. Where'd ya go?"

Graham smiled and shook his head. "Sorry. I can't say."

"Why not?" challenged Derek.

"Because Capt Conkey asked me not to say," Graham answered.

"Oh yeah? Are you snivelling for a stripe already then?" Derek sneered.

Andrew watched this exchange with interest and some concern when he saw that the jibe obviously hurt Graham's feelings. He found himself curious to know what had happened as well but did not ask him. Instead he asked Stephen Bell, but Stephen just shrugged and said he did not know. He was obviously peeved that Graham had been on some sort of a reconnaissance trip with the adult staff but would not say where to.

The teasing continued at lunchtime. This time Derek had his crony Wally Dru with him and both made unkind digs at Graham. Wally jeered and asked, "Heard you were camping with the officers on the weekend. What did they want you along for?"

Derek answered this, "He must be their bum boy, why else?"

This caused some cruel laughter from the assembled boys and Andrew saw Graham blush angrily. Graham retorted, "It wasn't like that!"

"Oh yeah? So what was it like?" Derek taunted. He stood over Graham in a threatening posture, thumbs hooked into his belt.

By then Andrew was angry. He moved over and stood behind Graham. Derek looked at him in surprise. "What do you want?"

"Leave Graham alone," Andrew heard himself say. He was breathing fast by this, expecting to have to fight.

Derek looked surprised and then doubtful. He curled his lip and said, "You'd know all about bum boys, being an Anal Cadet."

That sort of insult really annoyed and angered Andrew. The constant play on the spelling of naval and on words which implied that everyone in the navy was a homosexual was a red rag to a bull for him.

Wally added to this by jeering and saying, "Watch this, it's a navel salute."

Wally then saluted across his waist to his belly button. It took a minute for the play on words to sink in but then the others all laughed. Andrew gritted his teeth and determined to wipe out the insult. He clenched his fists and stood ready. Derek looked at him and Andrew saw him swallow. 'He's scared,' he thought. 'He doesn't want to fight.' Then he noted Wally's eyes flick over past his right shoulder. Both bullies drew back.

Two people ranged up on Andrew's right. He glanced and saw it was Blake and Luke. Both were looking hostile. Peter Bronsky came and stood on Graham's left. At that Derek gave a lopsided grin and said, "Only jokin'."

The two bullies then walked off. Graham turned and mumbled thanks. Andrew nodded, glad that it had not come to a fight. For the next few minutes the boys discussed the bullies. Blake then told Peter that he now outranked him.

"We've been promoted to Able Seaman," Blake explained.

"Able Seamen?" Stephen replied. "Able to do what?"

Blake snorted but Graham asked, "What rank would that be equivalent to in the Army Cadets?"

Blake didn't know. Andrew wasn't sure. Peter knew. "Lance corporal," he said. He then added his congratulations. Graham also did but Andrew thought his looks were tinged by either resentment or jealousy. 'Never mind,' he thought. 'He is in the Army Cadets now. Hopefully they will help him.' He then left him with Stephen and Peter and went off with Blake and Luke.

The other thing Andrew did note during the day was that Graham seemed to be more relaxed and did not muck up in class as much as usual. 'Maybe cadets is a good thing for him,' he hoped.

But what Andrew was really fretting about was Sub Lt Sheldon's report on the wreck near Townsville. Even though he was terrified of the diving

Andrew was willing to do it, if it meant being with Muriel. At home that evening he worked on his homework, waiting anxiously for the phone to ring. When it did it was just one of Carmen's friends. That got Andrew fretting even more and he made comments until Carmen ended the conversation and hung up.

There was then a half hour wait before the phone rang again. Carmen answered it. To Andrew's satisfaction it was Sub Lt Sheldon. Carmen called their mother and she listened. Andrew tried to eavesdrop but only got snippets of the conversation. Then his mother said, "Thank you Mr Sheldon. I will discuss it with my husband and ring you back."

"Oh Mum! What did he say?" Andrew asked. Carmen had joined him and brother and sister followed their mother through to the master bedroom.

"This sunken ship," their mother said to their father, who lay on the bed reading. "It is a steel-hulled cargo ship and is lying on a sandy bottom about seventy five metres off shore in a small bay on the North West corner of Cape Upstart."

'Cape Upstart!' Andrew thought. He had seen that name on his chart, and on the one he had been looking at on the weekend. 'I know where that is.' In his mind's eye he tried to picture the coastline to the south and east of Townsville.

His mother went on. "The wreck is in very sheltered waters, protected from the prevailing winds and is sitting upright in about twelve metres of water. The deck at the bow is in only eight metres."

"That doesn't sound too bad," their father responded.

"No. It is a lot shallower than that other one, the *S. S. Yongala*," their mother replied. "Sub Lt Sheldon says it only has three compartments and all open directly into the sea. There is no extra deck or anything like that. Also all the doors and hatchways are open or missing. He says that apart from a couple of rigging wires there is nothing much to snare a diver, no fishing nets or such like."

"Sounds OK. What is its name?" their father asked.

"Didn't say. I don't think they know," their mother replied.

"How did it sink?"

"No idea."

At that Andrew could not restrain himself any longer. "Oh Mum! Can we go for the dive trip please?"

His mother looked doubtful and looked at their father. He appeared thoughtful then nodded. "I don't see why not. If they don't we will never hear the end of it."

Their mother turned to them. "Yes, alright, but only if you promise to very careful."

"Oh thanks Mum!" Andrew cried.

He at once raced off to phone Muriel. That produced a shock. Muriel had the same information but said her parents still had not decided. "They are going to talk it over," she replied, sniffling. "I will let you know tomorrow."

"Oh I hope so!" Andrew replied. "I really want to be with you on the weekend."

"Me too!" Muriel answered.

They talked for a bit longer but then Muriel said that her father wanted to use the phone so she had to hang up. Andrew went off to tell Carmen, his hopes sinking as he thought of all the reasons why not. Then he went to his room and played on the computer till bedtime.

Tuesday passed in a state of gnawing anxiety. All day Andrew worried about whether Muriel would be allowed to go diving. Her phone call that evening did not settle the issue. "Grandpa doesn't want me to do it," she replied. "He is dead against me diving on a wreck."

"So when will you know?" Andrew asked.

"We have to decide tomorrow so that Sub Lt Sheldon can book the trip and make the travel arrangements," Muriel answered.

"Hope you make it."

"So do I. I'll keep working on it," Muriel replied.

So it was in that unsatisfactory state that Andrew passed the next 24 hours. The only good thing he remembered was after school on Wednesday seeing Graham wearing his army cadet uniform for the first time and taking part in the cadet unit's weekly 'Home Training' parade. 'I hope he settles down,' Andrew mused, watching from the sidelines as the platoon markers were called on parade.

By 8pm that evening he was in a state of restless anxiety. When the phone finally rang he pounced on it, beating Carmen by half a metre. It was Muriel.

"I can go," she said.

That was wonderful news to Andrew. He would have liked to talk to her for the next few hours but she ended the conversation saying she had to get all her assignments and homework done first. Andrew had the same requirement so he was driven, reluctantly, back to his own desk.

After that Thursday and Friday went more easily. Thursday evening Andrew packed and finished his schoolwork. That meant that when he came home on Friday all he had to do was put his toiletries in his kitbag and change out of his school uniform and he was ready. As usual his mother fussed and kept warning him about various perils of the deep. Andrew barely noticed and just gave her tolerant replies. His mind was taken up with Muriel and how he might get to win her affections even more during the weekend.

Thus, when the mini-bus driven by Sub Lt Sheldon pulled up outside at 5:45pm, he got a shock. Muriel was in the bus and she gave a friendly smile and waved, but she was sitting next to a youth and made no move to shift next to Andrew. It took him a few minutes to realize what the situation was, and it left him worried and upset. Sub Lt Sheldon took his gear and Carmen's and stacked it in the rear of the mini-bus, then introduced the people already on board. Andrew knew that the dive company would be taking strangers, to help pay their bills, so he wasn't surprised to see that the back two seats were filled by two Swedish girls named Kareena and Inge, sun-tanned backpackers in their early twenties. The next row forward were two English male tourists in their mid-twenties. Tod was solid and sun-tanned. Geoff was thin and pale skinned. Then there was Muriel and the youth.

She introduced him. "Hi gang! This is Doug. He's a Master Diver and works as a motor mechanic. He is training to be a dive instructor."

"Hello," mumbled Andrew, eyeing the youth with jealous resentment, as it was obvious that Muriel liked him. Doug was slim but muscly and had well-tanned skin and a shock of curly fair hair. His freckled face was lit up by a grin and he was busy telling jokes. Andrew at once sensed he was real competition.

When it became apparent that Muriel was going to stay seated next to Doug Andrew climbed into the empty seat in front of them. Carmen joined him and Sub Lt Sheldon introduced Michael, another local diver, who was travelling in the front.

Andrew tried to pretend that everything was normal and alright but inside he felt a sick sense of unease. Did Muriel not like him after all? How long had she known this Doug character? And how much did she like him? It was all very sobering food for thought and as they pulled out and he waved goodbye to his mother he felt deeply anxious.

'How can I win with Muriel?' he wondered.

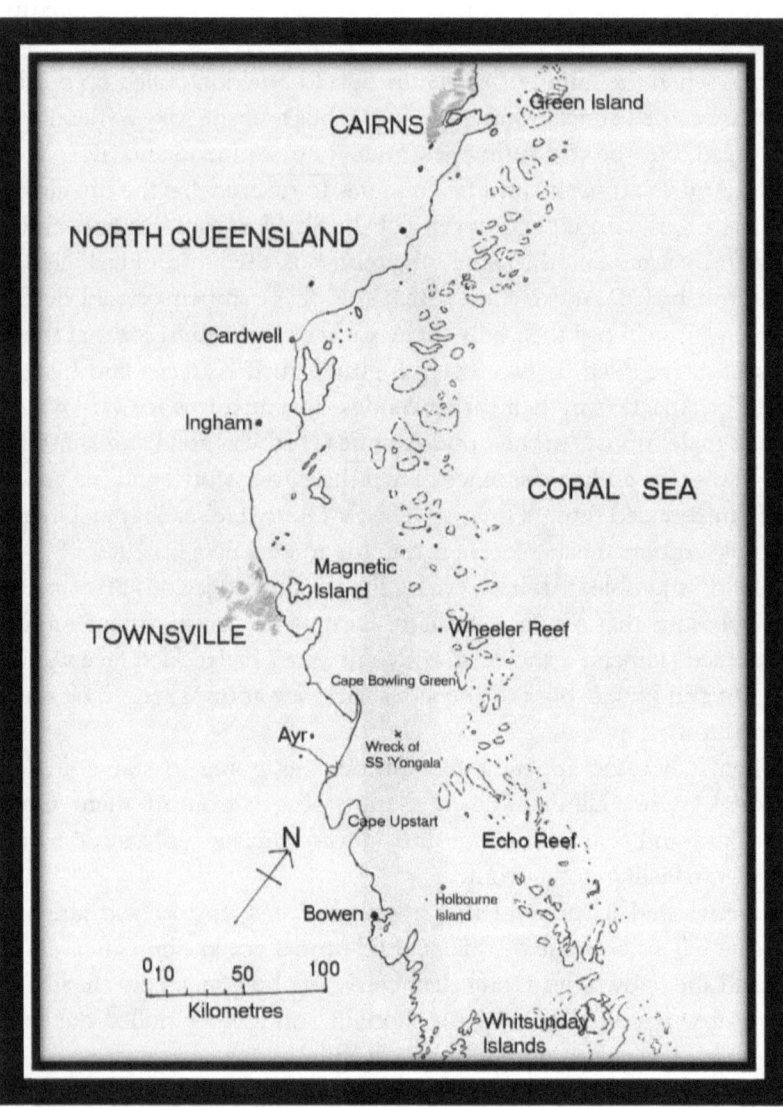

Map 2: The Reefs

Chapter 16

Jealousy

From the moment Andrew sat down in front of Muriel he was in emotional turmoil. Horrible suspicions bristled in his mind and he felt sharp stabs of jealousy. These were made worse by hearing Doug talking softly to Muriel and her gurgling laughter in reply. Having them behind made it even worse as Andrew felt extremely self-conscious, thinking that they were looking at him and that they were laughing at him behind his back.

'He must be ten years older than her. Surely she isn't interested in him?' Andrew fretted, remembering how friendly and passionate she had been with him only a few days earlier. Trying to tell himself that it was all nothing, that his imagination was making the situation into something it wasn't, he tried to relax.

The mini-bus drove south along Mulgrave Road and out of the city. It was a drive Andrew had done dozens of times before so hardly noticed until they were past Gordonvale. For a time he admired the huge bulk of Walsh's Pyramid, remembering the time he had climbed it with a Scout group two years earlier. In the russet glow of the last of the sunset it looked a most impressive mountain.

After that it was fields of sugar cane and hillsides covered with jungle as the highway and railway led southwards along the coastal corridor. Andrew thought this was a very pretty drive and even now, in the gathering dusk, he tried to take his mind off Muriel by looking across the flat fields to the jungle-covered coastal mountains.

The bus passed through the tiny settlement of Fishery Falls and a few minutes later the even smaller one of Deeral. It was just getting dark by then but Andrew was able to read the sign at the railway siding and knew where he was. Seeing that name 'Deeral' got him thinking about shipwrecks and about how his grandfather had died.

Darkness closed in and hid most of the scenery outside the windows but that made it worse for him because he could see Muriel and Doug reflected in the windows by the dim interior lighting. She seemed to be very attentive to everything Doug said and that twisted the dagger of envy even more.

Andrew had been to Townsville by road at least a dozen times before so paid no particular attention to where he was after that, merely noting the small towns as they passed through them: Babinda with its forest trails and refreshing rivulets, Mirriwinni, the bridge over the Russell River, then the jungle of the Eubenangee Swamp and Waughs Pocket before more open farmland: bananas as well as sugar cane, then the North Johnstone River and the larger town of Innisfail. They did not stop but drove on, across the South Johnstone River and through more canefields to the town of Mouri-lyan and on across more kilometres of sugar cane farms.

By 8:20pm they were stopped at Tully (another sugar mill town) at a Service Station and Road House for a snack. As they got off the bus Andrew hoped that Muriel would transfer her attention to him and was considerably hurt when she kept talking to Doug. Andrew was even more dismayed when he saw Doug buying Muriel a softdrink and snack. She allowed him to do this and kept chatting away, apparently oblivious to Andrew.

'Maybe I can organize it so that I end up with Muriel sitting beside me when we get back on the bus?' he thought. But he could not think of a plan to make this happen and knew that he was too hurt and too cowardly to make an issue of it. The best he could do was be first back on board, in the hope that Muriel would sit next to him. When she just smiled at him but made her way past him to her previous seat he was gripped by a cold feeling of despair. When Doug slid into the seat beside her and she resumed talking happily to him Andrew's jealousy grew to misery.

For the next two and a half hours he sat hunched up and pretending to sleep, hoping that Carmen had not noticed his unhappiness. Turning his head to the side and snuggling into his pillow he stared out the window at the dark fields and bush and tried to tell himself he was imagining it. 'She is just being friendly,' he told himself, in an unsuccessful attempt to cheer himself up.

They arrived in Townsville, at the end of the 350km drive, at about 11:00 pm. As they drove into the city Andrew sat up and cheered up a bit. His questing eyes picked out the lights marking the tops of Castle Hill (on his left) and Mt Stuart (a long way off on his right). Having stayed in Townsville for several school holidays and a Navy Cadet camp he knew the place reasonably well and now had some vivid memories. These were most particularly of the naked girls of Sheena's gang, and of the curvaceous and sexy Letitia. Just thinking about her made him squirm with desire and feel guilty at having thoughts unfaithful to Muriel.

There were other, less pleasant memories too- of the boy nicknamed 'Maggot' drowning; of the bullies being swept to their deaths from the flooded Black Weir. These thoughts made Andrew shudder and feel even more anxious about diving.

The route to the charter boat went past the rear of the local Navy Cadet depot, TS 'Coral Sea'. As they drove by Andrew felt quite excited and remembered the locals with warm affection. They had been very welcoming and helpful. The bus turned left to the Marina near the Casino and pulled up in a large, poorly-lit car park.

As Andrew and the others climbed out they were met by a cheerful, solid looking man in his early forties. He was one of the diving instructors from the local company and Andrew liked him on sight. His name was Dave and he led them with their gear down a sloping ramp and out along a narrow floating pier to where several large motor launches were moored at floating 'finger piers' set at right angles to the main one.

Their boat was named *Reefmaster* and Andrew liked the look of her. She was a large motor launch with a small focsle deck, then a cabin that ran for three quarters of the main deck aft to a dive deck. Above the cabin was a sun deck with a wheelhouse and rubber dinghy. Dave led them up the gangway and forward into the saloon to meet the trip director, an ex-navy warrant officer with a very efficient manner, who had them sit. He then checked their names and looked at their diving certificates.

While he was doing this, and discussing with Sub Lt Sheldon the training already done, Andrew kept looking around. There were people busy on the dive deck setting up gear, mostly young and looking like European backpackers (he was wrong, two were Canadian girls). Across at the next pier to starboard was an even larger dive boat which was also preparing to sail. Visible in the bright lights on its dive deck were a dozen people, all sorting out wet suits and air tanks and so on.

While he sat there Andrew's morale had gone up a notch because Carmen had sat on his right and Muriel on his left. The fact that Doug was sitting on the other side of Muriel was irritating and worrying but even so his hopes went back up. They went up even more when they were moved aft to the dive deck to check the fit of their gear and to set it up. While they did that Muriel stood next to Andrew and chatted happily to him.

Aft of the saloon on the dive deck were two long benches, one on either side of the aft companionway. On these were rows of air bottles held in place by elastic straps. Inside on the coaming were boxes of fins, snorkels, weight belts and so on. Hanging overhead were wet suits and BCDs.

Sub Lt Sheldon explained, "It is most important you get gear that fits properly now. If it doesn't then we can send a vehicle back to the dive shop and get some that does, but once we sail you are stuck with what is available."

Having spent a couple of hours with fins that were too tight Andrew knew how important that was. At the time he had not been able to credit just how agonizing those fins had become in such a short time. On another occasion he had picked a face mask that did not fit properly and he had spent an hour with water leaking in and a headache starting from a strap that was too tight. So now he pulled on a wet suit and made sure it did up easily, checked the fit of a BCD and secured it to a tank in the place allocated to him, then checked the fit of face mask, fins and snorkel. These were made up in a bundle for him. Then he set to work and made up his weight belt, aided by Dave and Sub Lt Sheldon. It restored his confidence to find that the equipment was familiar and that he could actually remember how to set it up and check it.

That was just as well because close alongside was the dark water and Andrew was having to fight down deep anxieties about diving into it. Fear of that night dive began to overlay his jealous anxiety about Muriel.

Having set up their equipment they were allocated sleeping accommodation. Forward of the dining table on the port side of the saloon a short set of steps led down to a small platform deck. From this gangways went down forward into the focsle and aft into a companionway. On the starboard side of the small deck was the galley and pantry. Andrew was directed to Cabin Number 3, aft on the starboard side. Carmen and Muriel were sent to Cabin Number 4, aft on the port side.

Andrew made his way down the short flight of steps and opened the narrow cabin door. Inside were two bunks, one above the other. A small porthole was set in the hull just above the top bunk. It was a tiny cabin and smelt of salt and stale air but he was satisfied, pleased he hadn't been put in the focsle. Opting for the top bunk so that he could look out the porthole he placed his gear in a small locker and swung himself up onto the bunk to try it out.

As he was wriggling to get comfortable, the cabin door pushed open and a head poked in. It was Doug. He tossed his duffle bag on the lower bunk and said, "Hi. I guess we are sharing. What was your name again?"

'That's all I need!' Andrew thought as he told Doug his name. Doug nodded and said, "What do you do?"

"I am still at school," Andrew replied.

"Oh yeah?" Doug answered, obviously neither interested not impressed. He then turned and made his way back out, leaving an irritated Andrew to lie there and feel hurt. The pain was exacerbated within a minute when he heard voices out in the companionway: Doug's and Muriel's. She laughed at something he said and Andrew heard her say, "I am in that cabin just there."

"Oh good!" Doug replied. He then said something that made Muriel giggle and which set all of Andrew's jealous thoughts in train again. Muriel then followed Doug up to the saloon. That sent Andrew into another bout of doubting and jealousy and he felt compelled to get up and to follow them up.

He found them in the saloon sitting on the benches aft of the cabin doors. Several others were there as well, including some of the people who had joined the trip in Townsville. Feeling shy and anxious Andrew sat and smiled. Inside he was annoyed and upset. What was particularly peeving him was that he had been really looking forward to being at sea and it was being spoilt. From the moment he had walked up the gangway he had been trying to savour the sights, smells and feel of being aboard a vessel. Even the small movements as the launch shifted with their weight and the tiny rippling waves made him feel better.

His interest in the boat was increased when he noted a small black and white photo of it before it was a tourist launch. Dave saw him looking at the photo and explained, "She used to be an RAAF crash launch."

"What's that?" Muriel asked.

"A rescue boat for the air force, to pick up aircrew who ended up in the sea. They use helicopters now so she was sold," Dave explained.

Doug joined them. "How would that happen here?" he asked.

Dave pointed to a chart on the bulkhead. "Just north of Townsville is the Halifax Bay Bombing Range. The air force practice attacking ships and things by bombing Rattlesnake Island and the rocks near it."

Muriel looked worried. "Rattlesnake? Are there rattlesnakes there?"

Dave shook his head. "Nah! It was named after a British gunboat which surveyed the area in the Nineteenth Century, the HMS *Rattlesnake*."

Andrew found all of that very interesting and he now devoted ten minutes to walking around along the narrow deck outside to the focsle and then back to the dive deck via the port side. As he did he sniffed the cool sea air and looked at the moored yachts and launches and watched the preparations on the neighbouring dive boat. It was all very interesting and enjoyable.

Then he got another rude shock. As he made his way forward again along the starboard side the door of the saloon slid open and Doug came out, followed by Muriel. They did not see him and made their way forward into the darkness on the focsle. That really hurt Andrew and he could only swallow and make his way back inside, pretending that everything was fine.

Carmen asked him if he wanted supper and insisted he drink some hot chocolate. Andrew was sure she was aware of the situation and that made him even more embarrassed. They were then instructed by Sub Lt Sheldon to take themselves to bed to get as much rest as they could. It was well after midnight by then and Andrew knew he was tired. Even so he did not want to go, his mind squirming with maggots of doubt about what Doug and Muriel might be doing outside.

Unable to relax Andrew stayed up until they returned. As they came back in Muriel met his eye and seemed to him to blush with guilt. Then she chatted happily and went to make cocoa. All Andrew could do was make his unhappy way down to his cabin and lie on his bunk in silent misery. It was a relief to him when he heard Muriel and Doug saying goodnight outside the cabin door. The sounds did not indicate any kissing or intimacy but it still hurt as she made no attempt to say goodnight to him. Doug then came into the darkened cabin and lay down without a word to Andrew.

That left Andrew to lie staring at the deckhead, brooding and wondering. Over and over he thought of all the times she and Muriel had been together, of the kisses and smiles, and it left him wondering what he had done wrong. The misery grew until tears of self-pity prickled in his eyes.

After a time he dozed off. Sleep was rudely interrupted by the sharp whirring noise of a starter motor, followed seconds later by the deep rumbling of the main engines starting. The huge diesels burst into life, making the whole launch vibrate. The movement of the hull and thudding sounds of footsteps overhead indicated that the lines were being cast off.

'We are getting under way,' Andrew thought happily. He was tempted to get up and watch but decided he should try to sleep. As the boat began to move he lay back and closed his eyes. A minute later he opened them again as Doug rolled out of his bed and quietly opened the cabin door. Out of half closed lids Andrew watched him slide out. The cabin door was then eased closed, the only sound the faint click of the catch locking. To him the movements seemed furtive. Horrible suspicions swirled in his mind. 'Is he sneaking out to meet Muriel?' he wondered. The thought made him both sick in the stomach and angry.

For another couple of minutes he lay there in jealous misery before he sat up. "I have to know," he told himself. With that he slid out of the bunk and moved to the door. For a moment he paused, listening. Hearing nothing he opened the door and stepped out, pulling it shut behind him. In the companionway he paused again. 'Which way?' he wondered. Had Doug gone up on deck or aft?

Three metres aft were three doors. The one directly in line led down to the engine room. The one on the port side led into Cabin Number 4-Muriel's. The one opposite it led to the shower and toilet. With his stomach churning with jealous uncertainty Andrew walked aft. For a moment he stared down the short flight of steps at the big yellow painted diesels. Then he stood and looked at the girl's door.

'Is Doug in there with Muriel?' he thought, feeling ill at the idea. Then Andrew shook his head. 'No. Carmen is in there too. They wouldn't risk anything like that.' Having decided that Doug must have gone on deck Andrew turned to go forward.

As he did the door of the toilet suddenly opened. Andrew spun round in surprise. Through the door came Doug. He merely nodded at Andrew and said, "Sorry. Didn't mean to wake you."

Feeling both incredibly silly and relieved Andrew seized on this. "You didn't. The engines did. I need to go too." He pointed into the toilet.

Doug nodded and made his way back to the cabin. Andrew went into the toilet and locked the door, then discovered he really did need to go. While he relieved himself he was able to look out through the port hole at the lights sliding past outside. Then he shuddered. 'You are a jealous bloody fool!' he told himself. 'Muriel isn't up to anything. She is just being friendly.'

Having finished relieving himself Andrew left the toilet and made his way up on deck. He was wide awake now and curious to see what the harbour looked like at night. As he stepped through the saloon door he was surprised at the strength of the wind, and at how cool it was. He was also reminded of just how confusing things can be at sea at night.

'All those lights!' he thought, staring at the flickering channel markers and the background lights from anchored ships and the towns on Magnetic Island. Making his way forward to the focsle he studied the lights, working out which was which and noting the lights of a small fishing boats sliding at right angles across their course to confuse things even more. After a while he had them all sorted out. By then the launch was well clear of the marina's rock breakwaters and was starting to butt into a head sea and to pitch. A shower of cold spray sent him back to the shelter of the port side of the saloon. From there he moved aft to the well-lit dive deck.

That allowed him a clear view out on either beam and also astern at the lights of Townsville. First he looked at them, picking out Castle Hill and Mt

Stuart. Then he studied the bright lights of the port. The port was separate from the marina and there were three big ships there, loading or unloading in the glare of floodlights. The ships held his attention for a while and he wished the Port of Cairns was as busy. That Townsville was much busier was obvious at a glance. The fact that three large ocean-going ships were anchored out in the bay waiting for a turn at the wharves reinforced this impression.

A revolving, flickering light in the distance caught Andrew's eye and he puzzled over this until the answer came to him. 'A lighthouse!' He rarely saw them around Cairns- not that he was often at sea at night. Now he studied the pattern of the light- the timing of the flashes. 'Must be Cape Cleveland,' he thought, remembering the bay from having sailed around it during the holidays with the Navy Cadets.

A thin, bearded man in his fifties, wearing old grey shorts and an open-necked, short sleeve shirt, came up the aft hatchway. He stopped and looked at Andrew. "You OK lad?" he asked.

"Yes sir. Just enjoying the view," Andrew answered, and he was.

The man introduced himself as Andy and as the skipper. He chatted to Andrew for a few minutes, confirming that the lighthouse was on Cape Cleveland. Then, apparently satisfied that Andrew was alright, he made his way forward and up to the wheelhouse.

Andrew now relaxed and began to enjoy the trip. He relished the pitching and rolling and even the occasional drops of cold spray that were flung up as the boat punched into a large wave. After satisfying himself that he knew where the life jackets and lifebuoys were Andrew looked out at the now distant lights and relaxed. He stayed there until they were abeam of Cape Cleveland and the lights of Townsville were starting to drop below the horizon. By then they were meeting larger seas and it quickly became both cold and uncomfortable.

Satisfied both with his sea legs and with the handling of the launch Andrew made his way back down to the cabin. Now the movement of the launch was so lively he had to use both hands to stop himself falling and it took picking the right moment to climb into his bunk. Once there he lay back, wedged himself securely in- and promptly dropped off to sleep.

Chapter 17

Wheeler Reef

When Andrew woke up he lay wondering where he was and what had woken him. Realizing he was aboard the diveboat he noted the grey light filtering through the grimy porthole. Then he registered the vessel's motion.

'We are rolling more than pitching,' he deduced. 'We have either changed direction or the wind has.' With that he struggled into a sitting position to look out of the porthole. This took some effort because the motion of the launch was very lively- not that that worried him. He was a good sailor and trusted the feel of the launch. As he peered out at the grey half-light of dawn the launch shouldered a larger than usual wave aside. The whole vessel shuddered and a shower of spray obscured the view. Seen from that level the waves looked enormous and quite daunting but Andrew knew from experience it was an illusion.

"About two metres," he muttered, estimating the wave height. He slid out of the bunk, noted that Doug was still asleep, then slipped quietly out of the cabin. The motion was so lively that he had to hang on tight as he climbed up to the saloon. With each wave he could feel his leg muscles working- one moment his weight pressing down hard and the next relative weightlessness.

There was only one person in the saloon; a middle-aged man who had joined them in Townsville. He looked tired and scared. Andrew gave him a cheery good morning and looked out. The sea was certainly rough, just tumbling waves as far as the eye could see. To get a better look Andrew slid open the leeward (port side) door and went outside. The wind was fresh and bracing and he breathed deeply and looked happily around, ignoring spatters of cold spray that were whipped in to his shelter.

A couple of miles ahead he saw a vessel bobbing on the waves. A few minutes observation revealed that the other vessel was anchored. 'We must be nearly there,' Andrew deduced.

He was right. Sub Lt Sheldon appeared from up in the wheelhouse and informed him that they were approaching Wheeler Reef. Andrew had been to the Great Barrier Reef a dozen times but found this one quite different and somehow scary. The Great Barrier Reef is actually thousands of smaller coral reefs, most formed in long lines with narrow gaps between them. But Wheeler Reef is nowhere near any other reef. It is just a pimple in the ocean, a few hundred metres across and surrounded by deep water. As a result there was very little shelter in the limited lee and the waves were unpredictable, sweeping in from either side. As well there was an obvious ocean current flowing away from the reef in a northerly direction.

This was not what Andrew had been expecting at all. At other reefs that he had visited, like Green Island, Oyster Reef or Michaelmas Cay off Cairns the boat had moved inside a shallow lagoon and anchored in calm, clear water. But here there was no lagoon at all, just a welter of foam where the waves broke over the reef.

The launch moored to one of the permanent buoys placed there by The Great Barrier Reef Marine Park Authority to protect the reef from anchoring. Andrew watched this bit of seamanship with interest, then looked across at the other vessel. It was the larger boat that had been tied up opposite them the night before.

Dave came by and, seeing Andrew's gaze, nodded towards her. "The *Trevally*. Rolls like a bastard. You are lucky to be on this one."

Andrew could see the other vessel rolling and could only agree. He turned and made his way back into the saloon, finding Carmen and Muriel among the others now gathered there. Muriel looked a bit pale and tired but she gave him a smile and came over to stand beside him.

"How are you Andrew? Sleep well?" she asked.

"Yeah, OK," Andrew replied. He managed a grin but was puzzled. She seemed different from the night before.

Dave called loudly to the group. When he had their attention he said, "We will have breakfast, then I will give you a dive briefing on this place before your first dive. Please be ready for the briefing by seven thirty."

A glance at the clock on the bulkhead told Andrew it was only just after six so they had plenty of time. The food was placed on the table by Dave and the Trip Director and they were told to help themselves. Andrew was hungry and quickly collected a bowl of cereal and two slices of bread, then moved to sit in the lounge section of the saloon. It was obvious that some of the others were having difficulty with the rapid rolling and rocking of the launch but that only made him feel superior, like a seasoned 'old salt'.

To boost his morale even more Muriel came and sat next to him. As they ate they talked, discussing the rough weather, the cold wind, and the fact that there was almost nothing of the reef visible. Now that the test was approaching Andrew felt himself becoming anxious but he concealed this and chatted happily with Muriel and Carmen.

His morale got an even bigger boost when a tired-looking and tousle-headed Doug appeared and Muriel barely acknowledged him. After a perfunctory good morning she seemed to ignore him. Then she concentrated on being friendly to Andrew.

Feeling considerably cheered he went below to go to the toilet and change. By 7:25 he was standing on the dive deck dressed in bathers and T-shirt. He then received another irritating little niggle from Muriel. She appeared wearing a white bikini, the bra cups of which were held by only a strap around her chest. The cups were made of some stiff material and barely covered more then half her breasts. They were very revealing. The fact that others must also be able to see them caused him a wave or embarrassed irritation.

She seemed oblivious to this and chatted happily until the Trip Director called for silence. Andrew stood beside Muriel and scowled at Doug, who was clearly ogling her bosom. To take his mind off this Andrew counted the people present. He was surprised to reach a total of 16 students and 6 staff, including the skipper.

The Trip Director hung up a blackboard with a sketch map of Wheeler Reef on it. He then explained the layout and the hazards. Andrew was dismayed to note that the area under the launch and astern of it (it lay head to the prevailing South East wind and facing towards the reef) was nicknamed 'Shark Alley'. Vivid images of Max Pullford's torn and bloody stump flooded his mind and he swallowed, doubting if he had the courage to go ahead with the diving.

The other features of interest were 'swim throughs' and a sand cay in the centre of the reef which appeared at low tide, and also a warning about the current. By the time the briefing was over Andrew was wondering how he could get out of the diving. So scared had he become that he was sweating and felt chilled. But pride was involved too.

'I can't let Muriel know I am a coward,' he thought miserably, feeling horribly trapped. So, when they were told to suit-up for an introductory dive, he just pretended he was happy and got busy. Concentrating on the technical aspects helped. So also did helping the others. But Muriel did not help by continually bending forward and by the way she did not fully zip up her wet suit so that it squashed her breasts up and made them even more obvious.

After struggling into his wet suit and buckling on his weight belt Andrew helped Muriel into her BCD and tank. She then helped him, her hands fussing about his body to check straps and to tuck in gauges and loose ends. It was nice but also irritating. So was the proximity of her trembling breasts close to his face. He found it a real relief when she finally zipped the wet suit right up. It helped him to watch Carmen being assisted by a handsome young English tourist who clearly thought she was nice.

Then Andrew's thoughts were moved from sex to the perils of the deep when Dave called the Advanced Course candidates into a group and briefed them for their dive. On hearing that they were going to remove face masks and also practice using alternate air sources Andrew became quite anxious. That was made worse by looking out over the tumbling waves at the sheer vastness of the sea, and then by having to enter the water by the 'giant stride' method. He had only done this once before, from the side of a swimming pool, and it was infinitely harder here, mainly because it was into such deep water. Not that it was the depth that worried Andrew- it was the things that might lurk in it!

Almost gulping and hyperventilating with anxiety Andrew pulled on his fins and shuffled along the narrow side deck to take his turn. With mounting trepidation he watched Carmen and Doug jump in. Then it was his go. 'Shark Alley!' he thought. But Muriel was close behind him and there seemed no way out. He adjusted his face mask, placed the regulator in his mouth and edged forward so that his fins were protruding over the side. Then, at a nod from Dave, he stepped forward, holding his regulator and face mask firmly as he did.

Andrew struck the water and went under, noting with half his mind how cold it was- and how wet. Amidst a flurry of bubbles he bobbed to the surface almost at once. Remembering to signal he was alright he at once inflated his BCD some more and looked around, very conscious that he was floating over Shark Alley, with his legs dangling down as attractive bait! Then Muriel jumped and his focus changed. It was borne upon him that the current was indeed strong as he was already drifting past the stern of the launch. To counter this he began finning backwards upstream. As he did he took off his face mask and spat in it, rinsed it and replaced it. Then he switched to using his snorkel and rolled onto his front to fin forwards against the current.

In doing so he had to look under the water and that scared him. By turning his head he could see the bottom of the launch. Its rudder and propellers were plain to see in the clear water. Studying them helped and he was amazed at how little of the launch seemed to be below the water. But looking down was scary. Way down underneath Andrew could just see the bottom- white sand, sloping down and shading off into murky blue-black depths. That gave him incentive to swim towards the shallower water of the reef in the wake of Carmen and Doug.

Muriel joined him and they swam together through the choppy seas until they reached a small dive buoy. By then they were a hundred metres from the launch. Carmen and Doug were waiting, clinging to the buoy. Dave joined them, then the other four on the course. By then Andrew was feeling puffed but he had no time to recover as Dave at once signalled dive and went under.

For a few seconds Andrew experienced a mild panic attack. Then he saw that he was the only one left on the surface so he lifted his arm and began releasing air from his BCD. Very gently he slipped under. For a second or so he had a waterline across his face mask- half sky and half underwater. Then he was below the surface. Suddenly it was easier. The water was crystal clear and he could see the bottom, the other divers and the coral outcrops.

Glancing around he saw that the place they were descending into was a circle of sand ringed by large coral outcrops. These sheltered them from the current and from the deep water. Andrew began to relax, noting dozens of brightly coloured small fish flitting around. He settled to a kneeling position on the sand beside Muriel, forming part of a line of divers. Dave came down in front of them and Doug and Sub Lt Sheldon behind them.

Knowing that he had to remove his mask got Andrew all flustered so he tried to think about something else. He looked around at the coral and the fish, rather than watching the others. To his own surprise, when Dave moved in front of him and indicated it was his turn, Andrew just calmly slipped the mask off, replaced it and cleared it.

'It worked!' he thought. 'The training really works.'

After that the practice at using another diver's alternate air source was easy. He and Muriel faced each other and did this. All the time her eyes seemed to sparkle and he was sure she was smiling. It made him feel much better. The testing done Dave led them on a swim, the depth averaging only 10-12 metres. To Andrew's surprise he really enjoyed this. First they slid out through one of the gaps in the coral and went along beside a steep wall of coral with the sandy sloped dropping away on their right into the blue depths. Here they saw a huge coral trout and dozens of smaller creatures.

Dave led them into a narrow 'canyon' in the coral. The width varied from only about three metres to about ten metres and the depth a fairly uniform ten. Andrew found it fascinating but gloomy, lots of shadows and the coral predominantly a brown colour. After checking remaining air they reversed course and swam back out of the twisting canyon to the open water. Once they were back in the sandy circle they then swam into a wide 'inlet' in the coral. Andrew liked this better as it was wider and there seemed to be more fish and prettier coral.

They swam up a side passage for about fifty metres, the passage winding and twisting but wider and nicer that the first canyon. There were some amazing coral formations along the gully and Andrew felt much safer from possible shark attack because of the protective walls. On returning to the main 'inlet' they followed this for about another seventy metres, swimming into ever shallower water until the rippling waves were only a few metres overhead. This 'swim through' was ten to twenty metres wide and Andrew liked it best of all. He was particularly struck by a shoal of several dozen large rock cod that they encountered. The fish were each a metre long and were just swaying almost stationary in the wave motion.

'This is what the tourists all pay to come and see,' he thought.

That was the end of the dive. Dave led them back to the dive buoy and signalled surface. That was a relief to Andrew, but only a small one as he realized he had been enjoying himself. On the surface he happily chatted to the others after inflating his BCD. Only later, as they allowed the current to take them back to the launch, did he remember to worry about sharks.

Trailing behind the launch was a float line and also the inflatable safety boat so it was easy to grab on and haul himself up to the stern. The Trip Director stood there on a small steel grating taking their fins and helping them to climb up the ladder. The effort involved was a rude shock to Andrew. He was amazed at how heavy all the gear felt. It was a genuine relief to have Carmen help him remove his BCD and air tank. Unbuckling the weight belt was also a relief.

He helped Muriel remove her air tank and pack the gear away. Then his jealous irritation returned as she peeled off her wet suit to reveal the bikini- or rather, her body. This emotion stayed with him when the group were seated in the saloon lounge. Muriel sat beside him but Doug sat opposite and Andrew could see his eyes continually flicking to stare at Muriel.

They had to calculate their residual nitrogen and the time they needed to stay out of the water before the next dive. Dave and Sub Lt Sheldon both checked their calculations and Andrew was pleased to find he understood and could work it out easily enough. Dive logs were then filled in and signed by buddies and instructors. After that they had an hour and a half to rest.

Andrew spent the break on his bunk sleeping. Then it was the second dive of the day. This was easier and Andrew found it much less stressful, even when they had to swim out into deeper water. The dive was navigation and they went out for a hundred metres from the edge of the reef with an instructor and had to find their way back to the boat, and then to the coral circle. They went deeper too, averaging 18- 20 metres but Andrew barely noticed that. It was that dark blue murk of 'Shark Alley' that held half his attention. Being a well trained navy cadet the actual use of the compass and keeping direction he found easy.

Another, longer break followed, during which they had lunch. By then Andrew was much more relaxed. He was almost resigned to Muriel flaunting herself, and was also feeling distinctly superior to the novices doing the basic course. He did feel a bit sorry for the middle-aged local who was obviously having a bit of trouble and did not look like he was enjoying himself. It was nice, Andrew decided, to sit in the lounge and eat corned beef sandwiches while listening to the foreigners talk about other places and other dives. It gave him a peculiar sense of belonging and of camaraderie. Despite his youth they obviously accepted him as a diver.

There was a long break after lunch, then the third dive of the day. This was both interesting and easy. It was the 'Marine Naturalist' dive. Before they went down they were given a long briefing on dangerous marine creatures: fish that bit, poisonous shellfish, sea urchins, blue-ringed octopi, stone fish, etc. They were then sent off in pairs. This time Andrew hardly noticed suiting-up, so frequently had he now done it. He was still aroused and embarrassed at the way Muriel was flaunting herself but tried to ignore it. Even jumping into the sea was no big deal. There was only a momentary hesitation, his mind focused on the technical aspects of holding mask and regulator and of breathing and signalling.

Once in the water there were a few twinges of anxiety about monsters of the deep but then he concentrated on finning to the dive buoy with Muriel. While clinging to it they discussed their dive plan and route before agreeing to slip under. They went down facing each other, just as a shower of rain swept across. Andrew expected the cloud and rain to cut visibility dramatically and was pleasantly surprised when it seemed to make little obvious difference. It became a bit gloomier, that was all.

For the next half hour the pair swam slowly along the largest of the 'swim throughs' and up a few small side alleys. As they went they recorded on wrist slates the different types of fish and corals they observed. Muriel was better at this than Andrew as he found he had a poor memory for the many fish types. Andrew was aware that he was coping well with the ordinary aspects of recreational diving and knew he should be enjoying himself more, but he was also aware of a niggling sense of unease. Even surfacing near the launch and climbing aboard did not dispel this.

He knew what was causing it- the fear of the night dive. The closer the time came the more anxious he grew. With it came some surprising changes in his personality. He found he was short-tempered and sarcastic and even snapped at Muriel a couple of times. She looked annoyed and was short in reply and moved to chat with Doug. That made Andrew curse himself as a fool. To allow things to settle he took himself down to his bunk and lay down.

That did not help. With nothing to do but lie and think all of his fears came squirming to the surface and he became so anxious he broke into a cold sweat. After half an hour of that he could stand it no longer and went up on deck. Most of the young people had congregated on the focsle in the afternoon sun. On arriving there Andrew got several shocks. The first was visual. The tide had gone down and a small sand cay was now showing in the middle of the reef. It was ringed with foam and the sand gleamed a pale yellow in the watery afternoon sunlight. The second was emotional when he found Muriel sitting on the cabin roof beside Doug. The pair were so close together that their legs and bodies were touching.

That really hurt but Andrew stubbornly remained to talk to her. He very quickly got the message that Doug wished him to leave but that just made him even more stubborn. For the next hour he chatted about diving and sailing, noting Muriel's little looks of irritation and Doug's obvious annoyance. He also found it hard not to keep glancing at the softly quivering flesh of the top half of her breasts.

'Bitch!' he thought. 'She is teasing us both, and playing games.' Then he regretted calling Muriel a bitch, even in his mind. Anxiety and jealousy gave way to anger, then remorse. But through it all the fear grew. By sunset he was almost in a cold funk, blaming it on the chilly wind. But in his heart he knew he was about to face one of life's real tests.

They were called in to eat and then all seated in the lounge for a detailed safety brief on night diving. Listening to that did little to reassure him. It was all very well for the instructor to say that sharks hardly ever bothered divers at night. That was the nightmare Andrew was facing. The thought that the creature could just rush out of the blackness and grab him with no warning at all made him break into a cold sweat. Desperately he tried to think of a way out. 'I could claim I am sick; or maybe that my sinuses are playing up,' he thought. Then he despised himself as coward.

To make matters worse Muriel teamed up with Doug. Carmen gave Andrew a knowing and sympathetic look, which increased his emotional turmoil. Instead he was paired with one of the Canadian girls: Kellie, from Alberta. When told to suit up Andrew just went out in numb misery, sure he was going to throw. He barely noticed putting on the wet suit and gear or the equipment checks. All he could see was that dark water flowing by in the boat's lights. It was all so vast, and so black!

Sub Lt Sheldon handed him a torch and helped him to secure it to his gear. "Are you alright Andrew?" he asked.

"Yes sir. Just cold," he said. Then he made a wry face, "And scared," he admitted.

"So am I!" Kellie commented. "Here, help put this on me." 'This' was a cyalume, a chemical glow stick. Andrew took it with trembling fingers and helped fasten it to her mask strap at the back. Then he turned and she did the same for him. Dave began urging them to move. Feeling sick to the pit of his stomach and shivering with fright Andrew pulled on his fins and shuffled along the side after Kellie.

There were splashes and Andrew saw divers go drifting or swimming by, their cyalumes glowing and torches shining down a metre or so into the blackness of the water. It was all terrifying and he seemed to freeze up. Then Kellie jumped in and it was his turn. With a sob he slid forward to the gap in the railings, and placed his regulator in his mouth. Out in the distance he could see the lights of the other dive boat. It was rolling wildly in the waves but there were divers jumping off it too.

'I can't do this!' he thought. He took his regulator out and took several deep breaths. Then he pulled down his mask but that made it worse. His already restricted vision seemed to become just a circle of black fog with a few glimmers of shifting light. He gripped the railing and began breathing deeply.

Sub Lt Sheldon tapped his shoulder and Andrew heard him say, "When you are ready. In you go."

Andrew glanced at him and then looked down at the dark water and fear froze him.

Chapter 18

Character Revealed

From what seemed like a great way off Andrew heard Sub Lt Sheldon's voice say, "In you go Andrew."

But all he could do was stand and stare at that black water. Waves of chill swept over him and he trembled, gripping the railing tighter. His breathing became deeper and he heard himself say, "I'm scared sir."

"We all are," Sub Lt Sheldon answered. "You will be alright. In you go."

From behind him Carmen spoke. "Let us go first Andrew."

Andrew knew that Muriel and Doug were both behind him, waiting, watching. 'She will be despising me for being a coward,' he told himself. Then he thought, 'I am despising myself!' Waves of hot shame and humiliation swept through him. A great sob was wrenched from his gasping, tightened-up throat.

So he jumped.

It wasn't a proper giant stride entry. He half landed on his front with a splash that would have stung if he had not been wearing the wet suit. The rush of water almost wrenched the regulator from his mouth and water flooded his mask. With the water came a gush of fear. Andrew struggled to the surface. As soon as he could glimpse the lights of the launch he spat out the regulator and pulled the mask off his face. Above him he saw a row of faint faces and he heard a voice cry, "step aside!"

There was a splash near him as a person jumped in but by then Andrew was sinking again. Panic swirled but he retained enough sense to grasp at his inflator. A quick press on the button and he heard the air hiss into his BCD. He felt the BCD tighten its grip on his back and sides as he pressed the button again. His head came up and he blinked water from his eyes- stinging, salt water. The stern of the boat slid past and he realized that the current had him.

Something brushed his arm and he flinched, and almost screamed, till he realized it was the float line trailing astern. With a convulsive jerk he grasped it and hung on. By then he had enough air and was floating so that his head was clear of the bobbing waves. A person splashed towards him.

It was Sub Lt Sheldon. "Are you alright Andrew?" he called.

Andrew felt sick, and ashamed. "Yes sir. Just a bit scared," he admitted.

"Turn your torch on," Sub Lt Sheldon instructed.

Another wave of hot shame engulfed Andrew. 'How could I forget something so elementary?' he wondered. He did so and then set about cleaning his mask and placing it on. A bobbing black shape with a cyalume on top approached.

It was Kellie. "We all set to go?" she asked.

"Andrew's just getting his torch sorted out," Sub Lt Sheldon explained.

Andrew pulled his mask on, blinking painfully from the salt and noting that he could hardly see anything clearly, other than the bright lights on the launch. He said, "I'm Ok now," and put his snorkel in his mouth. He put his head down and tried finning forward.

But that was more than his dissipated courage could face. Underwater it was all just gloom and blackness and a faint glow from the lights over-head. Within seconds he had begun to panic again and had to turn onto his back so that his face was out of the water. That was better, but his whole body felt like it was cringing, his legs working mechanically but very aware that they were under water, where anything- Anything- could just grab at them!

He was struggling to swim against the current past the port side of the launch by then. Other divers were jumping in, making him feel silly and ashamed. By then he had calmed down a bit and it was all just black fear, black waves, the lights of the launch getting further away by the second, the effort of breathing, gasping and coughing from water droplets in his throat, sore eyes, hurt pride. Having others swimming near him helped and he managed to keep pushing himself along.

They clustered at the dive float, bobbing black heads with glow sticks on top and torches shining down into the water. The torch did not do much to inspire Andrew. The glow of its beam seemed to die out after about a metre and he knew it was going to be infinitely worse once he was underwater.

'I should admit I am too scared and back out now,' Andrew thought mis-erably. He was afraid he would panic underwater. But pride stopped him. Instead he bobbed and swam while he recovered his breath. Dave joined them, then Doug and Muriel. Carmen came and asked if he was alright. Andrew nodded. Dave gave them a reminder to stay close together and to watch for their buddies all the time. That made Andrew blush with shame again as he wasn't sure which of the bobbing heads was Kellie.

He found her just as Dave gave the signal to dive. 'Oh no! I can't do it!' Andrew thought. But Kellie was there, facing him and smiling before she slipped her regulator in. Andrew did likewise and somehow summoned up the courage to start releasing air from his BCD. To his amazement he slipped under without any fuss. He was even more amazed to be able to see Kellie in the glow of her own torch, and to see her bubbles going up in a silvery stream.

It came to him that he had done it- he was underwater at night. He also realized he could see lights below him, grouped in pairs. The bubbles came up in clouds, looking dark and shadowy when silhouetted against a light, and silvery with the light on them. The cyalumes showed clearly and he even realized he could see the distant glow of the launch's spotlights on the surface. Knowing where the boat was made a big difference to how he felt.

'I am just going to endure this,' he thought. Gritting his teeth metaphorically he resigned himself to being terrified for half an hour.

Suddenly he was grabbed. The touch was so unexpected that he almost, as the saying goes, jumped out of his skin. Then he realized it was Kellie. She had grabbed his BCD straps and he lifted his torch. In its beam he saw her face, or at least her eyes. They were wide and staring and he realized she was scared too. Quickly he lowered the beam of his torch so as not to blind her and then he reached up and took hold of her hand and gave it a squeeze. She was trembling- he could tell that much, and she put her other hand across and held his.

He squeezed and patted her hand, then concentrated on equalizing pressure as they sank lower. She had to let go with one hand to do the same and then she reached down and picked up her own torch and shone it around. Andrew shone his down, noting that the clusters of lights below were getting closer and apparently not sinking deeper. Fearful that Kellie might panic and drown he kept hold of her hand and kept squeezing it.

Then they were on the bottom and Andrew gently squashed the last of the air out of his BCD to give himself negative buoyancy. Having settled firmly on the sand he helped Kellie to join him. She changed hands but he reached out and took hers and she gripped it tightly. Dave came along- or at least Andrew presumed it was Dave- and used his hands and torch to signal them to form a line. He then went along and shone his own torch on himself and made the signal for 'OK'.

Andrew turned his torch onto himself and gave the signal, having to let go of Kellie to do that. She then made the signal but quickly reached across. He took her hand again and gave it a reassuring squeeze. To his pleasure she pressed against him and squeezed back. While waiting for Dave to check the others Andrew shone his torch on his dive computer and noted the depth- 18 metres. Then he checked his air and indicated to Kellie she should do the same. 'Keeping busy will help her,' he reasoned. She let go and did so, then nodded. He took her hand again and they waited.

After that it was easier- scary, but easier. They swam slowly along in a straggling group in pairs, their torches swinging around on coral and fish and black nothingness- lots of black nothingness. Andrew found it was easier to ignore the open water and to concentrate on studying the coal and fish close underneath him. A prickling sense of unease about what might be out there never left him but he was able to cope.

It was an enormous relief to surface at the end of the dive but some- how swimming on the surface back to the launch seemed even scarier. To start with there was the fear of being swept away on the current and of not being found in the dark- despite the torch and the cyalume. He knew this was silly because the safety boat was manned and close by but he still felt anxious till he was holding firmly to the trail line. Only then did Kellie let go. Then Andrew could not get out of the water fast enough and he uncharacteristically pushed his way to the front and was second out.

As he heaved himself clear of the water he sighed. 'Safe!' he thought.

Kellie was next up and he steadied her and then helped her to remove her BCD and tank. She gasped with relief and then said, "Oh, thank you. I was so scared own there!"

"So was I," Andrew admitted.

They de-suited and packed away, then Andrew hurried below for a quick shower. He found it nice to wash off the sticky salt. After dressing in dry clothes he made his way back up to the saloon for debriefing. To his annoy- ance Muriel remained in her revealing bikini, continually leaning forward to give an even bigger show. That jealousy was fuelled again when Doug came and sat beside her.

Thus, when Kellie reappeared, dressed in a T-shirt and shorts and sat beside Andrew he gave her all of his attention, even though he guessed she must be ten years older than him. 'Two can play that game!' he thought.

They filled in dive reports and had them signed, then calculated their timings, even though they would not be diving again until the next morn- ing. Dave then debriefed them and complimented them on coping with the fear. "You all did well," he said. "It can be very scary diving at night."

He then told them to get some sleep as they would be doing a dawn dive and it would be their deep dive. Suddenly that did not particularly worry Andrew. 'I went down to 20 metres today. Another ten shouldn't be a problem.'

Feeling a deep glow of satisfaction he went out to help Dave and Sub Lt Sheldon rearranging air tanks. The empty ones were being moved four at a time to a compressor and that kept Andrew interested and busy for an hour. It took some skill on the sharply rocking boat to lift and safely carry the heavy air tanks but Andrew knew he had good sea legs and thoroughly enjoyed helping. At the end of that time he went back to the saloon. There were a couple of people there, drinking hot drinks and reading: the middle-aged local bloke who hadn't done the night dive and looked a bit sick, and a couple of young tourists.

Andrew made his way down to his cabin, and got a niggling surprise- Doug wasn't there.

'Where is he?' he wondered. With that came the uneasy suspicion about Muriel's whereabouts. The door to the girl's cabin was closed and Andrew knew there was no way he could knock and check. But where could he be? The launch wasn't very big. Unable to settle Andrew went back on deck and then outside.

Muriel and Doug were there, sitting together in the lee of the wheelhouse and talking. Seeing them caused a spasm of white-hot jealousy in Andrew but he was so stung he just turned and fled. He made his way back down to his cabin and flung himself on his bunk. For the next hour or so he lay there writhing in jealous agony.

Just before midnight the main engines rumbled into life and soon afterwards Andrew felt the launch moving astern. She then swung round and he had to satisfy his curiosity and go on deck. They were leaving Wheeler Reef and Dave told him they were now heading for Cape Upstart. "Be there by six tomorrow, unless the weather gets worse."

It was still blowing quite strongly and as they moved out from the limited shelter of the reef the launch began to roll sharply in a beam sea. That was most uncomfortable and even sometimes scary but Andrew enjoyed it. It at least drove Doug and Muriel in under cover. She gave Andrew a guilty look and a sickly smile before scuttling below. Doug ignored him and stayed to make a cup of coffee.

Andrew made his way back down to his bunk and wedged himself in, that being necessary as the launch was swooping and rolling sharply over quite high waves. The motion initially alarmed Andrew but he soon grew used to it and, despite his jealous misery, slipped into a deep sleep.

****

There was a bad dream in the night, one that caused Andrew to sit bolt upright, gasping and sweating. All he could remember of it was that he was diving at night and another diver had grabbed his wrist. Thinking to help and reassure the diver he put his own hand over the other diver's only to feel nothing but wet bones. He lifted his torch beam and saw that the other diver's face was a hideously grinning skull!

Sleep did not come easily after that. For an hour or so Andrew lay awake, brooding over whether Muriel liked him at all, and over whether he liked her! He thought he did, and he knew he was hurt and jealous, but was honest enough to admit that might have more to do with injured pride than with love.

Unable to sleep he went to the toilet, then on deck. In the saloon he found the middle-aged local sitting up reading, looking drawn and anxious. The weather had not improved and the launch was still rolling sharply, butting its way across an almost beam sea with sometimes sickening lurches. Outside all that was visible was a vast area of tumbling waves. The waves were rolling in from the South East in long, parallel lines.

So unexpected was one vicious twist of the rolling boat that Andrew almost lost his balance going back down to his cabin. He was flung heavily against a bulkhead and only just managed to stay on his feet. He found it a relief to hoist himself back into his bunk, but then had to brace himself against the motion. Eventually physical tiredness came to his rescue and he fell into a deep sleep.

It was a change in the motion of the launch that woke him. Now they were pitching more than rolling, and the motion was much less extreme. Andrew looked out of the port hole and saw that the waves were definitely smaller. It was still dark but he made his way up and looked out through the cabin door. To port were just tumbling waves but to starboard he thought he detected a darker line which might be land. By leaning out and looking ahead he saw the black outline of a rugged mountain range a few miles ahead and knew he was right.

'Cape Upstart,' he decided after a study of the chart pinned to the lounge bulkhead. Feeling sure he would not be able to sleep he sat and watched the sky to the east slowly turning grey. The middle-aged local was awake and looking out as well and they chatted for a while. Andrew learned that he was a primary school teacher and that he was doing his Basic Open Water Diving Course.

Dave and Sub Lt Sheldon climbed down from the wheelhouse (the instructors slept on the sun deck aft of the wheelhouse) and made themselves cups of coffee, then stood and chatted while looking out. When the first pink glow was showing on the eastern horizon they made their way forward to the focsle. Andrew went with them, staying on the starboard side of the cabin to get the benefit of its shelter. By then the mountains ahead were being bathed with a faint pink sheen, brighter at the top, and Andrew was surprised at how big they were, and how rugged. They appeared to be just one vast jumble of huge granite boulders, with rough scrub growing between them. The seaward slopes were steep cliffs.

As the launch moved into the lee of the cape the wind died away and with it the waves. It fascinated Andrew to note that what he had been taught in Geography about wave patterns actually happened. The waves refracted around the tip of the cape so that they curved into the bay behind the cape but they also lost height and force as they did. However this meant they were beam on the launch's progress which set her rolling sharply again.

This didn't bother Andrew and he watched with interest as the launch was conned to a point about a hundred metres out from a small cove with a tiny sandy beach. There was a much bigger and more sheltered bay just around the next headland further in and he did wonder why they did not go there, but then shrugged. 'This must be where the wreck is,' he decided.

An enquiry to Dave after the anchor had been let go confirmed this. Dave pointed out to sea. "Just as well we found this wreck. It is still much too rough out there for us to have dived on the *Yongala*."

This point was reinforced by him half an hour later when the Trip Director briefed all of the divers in the lounge, they having been routed from the their bunks. "We could have got you in the water and down to the wreck of the *Yongala*," he explained. "But we would never have been able to get you safely back on board."

Andrew pictured the stern of the launch rising and falling two or three metres, the water surging through the ladder and swirling around the transom and rudders and could only shudder and agree. It would be very easy to get injured in those circumstances.

Some of the tourists, having come half-way round the world to dive on the *Yongala*, expressed their obvious disappointment but they all had to agree that safety came first. One of the Englishmen then asked, "Do you know the name of this wreck, or any of its history?"

The Trip Director shook his head. "No. We only found it a month ago. We have dived on it twice and cleared away some fishing nets and lines to remove snags but we are still researching to find out the details." He then gave them the technical details, which confirmed what Andrew already knew: a small steel fishing boat or coaster with a single deck and the remains of a timber wheelhouse; a single mast, now broken off and lying over the starboard side; three hatchways or companionways and all open and with no covers or doors.

He added, "On this first dive the Advanced Course are going to do a deep dive to thirty metres and end up at the wreck, which is in only twelve metres. The Open Water Course will do a dive inshore to look at the rocks and marine life around the cove, ending at the wreck. Neither group is to attempt to enter the wreck, not even to stick your head in a hatchway. On their second dive, after a safety briefing, the Advanced Course will be allowed to enter the wreck under supervision. OK, now suit-up and let's get diving."

To Andrew's own surprise he found he was keen to get into the water. The idea of seeing a real shipwreck under water really gripped his imagination. Out on the dive deck he peeled off his shirt and tugged on his wet suit, noting as he did that Muriel was still wearing her revealing bikini. Now he just enjoyed the view, looking as much as he liked with her not apparently concerned. The sight got him a bit horny but by then he was in the wet suit and didn't care. There was still deep anxiety but he was able to push that to the back of his mind.

All the checks of straps and air pressure and so on went quickly as almost routine and within ten minutes they were jumping into the water. When it came to his turn Andrew barely hesitated. He was still scared but even that had become part of the routine- so in he went, heart in mouth. The sea was a dull grey colour still as the sun, while just above the horizon, was obscured by a band of cloud. Expecting visibility to be very poor Andrew was pleasantly surprised to be able to see all the way to a sandy bottom.

The safety boat had been launched and the Trip Director and another instructor went off in it seawards, testing depths with a hand line. At the 30 metre mark they dropped the anchor of a dive buoy. They then headed back inshore and began taking bearings with a hand compass. Andrew understood what they were doing, trying to position themselves over the wreck. When they were in the right spot they anchored the boat and both went into the water to check.

The float was the objective of the Advanced Course so Andrew waited till Muriel was ready, then swam with her out to it. Swimming so far from land- 200 metres at least, got him very anxious and he wished he hadn't overheard one of the others say that Cape Upstart was notorious for big sharks. That got him anxiously scanning the surface for the trademark fins. It also made bobbing around the dive float a tense few minutes.

'I'm not enjoying this,' he thought, then wondered how people could do it for pleasure.

Dave, Doug and Sub Lt Sheldon joined them and the group was briefed on the need to regulate their ascents and revised on how long safety stops should be at various depths to allow nitrogen to disperse from their bloodstream. Next they set their compasses to aim at the safety boat, just visible two hundred metres away. Then, satisfied they were ready, Dave gave the signal to go down.

Andrew felt safer going under. Now he could see better, he thought he would have a better chance of seeing any shark before it attacked, even though he kept thinking of the gloomy diver's lore that said that you never see the one that gets you!

What really struck him was how isolated he felt out there in ocean where no rocks or coral were visible- just blue water all round. It made him appreciate that thin cord running down from the float to its anchor and he emotionally clung to it as he went down. They did this slowly, stopping every five metres and the instructors checking that everyone was able to equalize and that there were no problems. At each stop they had to check their dive computers and report both their depth and their remaining air.

The bottom appeared at last and they settled slowly on it in a line. Here there was another check. As he knelt there Andrew looked up, watching his bubbles streaming up towards the rippling silver ceiling. Now it did seem a long way and he felt his chest tighten with anxiety. Suddenly it seemed harder to breathe and he became very conscious of the fact that only that regulator in his mouth was allowing himself to do so. The sound of his breathing seemed to him to very noisy and he was suddenly gripped by an intense desire to rip off the equipment and swim as fast as he could for the surface.

That alarmed him and he became agitated and started breathing very fast. His mind told him to stop but fear gripped him and he had to look at the others for help. Seeing Dave coming along checking for Oks was a real help.

'Calm down, or you will drown!' he chided himself. With an effort he held the regulator in his mouth and slowed his breathing. A thin trickle of water had been leaking into his mask and that annoyed him so he leaned his head back, pressed the top of the mask to his forehead and blew through his nose. Then he went back to kneeling and getting ready to signal OK to Dave.

Then it came to him. 'It works! The training works!' he thought, realizing how he had just cleared his mask without even thinking about it. That calmed him as well and he was able to read the depth on his gauge- 29 metres. 'I have to go down one more,' he thought. 30 metres was the safety limit for divers with the training he had. So, when he had signalled Dave and they began to swim along, Andrew made a short detour and went right down to touch the sand till his gauge read 30. Feeling immensely pleased with himself he rejoined the others as they began slowly finning on a compass course back towards the shore.

It took them twenty minutes to cover the 200 metres. Along the way they stopped twice for five minutes each time. Once was almost under the launch and it cheered and fascinated Andrew to see the black silhouette of its hull and the long thread of its anchor chain. During all of this he remained close beside Muriel and made sure he was swimming in the middle of the group. The whole time he kept looking anxiously in all directions for sharks.

Andrew knew he was still scared and thought, 'This is the last time I am ever going diving! I am certainly not taking it up as a sport!'

Once a ray of some indeterminate sort flitted past but apart from a few silvery-grey fish, they saw no other marine life. The bottom was just sand. But now Andrew became excited and interested. He was really keen to see the wreck and he kept peering ahead.

As he swam slowly along it suddenly came to him that he was able to do all the skills needed for safe diving. A warm glow of satisfaction filled him. 'I can do this!' he thought.

And there it was- the wreck.

Chapter 19

Facing Up to the Truth

The shipwreck first appeared as a vague, dark oblong in the murk. As Andrew got closer the shape became more apparent. This was still puzzling to him till he worked out that he was looking at the wreck from abaft the beam and that the outline was complicated by the remains of a mast or boom lying over at an angle towards him. Even so, he found it a thrilling sight.

'A real shipwreck!' he thought, his romantic imagination conjuring up stories and trying to work out what had happened.

The group gathered near the end of the old mast and Dave pointed to several weed encrusted wires- shrouds or stays or winch ropes- and wagged his finger in a determined negative. Then he led them slowly around the stern.

The wreck was sitting almost upright, leaning slightly to port, with its bow towards the beach. The whole structure was thickly coated with marine organisms, mostly seaweed of some sort, and a little coral. Dozens of small fish flitted in and out among the growths on the propeller and rudder. Andrew had read how old ships were now deliberately sunk to form artificial reefs for diving so wasn't surprised.

The group swam around the flat transom stern and then slowly up along the starboard side. By now the visibility was very good, the sun having come out. Soon they were at the bow and that was even more romantic. Andrew expected to see an anchor or anchors and noted that none was visible. To check he finned up a couple of metres and looked onto the foredeck. As he did a large coral trout swam up out of the black rectangle of a hatchway.

'I hope there isn't a bloody great groper lurking in there- or an octopus,' he thought.

They went back along the port side and then swam up above. The huge rectangular hole of a cargo hatchway was clearly evident, as was a smaller hatchway at the stern. The remains of a deckhouse were still evident but it had been made of timber and had either rotted or been smashed off by storms or trawler's nets. Andrew found the whole thing fascinating but also somewhat disappointing. It wasn't a very big wreck really, and certainly wasn't his romantic image of a wooden square-rigged pirate ship with treasure chests and skeletons and an octopus.

Then a horrible thought came to him- what if there were skeletons in the wreck? He shuddered but then shook his head. 'No, the crabs and fish would have eaten them all up long ago,' he reasoned.

At that moment dim shapes became visible moving towards them through the water. After a moment of alarm Andrew saw it was the Basic Course dive group. For a few seconds he imagined them to be enemy frogmen swimming to attack. Then he remembered the scene from the James Bond film 'Thunderball' and was able to pretend he was getting ready for a life and death struggle underwater. For a few seconds he shuddered at the image of how ghastly it must really be to fight underwater, of being hit by the flickering steel dart from a speargun or to have an air hose severed.

Dave ended that by signalling to surface. The group swam away from the wreck and towards the dive boat, angling up to ten metres. They stayed at this level till they came to the launch. A lead line had been dropped from the stern and a spare air tank with regulator hung on it at 10 metres, as an emergency supply for anyone who was running short. None were so they stayed drifting with neutral buoyancy for five minutes, then surfaced.

Up on deck, after storing their kit and getting out of their wet suits they made their way to the saloon. By now the sun was well above the horizon and the breeze had dropped to almost nothing. The motion of the launch was barely noticeable to Andrew. They filled out dive logs and then used the 'wheel' calculator to work out how long they had to stay out.

"Your next dive will be to twelve metres maximum when we go back and explore the wreck," Dave explained.

After going down to 30 metres Andrew thought that would hardly be a challenge. 'Only two more dives to qualify,' he told himself, nerving himself to keep going. After that he need never go underwater again in his whole life. There was also the delicious pleasure in continually glancing sideways down the front of Muriel's bikini top to watch how her breasts gently quivered, and in the hope of getting a glimpse of her nipples.

Breakfast followed, during which the Basic Course people returned on board. With nothing else to do Andrew joined the other young people on the foredeck, warming themselves in the sun. Muriel was there and he sat beside her. To his relief and delight she moved closer and sat so close that her legs and body touched his. Then Doug arrived and sat facing them. Andrew was irritated at the way Doug's gaze kept roving over Muriel's body. He was even more peeved at the way Doug tried to keep talking to her, and at her answering him in a friendly way. Nettled and anxious Andrew sat down facing them and joined in the conversation. The talk was all about diving- of the wreck, the big manta ray someone had seen; of a black-tipped shark one of the Englishmen had observed; of clams and coral.

To Andrew's annoyance Doug kept continually talking to Muriel. Andrew tried to give him the hint to buzz off but he did not seem to notice. To add to his discomfiture Andrew became aroused and had to remain seated so that this was hidden.

At 8:30 the Trip Director called them all for another briefing. Andrew waited till others were moving and then used his towel and shirt to hide his aroused condition. The need to squash into the saloon with the others and then the technical aspect of the dive briefing all helped take his mind back off sex but he was still feeling horny, mainly because Muriel sat pressing against him. What caused him to shudder were the stories, told as dire warnings by the instructors.

One was about how two divers entered the forward torpedo compartment of a sunken submarine but how their swimming around stirred up a cloud of fine sediment that had been deposited over the years. The sediment so lowered visibility they had been unable to find the narrow hatchway to get out again and both had died when their air supply ran out.

The other was by Dave about when he had dived on the wreck of a large Russian ocean liner, the *Mikhail Lermontov*, which ran on a rock in Picton Sound in New Zealand. "We swam into the superstructure and along the passageways," he explained. "Then, when we were three decks down, I saw that the vibrations through the water from our swimming had caused all the rotting chipboard wall panels lining the corridor to come adrift and the entire passageway was filled with floating rubbish. We had a lot of trouble finding our way back out in time."

The Trip Director reinforced this message by reminding them that many divers had perished in wrecks because they had got stuck in a narrow opening and had damaged their air supply, or been unable to get free. "I don't want any of the stuff you read about those mad cave divers doing like taking off equipment to pass it through narrow openings, then going through after it. If you won't fit easily, don't try to go through."

He then reminded them that divers always tended to underestimate their spatial awareness, and that angles and sizes were magnified and distorted by water. "So, you will only enter compartments one at a time and under the direct supervision of an instructor, got it?"

They said yes. The Trip Director then asked, "Any questions?"

One of the Englishmen then said, "Yes. Do you have some more basic data on this wreck?"

"No more than you have been given, but this time we will take torches and tools and tape measures and draw a plan of her."

"How did she sink sir?" Carmen asked.

"We aren't sure but we are going to look," the Trip Director answered.

"A storm perhaps?" suggested one of the tourists.

"Could have been. There is no anchor so she may have been sheltering here and dragged her anchor and hit a rock or something," the Trip Director replied. "Anyway, it is nine O'clock so let's get diving and you can look for clues."

Going down this time was easy for Andrew. He felt more scared swimming across to the wreck on the surface than in going under. The group descended and began exploring. Dave had them go into the main cargo hold one at a time. That was empty, except for a build up of silt. The hatchway was so large that Andrew felt no real fear going into it. The forward hatch led down into some sort of storeroom. The hatchway was just large enough for a diver to lower themselves vertically down. Inside it was so dark a torch was needed but Andrew was not alarmed, being the fifth person to enter the compartment.

The engine space aft was a bit trickier. The hatchway was just large enough but the signals and gesticulations of the others all indicated interest. Torch in hand Andrew went in when it was his turn. The space was mostly filled by a huge diesel engine, with smaller pieces of machinery and various pipes and boxes along the sides. He soon saw what had excited everyone's interest- a small octopus. The repulsive thing only had a head and body about the size of his fist but when it spread its tentacles it looked much larger. It was not one of the deadly poisonous blue-ringed variety but Andrew took good care to keep well away from it. He was also wary of the far end of the machinery spaces as he could see the head of a moray eel just poking out from a cranny among the pipes.

He found it a relief to get back outside. For the next ten minutes he drifted on neutral buoyancy and watched the others, while fantasizing about heroic adventures in bigger wrecks. While he did he idly watched the Trip Director and a couple of the Englishmen as they worked their way along the bottom of the hull, digging away sand and measuring. While he waited Andrew also kept making frequent checks that no shark had suddenly appeared.

In what seemed like no time at all the signal to surface was given. 'Good!' Andrew thought. 'Only one more dive to go.'

Back on board the dive launch they filled out dive logs and then calculated the times for their last dive. While they were doing that Dave and Sub Lt Sheldon checked the accuracy of their calculations. The Trip Director joined them, towelling his face. "Well," he said to the group a large. "That was interesting. We know a bit more now."

"What did you find out?" Sub Lt Sheldon asked.

The Trip Director pointed to one of the young Englishmen. "Young Jeremy here found the builder's name plate."

"Oh aye," Jeremy nodded. "Built on the Clyde she were, in nineteen forty four."

That got Andrew's interest. 'World War 2.' he thought.

What Jeremy next said caused him to stiffen with surprise. "She were an army workboat," he said, "Her number is A. V., one three, one three."

Dave nodded. "We should have no difficulty tracking her history now," he commented.

'AV 1313!' Andrew thought, surprise turning to puzzled shock. He looked up and met Carmen's eyes and he could see she was having the same reaction. Looking at her he said, "That was the *Deeral's* number."

Carmen nodded. A horrible feeling swept through Andrew, followed by intense interest. The others were all looking at him now.

Sub Lt Sheldon asked, "*Deeral?* What was she?"

"An ex-army workboat that my Grandad bought after the war," Andrew answered. "He was on it when he went missing at sea."

"Went missing!" cried Sub Lt Sheldon. "When? Tell us more?"

"Back in nineteen fifty eight," Andrew answered. "He and Muriel's Grandad went to sea looking for a sunken ship named the *Merinda*. The *Deeral* sank in a storm and Grandad was never seen again. Muriel's Grandad was the only survivor."

He glanced at Muriel, who looked puzzled but nodded. But Andrew was puzzled also and he could see that Carmen was too. Carmen spoke first, "But that doesn't make sense. I thought the *Deeral* sank somewhere east of the Whitsunday Islands. That is hundreds of kilometres from here."

Andrew's mind raced through possibilities and he tried to visualize the chart. He shook his head and said, "Maybe she didn't sink immediately? Maybe she drifted until she went down here?"

"Maybe," the Trip Director said, looking very thoughtful, "But this ship here didn't sink in a storm. She was scuttled using explosives."

There was a shocked silence. Muriel spoke first. "No! That's not possible!" she cried.

The Trip Director looked at her and shook his head. "It is. We found four holes blasted in her hull, one in each of the smaller compartments and two in the main hold, and both the steel hatch covers of the small compartments have been clipped open. If that ship had been in trouble in bad weather those would have been closed."

Once again there was a silence. Everyone present was interested but Andrew barely noticed them. His mind raced over the ugly possibilities. Explosives! Scuttled! Had there been an accident? What had happened?

Muriel spoke again, loudly and angrily. "Then it must be some other ship. Grandad said he was a long way east of Bowen when the ship hit a reef and sank, and he was washed ashore on Hayman Island."

The Trip Director shook his head. "There is no sign of this ship here hitting a reef," he replied.

"Then it must be another ship!" Muriel cried. She was upset now, as well as angry and Andrew moved to comfort her.

Jeremy now spoke up. "We can show you the maker's number," he answered. He looked as though he regretted ever raising the subject.

Muriel nodded but she looked so unhappy that Andrew put his arms around her and gave her a gentle squeeze. Carmen then asked, "Can we look at the wreck again on our last dive?"

The Trip Director nodded. "I was going to get you to study the marine life along the rocks but I think we had better clear this up. It is obviously causing some concern."

"There will be some perfectly simple explanation," Sub Lt Sheldon added soothingly.

Again Andrew patted Muriel's arm. "It will turn out alright. Let's have some morning tea while we wait."

They moved to the able to get drinks and biscuits and this helped ease the tension which had developed but while they ate Andrew remained puzzled. Something did not add up and it bothered him. Carmen obviously felt the same way because when she got Andrew alone she said, "This is really fishy. How could the *Deeral* be here when it is supposed to have sunk about one hundred and eighty nautical miles away? That is over three hundred kilometres. There is no way a sinking wreck could have drifted that far."

"Maybe this wreck isn't the *Deeral*?" Andrew replied. He was bothered by the whole situation and did not want to upset Muriel.

"We can check," Carmen answered. "We will take the details and see if they match."

There seemed nothing else to do. When it came time for the last dive- only for twenty minutes and no deeper than 12 metres- Andrew and Carmen set out with wrist slates and crayons. Muriel looked unhappy but came with them. The whole group jumped in and set out, Andrew barely noticing things like suiting up or jumping into the sea. Only when he was finning across the surface towards the dive raft did he realize that. Even then he only did a perfunctory search for sharks before pushing them out of his mind. He was now consumed by a gnawing curiosity to learn the truth.

This time the Trip Director came with them. Before they dived he said, "I will first show you the holes in the hull. Then Jeremy will take you into the engine room and show you the builder's plate."

Andrew nodded and then saw the look on Muriel's face and felt uneasy. 'If this is the *Deeral* then her Grandad might have some explaining to do,' he thought. Even thinking that made him feel ill and disloyal to Muriel. But he felt he had to know.

So down they went. The holes in the hull were right in underneath, below the sharp turn of the bilge, but by lying flat on the sand and peering into the hole scooped out by the earlier divers Andrew clearly saw a jagged hole. The hole appeared to be about 15 to 20 cm in diameter. But what really made him think was the way the jagged edges of the hole were facing downwards- outwards. Just seeing that was enough to cause him grave misgivings.

'It certainly looks like a hole blasted by explosives,' he thought, very aware that he had no experience or training in the field.

He wormed his way back out, bumping his air tank on the weed-encrusted hull several times as he did. Carmen went in to take his place. Others were clustered further along at another hole. Muriel was with them but appeared to be very reluctant to go down and look. She did so but just met his eyes blankly when she came back out.

Jeremy then led Andrew into the engine room. Both used torches. This time Andrew ignored the small octopus and just kept a wary eye on the moral eel as he and Jeremy swam past its lair to the far end of the space. Jeremy then shone his torch up on a stainless steel plate about 20 cm X 10 cm. He reached up and rubbed the mossy slime off it and pointed to the engraved letters and numbers.

Andrew moved closer and read the plate. As he did he felt his heart constrict and then speed up. It read:

A V 1313
Clydeside Shipyard
Job Number A 65478
6 April 1944

Reading those details caused Andrew a whole slew of emotions. He felt suddenly sad and could only shake his head as the possible implications dawned on him. Very carefully he copied the inscription onto his slate. Jeremy then took him to a pump bolted to the port side and showed him a number. Andrew copied the brand name and the number as well. Then he did the same for the huge diesel engine.

Once more Jeremy tapped his arm and pointed. Andrew saw a pipe which obviously led in from the ship's side to the pump. The pipe had been unscrewed and lay partly off. That made him feel even sicker. 'If it was sabotage someone deliberately set out to sink this ship,' he thought. But who? And why?

The ideas that followed were so ugly he shied away from even thinking them. He allowed himself to be led back outside so that Carmen could go in and look. Muriel was waiting there and while he could not see her mouth because of the regulator Andrew could tell by her eyes that she was worried and unhappy. When Carmen came back out Muriel appeared to be reluctant to even go in and look but she did.

As soon as Muriel was inside Carmen touched Andrew's arm to attract his attention and then took out her regulator to show a grim mouth. She put her regulator back in and shook her head. She looked more serious than Andrew could ever remember. Carmen then took his slate and printed on the back of it. When he turned it over and read the words he felt his chest tighten.

It read: Somebody is telling lies!

With that ugly thought churning his stomach and making his mind race Andrew swam back to the dive boat with the others. He helped Muriel up the ladder and with her air tanks and BCD but she looked thoroughly miserable. That made him feel worse. She made no move to help him so Carmen did. Andrew then helped Carmen off with her gear.

As she placed her air tank back in the rack Carmen said to Muriel. "If that is the wreck of the *Deeral* then your Grandfather has got some explaining to do."

Muriel looked aghast and then tears sprang to her eyes. "Oh that is a horrible thing to say!"

Carmen faced her squarely. "It might be. But someone has been telling lies, and as he was the only survivor, it must be him."

"Oh! How dare you! What a horrible person you are!" Muriel shouted, stung to anger by the accusation.

Through this Andrew stood appalled and unsure what so say, or whose side to take. He saw Doug, who had been hovering near Muriel all through the dive, step up beside her.

Doug fronted Andrew. "Leave her alone! You haven't any proof for such an accusation," he snarled.

Sub Lt Sheldon now stepped forward. "That's enough. Doug's right. We don't have the facts, so let the subject drop please. Wait until we have done some research and know what we are talking about before we make any legal accusations."

Andrew felt a cold chill at that word 'legal'. He understood that Sub Lt Sheldon was warning Carmen and him about things like slander. Through a mist of distress he saw Doug put an arm around Muriel's shoulders and lead her away to the saloon. Carmen turned to him and looked unhappy. So was Andrew, but he was angry as well. He was sure the wreck was the *Deeral.*

Carmen hissed to him, "Why would old Mr McGackey lie about a thing like the ship's number?"

Still trying to find excuses and wanting to help Muriel Andrew shrugged and said, "Maybe he is just an old man whose memory has wandered. Maybe the number was another ship he was on."

"We will soon be able to check," Carmen answered. "The government keep records of all ships registered."

Andrew could only nod and feel numb. He had a horrible sinking feeling that the truth, when it was revealed, might be really unpleasant. He also sensed that he and Muriel might now be separated by the need to face the truth. 'But I love her!' he thought miserably. Then tears came and he turned away to look out to sea.

Chapter 20

Suspicions

The Trip Director now came forward. "I'd like you two to move to the dive deck and wait there please. I don't want any arguing or fights on my trips."

Andrew and Carmen did as they were asked. Sub Lt Sheldon came with them, as did Jeremy and a couple of the tourists. Sub Lt Sheldon said, as they made their way aft along the narrow side deck, "And we don't need any splits or ill-will in our cadet unit either."

The Trip Director then said, "I'd like you two to stay here, away from that other girl until we get under way. Then I'd would like an explanation."

Andrew nodded and sat down, suddenly feeling quite exhausted. The Trip Director, Dave and Sub Lt Sheldon got busy recovering safety boats and dive floats and then the anchor was winched aboard. Normally Andrew would have been fascinated to watch these bits of seamanship but now he just observed them through a mask of dull confusion and misery.

"I think I have upset Muriel," he commented to Carmen when they were alone.

Carmen shrugged. "That isn't your fault. She is the one who can't face the truth."

"Be fair Car! You can't expect a person not to be loyal to their own family," Andrew replied.

"I suppose not. But one thing is for sure, when we get back I am going to investigate what happened to our grandfather," Carmen replied with a shrug.

It was almost midday by then. The launch turned and headed north at full speed, a good 12 knots. As they came out from the lee of Cape Upstart the waves increased in size and the launch began to roll and pitch, with an occasional slithering yaw down the side of a larger than normal wave. None of this bothered Andrew, but the middle-aged local stood looking at the sea with an anxious expression on his face and a couple of the tourists became sea sick.

Once everything was secured the Trip Director, Dave, Sub Lt Sheldon and a couple of others came and joined them. The Trip Director then asked for an explanation. Carmen did most of the talking but Andrew gave the detailed explanation of what Grandma Murchison had said. Carmen explained about the newspaper cutting and what old Mr McGackey had said, even to making excuses for an old man possibly getting his facts wrong. The adults listened with close attention, obviously very interested.

"So you can see why I think it is all very suspicious," Carmen concluded.

The Trip Director nodded. "Yes, I can see your point of view. But it isn't proof, so if I were you, I wouldn't say anything more. In fact, while you are on this boat, I am telling you not to. No more trouble."

"And none on the way home either please," Sub Lt Sheldon added. "Even if your suppositions are correct it wasn't Muriel who did anything, so don't start saying hurtful things to her."

"No sir," Andrew agreed. He then turned to the Trip Director, "Sir, are you sure that explosives were used to sink that boat?"

The Trip Director nodded emphatically. "Certain. I was a navy clearance diver for twenty years, a warrant officer when I retired. I am a demolition expert and in all that time I have seen the results of a lot of cutting charges on steel. The blast came from inside."

"Thanks sir," Andrew added. It was more food for thought.

The Trip Director then asked them to stay with Dave while he spoke to Muriel to get her side of the story. He also told them to wait outside until he told them to come in to have lunch. Andrew was feeling very hungry by now, as well and being physically and emotionally worn out but he could only nod and sit there, enjoying the view as the rocky mountains of the cape receded. As he watched the wavering foam line of the launch's wake he brooded on all that he had just learned, and on the fact that Muriel was angry with him.

As the launch rose and fell on the waves Andrew stared out over the tumbling waste of water and tried to imagine what it might have been like to have spent several days in such conditions with nothing but a lifebuoy to cling to. Having spent 15 hours drifting in the sea the previous year he had a good idea, but thinking about that just made him unhappier. 'The sea wasn't really rough when we were down in it,' he mused. 'If Old Mr Murchison was in it during a storm it would have been much worse. He would have got very cold and tired,' he thought, remembering how exhausted and cold he and his friends had become.

But that just introduced another niggling doubt that he did not really want to think about: was it possible to stay afloat in a lifebuoy in rough water for that long? 'To stay with one of those old-fashioned lifebuoys you actually needed to cling on,' he told himself, picturing how an exhausted person might slump through the middle if he lost his grip.

Andrew stared unhappily out to the South East. 'Out there somewhere it was supposed to have happened. So how did the *Deeral* end up at Cape Upstart?' Next, in an attempt to excuse Muriel, he pondered whether the explosives might have gone off by accident. 'Perhaps there was a fire in the galley- that might account for there being no superstructure?' But that did not fit very well either, and he had to accept that the explosives were not all in one place. He also had to reluctantly concede, from the evidence of his own eyes, that there was no indication of any fire in the engine room, the other most likely source.

Thinking thus made him more and more depressed but his curiosity was now fully aroused and he kept teasing at the possibilities. 'So, even if there was an accident, someone deliberately blew out her bottom with explosives. But who?' he wondered. After a moment he had to swallow and face the probability that it was Old Mr Murchison. 'And why? And why lie?'

Carmen was obviously thinking along the same lines as she said, "If Old Mr Murchison did sink the *Deeral* there, why did he do it? If there was some problem why didn't he try to sail to the nearest harbour? And why then make up a story and lie about it?"

Unwillingly Andrew answered her. "To cover up something, to hide what had happened," he said.

"That's what I think," Carmen agreed, "But what?"

In spite of his love for Muriel Andrew's mind had hatefully followed its own lines of reasoning and he had even thought about this. "What were Grandad and Murchison looking for?" he asked.

"The wreck of a ship called the *Merinda*," Carmen answered.

"And what was the *Merinda* carrying, other than some cargo and school-girls on their way to boarding school?" Andrew asked. The idea of pretty young girls drowning in a shipwreck appalled him. But the horrible suspicion in his mind appalled him even more.

"Gold," Carmen answered. "And people commit murder for gold."

"That's what I suspect," Andrew answered bleakly. "Maybe Old Mr Murchison murdered Grandad and the two black men, then sank the ship to cover the crime."

"That would mean that they found the wreck of the *Merinda* and recovered the gold," Carmen suggested.

"I think they did," Andrew replied, thinking about a certain chart he had seen. But he made no mention of that to Carmen. Instead he said,

"Having killed the others Old Mr Murchison may have sailed to Cape Upstart to unload the gold, to hide it. Then he sank the *Deeral* and made his way along the coast by boat. Then he told the story about the ship hitting a reef in a storm and of him drifting in the lifebuoy- and he even had the lifebuoy to prove it."

Carmen frowned. "But he was found at Hayman Island and we worked out that that is three hundred kilometres away. Could he have done that?"

"Easier to go three hundred kilometres in a small boat than float in a lifebuoy in rough weather for a few days," Andrew answered. Now he was feeling sick as well as miserable. He sensed that if the suspicions were true then his relationship with Muriel was headed for the rocks as well. What also bothered him was the realization that he would have to find out the truth, no matter what it might cost him! 'I will never sleep again for wondering if I don't,' he told himself.

Carmen bit her lip and nodded. "Captain Bligh went thousands of miles in an open boat. If Murchison did three of four knots he could sail it in about three days."

"That's what I calculated," Andrew agreed.

"What did he do with the boat?"

Andrew gave a short, harsh laugh. "If you've just scuttled a perfectly good ship then sinking a rowing boat wouldn't bother you, particularly if you had murder on your conscience."

Again Carmen nodded. "So you think that he later went back to get the gold from Cape Upstart?"

"Yes, and lied about finding it while prospecting up in Cape York Peninsula," Andrew said.

Carmen shook her head as though not wanting to believe it. Then she said, "I have to find out."

"So do I," Andrew agreed. "Otherwise it will gnaw at me for the rest of my life."

"How do we go about it?" Carmen asked.

Andrew had a few ideas and he suggested these, then added, "And we play it very quiet so as not to arouse suspicions. We don't want any surviving evidence destroyed."

Carmen agreed, adding, "And we don't want to cause any upset or grief if our suspicions are unfounded."

"No, you are right. I would hate to harm a person who was innocent," Andrew agreed, adding, "It might have all just been a ghastly accident or a mistake with a perfectly logical and reasonable answer."

Carmen nodded. "So we just act as though it was an interesting discovery at the time but that we have more important things in our lives."

'I do,' Andrew tried to tell himself, 'Muriel's love.' But even as he told himself this he sensed that it wasn't true. For a while he and Carmen discussed the strategy to try to uncover the truth but after a while Andrew had had enough. He was dismayed and sick at heart. To him it first and foremost meant that Muriel was angry and hurt and that he was on the outer. He began speculating on how he could win back her friendship.

The voyage back to Townsville took nearly six hours. During that time they saw only two other launches and one sailing yacht. Andrew was glad to have a chance to think about something else while he studied each one. As before he itched to be up in the wheelhouse where he could use binoculars and be more informed about where they were and what was going on. The course took them close along the length of Cape Bowling Green, a 14 kilometre long flat sand spit backed by a belt of mangroves and tipped by a lighthouse. Then it was across Bowling Green Bay and past the rugged mountains that terminated in Cape Cleveland and another lighthouse. The launch rounded that cape and swung to port, heading North West in the relatively sheltered waters of Cleveland Bay.

During the last hour Andrew and Carmen were asked to join the others in the saloon. Muriel was there, sitting beside Doug. She gave them an unhappy glance, then looked away. Seeing that caused Andrew some distress but he obeyed the orders not to talk to her and made sure he was well away from her. As they came into port all the dive logs were checked and signed and temporary certificates filled out and issued.

Andrew took his with mixed emotions. There was pride in achievement and deep satisfaction that he had mastered his fears and been able to do the course. There was also great relief. 'Good, now I don't ever need to go diving again,' he thought.

As the launch berthed Sub Lt Sheldon told them to get their gear and get it up on deck ready to disembark as soon as the gangway was across. "We've still got a five or six hour drive to get home," he reminded them.

Andrew and Carmen deliberately waited till both Muriel and Doug had collected their gear from the cabins before going below. Andrew had no desire to be alone with either of them at the moment. Back on deck with his kitbag he found they had already gone ashore. He and Carmen thanked the Trip Director and Dave and then hurried ashore.

Their minibus was waiting with the doors open. Sub Lt Sheldon loaded their bags in the back and then told them to board. As Andrew climbed in he saw that Muriel was seated at the back against the window, with Doug beside her in the aisle seat. She gave Andrew one unhappy glance, then turned her head and stared out the window. Doug gave him a hard look which also conveyed to Andrew feelings of malicious triumph. It really hurt but he did not feel up to any sort of a scene. Instead he slipped into a seat at the front next to the door and Carmen sat beside him on his left.

It was a long, uncomfortable and tiring trip back to Cairns. During it Andrew kept turning the suspicions over and over in his mind until he made himself very depressed and almost physically sick. For a time he dozed. At Cardwell they all climbed out for a rest stop. During this Muriel avoided him and stayed with Doug. That upset Andrew even more.

Carmen went to sleep after Cardwell and slumped with her head on his shoulder. That steadied Andrew when he saw how drawn and tired she looked. He tried to sleep but was unable to. Instead he tried to name every place they passed through, and to guess what the next section of the road was like. In spite of this he kept thinking about diving, and about the wreck.

Back in Cairns they went first to Muriel's. Andrew had never been there and studied the house with interest, noting the lights coming on at the front and then her parents coming out. Muriel climbed out past Andrew and stepped down. As she did she stopped and turned to face him. After looking him in the eyes for a few seconds she said, "Andrew, please don't hurt my grandfather. Please don't say anything about the wreck."

That made him feel very uncomfortable and he badly wanted to do what she asked. But he had to swallow and shake his head. "Other people are going to talk about it. Carmen will tell mum and dad and I will have to say something."

"If you love me you won't," Muriel replied.

That stung, but caused more anger than fear. 'And if you love me you wouldn't make such an impossible request,' he thought, but did not say. Instead he mumbled, "Goodbye, see you at cadets."

For a few seconds she gave him a look that set his emotions swirling- regret, love, sympathy. Then she said coldly, "Goodbye then." Picking up her bag she turned on her heel and walked away.

With a sinking heart Andrew watched her walk inside. By then the door of the bus was closed and then the bus began moving. It took all of Andrew's willpower to stop himself crying. To hide his distress he pretended he was tired (not difficult) and closed his eyes. Ten minutes later the bus stopped again and Carmen shook him. "Wake up," she said. "We are home."

Brother and sister climbed out. Andrew avoided Doug's eyes. Instead he concentrated on thanking Sub Lt Sheldon as he handed them their kitbags. By then his mother and father were making their way to the front gate.

As the bus drove away Carmen nudged Andrew and whispered, "Not a word. Save it till tomorrow."

Andrew knew exactly what she meant so, to his mother's question of how did it go, he just replied, "Very interesting. We both qualified."

"You managed the night dive?" his father asked him, obviously pleased.

The fact that his father had possibly noted his fears bothered Andrew as he thought he had hidden them fairly well. He nodded, then yawned.

His mother than asked, "And what about the wreck? Was that scary?"

"No Mum. Really interesting. Tell you about it tomorrow," he answered.

"Good idea," his mother agreed. "Bed time. School tomorrow."

They made their way inside and were offered hot Milo, which both accepted. Then it was brushing teeth and into pyjamas and bed. By then it was nearly 1am and Andrew was genuinely tired. He lay back, in the warmth and comfort of his own bedroom, sure he would sleep soundly- and didn't. For hours he tossed and turned, dozing fitfully. Several times he had bad dreams. The only one he could remember was being on the launch in rough weather, with the launch somehow shrinking to a small rubber boat. This in turn shrank to just a lifebuoy, and no matter how he tried to cling onto it, it kept tipping him up in the boiling seas. Suddenly he was underwater and he was terrified because it wasn't sharks or octopuses that were the dimly flitting shadows but skeletons.

So tired and washed out did he feel in the morning that he considered asking if he could stay home sick. But in the end he dragged himself out of bed and through his usual school day morning routine. During breakfast Carmen talked about the night dive but carefully avoided any mention of the wreck so Andrew followed her lead.

Their mother nodded and said, "Very interesting dears, now, hurry up or you will be late. You can tell us all about it tonight."

Andrew and Carmen made their way to school. Here he found an interested audience, especially Luke, but again he made no mention of the wreck. Instead he talked about the thrill of the deep dive, and of how scary he had found swimming in the sea in the dark.

Luke shook his head and said, "Not me mon. No way! You wouldn't get me in that sea at night, not even if the ship sank from under me!"

Blake and Simmo teased him and laughed, then paused to tease Willy Williams who was nearby throwing paper planes. "Is that the best the air force can do Willy? You should try adding an engine."

Simmo laughed but then cried, "No, a rocket motor. That would really make it go boom- I mean zoom!"

They laughed some more. Andrew then said, "Willy, there is a teacher over there. You had better take your paper planes out of sight in case you get into trouble."

Willy and his friends did so. Andrew resumed his tales of diving in the deep, enjoying the envy and adulation of his friends, even if he felt slightly fraudulent. As he talked he saw Graham walking along looking anxiously around. They exchanged good mornings but Graham was obviously distracted and only listened to his diving stories for a few minutes before wandering off, mumbling some excuse of looking for someone.

A few minutes later Peter and Roger joined them. "How did the diving go?" Peter asked.

"Great. What's wrong with Graham?"

Peter made a wry face and said, "Girl trouble I think. He is in love with Amanda."

"Amanda Howley, the regular army warrant officer's daughter?"

"That's the one," Peter confirmed. Andrew nodded. He had noted Graham talking to her and sitting next to her in Geography. When he went to Geography later in the day he saw that Graham was sitting next to Amanda in a seat near the back of the room. Andrew seated himself next to Angus MacDougal and pointed towards Graham. "Is Graham doing a line for her?" he asked.

Angus nodded. "I suspect so," he replied in a broad Scottish accent. "For sure he's been teased about it. I heard there was a wee bit of hanky panky on the weekend but that's all I know," Angus explained.

Thinking of his own girl troubles that information just depressed Andrew still further. 'A bit of hanky panky eh? Lucky Graham!' he thought wistfully. Then he thought more about Muriel. 'I hope she phones me,' he thought.

With that in mind he hurried home as soon as school was over. Once there he had afternoon tea, during which Carmen came home. She said, "I've just been organizing with Gran to go and visit old Mr McGackey again. Be Wednesday afternoon. Do you want to come?"

Andrew did but didn't. What nagged at him was Muriel's pleading not to do anything to hurt her grandfather. But how to avoid that? It was plain that Carmen was going to follow up with her own enquiries. For an hour he lay on his bed and thought hard about all he had seen and heard- and promptly slipped into a deep sleep. He was roused from this by his mother for tea at 6pm. After washing his face he joined the others in the lounge-dining room. As usual they ate their tea watching the TV news. Afterwards Carmen turned the TV off, much to their father's surprise.

"I wanted to watch the current affairs program," he protested.

"No you didn't," Carmen replied in a very determined voice. "You really wanted to hear what Andrew and I have to say." Then she insisted they listen while she told them about the wreck.

As she talked, backed up by Andrew from time to time, Andrew saw the look on his father's face change from polite listening to acute interest, his features marked by a peculiar drawn look. The story was certainly a shock to him, and Andrew could see that his father was having the same reaction he had - a burning desire to know the truth. It dawned on Andrew that if he was curious about what had happened to his grandfather, how much more interested must his father be in knowing the fate of his own father!

Sadly he shook his head. 'There is no way I can stop this hurting Old Mr Murchison,' he realized.

His misery was compounded by waiting for hours in the hope that Muriel might telephone. But there was no call and he lacked the courage to go against her wishes and call her. Instead he did his homework and moped off to bed- to sleep soundly right through the night.

Chapter 21

Shocks and Recriminations

Nor could Andrew protect Old Mr Murchison. At breakfast the next morning Andrew's father held up the morning newspaper.

"Well, the secret is out now," he said.

Andrew stared at the headline appalled.

LOCAL MARITIME MYSTERY SOLVED? it read.

'Oh no! Muriel is going to be very upset. I hope she doesn't blame me,' he thought.

The newspaper article was all about the wreck of the *Deeral*. It went over the story of the sinking of the *Merinda* and of how the *Deeral* had set out with four men on board to search for it. Andrew noted that his grandfather's name was there, along with Murchison's and the names of the two crewmen. There followed a word for word copy of the 1958 article that he had read. Then there was a detailed description of how the wreck was found and of what it looked like. The concluding sentence set Andrew's heart in his mouth with interest and anxiety. It read: 'Now at last, after all these years, it seems that the sea might be going to give up the secret of what really happened on that fateful voyage.'

As he looked up from reading Andrew's mind raced. Who had written the article and put it in the paper? His first thought was that it must have been Carmen. Then he considered his father. He looked at him and asked, "Did you write this Dad?"

His father looked surprised. "Not me. I'm interested, but not that much."

"Car?"

Carmen shook her head. "I wish I had but it never crossed my mind. I wanted to do some quiet detective work first but now it looks like it will all be out in the open."

Remembering Carmen's comment about evidence being hidden or destroyed Andrew could only nod. "I wonder who wrote the article then?"

he said, ticking off in his mind possible candidates. The article had a name under it he did not recognize and which was no help. They discussed who it might have been, then once again speculated on what might have happened on the *Deeral* on her fateful last voyage. All they could do was go over the same theories as before and nothing was resolved, except the obvious determination to find out the truth.

This time when he got to school Andrew told his friends about the discovery of the wreck but was careful not to put forward any of his ideas or suspicions about what might have happened.

Peter nodded and said, "I saw the name Herbert Collins and wondered if he was a relative. Your Grandad eh? Sorry about that."

The person Andrew thought would be most interested was Graham but he seemed preoccupied and soon left, to go and talk to Amanda. This occasioned some cruel jibes from some of the others about 'dogs' and 'going for the ugly ones because they are grateful'. Andrew thought they were being quite unkind. Amanda was plain but she appeared to him to have a very full bosom and a shapely figure. 'She's probably a very nice person,' he thought. Later, in Geography, he cast a few glances back at where Graham and Amanda sat side by side. They were obviously so close together that their bodies must be touching. Seeing them putting their heads together and the way they were whispering and looking at each other made him quite envious. With memories of doing just that with Muriel he wistfully wondered if he had any chance of recovering her affection.

That hope seemed to vanish to almost nil that evening. The phone rang and when his mother answered it and said, "Yes, Andrew is here," his hopes shot up.

It was Muriel, but her first words were biting. "Oh Andrew, how could you! I asked you not to. I thought you loved me."

"How could I what?" Andrew asked, mystified.

"Write that newspaper article," Muriel answered.

"But I didn't," Andrew replied, hurt that she thought so.

"Then it was that sister of yours," Muriel snapped. "It is so cruel! There have been media people over at Grandad's badgering him and Grandma all day. They are very upset and hurt."

"It wasn't Carmen," Andrew answered, angry that Muriel was making the accusations without any proof.

"Then who was it?" Muriel asked angrily.

"I don't know. Look Muriel, I am sorry about all this but we didn't tell anyone, except our parents," Andrew explained, trying not to let his emotions obvious.

"Then it was them!" she snapped.

"It wasn't! Dad was quite surprised to read it in the paper. Anyway, he wouldn't have had time. He only learned about the wreck a few hours earlier."

"He could have," Muriel said.

"He didn't! He told me," Andrew replied. He was getting annoyed now and it hurt to hear her speak that way.

There was a silence and Andrew distinctly heard muffled sobs. It made him realize that Muriel was crying. While he was groping for the right words to say she said, "Please let it drop. Please don't talk to people about it, and don't hurt my Grandad."

That was food for thought and all Andrew could say was that he would not raise the issue with anyone. "But if people ask me I will have to tell them," he added.

"Then you are no friend of mine!" Muriel cried, slamming down the phone.

Feeling hurt and puzzled Andrew made his way back to his room but was quite unable to settle to his homework. What he did instead was take out his chart of the Barrier Reef and pencil on the actual location of the wreck of the A V 1313 and then circle an approximate area for where Old Mr Murchison said the *Deeral* had gone down. He carefully measured the distances and found it still matched what they had previously calculated. He also thought hard about the pencil lines he had seen on the chart at Bosuns Bay and did some more speculating.

That night he had another horrible nightmare- diving again and swimming around a huge wreck full of moray eels and skeletons- and his air suddenly running out and no-one there to share with! Muriel should have been close but she was nowhere to be seen.

He woke up gasping for breath and sweating, then had trouble going back to sleep again.

The next morning it was their turn to be badgered by a newspaper man. Andrew and Carmen were only allowed to answer questions with their parents there and both, by silent agreement, kept their suspicious theories to themselves. Their father did most of the talking and merely said that it had always been a family mystery what had really happened to Herbert Collins.

The paper that morning had another article. This was obviously the result of the interviews with Old Mr Murchison. "I can't explain how the ship ended up where you say it is," he was quoted as saying. "I didn't actually see her sink. The waves were huge and it was dark and I was washed overboard and was lucky to grab a lifebuoy."

Carmen read this aloud to Andrew at the breakfast table. Her whole voice was doubting in tone. She read on: "Old Mr Murchison could offer no explanation to reports of the ship possibly being sunk by explosives. 'We had no explosives on board. I know nothing about that,' Mr Murchison said. Oh I don't believe that!" she snorted.

"How could we prove that?" Andrew asked.

"We could ask old Mr McGackey. He was a crewman on her," Carmen answered.

Andrew had forgotten about the arrangement to go and speak to him that afternoon and was pleased to learn that his father was going to join them. He was obviously intent on discovering the truth about his father's death.

School that day was ordinary. Andrew later only remembered two incidents. One was seeing Graham and Amanda being all lovey-dovey in class. The second was finding Willy Williams and his mate 'Stick' Morton sitting outside the Deputy Principal's office.

"What are you here for Willy? Are you in trouble?" he queried.

Willy nodded. "Yes, over a paper plane," he replied.

Stick chuckled. "It hit Miss Hackenmeyer," he interjected.

"Oh silly boy!" Andrew commented, shaking his head but grinning.

Willy couldn't help it. He grinned back. "Stick hit her with it in class," he replied.

Andrew looked at Stick and then back to Willy. "So if Stick threw it why are you here?" he asked.

"Because I made it," Willy answered. Then the memory of Stick's face as he saw the plane hit Miss Hackenmeyer came to him and he chortled. For the next few minutes he related the incident in the class room. The story cheered Andrew a bit and he went on with the errand he had been sent on.

After school Andrew made his way home with Carmen. Their father was waiting for them. "No afternoon tea," he commanded. "Get in the car. We will have afternoon tea when we get there."

They were driven over to Gran's. She joined them in the car and they continued on to the Retirement Home. Mr McGackey offered them tea and biscuits and then sat and listened to their story. As they spoke he kept nodding and his lips were pursed. At the end he said, "So that is a real mystery. Old Joshua comes back from the sea and tells everyone the ship sank in a storm way out on the Barrier Reef, and here she is scuttled in shallow water close inshore. Very fishy! Very fishy indeed!"

Andrew now asked, "Mr McGackey, are you positive that the *Deeral's* number as an army workboat was A. V. one three one three?"

Mr McGackey nodded vigorously. "Absolutely certain. As I said, us old sailors were real superstitious. To be on a ship with one thirteen was bad enough, but two!"

Carmen then asked, "Mr McGackey, would the *Deeral* have been carrying explosives?"

Mr McGackey nodded. "Of course she were. We were a salvage outfit. We always had some gelignite and detonators with us. Not a lot, but always some. You never know when you have to blast a bit of reef or rock like when you are trying to refloat a vessel what's aground. We even blew a bent rudder off a ship once."

"So you don't believe what Mr Murchison said to the newspaper today?" Carmen asked.

Mr McGackey gave a snort of disbelief and shook the newspaper which lay on the table beside him. "Joshua Murchison is a bloody liar! I always thought his story sounded a bit fishy. Never did like the man, nor trusted him either. There were a few times I thought he was pullin' the wool over Bert's eyes about a couple of business deals. But Bert were a good, trusting man, honest as the day is long, and he could see only good in other people."

Hearing that praise made Andrew glow deep inside and he could tell that it pleased his father and Carmen as well. He asked, "How could we check whether the wreck we found is actually the *Deeral,* to match up the maker's number and so on?"

Mr McGackey looked thoughtful for a minute, then said, "Well, she were registered here in Cairns. You could ask at the Harbour Board offices. Or you could try to contact the builders in Scotland- if they are still in business that is."

Both of those ideas were accepted as a plan. They agreed that the first step must be to prove that the AV1313 actually was the *Deeral.* "Otherwise we could be doing Old Mr Murchison a great injustice," he said.

Andrew's father said that he would get on to that the next day. They then thanked Mr McGackey, who said, "Anytime. Always nice to have a chat about the old days."

That made Andrew realize just how bored and lonely the old sailor probably was and it saddened him. It made him even more aware of the other old people in the home and he tried not to look at them, feeling both self-conscious and very aware of his youth and good health.

The family made their way home and Andrew settled to his homework. In particular he began a rewrite of his History assignment, to include a paragraph on the mystery of the *Deeral.* That evening he sat watching TV, all the while hoping Muriel would ring, but dreading what she might say if she did. She didn't, so he went to bed feeling depressed and irritated. The next chance of speaking to her would be at Navy Cadets on Friday night and he began to half-dread that.

'Oh, I hope I can make it up with her!' he thought unhappily, still trying to come up with a strategy to win back her affection.

There was no mention of the wreck or the mystery in the newspaper the next morning. That concerned Andrew but did not really surprise him. 'It is not important to other people,' he thought. But it was a sad comment. Carmen was both angry and vocal about it. "They should open an enquiry into it," she said at breakfast.

"An enquiry? What sort of enquiry?" her mother asked.

"A police investigation," Carmen answered.

"Oh fair go!" her father said. "There is no proof that would justify that."

"But Dad there is!" Carmen insisted.

"Maybe, but I can't see the authorities wasting time and money looking into something that might have happened half a century ago when there isn't any real evidence of wrong doing," her father replied.

Carmen almost scowled. "I call the wreck of a ship in the wrong place pretty firm evidence," she cried.

Her father shook his head. "Not till the wreck is definitely identified. Then we will need even more evidence."

Carmen pressed her lips firmly together, "Then we will just have to find some evidence," she said.

Her father nodded and wiped his lips with a serviette. "We will. Now eat your breakfast."

"Don't forget to go to the harbour people or whatever," Carmen added.

"Cairns Port Authority is the name now. No, don't worry. I won't," her father replied.

Andrew, who had been listening but not really wanting to get involved, lest he turn Muriel against him permanently, sadly took himself to his room to get ready for school. Thursday was a nothing much day. Other than noting Graham and Amanda arriving late at History it was a dull day. Nor did his father have any new information.

"I have applied for information," he explained. "If they can find it they will send it to us."

"What about the builders?" Carmen asked.

Their father shook his head. "According to my internet inquiries they went out of business years ago. I don't think we will get much that way."

So there was nothing to do but wait. In his room Andrew worked on his assignment and brooded. To his great relief he slept well that night without any nightmares. Friday dawned dry and clear and with Andrew suffering butterflies in the stomach from anxiety. Would Muriel be at Navy Cadets that evening? Would she speak to him? It was all very upsetting. On top of that it was the annual school Sports Day and Andrew was nominated for half a dozen events and wasn't really looking forward to them.

Despite that he tried his best, coming second in the 400 metres race, 5th in the 800 metres, and gaining points for his house in the discus, javelin and shot put. He did enjoy seeing all the girls in their short sports dresses. He also noted Graham, Amanda, Stephen and Rosemary wandering around as a group, obviously not participating. 'Graham must be winning with Amanda,' he decided, feeling a spurt of envy and then brooding over whether he ever had any chance of winning with Muriel.

Then it was Friday evening and time for cadets. By tea time Andrew was almost nauseous from anxiety. It took an effort to eat and he dressed with particular care, making sure his teeth were cleaned, washing his mouth with a gargle to remove any possible bad breath, and using deodorant.

All the way to Navy Cadets in his mother's car Andrew was tense. On arrival he anxiously scanned the yard and then inside. But there was no sign of Muriel. All the worry had been for nothing, to be replaced by another concern. 'I hope she isn't going to drop out of cadets just because of me,' he thought.

Sub Lt Sheldon was there. After the first parade Andrew took the opportunity to speak to him. "Sir, did you see the newspaper articles about the wreck?" he asked.

"Yes I did. I wish they hadn't been written. Do you know who the author was?" Sub Lt Sheldon asked.

"No sir. It wasn't anyone in my family. We were quite surprised and shocked," Andrew replied, nettled by the implication that he might have been responsible.

Sub Lt Sheldon nodded and looked thoughtful. "I think it was one of those English tourists. One of them was a journalist, but I haven't been able to check yet. But I wish he had waited to check a few facts before stirring things up like that."

"Yes sir. It has really upset Muriel and her family," Andrew agreed.

"Seaman Murchison? Yes, I noted she wasn't on parade. Do you know where she is?"

"No sir."

"I will phone her home to check," Sub Lt Sheldon said. "Now you had better get along to your lesson."

"Aye aye sir,' Andrew replied, saluting. He really wanted to stay and find out where Muriel was, but had no excuse to remain. So he about turned and marched away. Splicing was the lesson, something Andrew already knew how to do but was still required to demonstrate his skill at. After that there was a lesson on First Aid- serious bleeding, and then drill. Andrew settled back into the routine of the training and was able to relax somewhat. However worry about Muriel remained to niggle at him.

Jennifer was there but she did not know where Muriel was. "She has been away from school most of the week," she said.

Nor did Shona know. Andrew even asked Tina, noting a hurt look on her face as he did. That made him feel uncomfortable as he was dimly aware that Tina liked him. Carmen had no news either. "Pity," she said. "There are a few questions I would like to ask her, and I would like to talk to her grandad again."

"Not much chance of us being invited over there at the moment," Andrew replied bitterly. He also wanted to visit the house at Bosuns Bay. In particular he wanted to have another look at that chart. He did not trust his memory and had not been focused on the thing at the time, but now it was starting to loom larger in his thoughts all the time. 'It had a pencil line from out on the Great Barrier Reef in to Cape Upstart,' he remembered, 'and with some numbers written beside it. Were they the magnetic bearings to steer?' he wondered.

Carmen made a face and said, "Then we might just go uninvited."

"Muriel wouldn't like that," Andrew replied, aghast at the thought of offending her even more by such obvious prying.

"I think you've cashed your chips anyway," Carmen replied.

Andrew gave her a bleak look and nodded. His intellect told him that, but his heart still hoped. Carmen obviously saw how down he was because she patted his shoulder. "Never mind Little Brother, plenty more fish in the sea. Now, are you game to come with me?"

Chapter 22

Out!

For a few seconds Andrew felt alarm. How to say no without Carmen guessing his true motives? But then he remembered his own plan and shook his head. "Yes, but not this weekend," he said.

"Why not?"

"There are a few facts I want to check first, facts that might strengthen our case," Andrew replied. "I am doing a bit of research and don't have all the information. I am hoping to get it next week. For one thing we need to be sure that the *Deeral* really is the AV1313."

"Oh alright," Carmen conceded.

"Anyway, we are going to see Aunty Jean in Mossman this weekend," Andrew added.

So the weekend passed quietly. Andrew did all his chores and even some study for the exams that were coming up in the next few weeks. He also did quite a bit of sleeping, catching up after the exertions of the previous weekend. On Sunday the family drove north to Mossman. Travelling along the Cook Highway beside the sea gave Andrew some sharp memories of when Carmen had been kidnapped by the smugglers in April and he could see she was affected too.

On Sunday night he was both surprised and delighted when he got a phone call from Muriel. "Oh Andrew, I am so sorry I was mad at you," she said. "Sub Lt Sheldon explained that it was one of those English tourists who wrote those newspaper articles."

Hearing her got Andrew all confused. She sounded all bright and cheerful but he did wonder if it wasn't a little strained. "Thanks," he said. "Will you be at cadets next Friday night?"

"I should be," Muriel answered. "I just wasn't very well last Friday."

"It has been a long couple of weeks," Andrew agreed.

"Can we be friends again?" Muriel asked.

On hearing that Andrew's heart leapt with hope. "I'd like that," he replied. He then talked about cadets, before branching off onto gossip about school. Despite feeling elated he still felt a reserve that kept him from mentioning the wreck and he was careful to keep the conversation light and happy. 'No point in risking annoying her again,' he reasoned.

That night he was happy and slept very well.

Monday went by quickly. Andrew concentrated on studying for the coming exams. The only unusual thing was that neither Graham nor Amanda was at school. That afternoon he made some discreet enquiries in his research into the loss of the *Deeral*.

Next day at school Andrew was still in high spirits. These were dampened slightly when he noticed during Geography that Graham was there, but was sitting on his own and looking very gloomy. Amanda was also looking unhappy and was seated on the far side of the room from him. 'Uh oh!' Andrew thought. 'Something has happened.' But he did not think it was his business to ask what so he concentrated on his work.

His concern returned when he overheard Mr Conkey say, "Come on Graham, it isn't the end of the world. Get on with your work."

On hearing this Andrew glanced over his shoulder and was just in time to see a look of bleak misery cross Graham's face. 'Definitely something gone wrong,' he concluded. Further confirmation was added ten minutes later when he looked back and saw Graham looking towards Amanda with a wistful expression on his face. Then Graham glanced around and his eyes met Andrew's. He hastily looked away but Andrew was sure there was misery and even guilt in them. 'I hope he isn't going to have one of his fits of the dejections again,' he mused.

But at lunch time, when he meant to talk to Graham, Andrew found himself diverted by another incident involving Willy Williams. Willy was sitting under 'G' Block with two of his friends: Stick and Noddy, and was being teased by two Year 10 bullies: Scranton and Carstairs. The cause was a plastic model kit of an aeroplane which Willy was showing his friends.

Scranton snatched the lid of the box off Willy and looked at the picture of an aeroplane on the cover. "What's this Williams? Are you still a little kid who plays with toys?" he said sneeringly.

"Plays with himself more like!" Carstairs added, reaching out for the box. This was held by Noddy and was full of dozens of tiny plastic parts. "Give it to me shitface!" Carstairs snarled.

Scranton grabbed the box. Noddy tried to pull it away and said no, at which Carstairs hit at him with his other hand. Noddy ducked, but in the process the box was torn and tipped up. The tiny pieces cascaded onto the concrete.

By now Andrew had seen red. He hated bullies and found this pair more than normally objectionable. Without conscious thought he veered across and stopped beside Carstairs and Scranton. As Carstairs went to stamp on the pieces on the concrete Andrew blocked his leg. Carstairs look at him astonishment, then snarled, "What the buggery are you doing? Mind your own business."

"Leave them alone," Andrew replied evenly. By now his heart rate had shot up and he was scared, fully expecting to be bashed.

Both Scranton and Carstairs turned and adopted threatening gestures. By then Willy had stood up and raised his fists and both Noddy and Stick reluctantly stood as well. Carstairs snarled, "Bugger off Collins, before we rearrange your ugly face."

Andrew tensed, ready for a blow, but then almost laughed because he thought that Carstairs' tone indicated a degree of anxious bluster. He looked at Scranton and said, "Give Willy back his box."

"Get stuffed! Make me!" Scranton retorted.

Andrew placed his fists on his hips and faced Scranton, then said to Willy, "Willy, pick up the parts before they get stood on."

"You'll get stood on!" shouted Carstairs angrily. "Leave 'em where they are Williams, or else."

Another person came and stood beside Willy. It was Stephen. He took his glasses off and put them in his pocket, then stood blinking at Carstairs, plainly taking sides and ready to fight. That action really sent Stephen up in Andrew's estimation, although he still thought he was bad influence on Graham. Then another Year 8 arrived and joined Willy. Andrew did not know his name but knew he was in Willy's class, and he also had a plastic model aircraft kit under his arm.

There was a minute's tense stand-off, then Andrew said, "Give back the model kit Scranton."

Scranton glanced around and licked his lips nervously, then tossed the box at Noddy. "Here! Take yer stupid toy, little boy!" he cried. Then he quickly turned and walked away.

Seeing he was left alone Carstairs quickly retreated as well. "We'll get yez later," he threatened.

"I wouldn't advise it," Andrew replied. He then turned and told the others to pick up the plastic parts. While bending down to help he said, "What is it a model of Willy?"

Willy showed him a picture of a World War 2 British aircraft. "A Beaufighter," he answered.

"Have you got many plastic models?" Andrew asked.

"Yeah, about a dozen," Willy replied. Then he gestured towards the last boy to arrive. "John here has got hundreds. They are great!"

"I think that is all," Andrew said, his eyes scanning the concrete for any more tiny parts. "Are many broken?" he asked, studying the pieces piled in the box.

Noddy shifted a few with his fingers, then shook his head. "Don't think so. Most are still attached to the spruing."

"You shouldn't bring models to school," Andrew commented.

John (John Ruddock Andrew now remembered) said, "That's what I told them. Stick had one broken last week."

"I like them," Stick defended.

Willy nodded. "I didn't mean to. It was in my bag from yesterday," he explained. Then he looked at Andrew and Stephen and said, "Thanks."

Andrew went on his way but by then he had forgotten about Graham and did not remember till later that afternoon. Once at home study and chores then took up Andrew's attention. He then walked the dog, had tea and washed up, then watched TV. All evening he kept hoping that Muriel would phone but she did not. Still hoping and planning he took himself to bed to daydream and fantasize. Unfortunately the fantasies were clouded by a growing sense of anxiety about how he and Muriel might relate on Friday night.

During school on Thursday Andrew was concerned to note that Graham looked desperately unhappy. 'He looks really sick and miserable,' he thought. That made him look around to check where Amanda was sitting. There was no sign of her and that bothered him. 'I wonder if that is a coincidence?' he pondered.

This time Andrew's concern motivated him to act. When he saw Graham moping along at morning break he joined him. "G'day Graham. You OK mate?" he asked.

"Yeah, why?" Graham mumbled back.

"You look a bit down, that's all," Andrew replied. He did not want to pry and was feeling quite uncomfortable by this.

"I'm alright," Graham replied without looking up. The pair walked in silence for a few minutes, Andrew feeling even more uncomfortable. To escape he pointed to where a group of Year 8s led by Willy were running in circles pretending to have 'dogfights' with model fighter planes.

Andrew gestured towards them. "Silly little buggers. I told them the other day they will get into trouble bringing model planes to school," he said. When Graham just grunted and did not respond Andrew became irritated and gave up. He peeled off and went over to talk to Willy. This meant admiring half a dozen plastic kit aeroplanes. All were 1:72 scale and most were very well put together and painted. "These are really good!" he said, studying Willy's model Spitfire. And he was sincere. They were good.

Andrew studied a German Me 109 held by Noddy then asked, "Do you make ones that fly?"

Willy shook his head. "Not yet, but we are working on that."

By the time Andrew had looked at all the model planes he saw that Stephen had joined Graham and that the two were talking. With that he shrugged and went off to the library. Study and schoolwork took his focus away from Graham and his problems for the remainder of the day. At home that afternoon he had afternoon tea and then settled to reading the 'set' novel for English. In the evening he sat studying or watching TV, all the while hoping that Muriel would phone. She didn't and he was left feeling flat but relieved.

On Friday at school Andrew was again made anxious about Graham but this time he tried to find out what had happened. While placing his books in his school bag after class he noticed three of the girls glancing at Graham and whispering. They were obviously discussing him. One was Gwen Copeland, who was in most of Andrew's classes. Andrew liked her and had a healthy respect for her intellect and her personality. So, when Gwen detached herself from the others and came walking towards Andrew, he took the opportunity and held up his hand to stop her.

"Excuse me Gwen. It's none of my business really, but I'm worried about Graham. Do you know what has happened?"

Gwen glanced back at Graham and then shook her head while tut-tutting. "I don't know any details," she said. "Rosemary and Louise both say that he and Amanda Howley were being very... er.. very naughty on Saturday night at the movies and again at the swimming pool on Sunday. Apparently they both went off together and the girls were sure they were going to try to.. to ..er... to have a ..a.. you know!"

Andrew did and he blushed bright red. "So what happened? Obviously something has gone wrong."

"We don't know. But Amanda hasn't been at school for four days and the word is she has gone to another school. Louise heard she'd been sent to a convent."

Andrew was astonished and could only speculate. "If that has happened then her parents must know about it. Were they caught in the act?" he suggested.

"Probably," Gwen agreed. "Well, serve her right, if she is going to behave like that."

That opinion made Andrew feel uncomfortable but he nodded. "Thanks," he said, and walked on, deep in thought. 'If Graham has done something he shouldn't have to Amanda and her parents know about it, then he could be in deep trouble,' he mused. Concepts like police, court and jail all flitted across his mind although he was quite unsure what really might occur. 'No wonder he looks unhappy!' he thought. That got him wondering if there was any way he could help Graham, and even if he should.

At home that afternoon after school Andrew tried to study but was unable to settle to his homework and could only sit and brood, trying to work out what to do about the wreck and how to win back Muriel's affection. He became more and more anxious as the time for cadets drew closer. The situation was made much worse when his father came home from work. He called both him and Carmen in and said,

"I've checked with the Port Authority. The *Deeral* was the A. V. one three one three. They even gave me the manufacturer's number of her diesel engine."

Andrew felt a spurt of satisfaction, rapidly succeeded by one of anxiety as it could mean trouble with Muriel. At his father's request he went and found his notes and they compared the engine number he had written down while diving on the wreck. The numbers were identical. Seeing them line up like that caused Andrew a chill of dread. 'It means something really odd has happened,' he thought.

But what to do about it? He put this to them and Carmen said, "Nothing yet. Wait till I have finished some research Mum and I are doing tomorrow." She would not explain what this was saying that, if it turned out to be wrong, then speculating about it beforehand could prejudice people.

That was very unsatisfactory but Andrew had to leave it like that. He went to have his shower and to get ready for cadets. Once again he took particular care with his personal hygiene and appearance, hoping that Muriel would be there.

She was, and she smiled, but the smile did not seem to reach her eyes. It was immediately apparent to Andrew that something fundamental had gone out of their friendship. There was a wary barrier of reserve, and not all on her side either. All he could do was act light-hearted and to chat about anything but the wreck. But avoiding the topic seemed to make it loom even larger in his mind and, he suspected, in hers. It was a relief to be separated during the lessons and drill.

During the dismissal parade Lt Cdr Hazard again reminded them about the courses camp in Mackay, and about having their Permission Forms and

Next-of-Kin Forms returned beforehand. He added that, as far as he knew, the plan for them to travel on the HMAS *Tobruk* was still going ahead. That was really good news to Andrew and he hoped that nothing would come up to cancel it. Travelling on a ship had infinitely more appeal than going by coach.

After being dismissed Andrew plucked up the courage to go and speak to Muriel. "Can I see you this weekend?" he asked, fearful of being told no.

Muriel looked unhappy and that worried Andrew even more. 'She is trying to find a way to say no without lying,' he thought. She then shrugged and said, "We are going over to Grandma's for the weekend."

"Could I visit you there?" he asked.

She looked even more doubtful and then, after biting her lip, said, "You couldn't stay, not a sleepover."

"No. Just a short visit," Andrew replied. "We could sail over and just meet for a little while." He wanted to say an hour or so and suggest they might go for a walk together but could not find the courage to say it.

Muriel nodded, but then looked him hard in the eyes. "Only if you promise not to ask my Grandad any questions about.. .about what happened."

That was an awkward one. Andrew realized that that was one of his main motives for wanting to go to Bosuns Bay. Reluctantly he nodded and said, "No. I won't." 'If that is the price of her friendship, I will pay it,' he decided. But having decided he knew he did not feel good about it. Somehow it seemed both a lie and a betrayal.

They said goodbye and Andrew went to join Carmen. Their mother picked them up and drove them home. On the way Andrew put to Carmen the idea of sailing to Bosuns Bay. Carmen nodded but said, "Have to be Sunday. Mum and I are going to the university tomorrow afternoon and we have chores tomorrow morning."

"And you have study for your exams," their mother added.

Later, when they were out of hearing of their parents, Andrew turned to Carmen and said, "Are you going to come in to the house when we visit Bosuns Bay?"

"Yes, why not?" Carmen replied. "I don't feel like twiddling my thumbs on the beach for a couple of hours while you pursue a lost cause."

That comment hurt but Andrew ignored it. He said, "Because Muriel asked me to promise that if I visited I wouldn't upset her grandfather by talking about what happened to the *Deeral*."

Carmen shook her head and curled her lip. "Boy! Has she got you twisted around her little finger! I would have thought your own family was more important."

"If that is how you feel then I will go on my own," Andrew replied angrily.

"OK, keep your shirt on!" Carmen answered.

"If you come I want you to agree not to raise the subject," Andrew said firmly.

"Yes, alright."

It was an anxious boy who took himself to bed an hour later. He knew he should be happy but inside he felt a sense of gloom and a nagging feeling of things not being right. This stayed with him all of the next day. There was also a feeling of mild envy, knowing that the army cadets were taking part in a weekend 'bivouac'. 'I wish the Navy Cadets did more weekend camps,' he thought. He tried to study for his exams but found it hard to concentrate.

There was also curiosity over what Carmen was researching at the university. Their mother was doing a part-time course in Business Studies so they had access to the library but Carmen had made no explanation. When she arrived home Andrew asked if she had found what she wanted.

Carmen nodded and said, "I think so."

"What was it?" Andrew asked.

"Tell you when I have all the facts," Carmen answered. "If I tell you now it might make you angry."

That didn't help. It just made Andrew more anxious and curious but Carmen would not relent. He went to bed feeling mildly unhappy. His main worry was over how the social meeting with Muriel and her family might go.

The anxiety was even more pronounced when he and Carmen set sail from the Yacht Club on Sunday morning. The closer they got to Bosuns Bay the more Andrew wished he hadn't suggested the meeting, or at least not at her grandparent's house. What made it worse was that it was a beautiful day, the sort the tourists flocked to North Queensland to enjoy: clear blue skies, sunny but not too hot; a gentle, cool breeze.

It took them over an hour to sail the six kilometres. That made it worse as Andrew's emotions were heightened by the tension. By the time the catamaran slipped around the rocky headland into the small bay he was deeply regretting the decision to visit but still clinging to faint hope that somehow Muriel and he might repair their friendship.

Carmen steered the catamaran through the outlying rocks and then tacked her up the length of the short bay to the beach. While they did this Andrew scanned the house but saw no sign of anyone. He had half expected to find them on the back patio, or in the garden. 'I hope they are home and we haven't come all this way for nothing,' he thought. A check of his watch told him it was just after 2pm. He was also worried about Carmen. She seemed to be in a funny mood and he did not want her asking questions and upsetting Muriel or her family. However he knew she would resent any reminder. To her a promise, once given, stood for ever.

The catamaran was beached and the sails lowered and roughly furled. Andrew placed the anchor among the exposed roots of one of the big trees. Then he turned and looked up the driveway, his heart beating with what he recognized as fear. But there was no backing out so he set off up the driveway, Carmen following along behind.

As he passed the closed side door to the boathouse Andrew wondered if the old lifebuoy was still there. So strong was his curiosity that he stopped, tempted to risk a peek. However all of his upbringing had made him shy of making free with other people's possessions or homes. With an effort of willpower he resisted the temptation. Shaking his head he started walking again, Carmen now beside him.

When he reached the steps leading up to the back terraced garden he turned to go up them, then stopped, his left foot on the bottom step. Carmen pointed up the driveway. "Better go to the front of the house. Visitors don't usually come in the back way," she said.

The thought of having almost committed such a beach of manners caused Andrew to blush. He even felt guilty walking up the driveway beside the house. They passed the open doors to the garage and looking inside cheered him up. There were no people visible but there were two cars parked there: His and Hers; and Muriel's family car was parked off the side of the driveway under a tree up near the front of the house. 'There must be people home,' he thought.

There were. In the front garden were four people: Muriel, Old Mr Murchison, Grandma Murchison and Muriel's mother. They were busy pruning rose bushes. Old Mr Murchison was peering among the foliage of a rosebush, a spray in his hand. There was a side gate and Andrew stopped outside it and waited till Muriel's mother saw them.

"Oh hello. What do you want?" she asked, her voice far from friendly.

To Andrew's relief Muriel looked around and then said, "It's alright Mum. I invited them." She gave a smile and said, "Come in. How was the trip over?"

"Good," Andrew answered, opening the gate and going in to the front garden. "Bit slow. There wasn't much wind. Hello. Hello." These last to Old Mr Murchison, who had straightened up and was peering at them through his glasses and to Grandma Murchison. So emotionally sensitive was

Andrew that he fancied the old man was glaring at him. Certainly Grandma Murchison was only being polite, not warmly welcoming.

There were a few moments of embarrassed silence, then Muriel said, "Would you like a drink?"

They never got a chance to answer. Through the front door of the house came Muriel's father. He stopped and looked at them in surprise. "What are you two doing here?" he demanded.

Andrew went hot with embarrassment. Carmen gestured to Muriel, who said, "I invited them Daddy. They are my friends."

"Funny sort of friends," Muriel's father replied, compressing his lips into a thin line. "You should have had more sense than to invite them here."

At that Carmen bristled. "Excuse me! What have we done wrong?" she demanded to know.

"What!" exploded Muriel's father, his face mottling red. "What? You stir up all these lies and accusations and go around making up wild tales that hurt my father and you have the hide to ask what you have done!" he shouted.

"We haven't made up any wild tales," Carmen cried angrily. "All we have said is what we have seen."

"What about those insinuations in that newspaper article?" Muriel's father snapped.

"We didn't write them!" Carmen cried. She looked to Muriel who nodded but also looked upset and angry.

"So who did then?"

"Sub Lt Sheldon said it was one of the English tourists on the diveboat," Carmen answered.

"So you say! I don't think I believe you!" Muriel's father cried.

"Are you calling me a liar?" cried a very angry Carmen.

"Yes I am," Muriel's father snapped back.

Carmen gasped and sucked in her breath. "Well! I know one thing for sure, that someone has been telling lies." At that she looked directly at Old Mr Murchison. Andrew saw the old man blanch and then his face mottle with emotion. He shook his head and muttered, "Go away please."

To Andrew's growing dismay Carmen stood her ground. She faced the old man squarely and said, "I would like to know what happened to my grandfather."

Old Mr Murchison seemed to shrivel and wilt. Again he shook his head. Andrew saw his hands shaking. Old Mr Murchison trembled and said, "I don't want to talk about it. I can't help you. Go away."

"Can't? Or won't?" Carmen snapped

Muriel's father took a step forward. "How dare you make accusations like that! Get out!"

"Accusations!" Carmen shouted. "Facts I would call them." She turned back to face Old Mr Murchison and went on, "According to you the *Deeral* encountered bad weather on the twelfth of February, Nineteen fifty eight, at which time she was approximately a hundred nautical miles east of Bowen. And you said she sank in a storm during the night of February the fourteenth, two days later. And you claim that after she sank you drifted in the sea in a lifebuoy for the next three or four days. So how come the wreck of the *Deeral* is at Cape Upstart?"

"That is not certain," Muriel's father yelled, "Now get out of here!"

By now Andrew was both distressed at the turn of events, and afraid. He backed through the gate. Carmen however stood her ground, glaring at Old Mr Murchison. "Well Mr Murchison, how do you explain that?"

Old Mr Murchison shook his head and appeared to Andrew to shake with emotion. "I can't," he croaked.

Carmen then pointed at the old man and said coldly, "I think you are liar Mr Murchison. You said there were storms for four or five days, but I have checked the weather reports for Bowen and the Whitsundays during the period from February the tenth to February twentieth that year and there wasn't a single day when the wind got above fifteen knots, and no storms at all, just a bit of rain."

At that Old Mr Murchison seemed to choke up. He gobbled and then clutched at his chest. Andrew feared that he was going to have a heart attack. So, obviously, did others as Grandma Murchison and Muriel's mother both hurried to him. "Inside!" Muriel's mother said. The two women helped the trembling old man through the door.

By then Muriel's father was almost beside himself with rage. "Get out of here!" he shouted, stepping forward.

Chapter 23

Plans

This time Carmen did retreat. She stepped back through the gate and swung it shut but remained defiantly angry. To Andrew's added distress Muriel now waded into the argument. "You horrible person!" she screamed at Carmen. "How could you hurt my grandfather like that!"

"Because I don't have a grandfather," Carmen retorted, "Something happened to him and I'd like to know what. And your grandfather knows the truth and won't tell." Then she turned on her heel and said, "Come on Andrew."

Andrew met Muriel's eyes, his emotions all in a jumble. Muriel glared at him. "You promised Andrew!" she shouted. "Now get! I hate you! And I never want to see you again!"

Muriel's father advanced to the gate and shouted at them, "Get out of here, and don't ever come back! And stop spreading malicious lies or I will get my lawyers to sue you for slander."

At that moment Muriel's mother came to the front door and called to Muriel's father. "Basil, you had better come quickly. Your mother has fainted."

Hearing that made Andrew swallow with anxiety. His stomach had already turned over from fear caused by the mention of legal things. Now his stomach heaved again. The thought that the argument might have harmed the two old people made him feel sick. On top of that he was feeling stunned and hurt by Muriel's rejection. He saw both Muriel and her father hurry to the front door and inside as he hurried down the driveway behind Carmen. But he was also feeling angry as well. What Carmen had said about the weather had shocked him but had caused his suspicions to gel.

Being abused and called a liar also stung. Andrew felt broken hearted over the loss of his love but he was also upset at her being unfair to him. 'I didn't raise the subject, and nor did Carmen,' he thought, the injustice burning.

Brother and sister hurried down past the garage and terrace to the beach. As they did Andrew kept glancing back, half hopefully, half fearfully. However they reached the beach without seeing anyone back at the house. In silence they unhooked the catamaran and slid it down into the water. Within a minute they were afloat and busy raising and trimming sails.

Only when they were under way did Carmen speak. "Well, that put the cat among the pigeons! Sorry Andrew, but I wasn't going to take that sort of abuse and false accusations lying down."

Andrew shrugged and looked back at the house. As he did his mind seemed to clear. "You were in the right," he said. "I agree with you. They had no reason to be nasty like that."

"Some guilty consciences back there I reckon," Carmen observed. "Old man Murchison knows what happened to Grandad alright. Did you see the way he went pale and started to shake? That is a guilty conscience if ever I saw one."

"I was worried he might be going to have a heart attack," Andrew replied.

"Good!" Carmen snapped. "Be only justice. I think your theory about the gold is the right one; and I suspect that Old Mr Murchison murdered Grandad and the others."

Despite his distress over Muriel Andrew thought so to. He said, "We would have a hard time proving it."

"Oh, I don't know. We are doing a pretty good job so far," Carmen replied.

At that moment Andrew knew that he just had to find out. 'If I don't it will eat at me from inside for the rest of my life,' he thought. "I am going to try to find out," he said.

"Good! We both will," Carmen answered. "And I know Dad really wants to know too."

But how? Discussing that kept them going all the way back to Cairns. They reached the Yacht Club without any clear plan at all. To Andrew it was intensely frustrating. They had a certain amount of proof, but none of it was conclusive. When they discussed this with their parents and he suggested asking the police to investigate, his father again shook his head and said no. Nor did his father think that the civil maritime authorities would be interested in opening an enquiry into what happened. All the family could agree on was to go quietly and secretly, to pretend that they had lost interest.

That night in his bed Andrew cried himself to sleep. He mourned his broken friendship with Muriel, but he was also hurt by the injustice of her accusations and wondered if he had known her well enough. 'I think I was blinded by her good looks,' he decided. But that didn't help much. He still felt hurt and rejected.

Next morning as he sat down breakfast his dismal thoughts were interrupted by his father holding up the newspaper for him to look at. "Isn't this one of your friends from school?" he asked.

Andrew's eyes noted the coloured pictures of a large, burnt-out vehicle and of people in army uniforms sitting beside a road being tended by ambulance personnel.

HEROIC RESCUES read the bold headline. Underneath it said, 'Army Cadets rescue people from blazing fuel tanker on Kuranda Range.'

On reading that Andrew leant closer and read the caption to the second photo. 'Paramedics provide treatment for minor burns to cadet heroes Graham Kirk and Stephen Bell'. "That's Graham alright," he commented. His own unhappiness forgotten he sat and read the article. As he did Carmen joined them and he showed it to her. He then read with interest how the previous afternoon a van with five people in it had tried to overtake a fuel tanker coming down the range road. The van had collided with a sports car coming up the mountain. The driver of the sports car had been killed in the crash and his car had erupted in flames. This had set fire to the petrol tanker. Warrant Officer Howley, who was the driver of an army Land Rover which had been following the van down the mountain, had dragged four people from the van, which had crashed on its side amid streams of burning fuel. Warrant Officer Howley had become trapped but Graham, who had been helping the people to safety, broke the windscreen and dragged both the driver of the van and Warrant Officer Howley to safety. They had managed to get clear just before the petrol tanker exploded.

"Graham really was a hero," Carmen commented.

"Yes," Andrew agreed. 'But it won't make him any friends. People will be jealous,' he thought. Curious to know more he hurried to school, almost forgetting his own troubles.

The first person he met there was Peter. Peter was not able to tell him any more than he had read in the paper. "I didn't see any of it," he explained. "I was in a coach with the main body of cadets and we were stuck in traffic way back up the road. We had to come home via Mareeba and the Rex Highway, then along the coast."

"It said Graham and Stephen both helped that army warrant officer," Andrew said.

Peter frowned. "Yeah, I read that, but I don't understand it. Neither Graham nor Stephen was at the bivouac and I didn't see them in the Land Rover before we left."

"Maybe they were picked up later," Andrew suggested.

"Hmm," said Peter. "Maybe, but it sounds funny to me."

That got Andrew worried. "Are they in trouble for something?"

"Don't know, but here comes Graham now. Let's ask him," Peter replied.

As Graham arrived Peter stood up and shook his hand. "Bloody well done mate! You and Stephen both. Really well done," he said.

Graham blushed and said 'Thanks,' then managed a weak grin as Roger stood up and congratulated him. Andrew joined in, being careful not to touch the bandaged forearm. Peter then asked, "Where were you blokes on the weekend? I didn't see you at the bivouac, yet you were with Warrant Officer Howley at the crash?"

For a few moments Graham looked quite sick. Then he shook his head and replied, "Sorry. We've been ordered not to say."

To Andrew's mystification Peter nodded and said, "Like that other weekend when you went off with the officers eh? They must be planning another one of those really good week long exercises. I hope so."

Graham nodded but did not answer. Andrew felt a genuine surge of jealousy. "I wish we could come on them. I've heard they are great," he commented.

That got them talking cadet exercises and army versus navy rivalry became a major part of the conversation. Andrew didn't resent it from people like Peter but he was still envious. There was no more discussion of the weekend accident when Graham indicated he didn't want to talk about it. "I saw that guy in the sports car get killed and then incinerated. It was horrible," he explained.

The thought of being burned to death made Andrew squirm with revulsion and he was happy to drop the topic. Blake and Simmo next appeared and he went off with them. For the next ten minutes, until the bell went, they discussed the tanker crash and also the upcoming camp.

During Geography in Period 1 Andrew noted that Graham was again sitting next to Angus, and that there was no sign of Amanda. Out of curiosity he asked Louise, who was sitting across the aisle at the next desk, "Where is Amanda?"

Louise shrugged and said, "Don't know. I heard she has been sent to another school."

"She is the daughter of that army warrant officer who is in the paper this morning isn't she?" he asked.

"Yes she is," Louise agreed.

"Weren't she and Graham going together?" he asked.

"Sort of," Louise replied, sounding very off-hand.

Her apparent indifference piqued Andrew's curiosity. "Did something happen?" he probed.

Again Louise shrugged. "Don't know," she said. She turned back to her work, indicating that the conversation was over.

'Hmm!' Andrew thought. 'She knows something but isn't going to say. There is a story here!' (And there is but you will have to read 'Fourteen' by C. R. Cummings to find out what it is!)

At the conclusion of the lesson Capt Conkey reminded them all that exams were coming up the following week, and that their assignment was due the next Monday. That was mildly worrying to Andrew as he had not really started the Geography assignment. There was another reminder during History and that did get Andrew thinking. What was worrying him about that assignment was how much to include about the *Deeral* and how much about the *Merinda.*

'I don't have very much on the *Merinda,*' he mused. He knew he could not include any of his suspicions about what became of the *Deeral,* other than to hint that where she was found was unexplained and peculiar. That got him mulling over his suspicious theories again and from that he fell to lamenting his broken relationship with Muriel. Again he wondered if there was any hope of repairing it.

That afternoon when he got home he found a large package waiting for him. It had come in the post and when opened revealed a dozen A4 pages of photocopied ship plans and specifications.

"It is the plans of the *Merinda!*" he muttered. He spread the pages out on the table and sorted them, then fell to avidly studying them. Once again all his horrible suspicions and theories swirled in his head. What he was particularly interested in was where a shipment of gold bullion might have been secured in the ship for safe transport. He saw that she was a steel vessel of 550 tons gross, and 275 tons deadweight. For a while he puzzled over the difference and had to look it up in a reference book.

'Ah! Gross is enclosed cargo space, measured by volume, not weight, and deadweight is the actual weight of water the ship displaces,' he read. He noted that there were several types of deadweight such as normal and full load and so on. Having satisfied himself he understood he went back to the plans. The *Merinda* was 195 feet long with a beam of 40 feet and a draught of 16 feet. These dimensions he had to convert to metres to better imagine them (60m X 12m X 4.9m). He saw that she had a raised focsle with three decks below it, a main deck which was open for a cargo hatch aft of the focsle. The superstructure took up about half of the main deck, extending almost right to the stern. The superstructure was only one deck high with a small wheelhouse on it, a single funnel and two lifeboats. Under the superstructure was the engine room and coal bunkers and water storage. This took up about half the space. Aft of that were two lower decks. The lowest one was fuel storage and the shaft tunnel. Above that was the tiller flat, steering engines and three cabins.

Andrew's attention then focused on the writing. It was all in old fashioned running writing and he had trouble deciphering it but at last made out the names of the various compartments: captain's cabin, saloon and so on. Then his eye lighted on the words 'strong room'. It was on the lower deck aft below the saloon and was next to the purser's cabin. 'There!' he thought. He knew that the purser was responsible for stores and finance. Seeing that word fired him with a sharp wish to actually find the wreck, to check if the gold was still there or not.

Carmen, when she came home, joined him and he put this notion to her. "It's a good idea," she agreed. "But first we have to locate the wreck. Then we can dive on it."

Only when Carmen mentioned diving did Andrew realize what he might be letting himself in for. Intense feelings of anxiety coursed through him as the memories of diving came back to him. Having told himself he would never dive again he now found himself torn. 'Maybe I might have to,' he conceded, but it was an ordeal he wasn't looking forward to. 'Anyway, the chances of us finding the wreck are so small it is not worth worrying about,' he told himself, even though one of his theories was even then niggling at the back of his mind.

That night he settled to redrafting his assignment on the *Merinda*. He also began work on the Geography assignment. While he worked he was gnawed at by a hope that Muriel might phone. He even considered phoning her but vivid memories of her angry father and his legal threats soon killed that idea. He went to bed both depressed yet somehow hopeful.

Tuesday presented no solution to the problem of ever finding the *Merinda*. Even just thinking about the practical difficulties soon depressed him. 'We would need a good seagoing boat and I have spent nearly all my money doing the diving courses,' he mused. He could not imagine his parents providing the large sums of money he was sure it would cost to hire a big launch, possibly for days. Having thought that out Andrew reluctantly pushed his hopes to the back of his mind.

At school the only event of note was a discussion between the army cadets and navy cadets about their upcoming camps. "Only eleven days to annual camp," Peter commented.

"Ten for us," Andrew answered. "When do you go?"

"On the first Saturday of the holidays," Peter replied.

"We go on the Friday night," Andrew answered. "By ship."

"Ship?" Stephen asked. "What ship?"

"HMAS *Tobruk*, a Landing Ship Heavy," Andrew answered. As he said this he saw Graham lift is head and look at him for the first time. A look of bitter regret (or was it envy?) crossed his face, making Andrew feel sorry for him. 'Poor old Graham, he is wishing he had stayed in the Navy Cadets,' he thought. It made him feel a bit guilty while he described the *Tobruk* and what he expected to happen.

Blake added to this and said, "I'm really looking forward to camp. I'm going to train as a quartermaster gunner."

"Gunna train as a quarter of what?" Stephen teased.

"Phffft!" retorted Blake. "You are just jealous. We will get to fire rifles at the range."

Stephen sniffed and said, "So will we!"

"Where are you going for your camp?" Andrew asked.

"Some place in the bush west of Townsville," Stephen replied.

Peter supplemented this by saying, "Speed Creek it is called." Then he turned to Andrew. "Where is your camp?"

"Mackay," Andrew answered.

"How long for?"

"Nine days, including the travel to and from," Andrew replied. "How long is yours?"

"Eight days I think," Peter answered.

"More than that for me," Stephen Bell answered morosely.

Andrew asked, "Why is that?"

"Graham and I have to go on the Thursday as part of the advance party," Stephen replied.

"Advance party? What do they do?" Blake asked.

"Load trucks with stores and put up tents and things," Stephen answered. "I'm not looking forward to it."

"Why not? You are getting two days off school," Andrew replied. He was intrigued by the mention of Graham going as well and glanced at him. Graham just nodded and looked unhappy. To satisfy his curiosity Andrew asked, "How come you and Steve are going in the advance party Graham?"

Graham made an attempt to smile and replied, "Ordered to."

When he did not amplify it there was an embarrassing silence. This made Andrew suspect that there was in fact some other reason but he could not think of a tactful way to divert the conversation.

To his relief Peter changed the topic by asking him, "Are we going to have any sailing races these holidays?"

During the previous school holidays in June they had raced almost every day during the second week while competing for the 'Mudskipper Cup'. Andrew smiled at the memory but shook his head. "Sorry. Don't think so." He did not explain but he still had secret hopes that somehow he could spend that week looking for the wreck of the *Merinda*.

That night he finished his History assignment. To add to it he scanned in the ship plans and also several photos, including the last one of the *Deeral*. Next day during History he handed it in. By then the pressure of impending exams had most of the students in its grip. Andrew isolated himself during the breaks so that he could study without interruption. The only gossip of interest he picked up was more intriguing news about Graham. Apparently the night before he had travelled to the local Army depot, Porton Barracks, with Warrant Officer Howley and had attended the Army Reserve weekly training parade, training with the soldiers.

'So how come this Warrant Officer Howley is treating him like this? Is it punishment of some sort?' Andrew wondered. It certainly puzzled him. Then another thought came to shock him. 'Maybe Graham has made Amanda pregnant and he is going to be forced to marry her?'

There was no easy answer, short of asking Graham directly, and as it was really none of his business Andrew did not. Instead he kept on studying and puzzling how to solve his own problems. To dull the ache of his broken heart Andrew threw himself into study and assignment writing- Geography this time.

Exams began on Thursday. History was first and Capt Conkey supervised, again reminding those who had not yet handed in their assignments to make sure they did on Monday. That night Andrew finished his Geography assignment. To add to his mix of emotions both he and Carmen made sure that their mother had filled in the permission forms and medical forms for the cadet camp. That got Andrew all keen in anticipation but then he found he was having trouble sleeping and when he did drop off to sleep he had bad dreams. These were all similar to the ones he had been having recently- sailing on a boat which unaccountably shrank in size until he was swimming in the sea- deep sea with a strong current and large waves- and in which lurked shapeless monsters.

The Geography exam was first up on Friday. Andrew handed in his assignment and was pleased to note that Graham also handed his in and looked a lot happier. That made him feel a bit better. 'If he is getting his schoolwork done then things can't be that bad,' he reasoned. During the day he became more and more anxious, wondering how Muriel might treat him at cadets that evening.

She wasn't there, which was both a relief and source of sadness. 'I hope she isn't going to drop out of cadets just because off me,' he thought. There was a lot of regret and mulling over the might-have-beens and wondering if he had done things differently whether they might not still be friends. It was very depressing and he slept badly, again suffering several nightmares.

The weekend was a real drag. Andrew did not go anywhere. Instead he stayed home and did chores around the house and studied. He finished an English essay and worked his way through his mathematics text book. Thinking about Muriel got him all dejected but he forced himself to do things, so as not to think about her.

The following week followed a similar pattern. Exam followed exam. Nights were spent studying and having bad dreams and bouts of bitter regret. On the positive side Andrew noted that Graham seemed to be a lot happier, and that he was obviously in good health and looking forward to his army cadet camp.

Wednesday came and with it the last exams. By then Andrew was becoming excited at the prospect of going to cadet camp. A general sense of excitement gripped the groups of friends. There was also the relief that the exams were over and that holidays were upon them. This was marred by the fact that Andrew had not managed to me up with any sort of plan to try to find the wreck of the *Merinda* and he was sadly resigning himself to the probability that he would never manage to do so. 'Nor win back Muriel either!'

Then, during History on Thursday, Capt Conkey said something that opened up a glimmer of hope.

Chapter 24

Coincidence

History was first period after lunch. Andrew had already confirmed that Graham and Stephen had gone early that morning with the army cadet advance party so was not surprised to note that their seats were empty. When Capt Conkey came in he first handed back the exam papers. To Andrew's relief he had scored very well- 92%. That cheered him up as he knew he needed to aim at consistently high scores in all subjects to hope to be selected at the end of Year 12 for entry to the Australian Defence Force Academy. Despite the recent failures in his personal life his ambition to become an officer in the navy was still burning strongly.

Capt Conkey then sat and thumbed through a bundle of assignments. Having extracted two and placed them side by side he looked up. "Andrew, Luke, would you two come out here please?" he asked.

Mystified Andrew walked to the front of the room. Luke joined him, the two friends standing side by side next to the teacher's desk. Capt Conkey looked at them with a quizzical expression. He then said, "Now, I know you two are friends, but I have to ask if you have been in collusion over your assignments."

A cold liquid seemed to seep into Andrew's lower stomach. 'Mr Conkey thinks we have been cheating!' he thought in dismay. He knew that plagiarism and the copying of other people's work were dishonest and that Capt Conkey held very strong views on the subject. Equally, he himself was firm about it. A feeling of guilty shame started to engulf him even though he was mystified.

He shook his head. "Sorry sir. I don't understand. We haven't discussed our assignments at all," he said.

"Nor me," Luke added, also looking worried.

"I believe you but I will show you why I asked," Capt Conkey said. He opened Andrew's assignment to a page of photos. Then he opened Luke's. "Three photos the same," Capt Conkey said. "And no reference to their sources. I think that is a real coincidence."

Andrew stared at the photos in Luke's assignment on Pearl Diving. There was the photo of the *Pearl Reef* at the Cairns wharf. Next was a photo of a helmet diver standing on the deck of a lugger in his diving suit and holding his helmet and assisted by several Torres Strait Islanders. The third was the last photo of the *Deeral,* the one that showed his grandfather, Old Mr Murchison and the two 'T.Is'. Amazement replaced apprehension.

"These are from my family album," Andrew exclaimed.

Capt Conkey looked at a surprised Luke. "Where did you get yours Luke?"

"From my family's photo album," Luke answered. He pointed to the photo of the *Pearl Reef* in Cairns. "My grandad and my great uncle, they both sailed in this lugger for a coupl'a years. And this one," He pointed to the lugger with the diver standing on deck. "That my grandfather Solomon, and that other fella there, the one holdin' the air hose, he a man named Francis Sailboat."

Andrew stared at Luke and then pointed to the diver in the photo. "We have this photo in our album and the writing on the back says that the diver was my grandfather, Herbert Collins in nineteen fifty six."

Luke went wide eyed. "No kidding man! These fellas here (He pointed to the two Torres Strait Islanders on the *Deeral*), they my grandad and Francis Sailboat."

This time Andrew shook his head in amazement. He pointed at the same photo. "That man there is my grandfather, and the man next to him is Joshua Murchison, Muriel's grandfather."

"So our old folks knew each other," Luke cried. "Hey man, ain't that grand!"

"Do you know what happened to your grandfather?" Andrew asked.

"Family story say he die at sea when some boat he was on go missing," Luke answered.

Andrew looked hard at Luke's photo of the *Deeral.* The caption only named the men, not the ship. He pointed to it. "This ship is the *Deeral,*" he explained, his mouth settling into a hard line. "She went out to look for the wreck of the *Merinda* and she allegedly sank in a storm out on the Barrier Reef. But that is the wreck we dived on two weeks ago at Cape Upstart. And it is mighty strange how she came to be where she is."

"You sure it is the same ship?" Luke asked.

"Certain," Andrew replied. He then described how his father had checked the details taken from the wreck with the Port Authority.

"What you sayin' man?" Luke queried.

"That something doesn't add up," Andrew answered.

Capt Conkey now interrupted. "You hint at that in your essay Andrew. Just be careful you don't make any accusations in writing without any real proof."

Andrew nodded. "No sir, but the whole story is mighty fishy, and I'd like to try to find out what really happened." He meant Murchison's story but managed to change it as he spoke.

"So would I," Luke added. "My ma, she always wondered what happened to her dad."

"What was his name?" Andrew asked.

"He that fella there," Luke answered, pointing to a large Melanesian in the middle photo. "His name was Solomon Tapau."

Capt Conkey held up the two assignments. "This seems to be a remarkable coincidence. I am sure you want to discuss it, however there are other people in the class so I will give these back to you and you can compare notes later. They are both very well done by the way, excellent research."

Andrew noted that he had a very good mark but at that moment all he wanted to do was talk to Luke. However they sat on different sides of the room and had no chance to talk until the end of the period. During the break Luke asked if he could borrow Andrew's assignment. "I'd like to take it home for Poppy to read," he explained.

A strong temptation to tell Luke all of his suspicions gripped Andrew but he managed to resist it and instead just asked if he could take Luke's assignment home. 'I don't want to start a wild goose chase,' he thought. He said, "I will bring our family album tomorrow and you can see the other photos."

"Thanks man. I'll do the same," Luke answered.

That afternoon and evening Andrew could hardly think straight. As soon as he got home he took out the family album and carefully studied the old photos. Then he read Luke's assignment. When Carmen came home he showed her and explained the coincidence. She had to hurry off to her part time job but was very interested. So were their parents when they returned home. That evening there was a lot of discussion and speculation, in between which Andrew had to pack for camp. That got him even more excited.

Not only excited but decidedly anxious. Would Muriel be coming to camp? How should he act towards her? How would she treat him? It was all very worrying. As he placed each item of clothing or equipment in his kitbag and ticked it off on the 'What to take' list he felt the thrill of possible adventure growing.

Next morning Andrew remembered to take the photo album when he went to school. As soon as he saw Luke he gave him back his assignment and the two sat to look at the photos. Luke also had his album but as he opened it he said, "Sorry but most of the pictures have no names. Nobody wrote on them all them years ago and now nobody can remember much who they of, or where. That's why we did not know the name of that little ship, the *Deeral*."

Andrew smiled and then said, "We had the same problem. Carmen sat with our Gran and asked her, and then wrote down the things Gran could remember. Now we write on the back of all photos as soon as we get them."

"Good idea," Luke agreed. "But you gotta remember to do it eh?"

"And find the time," agreed Andrew. "Gee, this is a great photo of a diver getting ready."

Luke nodded. "That my great uncle Absalom. All them old fellas were divers."

Andrew nodded and felt quite ashamed. He was now struck by the difference between the albums. Never in his life had he seen one full of pictures of black people and it was only from reading Luke's assignment that he had learned that most of the pearl and trochus shell divers back in the 20th Century had been either Torres Strait Islanders or, before World War 2, Japanese. Very few had been Europeans. Looking at the pictures made him uncomfortably aware of just how ethnocentric he and his group were, although he had always prided himself on not being racist. Yet here before his eyes was the evidence of another strong and vibrant culture with its own proud traditions and heritage.

While they looked at the photos Blake and Simmo joined them. They also leaned over to look. It was when they reached the photo of the *Deeral* that the conversation turned back to the mystery of what happened to her.

Luke pointed to the photo of the *Deeral*. "My Nanna say that my Grandad, he went missing when he sailed on that ship. They were looking for the wreck of the *Merinda*," he said.

Andrew was astonished at the coincidence. "Which one was your grandad?" he asked. Luke had told him the previous day but he had forgotten.

"That Solomon Tapau fella," Luke replied, pointing. "He was my ma's dad." The two boys looked at each other. "And you are sure that the wreck that you found at Cape Upstart is the *Deeral*?" Luke asked.

"Positive," Andrew replied. He then detailed again how he was sure of that.

"And definitely scuttled by explosives?" Luke queried.

Again Andrew described the wreck and what he had seen and been told by the Dive Trip Director. Luke looked very thoughtful and shook his head. "This don' add up. It don' square with the newspaper article you quote."

"That's what Carmen and I think too," Andrew answered. What he was still reluctant to do was voice his theory so he remained silent.

Luke opened up Andrew's assignment, which included the news articles about the *Merinda* and *Deeral*. They reread these and Luke kept shaking his head. "My Nanna, she thinks this is really sus. She would like me to show this to my uncle Moses. He will be real interested I reckon."

"I didn't know Moses was your uncle," Blake quipped. "Has he still got the Ten Commandments?"

"Very funny!" Luke replied. He looked at Andrew. "Would it be alright if I borrow this assignment until after the holidays?"

"Sure. Where does your uncle live?" Andrew asked, his hopes of getting another lead going up.

"Mackay," Luke replied.

That really got Andrew's interest. "We are going there for camp tomorrow. Maybe you will get a chance to see your uncle then?"

"That's what I was thinkin'," Luke replied. "He might be able to tell us more."

"I hope so," Andrew said. "And I will see what else I can dig up."

"Dig what up, skeletons from the family closet?" Blake added with a laugh.

Andrew gave a wry smile and changed the subject. There were times when Blake could be a bit of a pain. Then another worry crossed his mind. "Don't you blokes talk about this please. I wouldn't like anyone's feelings to get hurt, ok?"

"Because of Muriel's grandad?" Blake queried.

Andrew nodded. Blake then asked, "How are you getting on with her? I heard you had a bit of a bust up."

That hurt, and the public shame made it worse. "We did," Andrew answered, colouring crimson with embarrassment. "It was over the location of the *Deeral* and the discrepancies in her grandad's story. So I'd appreciate it if you didn't mention any of this to her. I want to try to get back into her good books."

They left it at that and made their way to class. Geography was first up and Andrew made a point of showing Capt Conkey the photo album. He was also pleased to learn that he had achieved 95% in his exam results and a VH for his assignment. Capt Conkey looked at the album with evident interest and then said, "You off to camp these holidays Andrew?"

"Yes sir. We leave tonight on the HMAS *Tobruk*. We are going to be in Mackay for a week. I am doing my quartermaster gunners course."

"That sounds interesting. I hope you have a good camp, and a good holiday."

"Same to you sir," Andrew replied.

For the rest of the day Andrew was in a mood of tingling anticipation and apprehension. As soon as school was finished he hurried home and completed packing. By 4:30pm both he and Carmen were ready, dressed in their navy grey and black camouflage work dress with grey caps. Their mother arrived a few minutes later and they loaded themselves and their gear into the car. 5:00 pm found them unloading at TS 'Endeavour'.

After farewells to their mother brother and sister shouldered their kit-bags, picked up their hand luggage and walked inside. Already half a dozen other cadets were present, as well as several of the adult staff. Andrew looked anxiously around to see if Muriel was there but saw no sign of her. He went to join the others and was at once directed to PO George, his watch Petty Officer, to help load stores into a truck.

While he was doing this with Percy Parsons and Simon Creswell Andrew saw Muriel arrive. Just once she glanced in his direction so he wasn't sure if she had seen him or not. He was actually surprised to see her as he had thought she would not go to camp. Worrying about what she now thought of him got him all in an anxious state; half hopeful, half fearful.

He got a clue when they were called on parade for roll call at 5:30pm. Once again Muriel glanced briefly in his direction but she then went and stood with the starboard watch. Knowing she could not do that without having been transferred Andrew began to worry what she might have told the officers. It was a blow to his hopes but he tried to ignore it and resolved to just get on with doing his best on the camp.

The events of the next hour helped drive such unhappy thoughts from his head. Andrew had been on two navy ships before, the patrol boat HMAS *Fremantle* for a couple of hours, and the Landing Craft Heavy HMAS *Tarakan* for a day trip out to the reef and back. But going on board the Heavy Landing Ship HMAS *Tobruk* was an altogether different experience. After checking that all unit gear and stores had been loaded onto the truck (which was driving to Mackay) the cadets shouldered their gear and marched out the gate and across the hundred metres to the front gate of the naval base, HMAS *Cairns*. From there a naval rating acted as guide and led them through to the main wharf and then up a gangway onto the *Tobruk*.

As they approached the ship Andrew's interest and excitement rose to a new pitch. Just the sight of those high grey steel sides and of the masts, rigging and other nautical details got him looking eagerly in all directions. He was gripped by a fierce desire to soak up as many experiences as possible. This was the world he wanted to be part of and he intended to learn as much as he could and to savour every moment of it. Just struggling up the gangway under the cynical gaze of the real sailors was a small adventure. He could imagine he was actually a hardened old salt returning aboard with vital orders to sail on a desperate rescue mission.

He knew already that *Tobruk* was one of the oldest ships in the RAN but that did not bother him because he was also aware that she was one of the navy's most useful ships and had a very proud record of operational duty: taking troops to Somalia, Kuwait, Bougainville, East Timor and Makasang. He also knew her main characteristics so only half read the pamphlet they were all handed when they were assembled in a flat.

A regular Petty Officer briefed them on the ship: a displacement of 5800 tons, length of 164 metres, beam of 18 metres and a draught of only 4 metres. "That is so we can get right in close to the shore to land tanks and vehicles across the bow ramp," the petty officer explained. Andrew was surprised to learn that the ship could carry up to 18 main battle tanks or 35 APCs on her main cargo deck. She could also carry troops and in fact was transporting an army engineer squadron and its plant and vehicles back to Brisbane after a deployment to the Solomon Islands.

The petty officer then handed over to a lieutenant. The lieutenant wore his dress white uniform and Andrew studied him with hungry ambition. His eyes took in every detail of the peaked cap, tanned and handsome face, the black epaulets with their two gold bars, the obviously fit body in the brilliantly white uniform. The lieutenant looked exactly like what Andrew thought a naval officer should look and he at once hero worshiped him and hung on very word. Even that impressed him. The man spoke very clearly and precisely and was so obviously master of his profession that Andrew felt great confidence in him.

The lieutenant gave them a detailed safety briefing. At the end of this he called over several ratings who distributed lifejackets to everyone. The cadets then practised putting the lifejackets on, the ratings checking every cadet. After the lifejackets were taken off and stowed the cadets were split into groups, each group in the charge of a rating. The rating then led them to their allocated mess deck.

All of the boys in the port watch were berthed in the same quarters- bunks in the troop space but separate from the adults and the soldiers. The glimpse of the camouflage uniforms of the regular army engineers added another dimension of interest to the event. The cadets having stowed their kit in lockers the rating then led them on a guided tour of those parts of the ship not out of bounds at that time. As the ship was preparing to sail this did not include the bridge, control room or engine spaces and even the focsle and upper deck were off-limits.

They did tour the flight deck and part of the upper deck to be shown their 'abandon ship' emergency station. They also went down to the tank deck. This was an eye-opening revelation to Andrew. To his eyes it was huge. It was lit by electric light but still gave the impression of being a vast gloomy steel cavern. The lines of dark green military vehicles and the usual festoons of pipes and wires all gave an impression of power and efficiency.

After being shown the 'heads', showers, mess and rec rooms they were led back to their berth space. By then it was 6:45 pm (1845 as the rating put it). "Ship is due to sail at nineteen hundred," he said. "By then you are to be formed up on the flight deck in your S. Eights."

There was a hurried changing into white shorts and shirts, white caps and dark blue long socks and black boots. Andrew was a bit shy of changing in front of the others, being used to the privacy of his own bedroom, but he did it as quickly as he could and then adjusted his cap in front of a full length mirror on the end bulkhead.

Luke joined him, giving a big grin as he did. "My Ma, she has rung Uncle Moses," Luke said. "He is going to visit us in Mackay."

Being reminded of the mystery at that moment was a slightly irritating jolt to Andrew as he had become absorbed by the experience of being on the ship but he gave a friendly reply and then led the way up to the flight deck.

Even just walking along the corridors he enjoyed. It was all so novel: the smells of paint, oil, diesel, and a hundred other softer odours; the sight of all the pipes, wires, boxes, fire hoses, and so on that lined the bulkheads (He almost called them walls and had to correct himself); the feel of the forced draught air conditioning, the vibration from machinery. It was a distinct change in the tremor from what he assumed were the main engines that got him hurrying. There was no way he wanted to miss the experience of sailing out of his home town while standing on the deck of a navy ship.

On reaching the flight deck the cadets were marshalled into lines five paces back from the deck edge (even though it had safety netting beyond that) by the adult staff. Luckily, being Port Watch, Andrew was lined up on the side facing the city. By the time the cadets were ready the shore lines had been singled up and the ship's engines increased in tempo again. From where he stood Andrew could not see either the wharf or the water astern so he had to imagine the scene as the last lines were cast off and the ship began to swing out from her berth.

On sensing that first movement Andrew experienced another spasm of excitement. This was the real thing! This wasn't just a little day trip or a dive trip in a small launch. This was a famous navy veteran setting sail and he was on her! His imagination began to conjure up all sorts of romantic and exciting stories. But that almost spoilt it. Into his mind crept images of rescuing a pretty girl from rebels on a tropical island like Bougainville. But the face that he conjured up was Muriel's. That made him risk looking over his shoulder to where she stood on the other side of the flight deck. Luckily she had her back to him so did not see his glance but there was still a sharp spasm of regret.

The ship slid quietly down the Inlet past the oil wharf and the main wharf and marinas. By then it was almost a dark and, to his disappointment, there seemed to be almost no-one watching from the shore. He did see a few people waving and he knew that his parents would be among them, but he could not tell if they were or not. Nor did he relax his self discipline to wave. He just stood to attention when ordered and stayed that way till 'stand easy' was given out past the first harbour beacon.

On being told to fall out and make their way to the dining mess Andrew paused for a few seconds and looked around, sniffing the sea and air and relishing being afloat. He had a strong feeling of adventure and happily enjoyed the sights. Then he turned to follow the others- to almost immediately have his bubble of joy pricked.

Chapter 25

South by Sea

Andrew made his way below, then joined the others from his watch in a queue at the dining mess. Blake stood in front of him in line and Luke behind. As the queue shuffled into the mess Andrew was talking to Luke. At the door he paused to look around the space, feeling both shy and inferior in the presence of the seated regular seamen and soldiers. While not being overt about it they radiated such a sense of superiority that Andrew had an urge to hide in the crowd.

Then he noted Muriel further ahead in the queue. The queue went along the passageway and then turned to cross the front of the cafeteria style servery. Muriel was at the start of the servery. As he looked at her he noted that she was talking to Shona and that both were looking in his direction. Even as he watched they both looked away, then glanced in his direction again, then away. Muriel had an unhappy expression on her face, almost a scowl. Andrew felt a peculiar sensation in his skin and he shivered.

'They are talking about me,' he thought unhappily. From the look on Muriel's face he was sure that what they were saying was not good and it caused him to feel a sick sensation in the stomach. Wondering what he had done to upset her now sent his mind back over the day's conversation. 'I hope Blake hasn't told Shona about what Luke and I were discussing,' he thought.

He never did find out, but it almost spoilt his meal. The food was excellent, with three choices of main course, but somehow his appetite was gone. Muriel, he noted, sat with her back towards him and he was careful after that not to look at her in case he annoyed her even more. 'I will never get her to like me again if I do,' he reasoned.

After the meal the groups were again taken on a guided tour of the ship, this time taking in such places as the engine and machinery spaces, the bridge and hangar. By then the ship was out of the channel into the open sea beyond Cape Grafton and had begun to move with quite a lively motion. Andrew was amazed at how such a large vessel could pitch so much but the motion had no effect on him. Not so on others. The first shamefaced victims of seasickness went off to their bunks. This included several older cadets with rank and caused Andrew to experience a spasm of relief, and of superiority.

To his regret the cadets were not allowed out on the open decks after nightfall so he only got a few glimpses of the dark sea and the odd flickering light when they visited the bridge. They were then led back down to a briefing room and shown several videos about the navy and its ships. By the time they were over it was 2130 hrs so they were ordered to bed, to be ready for check parade at 0600.

Back in his mess on the berth deck Andrew cleaned his teeth and changed into his pyjamas before climbing into his bunk. His was above Blake, with Simmo opposite him and Luke beneath Simmo. By then the ship was rolling as well as pitching and even more cadets were looking a bit green around the gills. Andrew merely wondered if he might roll out of his bunk during the night. For a while he studied his chart, calculating the ship's probable course and progress. Satisfied he knew where they were he snuggled into his sleeping bag and joked with his friends while enjoying every second of the experience. Even after grouchy old Chief Petty Officer Walker had come round to enforce 'lights out' he was still happy. He lay back, daydreaming about being at sea in wartime in a convoy of troopships on their way to land a force under fire on a hostile shore.

With happy fantasies of how bravely he would save the ship and help the assault to succeed he drifted into a restless sleep, broken by the unfamiliarity of his surroundings, the motion of the ship, and the fidgeting and movement of the others.

The morning check parade and roll call was on a cold and windy flight deck. To Andrew it was really enjoyable but he could tell that many cadets were feeling tired and miserable, if not actually seasick. The thing that he was not prepared for, even though he had read about it often enough, and experienced it several times in smaller vessels, was the way the horizon moved- or rather, the way it appeared to move as the ship rolled and pitched. The weather was not bad, just brisk, and the waves only one or two metres but there was a long swell that the ship was quartering and that made the movements seem enormous.

To some it was obviously a frightening experience, to judge by their pale and anxious faces. A couple fell out, including Leading Seaman Holloway, Andrew's immediate, and disliked, superior. As he did Andrew was careful to avoid his eye or to show any of the very real satisfaction the sight gave

him. Once the roll was marked they were briefed on the morning's program and then fallen out to carry out their morning routine and to have
breakfast.

While he'd been standing in ranks Andrew had been noting the landmarks that were visible. Only a couple of miles off the starboard beam
was a large, mountainous island. Later, as they were being briefed that they
would be entering Townsville soon he had guessed it was Magnetic Island.
Out of curiosity he walked across to the starboard side and looked forward. Beyond the end of Magnetic Island a large mountain was visible in
the distance. Even as he looked forward the ship changed course to starboard. Into view beyond the end of Magnetic Island Andrew glimpsed the
distinctive shape of Castle Hill and in the distance the even more familiar
shape of Mt Stuart. For a few moments he experienced a wave of pleasur-
able memories about the holidays in January and the adventures that had
befallen him.

The superstructure now blotted out the view forward as the ship kept
turning into the main shipping channel so Andrew made his way below
to 'lash up and stow' his bedding, shower and shave (He was immensely
proud of having to shave at 14!), and to dress in the work dress for the day
(W 9s- Navy camouflage shirt and long trousers). Then he made his way to
breakfast. He was a bit anxious about that, worrying about meeting Muriel,
but she was nowhere in sight. Feeling somewhat relieved he collected a full
breakfast of bacon and fried eggs with toast and sat with Jennifer, Tina and
two boys from the starboard watch.

By the time Andrew had eaten it was time to quickly change into whites
and to assemble on the flight deck again for entering harbour. By the time
Andrew came on deck the ship was close in to the rock breakwaters which
formed the artificial port for Townsville. For the next half hour he watched
with great interest as the ship was swung, then berthed stern first to allow
some of the army vehicles to be driven off via the stern ramp. Then he was
granted the pleasure of feeling like an old salt when the Townsville Navy
Cadets from TS 'Coral Sea' joined the ship.

There was also the pleasure of seeing friends among them, and of feeling comfortably superior, having been aboard much longer. In particular he
greeted new recruit Martin Schipholl, whose big sister Letitia, nudist and
flirt, was the object of many of his heated fantasies. Also with them was
the really nice girl who had shared the adventures on Endeavour Island:
Anne Maudsley. She had been Martin's girl friend but from casual appear-
ances the pair were now just friends. Not wanting to cause embarrassment
Andrew did not pry.

By 0900 the *Tobruk* was on her way out of harbour again. The cadets were again stood to attention on the flight deck. As the ship steamed down the channel Andrew noted that the wind had dropped and with it the sea so that it was almost a glassy calm. The newly joined Townsville cadets were then taken off to have their safety briefings and guided tours while the Cairns cadets changed into camouflage work dress and were divided into four groups for training. Those cadets who were gunners were led right forward across the upper deck under the huge cranes and past the lashed down LCM8s to the focsle. Here they were introduced to two real 40mm Bofors guns and real navy gunnery instructors.

For the next three hours the cadets toiled and sweated: safety precautions, how the gun works, loading, unloading, aiming, 'training', misfire drills and stoppages, everything except actually firing, which of course the cadets all itched to do, or at least to see! Andrew enjoyed every second of it and made a conscious effort to imprint the knowledge and skills into his very being. When it was his turn to act as the gun aimer he was able to conjure up images of enemy planes diving on the ship, with him valiantly shooting them down. The only distractions that really took his focus away from the training were landmarks he noted while he was one of the group watching and waiting, there being too many cadets for two gun crews.

Thus he was able to study Cape Cleveland as they rounded it heading south, his mind filled with images from the dive trip a month earlier. By 1000 Cape Cleveland had slipped astern as the ship stood out to sea across the mouth of Bowling Green Bay. By the time they were level with the lighthouse on Cape Bowling Green they were so far out to sea that all Andrew could see was an occasional glimpse of the lighthouse itself, a tiny, white sliver, and mirage like dots which were the tops of trees on the flat, sandy spit.

Soon after that they passed, at a distance of about two miles to port, three large launches apparently anchored out in the open sea. Andrew suspected what they were but this was confirmed by Sub Lt Sheldon. "They are dive boats moored over the wreck of the *Yongala*," he said. "That furthest one is *Reefmaster*."

Andrew shielded his eyes against the glare and peered at the launches. In spite of himself he felt a surge of affection for the dive boat and realized he was glad he had done the advanced course. It gave him a real sense of achievement and pride in himself for having faced up to his fears and won. 'But I don't want to do any more diving,' he told himself, shuddering at some of the memories.

Sub Lt Sheldon said, "Pity the sea wasn't as kind as this when we were here. I've never dived on the *Yongala*. I'd really like to. Maybe we could organize another dive trip one weekend?"

At that Andrew swallowed and scratched around in his head for an excuse. What he did not want Sub Lt Sheldon to think was that he was a coward. "I liked the wreck we dived on sir," he said. "That was really interesting."

"Oh, the one your grandfather was on? Was it really the *Deeral* like you thought?" Sub Lt Sheldon asked.

"Yes it was sir," Andrew answered. He described the way they had proved the identity of the wreck, but was very careful not to repeat any of his suspicions, nor to hint that he and Carmen were still interested in finding out what actually happened.

At 1200 the cadets were sent below to have lunch and rest. Luckily the port watch did not eat at the same time as starboard watch so he did not see Muriel. That made the break more relaxing and the friends could discuss the Bofors guns and training as well as tell jokes. Then they were called out again and mustered for more lessons.

The first lessons were on the .50 calibre machine gun. During the training Andrew noted the top of an isolated mountain many miles away to starboard. He suspected it was Cape Upstart and that got him thinking hard about the dives on the wreck of the *Deeral*. 'What really did happen?' he asked himself.

But his mind was soon taken off speculating about the past by the more interesting present of learning safety precautions and how the machine gun worked. Lessons on holding and aiming, on loading and firing followed. This time the cadets of both units were mustered at the starboard rail and the machine gun was actually fired. Much to Andrew's regret this was done by the ship's gunners and none of the cadets was allowed anywhere near it. Even so it was a thrill to hear the rat-a-tat-tat hammering of live rounds being fired, and to see the little pillars of white spray flung up by the bullets hitting the water.

That really got Andrew's imagination going and he quickly conjured up a daydream of him manning the gun under fire and of beating off attacks by radio controlled explosive motor boats. These were sent in by fanatical terrorists who also tried to hit the *Tobruk* by firing guided missiles. Then he was brought back down to earth with a bump. The machine gun had to be cleaned- and the regular navy gunners were more than happy to instruct the cadets on how to do this while keeping their own hands clean! Andrew now learned some of the realities of gun oil and elbow grease.

Next was a first aid lesson which involved treating a dummy and then lashing it to a stretcher and hoisting it up several decks to the flight deck. While they were up there Andrew noted a rocky, conical island several miles to port. An enquiry of one of the navy POs elicited the information that it was Holbourne Island, off Bowen. For a few minutes Andrew studied the distant shore while pondering his grandfather's fate.

After that they had a lesson on the fire fighting equipment so that by 1700 all of the cadets were feeling quite worn out. They were fallen out for the evening meal and then allowed a 'stand easy' till 1900. During that time Andrew went on deck with his chart and was rewarded by seeing islands appearing. He knew they must be approaching the famous Whitsunday group and was curious to see them. Having never been there, and only having read about them, he was keen to get a close look.

In particular he wanted to see Hayman Island. In this he was lucky on two counts. Firstly, several of the regular navy personnel, seeing his chart, came over and asked to look at it. They were then able to assure him they were in fact entering Whitsunday Passage and that the large mountainous island he could see to port was Hayman Island.

'So Old Mr Murchison came ashore on the seaward side of that,' Andrew mused. He looked around, noting how sheltered the passage was, and how many smaller islands there were. Several quite small boats were visible, either anchored or powering along, and that helped form his opinion. 'It would be quite easy to get across to Hayman Island from the mainland in a small boat,' he decided.

While thinking such grim thoughts he had pointed out to him the equally famous Daydream Island. 'I must go there one day,' he decided. That got him remembering the holiday on Endeavour Island in April. The memories of all the sex and nudity he had seen caused him to became quite aroused and then guilty when Carmen and Tina both joined him. For the next hour they sat and admired the sunset amid the beautiful scatter of islands.

By 1900 the ship was well down the passage and passing Hamilton Island with its famous tourist resort. Darkness was setting in by then and the resort was plain to see by the twinkle of its lights. Evening lessons began- more fire fighting and first aid. Training ended at 2100 and they were allowed to go to the canteen. That was the only time Andrew really saw Muriel at all that day. He met her at the entrance to the canteen and she at once looked away and walked past him without a word.

Feeling very mixed emotions, with the hurt of rejection predominating, he went in to the canteen. There he had to pretend that everything was normal while he talked and joked with his friends. For the next two hours the cadets had to remain in the rec spaces or mess decks. The standing order about no personnel on the upper deck after dark prevented Andrew from looking out for more islands such as Brampton, much to his regret.

The *Tobruk* entered Mackay harbour just before 2300 hrs but again all cadets were kept inside so all they could do was talk and tell jokes while imagining what was going on. The ship was swung and then berthed and the main engines eased back to a distant vibration. Lt Ryan, the XO, of the unit, then appeared and got them all moving. Lugging their kitbags they shuffled wearily along the steel passageway and then down the long gangway to the wharf.

On the wharf, under the glare of floodlights, kitbags were tossed up into a truck. The cadets were then shepherded into waiting coaches. By then Andrew was feeling decidedly jaded and was glad to be able to slump into the seat beside Simmo. Despite being tired however he remained interested and looked back at the *Tobruk* with real affection. It had only been 30 hours but it had confirmed for him that the navy was the place he wanted to be.

For Simmo it had had the opposite effect. "I found it too claustrophobic," he admitted. "All closed in with no windows or portholes and hardly any doors. If it was wartime I don't think I could stand it."

"I'm not sure if I could either," Andrew confessed. It was certainly sobering food for thought and not something he had been aware of until it was brought to his notice.

The coaches moved off and drove via North Mackay and across the Pioneer River to the cadet multi-user depot. Here they debussed and lined up to unload the truck. When everyone had found their kitbag and hand luggage they were led inside. Andrew found it was a large hall with offices, classrooms, kitchen and storerooms around the sides. As the facility was shared with the Army Cadets half of the offices were locked. Areas along the sides had been screened off with Hessian and plywood screens. These were the living areas.

After a quick safety brief the cadets were allocated to living areas by courses and then taken to their bunks by guides. They were shown the location of the showers and toilets and then told to get to bed. As it was well after midnight by then Andrew was more than willing to obey. He was feeling genuinely tired, though still excited. Within minutes of sliding into his sleeping bag he had slipped into a deep and dreamless sleep.

Chapter 26

QMGs Course

Harsh cries and the shrilling of Bosun's pipes wrenched a bleary eyed Andrew from sleep. Nearby stood a lad he had never seen before, a petty officer by his rank badges. He was shouting a polite variation of the traditional navy call to get out of bed. "Wakey, wakey, wakey! Into your eights and don't be late. Wakey, wakey, wakey! Show a leg there! Out you get and lash up and stow."

With a groan Andrew sat up and looked around. From two long rows of stretchers which lined the screened off male cadets sleeping area tousled and sleepy heads appeared. The petty officer strode along giving kicks to the legs of any stretchers whose occupants did not show definite signs of waking up.

"Out you get! Get yourselves decent and get on parade for roll call," he barked.

This was what Andrew expected and he had no problem with it. Slipping his feet into his sandshoes he hurried out to the parade area. That meant seeing Muriel but he avoided direct eye contact. Instead he gave Carmen a smile and waved to Anne Maudsley and Jennifer. He even gave an anxious looking Tina Babcock a sympathetic nod.

So began Andrew's Quartermaster Gunners Course. For the next week he threw himself into the training, hardly thinking about the mystery of his long-dead grandfather's disappearance. The only real fly in his ointment was Muriel. Still hoping to somehow regain her favour he stayed away from her. When they did meet he gave her a friendly nod and smile but made no overt moves to restore their relationship.

'Time for that after the course,' he told himself. Besides, fraternization was strongly frowned on so he kept a distant state of friendship with the girls. It was made easier by the fact that Muriel was doing a seamanship course. The way the camp was organized grouped cadets from all three units: TS 'Endeavour'; TS 'Coral Sea' and TS 'Pioneer', into their specializations. Thus Muriel was gone most of the day, sailing and canoeing.

For Andrew most of the camp was in the depot or its grounds. The QMG Course only had 12 cadets on it, so Andrew soon knew all their names. His close friends were all doing other courses but he did not really mind that. Blake was on the Seamanship and Coxswains Course, Simmo on the Technical Course and Luke on the Signals Course.

On the Sunday morning they had a parade for 'colours'. Following that was an inspection of the living areas and dining mess, then administration and detailed briefings on safety, fire drills, 'Out of Bounds' and so on. The training sessions then began. For the QMG course this alternated between drill with arms and training with the Steyr rifle. The lessons followed the usual sequence but in great detail and with a lot of repetition so that the cadets became safe weapon handlers who were competent with the rifle. Safety precautions were followed by stripping and assembling, then cleaning. The afternoon drill was a rehearsal for the 'Ceremonial Sunset' parade that the course was to take part in on the last afternoon. The QMG Course was to provide the armed guard and Andrew was determined that he at least would not let the guard down by poor drill.

That evening the course had revision lessons on First Aid and Fire fighting. This included the cadets detailed as members of the fire fighting team donning flash protection and safety helmets and then testing the fire hoses in the compound outside. 'Lights Out' was at 2200 and a 'Watch on Deck' then mounted duty: 8 cadets under a cadet petty officer and with an adult officer as Duty Officer. They mounted guard at the door as the Duty Quartermaster and provided a fire and security sentry inside. It was a duty Andrew was looking forward to but he was thankful he wasn't on that night as he was still tired from the voyage down.

Monday was similar except that the afternoon was spent on the water in 'Corsairs'. This was to select the course crew for a sailing race between the courses on the Thursday. In the morning the drill and rifle training continued. There was marching, holding and aiming the rifle in the lying position, degrees of weapon readiness, unload and stoppages. The sailing was just fun and Andrew was pleased to be in one of the two crews selected. He was sure this was on the basis of all the sailing he had done over the previous few months. That night they had lessons, including a video of current naval weapon systems. The lessons were on the theory of naval gunnery and the types of guns in current service in the RAN.

By the time he went to sleep Andrew was really enjoying the camp. He had made new friends in both the Townsville and Mackay cadet units and was finding he could do all of the training well. He even dreamt about rifle training that night, only spoiled by one of his usual dreams where he ended up on a beach and the waves suddenly got bigger and bigger and suddenly he was washed off his feet and sucked into deeper water by the backwash. He struggled to swim to shore but was carried rapidly out into deep water, with darkness setting in and the waves getting even bigger!

As usual the hands were called at 0600 the next morning. By 0800 all were standing in their divisions on the parade ground for colours. This time the QMG Course went on parade with their rifles and presented arms when the flags were hoisted. That made Andrew feel quite proud and he was glad he had chosen that course.

Tuesday's training Andrew also found interesting. The morning was devoted to training as lookouts. This began with lessons on the care and use of binoculars and telescopes, then continued with practical training. For this the cadets were moved by bus to the harbour where they boarded a large civilian launch hired for a short sea trip. The Seaman and Coxswains Courses provided (under supervision) the people to handle the lines and to steer the launch. The Technical Course worked in the engine room and bridge, the Cooks worked in the galley and the Signallers got to practice communicating by flag, light, semaphore and various types of radio with a shore signal station at the end of the harbour breakwater, and with a team of instructors who moved by minibus from place to place along the shoreline.

For the medics and gunners it was lookout duty most of the time, although the Seaman and Coxn's courses also did some of this. Andrew enjoyed the trip. It was only for three hours, out around Flat Top Island and along the coast for a few miles but it was a lovely day: sparkling blue water, bright sunshine and the ocean dotted with distant islands. What did annoy Andrew was finding that he had great difficulty actually holding his binoculars steady enough to focus on objects as the launch yawed, pitched and rolled. To his surprise he found it harder to focus on close objects than ones further away and he felt some sympathy for those on the Signallers Course as they worked in pairs, one cadet trying to read the messages while the other wrote them down. When he looked at one of the tiny semaphore stations in the distance Andrew could barely distinguish the movements. Likewise with the signal flags being sent up a flag pole on the seashore. The wind was at the wrong angle ("Always bloody is!" said the navy instructors) so that the flags blew straight out away from the observers, making the colours very hard to distinguish.

Lunch was eaten on board and during it Andrew had to sit near Muriel but he just gave her a friendly nod and kept talking to Blake. After lunch the launch took them back to the harbour. Then a bus took them back to the depot. The bus trip at least allowed them some chance of seeing a bit of Mackay in daylight. He decided it was very similar to Cairns, being green and tropical but without the close ring of mountains. Andrew was also struck by the large number of pretty girls there seemed to be.

From 1500 hrs to 1600 hrs there was a rehearsal for the Ceremonial Sunset parade. They were then able to fall out after 'secure' and have an hour to themselves. Andrew used this to get his washing done and to play handball with Simmo, Blake and Luke. By then he had settled well into the routine so that changing into night clothing (W 9s- cam work dress), supper, cleaning up ready for rounds, and rounds all just flowed.

The night lessons were on lookout duties in the dark and included another bus trip. This was down to the shore to try using binoculars at night. Adding greatly to the interest was a chance to use the latest army night vision sights, brought along by members of the local Army Reserve unit. Seeing those really clear green images of people in the blackness of the night gave Andrew the shivers. To him it was an awesome revelation of the importance of modern technology.

While travelling back through the brightly lit streets of the city Andrew could only agree with Blake when he wistfully wished they could have some local leave. "Lots of pretty girls in this town. I wouldn't mind getting to know some of them," he commented.

"What about Shona?" Andrew replied.

"Humpff!" Blake answered, adding, "No fraternizing at camp."

The way he said that made Andrew suspect that Blake was having girl trouble too so he tactfully dropped the subject.

Apart from a Fire Drill half an hour after 'lights out' the night was uneventful. Andrew slept soundly the whole night through.

Day 4 was not as interesting. During it there were lessons on the safe handling of 9mm pistols (that was good), and various other small arms such as civilian shotguns and sporting rifles. Then there were lessons on identifying all the types of ammunition used by the navy. Mostly this was done by video and Data Projector but there were some 'Drill Rounds' for them to practice on. The course covered the recognition, storage and safe handling of 4.5" and 5" shells, 76mm, 40mm, 0.5" MG ammo, 81mm mortar bombs of various kinds, types of explosives, pyrotechnics, Man Overboard Marker Smoke flares and Lights. Andrew found it all interesting enough and was amazed at the variety of types.

The physical aspects of safely carrying shells and of loading and unloading the old 'drill purpose' 40/60mm Bofors gun in the front yard tested his muscles and left a few aching unpleasantly. The hour of drill at the end of the day increased his sweat so that he was glad to fall out at 'secure' and head for the showers.

That evening there was another movie about the modern navy and revision but Andrew missed most of this because he was rostered on as part of the Duty Watch. For two hours at a time he stood at the front door as Duty Quartermaster. This went on all night, with a four hour break to sleep, then another stint on watch from 0200 to 0400. The boredom he dealt with by talking quietly to the other cadet on sentry, or by fantasizing about guarding the depot from rebels or fanatical terrorists. But that got him into thinking about rescuing girls, or at least impressing them mightily with his bravery and brilliant tactics. That led to picturing Muriel and then to confused and unhappy thoughts.

Thursday dawned cool and overcast, which caused a deal of gloomy speculation as to whether the sailing race scheduled for that afternoon would go ahead. But Andrew did not particularly care and was not focused on that. During the morning the QMG Course was going to the rifle range to fire live ammunition and he as really looking forward to it.

There was another bus trip. This time it was out into the country. To Andrew the flat sugar cane farms of the Pioneer Valley reminded him of the country around Innisfail, except that there was more of it and the mountains were further away. At the rifle range they were revised and tested at their safe weapon handling and the Tests of Elementary Training. To assist the adult Navy Cadet instructors run the shoot there were five army NCOs.

Andrew enjoyed the shoot and was gratified to find that he was a good shot- scoring 20 out of 20 on the first practice at 50 metres and 19 out of 20 at the next, which was at 100 metres. He found the Steyr easy to use, except for the barrel replacement after unloading, and was satisfied he could use one if he had to. His only disappointment was that it did not match his expectations of drama. There was almost no recoil and the sound was trivial, not at all like the descriptions from older relatives who had fired the obsolete weapons of the 20th Century: the .303 and the 7.62mm SLR.

There was a third shoot after lunch, during which they fired at ranges up to 300 metres. That was a lot more testing and Andrew only scored 15 out of 20. After that they cleaned the range, picking up all the spent brass cartridge cases. By then the clouds had cleared away, the wind had dropped and the heat increased until they were all perspiring freely.

Another hire bus took them back to the depot at Mackay. By then it was 1430 hrs but they now had to clean the rifles. Andrew even enjoyed that, although he was called away half way through to go off for the sailing race. The race was only a short one and was won by the Seamanship Course.

That evening the lessons for the QMG Course were on Gunnery Communications. By the time that he went to bed Andrew was feeling both keyed up with tension over the next day's testing, and also aware of a feeling of sadness because the camp was nearly over and he was really enjoying it. He went to sleep wishing he was already grown up and in the navy.

Friday was a very busy day. After 'colours' all the courses were drilled as a rehearsal for the ceremonial parade planned for that evening. The QMG Course then spent an hour doing practical tests on the Steyr rifle. After that there were oral and practical tests on the 40/60mm Bofors, on ammunition handling and safety, on lookout duties and on gunnery communications. There was then a break for lunch, followed by one hour of written tests.

1400- 1500 hrs was set aside for retests. As Andrew had none to do he was able to sit on his stretcher and polish his boots and brass ready for the parade. There was then another rehearsal between 1500 and 1600 hrs. As soon as the rehearsal was over there was a frenzy of polishing, ironing and quick showers so that by 1700 everyone was dressed in their best Ceremonial S1s ready for the 'Ceremonial Sunset' ceremony.

To Andrew dressing in the full ceremonial uniform for the guard: white cap with the cloth band down under his chin; white long-sleeved jacket with the traditional 'silk' and collar; white web belt with polished brass; white longs worn tucked into white gaiters; and all ending in highly polished black boots was an almost mystical ritual. When fully dressed and armed with the rifle he felt very proud and determined to do his best.

The armed guard was formed up to one side and was commanded by a Cadet Midshipman from Townsville, Cdt Mid. Mainwaring, whom Andrew thought was just the most perfect example of what a young officer should be like. While waiting to march on Andrew watched with interest everything that went on. He was particularly struck by the number of official guests and parents. Among the official guests were the local mayor and member of Federal parliament, the local Army Cadet major and the Air Cadet squadron leader. There were even a few army cadets and air cadets among the crowd that assembled at the front of the parade ground. Seeing the other cadets really added a fine edge of determination to Andrew's desire to do good drill.

'There is no way they are going to have anything to criticise about the Navy Cadets,' he told himself.

The ceremony began at 1715. First the unarmed divisions marched on and were right dressed by the Cadet Warrant Officer from TS 'Pioneer'. Once he was satisfied he handed over to the Cadet Midshipman commanding the parade, a girl from Mackay. She posted the four Cadet Midshipman who were in command of the divisions. Each carried a drawn sword and the blades of these twinkled and glittered in the sun.

Seeing the officers with swords fired Andrew's ambition. 'That is what I am going to be,' he told himself. 'First I will get to be a cadet midshipman, then I will become a real midshipman in the navy and then an admiral.'

Next it was the turn of the armed guard and the sweating and stiff self-discipline came into full play. The guard marched on, faced the front and were right dressed. Once they were exactly lined up they were also stood at ease. When the RAN Captain commanding Queensland, plus two Commanders, one RAN and one ANC, arrived by car the guard were called to attention. The captain, who was the Reviewing Officer, was met by Lt Cdr Hazard, who was the camp commander. The captain was then given a present arms by the armed guard.

As Andrew stood rigidly holding the present arms he looked at the captain in his dress whites and was even more determined to become a naval officer. To Andrew the peaked cap with its gold badge and old oak leaves on the shiny leather brim, the crisp white uniform with its gold badges and bright display of medals, and even the white shoes, all looked splendid.

'That will be me in twenty years time,' he vowed.

After the present arms came an inspection. This seemed to go on for a very long time and as Andrew stood there sweating he became alarmed lest he faint. Remembering what the drill instructors had kept advising he continually wriggled his toes inside his boots and bounced his knee caps. He also kept his head up and took a close interest in the audience, noting a number of very pretty girls.

'This Mackay place seems to have lots of good looking chicks,' he decided.

Then the inspection party was in front of him and he swallowed and stiffened into immobility. All he noted were the blur of white uniforms, the bright splashes of colour which were medal ribbons and the shimmering glitter of sword blades and medals. Just for a second the captain looked him right in the eye. The captain gave a nod of approval and moved on, allowing a relieved Andrew to relax a little.

The inspection was followed by a march past. This was done to music from a loudspeaker and that embarrassed Andrew a little as he was sure the army and air cadets were sneering at that. Some of the marching from the junior divisions wasn't very good either and that further embarrassed him.

A long speech followed during which several cadets fell out. Even the cadet next to Andrew left the ranks and he began to sweat with anxiety that he might not be able to stay standing himself. He was sure he was saved from this humiliation by the award of prizes. To his delight he was named as having topped the QMG Course. He fell out and marched across to where the captain stood. After saluting and shaking hands he was presented with a small trophy. Still without it really sinking in he saluted again, turned left and handed the trophy to a waiting officer, then resumed his place in he ranks.

After the prizes there was the ceremony of 'sunset', again with piped music to play the famous bugle tune. Standing rigidly at attention at the present arms Andrew watched the flags and colours coming slowly down the halyards and felt a great surge of pride. Watching the last of the sunlight lighting up the red, white and blue of the Australian flag made him feel very patriotic.

There was another present arms as the VIPs departed and then the guard marched off. They were halted inside the depot and Cadet Midshipman Mainwaring turned to face them.

"Well done guard," he said. "That was an excellent effort." He then handed command to the Petty Officer, a burly lad armed with a silver bladed cutlass. The P.O. marched them over to the armoury to return the rifles to secure storage. They were then dismissed.

The evening meal was a barbeque out on the side lawn. As Andrew made his way out to join the queue of cadets he looked happily around, pleased that the parade had gone off well. He noted that all the parents and friends were now mingling and eating. Some of the VIPs were still there being social and even the army and air cadets were part of the crowd. Andrew particularly wanted to talk to them.

He never got the chance. To his surprise Luke came along the line and took his sleeve. "Come with me man," he said. "I want you to meet my Uncle Moses and his friend Jordan."

The request came as quite a shock to Andrew but he allowed himself to be led towards a group of Torres Strait Islanders. He had noted them during the parade, their black skins making them stand out in such a gathering, but he had not connected them with either Luke or himself. Now his thoughts began to race with speculation.

"Do they know about the wreck of the *Deeral*?" Andrew asked as he and Luke made their way through the small crowd.

"Too right!" Luke replied, nodding vigorously. "I mailed them a copy of your assignment. They really interested. They want to talk to you man. They both really like to know what happened to their grandfathers too."

"So do I," Andrew answered, suddenly gripped by a feeling of intense curiosity. "But I don't know how to go about it."

"They got a few ideas," Luke replied. "So come and meet them and hear what they got to say."

Chapter 27

Unexpected Allies

As he and Luke made their way through the crowd towards the group of Torres Strait Islanders Andrew felt unaccountably nervous. He was used to talking to Luke, and was also used to seeing black people, at least ten percent of the students at his school being of either Aboriginal or Torres Strait Islander origin. But facing up to being the only white face among such a group of very black ones made him feel uncomfortable. There was an uneasiness which sprang from the knowledge that here was a complete culture about which he knew very little and because he did not wish to offend. His ignorance made him feel ashamed.

Then he spotted Carmen talking to Shona and Tina Babcock. "Hey Luke, let's get Carmen to join us. She will be interested in meeting your relatives," he said.

"Yeah, ok," Luke agreed.

The two boys detoured across. Andrew gestured to Carmen who asked what he wanted. Andrew pointed to the group of T.Is and said, "Come and meet Luke's uncle. He is the son of Solomon Tapau who vanished with the *Deeral*."

Carmen looked surprised. "His son! Does he know what happened?"

"No. But he has read my assignment and is very interested in finding out, so Luke says," Andrew answered.

Luke nodded. "That's right. He always wondered what happened to his poppy and he says he might be able to help us find out."

Carmen nodded with satisfaction, then turned to the other two girls. "Excuse us please you two. This might be very important."

Leaving Shona and Tina to the attentions of two male cadets from Mackay the three made their way across to the group of T.Is. As they did Andrew received a vivid impression of very black, very vibrant people. They were all well dressed and seemed very cheerful and were quite happily joining in the social activities. It reminded Andrew of comments he had heard about the differences between the Aboriginal and Torres Strait Island people. The T.I s had retained much of their culture and pride to a much greater extent and had more readily adapted to the changing economic and social systems. They had an excellent reputation for being very reliable and hard working people and it was obvious they intermarried much less.

Andrew found himself shaking hands with a large man who had almost coal black skin, his grizzled face topped by a whitening thatch of the fuzzy 'steel wool' looking hair of a typical Melanesian. The man was about fifty and was quite fat but still looked fit and strong. He was Luke's uncle: Moses Tapau.

Moses gripped his hand and shook it vigorously, grinning happily while he did. Andrew was next introduced to another man; a very strong and fit looking man in his thirties named Jordan Wania. "He my cousin," Moses explained.

So apparently were several other people. Luke was embraced and kissed by two big strapping girls with bold, flashing eyes and jutting bosoms. They looked a couple of years older than him and he explained they were his cousins Bernice and Amy.

The two girls gave Andrew laughing smiles that made him blush deeply, much to their obvious amusement. Next he met several older women. They all had the characteristic bulk of their race and several had young children. Carmen was more at ease and even got several of the young children to give her shy smiles. Luke shook hands with more cousins, big lads named David and Reuben.

Then Moses called to a wizened old man who was seated on a folding chair. "Hey Absalom, you come meet this fella here eh?"

Old Absalom hoisted himself to his feet and hobbled over on twisted legs. He peered at Andrew through eyes that looked amazingly bloodshot and also yellowed. For a moment a puzzled frown formed on his face. Then his eyes went wide and his lips opened. He gave a shrill cry of astonishment then said, "Bert Collins! You be just like Bert Collins."

"I'm his grandson," Andrew replied, the hair on the back of his neck prickling in reaction.

Old Absalom looked stunned. He muttered and shook his head and Andrew feared he was going to faint. One of the ladies came and held his arm. Old Absalom then nodded. "Luke boy was not kidding when he say you a Collins then. You the dead spit of Bert Collins."

"I'm Andrew Collins. This is my sister Carmen," Andrew said.

Old Absalom bowed and shook her hand, then turned back to Andrew. "Yeah, I read that paper you wrote. Really got us thinking it did."

"Did you know my grandfather well?" Andrew asked.

"Too right! We dived together for years, off the old *Pearl Reef*," Old Absalom replied, his eyes misting with memory.

"So you knew Joshua Murchison too then?" Andrew asked.

Old Absalom snorted and curled his lip. "Him! That no good for nuthin'. Yea, I knew him. Never liked him though and didn't trust him. Used to feel real uneasy when I was on the bottom an' him workin' the pump and lines up top."

Andrew was surprised at the venom in the old diver's voice. He said, "We want to find out what really happened to our grandad. You know they found the wreck of the *Deeral*?"

Moses answered him. "We read about that an' it got us all speculating. She not anywhere near where the Murchison say she sink. Somethin' mighty strange about that."

"We dived on the wreck," Carmen added.

"You a diver eh?" Old Absalom queried, looking surprised.

Carmen nodded. "Yes, both Andrew and I have qualified as Advanced Open Water Divers. Luke is an open water diver too."

"Lukey a good boy," Old Absalom said with evident approval. He then gave a sidelong glance at Moses and added, "Not like some. Back in my day all men were divers- but not women eh?"

Andrew sensed there was some cultural, gender issue here but all he detected was Moses looking a bit uncomfortable and irritated. Old Absalom went on, "So you tell us about this wreck eh?"

This led to a description by Andrew and Carmen of the wreck of the *Deeral* and its location and condition. When the fact that scuttling charges had sunk her was mentioned all of the listeners nodded their heads and looked serious.

Moses said, "Luke tell us that and we read your paper. Makes us think that there was foul play."

Luke spoke next. "I reckon they found the gold in that *Merinda* and then Murchison he bumped them all off to keep it all for himself."

On hearing his own theory put like that Andrew stared with surprise. He nodded and said, "That's what I think. But how do we prove it?"

Moses said, "If we could find the wreck of the *Merinda* we could check to see if the gold is still there. If it isn't then maybe it was taken."

At that Jordan gave a chuckle and said, "Finding some gold wouldn't be a bad thing either."

"Yeah, but how do we find the wreck of the *Merinda*?" Moses said. "Lots of guys have tried an' she sure ain't layin' anywhere near where people think."

"I've got an idea where to look," Andrew commented. "But we'd need a boat." As he said that he looked around to see where Muriel was. Even as he did he saw her and their eyes met. She was looking in their direction and had a sort of frozen glare on her face. For a full second she held his gaze, then looked away. That sent a wave of uneasiness through Andrew. 'I hope she doesn't know what we are talking about,' he thought.

Unaware of this by-play Moses answered. "We got the boat, but we fishermen, not divers."

At that Old Absalom snorted, to show what he thought of the soft younger generation. "In my day all warriors worth their salt was divers," he said.

That obviously stung Moses who retorted, "Yeah well, I got more sense. I seen what live in that sea, an' it all got big sharp teeth!"

"Huh!" sniffed Old Absalom.

It was obviously an old argument. Andrew wondered how to lead the conversation back but Carmen did it for him. "Never mind that," she said. "Would you be willing to help, to use your boat?"

"Too right!" Moses agreed.

That made Andrew a bit anxious. "What sort of boat is she? Could we go right out to the outer Barrier Reef in her?"

"Too right. The *Moa Mermaid*, she a forty foot motor launch. She old, but she seaworthy. She often been out to the reef. But where do we look, and who do the diving- you kids?"

"That's right," Andrew replied. Only then did it dawn on him that he had possibly committed himself to more terrifying dives beneath the sea. The thought made him shiver but he pushed the fear into the back of his mind. 'I want to know,' he told himself.

"Yeah, but where to look?" put in Jordan, who had been listening with interest. "We can't just search every reef for hundreds of kilometres. We got a living to make."

"I've got an idea where," Andrew answered.

"Where?" Moses cried.

"I'd rather not say yet," Andrew replied. "I have to check something first. If I am right, we can go ahead and do some proper planning."

Carmen then said, "But it has to be next week, or we leave it till the holidays at the end of the year."

The thought of waiting another three months filled Andrew with impatient dismay. To his immense satisfaction Moses looked at Jordan and said, "We could go out for a few days next week eh Big J?"

Jordan looked thoughtful and then nodded. "S'pose so. Could do some fishing at the same time as like as not."

Andrew's mind had been racing, images of charts filling his mind. He nodded and said, "That would be great, but you would need to be in the Bowen or Whitsundays area."

Moses nodded. "We figured that. Haven't been to Bowen for a coupl'a years. Be a nice change. What you say Big J?"

"We couldn't get there before Monday or Tuesday next week," Andrew said.

At that Carmen cried, "Steady on Andrew! We have to ask Mum and Dad for permission and we will have to organize buying or hiring diving equipment and so on."

Moses nodded and said, "OK, you kids ask your parents for permission and then we organize. No point in sailing all the way to Bowen only to find you can't come."

They had to leave it at that. The cadets were called to start cleaning up and the guests were requested to leave. After a few final questions and an exchange of phone numbers and addresses they parted. As Andrew and Carmen walked back with Luke to where the cadets were being formed up he was gripped by a fierce desire to learn the truth.

He also got another uneasy qualm when he noticed Muriel looking hard at them. He said, "We had better keep all of this quiet. We don't want to cause trouble with Muriel."

As she swerved off to join her division Carmen gave Andrew a half pitying look but nodded. That upset him as he still harboured vague hopes of making it up with Muriel.

There followed several hours of cleaning, packing and loading vehicles. During all of this Andrew fretted with the urgent desire to get to a telephone to call his parents to ask for permission to go looking for the wreck of the *Merinda*. The possibility that they might forbid any such thing was strong and that gnawed at him. It also made him guiltily aware of Muriel whenever she was near him.

When all the work was done the cadets were allowed free time to socialize. Along with a dozen others Andrew made his way to the public telephone available to the cadets. To his intense frustration he was about tenth in line and could only sit and fret with impatience. As he did his hopes declined by the minute as gloomy negative thoughts crawled into his mind.

'We had enough trouble persuading Mum and Dad to allow us to do the diving courses,' he mused, 'and they were properly conducted by experienced professionals with all the right gear. This will just be us and a couple of fisherman.'

After waiting half an hour, when he was only second in line, Andrew saw Carmen approaching. She smiled and said, "I thought I would find you here. You can come away."

"Why? I don't want to lose my place in line," Andrew answered.

"It doesn't matter if you do," Carmen replied. "I have already spoken to Mum and Dad."

"How?" Andrew asked, annoyed that he had wasted that much time and energy.

"Shona's mobile phone," Carmen answered.

"What did they say?" Andrew asked anxiously.

"They said they wanted to know exactly what was being proposed and that we would have to wait till we got home and could tell them in person," Carmen answered.

That was what Andrew had expected. It clashed with his fierce desire to find out the truth. This was now so strong that he had even begun to consider wild schemes to try to achieve that goal: schemes such as getting off the bus in Bowen on the way home, or of running away from home. The idea of somehow leaving the bus in Bowen he quickly shelved. 'It would cause too much trouble to the cadet officers,' he decided. And there were all the practical difficulties of food, money and accommodation, and so on.

Even so the idea kept recurring and as the coach taking them home passed by Bowen the next morning Andrew looked intently out and kept wondering how he could find out the truth. All the Townsville and Cairns cadets travelled home in two hire coaches, along with most of their officers. After the usual farewells they had left Mackay at 0715. It was only as the coach was pulling out of the depot yard that Andrew realized he had forgotten to feel sad about the camp ending, so engrossed was he now in his quest for the truth.

The trip from Mackay to Townsville took five hours, broken by a stop at the Don River Roadhouse just north of Bowen. There was a delay of an hour in Townsville while they had lunch. During that there were more farewells, this time to the Townsville cadets.

"You must come and visit us next holidays," Martin Schipholl said. This sentiment was echoed by Anne Maudsley, much to Andrew's embarrassed discomfiture as he thought it was fairly obvious that she was meaning him. That impression was reinforced by the stony looks the suggestion engendered on the faces of Tina and Jennifer. For a moment Andrew was tempted to tell Martin and Anne about the proposed search and to suggest they join them but then he shook his head. 'No, loose lips sink ships,' he told himself. 'They wouldn't be allowed and would only get in the way. They aren't divers.'

Then it was another tiring four hours to Cairns with a stop at Cardwell. It was nearly 6pm when the coach arrived at TS 'Endeavour'. The parents were mostly waiting but another forty minutes went by while stores were unloaded and packed away. Only when that was done were they paraded. Lt Cdr Hazard then congratulated them and thanked them for their good behaviour. Finally they were dismissed.

As they made their way towards the gate, struggling under kitbags and suitcases there was another worrying little incident. Andrew saw Muriel ahead of them and after she greeted her parents she said something that made them turn their heads to look towards him and Carmen. 'I think she suspects something,' Andrew thought. Rather than risk an embarrassing incident he looked away and hurried to meet his own mother.

Chapter 28

The Chart

By 11:15 the next morning Andrew and Carmen were afloat on their catamaran, heading down channel towards Trinity Bay. When, after their chores, they had told their mother they were going to the Yacht Club, she had shaken her head and muttered that she would have thought they would have had enough of sailing by now. But, to their great relief, she had not said no, so they had hurried away. Now, dressed in old clothes and carrying a haversack of things they thought they might need, they were on their way to commit a possible crime.

That thought had Andrew in a sweat of anxiety. Normally law abiding he was worried just on that account but there was also the possibility that getting caught and having a criminal record would exclude him forever from his cherished ambition of being an officer in the navy. He did not voice these fears to Carmen as he knew she would at once offer to go in his place and there was no way he would place his sister at risk, not just to save himself!

It was a pleasant day with no clouds and with light winds so the sailing was simplicity itself and he barely noticed it. So skilled and practised were both of them that they instinctively handled the cat as it slid quickly but without fuss over the gentle waves in the lee of the mangroves on the eastern side of the waterway. That was the course they had agreed on, to slip along close to the shore so that for most of the voyage they would be hidden from any watcher at Bosuns Bay. It had the risk that they might be observed by people who knew them (Muriel!) driving in a car along the coast road but, as this only came close to the sea at two points, Andrew did not think that was a big risk.

By 12:40 the cat was passing the group of houses nestled in the little cove just to the south of Bosuns Bay. A small boat ramp and vehicle turn-around had been built on the end of the rocky headland that divided this cove from Bosuns bay. Carmen steered in to the beach near the boat ramp.

The cat was beached and then secured to a mangrove that was struggling for existence in the sand. Close above them was the main road, making this the period of greatest danger of being discovered on the approach voyage. Despite this they had agreed the risk had to be run. To try to secure the cat among the rocks of the headland itself was to run the even greater risk of waves grinding it on the rocks, possibly damaging it.

They had of course agreed that sailing into Bosuns Bay in broad day-light would be very poor tactics. So now they set out to make their way around the end of the headland by scrambling across the rocks. This was not particularly difficult but it was hot. Being in the lee of the mountains there was almost no breeze so both were soon perspiring freely. As it was the 3rd of October and thus the start of the Hot Dry Season, this was only to be expected.

As they got closer and closer to Bosuns Bay Andrew became more and more anxious. He was scared and regretted suggesting the raid. However he knew he could not easily back out. Both Carmen and his father wanted to know the truth too and if he backed out he suspected Carmen might try to do it on her own. So, reluctantly, he continued on. As they rounded the end of the headland and more and more of Bosuns Bay came into view the slower he went, pausing behind trees or rocks to scan the view ahead for any sign of people. Seeing no-one he continued on, creeping from rock to rock.

Ten minutes of careful approach had brother and sister among the big boulders near where the small creek came down to the beach. It was only then that Andrew realized they had both walked on the beach and left a trail of very clear footprints. "We must brush these out as we leave," he whispered to Carmen.

Their plan, already agreed on, was to creep up the creek line and study the house before trying to sneak in (How Andrew hated that word sneak!). From where they were they could just make out the boathouse but the main house was not visible. By creeping forward through the trees and bushes Andrew was able to ascertain that the boathouse was closed up and locked. That was a mild disappointment as he was curious to know if the lifebuoy was still hanging inside. His supposition was that, if Old Mr Mur-chison really had something to hide, he would have now disposed of it, in an attempt to get ready of any incriminating evidence.

It was exactly that fear that was now motivating Andrew to make this attempt to find the old chart- if it was still there. 'And if it actually has anything to do with the mystery,' he thought, unhappily aware that a pencil line on an old chart might mean nothing. 'It might be pure coincidence and have nothing to do with the disappearance of the *Deeral* at all,' he told himself.

Having often seen old pencil lines on other charts Andrew was only too aware that this might be a wild goose chase. Worse was the thought that he might be about to wreck his whole life over a mere hunch, a supposition that had no foundation in fact. Glancing back at Carmen and seeing her urging him to go on did not help. He had put all these gloomy thoughts to her and she had insisted they still had to try.

The creek was easy to move up. There was only the tiniest trickle of water and the rocks were dry and easy to climb over or walk on. Five minutes of slow scrambling had the pair up level with the house. This was just visible all the time, glimpsed through the foliage. Andrew now crept out of the creek line to a better point of vantage and carefully studied the house. What he found was that he was actually too close to it to see much. From the edge of the scrub he could see the side and roof but not the back patio or garden.

What he did note with real satisfaction though was that the doors of the garage were open. 'All I have to do is slip in there for a minute and it is done,' he told himself. But he also discovered that it was a lot easier said than done. He found that his heart rate had shot right up and that his palms had gone sweaty.

Making his way slowly and carefully back to where Carmen waited (and annoyed at the unavoidable crackling of dead leaves under his gym boots) he told her what he had seen.

"I will just nip in now," he whispered.

"Not yet. Let's go right up to the road and check the side windows and the front of the house first," Carmen cautioned.

Andrew agreed that was sensible so they continued up the creek to the small concrete bridge. Seeing it caused Andrew a flood of memories of Muriel. It seemed only yesterday that he had followed her under it. That thought caused a sharp pang of regret that hurt more than seemed fair.

Carmen studied the front of the house and the driveway, then said, "No other cars parked outside. That should mean that only the two old folks are at home."

Andrew nodded. What he had feared was finding Muriel and her family there. If there were only two elderly people in the house then that improved the chances of successfully carrying out the raid (He preferred to use that term with its military connotations as a sop to his conscience). Heartened by that thought he led the way back down the creek until they were level with the open garage door.

Once there he crept forward from tree to tree, pausing frequently to study the side windows and to listen. The only sounds he could hear were the gentle rustle of leaves in the breeze, the swash of small waves on the beach, and the hum of insects. The house appeared silent and deserted. Tensing himself for action Andrew glanced back at Carmen and nodded. She was to stay outside on watch.

Feeling sick with guilt and with his heart now hammering in his mouth Andrew steeled himself and stood up. For a few more seconds he paused in cover. Up till now they could deny and bluff and talk their way out of any encounter but once he entered the building he would have broken the law- trespassing at the very least but probably (as he had heard on the TV News) 'entering with intent to commit a crime'. It was a sickening thought and he almost did not go on with the plan. For a few seconds he again wondered whether he shouldn't put on a mask or cover his face somehow. But that seemed even more criminal and dishonourable so he rejected the idea.

Taking a big breath he nerved himself to walk quickly out of the trees and across the driveway. Here he paused with his back to the wall. After looking both ways along the driveway he edged sideways and peeked around the doorpost into the garage. As he did he strained his ears to try to detect if there was any one inside. The problem was that his heart was beating so hard that the pounding was causing a swashing sound which made it difficult to hear.

'I will look bloody silly if Grandma Murchison is in the laundry doing the washing and I get seen,' he thought. And thinking of her did not help as he genuinely liked the old lady and had no wish to cause her any harm. That thought almost made him give up. As yet he hadn't entered the house. 'I could still just walk away,' he argued with his conscience.

But he saw Carmen's frowning face peeking from behind a tree so he nerved himself to act. She gestured to get moving. That helped. He told himself that there were other people involved as well. So in he went. It was like taking a dive from the high diving board into cold water. He gulped and almost scuttled inside.

The interior lights were not on so it was quite gloomy but as he knew the way that was not a problem to begin with. Both cars were parked there. Keeping low he went between the Mercedes and the end wall at a crouch. At the front end of the car he paused again to listen. There was no sound from the laundry, the door to which was open. Reflected light came down the stairway from the patio but Andrew did not want to go that far into the room. Instead he angled right and made his way the five paces to the door of the small office.

The office was in darkness but he had anticipated that and from his small haversack he took out a torch and clicked it on. A quick sweep with the beam showed that the room appeared to be as he had last seen it, the map cabinet still in place against the far wall. For a few seconds more he stood and strained his ears to listen. Hearing no sounds at all he moved forward to the map cabinet.

The next problem was to find out which of the eight or ten sliding drawers was the one? Andrew tried to conjure up the image of Blake sliding the drawer open all those weeks ago. All he could decide from that was it was one of the bottom ones, but not the lowest. So he knelt and placed his torch on the floor, then gently used both hands to pull out the third drawer from the bottom. The drawer obviously was rarely used as the slides squeaked and the drawer was stiff and difficult to move. Fearing he had made too much noise Andrew stopped to listen, then inched the drawer out a few centimetres at a time.

Then he discovered another problem. To look at the lower charts he had to hold the ones above up with one hand. To his annoyance he discovered that it was really a two handed job. After putting his torch on the floor three times and then struggling to hold the top chart up with one hand while he picked the torch up and scanned the next chart he stopped and wondered if he should not take the risk of turning on the light.

He was also fairly sure after six charts that this drawer was not the one as all the ones he had so far seen were of the Gulf of Carpentaria. As there were no labels on the outside of the drawers he could not easily check, other than by sliding all the drawers out. He persisted for three more charts but when they showed Arnhem Land he stopped.

"No good!" he muttered with annoyance. He was sweating now and feeling really anxious. Carefully he slid the drawer back in, not an easy task as it jammed several times and made screeching noises. That, more than anything, convinced him it was not the drawer Blake had pulled out. That one had slid out easily. After once more placing his torch on the floor Andrew gripped the two handles of the fourth drawer and tugged.

It came out with no real noise and very little stiffness. A check of the top chart showed it was the northern tip of Cape York Peninsula and the east coast as far south as Cooktown.

'This looks more like it,' he thought.

But once again he had the problem of having to put his torch down while he lifted the top chart to expose the next below. Just holding the large sheets of paper up was awkward. However he decided against turning on the light and persevered. The thought of taking the charts out one by one and then putting them back again later he rejected. 'If someone comes I wouldn't have time,' he reasoned.

And there it was- the chart he remembered!

As he tried to shift the charts above it he trembled with emotion and had trouble focusing his eyes. Frustration and fear were then almost his undoing. To get a good look he needed to roll the five charts above it out of the way but the drawer wasn't far enough out. Grunting with annoyance he lowered them onto his torch as a 'place mark' and then pulled the drawer further out. To his dismay it rolled sharply out and came to a jarring stop, half hanging down.

For a few seconds Andrew crouched, heart beating rapidly and ears straining. However there was no sound from above so he carefully rolled the charts aside and began the next stage of the plan. Reaching into his haversack he took out a camera, set the flash and stood up. It was a cheap camera with a fixed focal length of a metre so he hoped he was more than a metre from the paper as he clicked the shutter.

The sound of the shutter quite alarmed him, as did the brilliant flash of light. He quickly took another photo, then put the camera back into his haversack. Taking from the bag his own chart and a pencil he crouched to study the pencil line. No doubt about it- the line ran from the Great Barrier Reef to the northern tip of Cape Upstart. Written on it in smudgy pencil was 264° MAG. The calculations were on the side- converting from Latitude and Longitude to a magnetic compass bearing. −7° was the variation used.

Andrew now knelt to stare at the reef end of the line. There were several large reefs in the area: Old Reef, Stanley Reef and several smaller ones with names like Faith Reef, Hope Reef and Charity Reef but the line ended at a small one with the pencilled name Echo Reef beside it. When Andrew and Carmen had discussed what to do once he was inside the office their first idea had been to find the chart, grab it and bolt. Then they had decided that was not a good plan as it would betray the fact that someone had been there and taken it, thereby putting Murchison on his guard. It would also be theft. Instead the camera and a copy were opted for.

So now Andrew crouched low and tried to match his own modern chart with the old one. He bit his lip with concentration as he slowly slid his pencil across the paper from reef to reef. Suddenly he froze. 'Was that a voice?' he wondered.

Within seconds he knew it was. Quite clearly he heard Old Mr Murchison's voice say, "I'll just look."

'Look at what?' Andrew wondered. In a fluster of near panic he quickly pocketed his pencil and then tried to close the drawer. To his dismay he found that he had dislodged the top charts so that they would not fit.

Quickly he placed the torch and his own chart on the floor. With fingers all shaking from fear he hurried to push the charts back into place, actually making a hash of it in his haste. As he did he thought he heard footsteps on the stairway down from the patio but wasn't sure. Resisting the urge to run he lifted the front of the drawer and got the thing back on its runners, then tried to slide it in.

With the perversity of such things it jammed when nearly closed. To his dismay Andrew saw the corner of a chart stuck in the runner. But as he bent to free it he heard Muriel's voice call clearly down the stairwell. "Wait a moment Grandpa," she said.

'Old Mr Murchison is coming downstairs!' Andrew thought in alarm.

Chapter 29

Out in the Open

Snatching up his satchel, the torch and his own chart Andrew hurried to the door of the office and looked around the corner. Seeing no-one he stepped out and started walking across towards the garage door.

Suddenly the lights came on, half blinding him. From near the bottom of the stairs Old Mr Murchison called out, "Hey you! Who are you? What... What the? What are you doing here?"

Andrew stopped in shock, but then resumed walking even as he heard footsteps clattering down the steps. Old Mr Murchison cried out again, louder and more angry this time. "You! Young Collins! How dare you! What are you doing sneaking into my house?"

Again Andrew made no answer. By then he had reached the front of the Mercedes. From behind him he heard Muriel ask, "Grandpa, what's wrong?"

Old Mr Murchison called out again, shouting angrily this time. "Stop thief! Put down that chart!"

Only then did Andrew remember that he had his own folded chart in his hand. He glanced at it but kept on walking, fear and shame making him hurry. From behind him Muriel also called out, "Andrew! What are you doing here? What have you done?"

Old Mr Murchison answered that. "He's stolen one of my charts. Stop him!"

By then Andrew was at the open garage door. To his shame he had to suppress an urge to run. Instead he was stung by the accusation and turned to face Muriel, who was now hurrying past her grandfather. "It isn't yours!" Andrew shouted, waving the chart in the air. "It's mine. I bought it from Commander Hazard."

Muriel came running over, halting when only a metre away. "Give it to me!" she snapped.

"It's mine I tell you!" Andrew retorted.

"Grandpa called you a thief. What have you got in that bag?" she demanded, reaching out towards it.

"Nothing of his," Andrew replied, holding the chart away from her. She stepped closer and again tried to reach it. Then, before Andrew realized her intention, her foot kicked up into his groin. Searing pain shot through him and he doubled up in agony, clutching at himself. As he did her hand snatched the chart from his grasp. All Andrew could do was gasp and crumple up. The shock was as bad as the pain. 'She kicked me!' his stunned mind told him.

Into his blurred vision as he sank to his knees came Carmen. Muriel saw her coming and tried to turn and run but she was too late. Carmen grappled with her. "Give that back!" she demanded. "It doesn't belong to you. It is Andrew's."

"Let me go, you sneaky bitch!" Muriel screamed.

Andrew now lay on the driveway, sucking in shuddering gasps of breath as waves of pain swept through him. Part of his mind noted the two girls clawing and wrestling with each other. The other part was still trying to comprehend that Muriel had actually kicked him. It was such a blow to his pride that he had difficulty accepting it.

Old Mr Murchison arrived at the garage door but he just stood waving his hands ineffectually and looking aghast at the two girls. Andrew rolled further away and struggled to his knees. The pain was still so intense that he remained doubled up. He could not believe how much it hurt, or how instantly it had rendered him helpless. Tears ran unheeded down his face. Now Carmen's size and strength showed. She grabbed Muriel's little finger and jerked it hard, causing her to drop the chart.

"Grab it Andrew!" she cried.

Andrew gasped in pain but managed to hobble over bent double. He picked up the chart just before Old Mr Murchison. As he straightened up and backed away Andrew looked at close range into the old man's eyes and was appalled. A look of pure hatred glared at him.

Old Mr Murchison's clawing hand reached for him and the old man shouted, "Give it to me boy! Give it to me or else!"

"No!" Andrew shouted angrily. He was recovering from the agony and anger and outrage were replacing the humiliation and feelings of rejection.

"I'll get the police onto you!" Old Mr Murchison shouted, his face a mask of fury.

"Good!" Andrew retorted. "That is exactly what we want. Then you can explain why you lied about what happened to the *Deeral.*"

"Why! How dare you! You... you.." Old Mr Murchison spluttered.

Andrew retreated another step, Carmen joining him, while still fending off a furious Muriel. Andrew stood his ground now, chest heaving and burning with embarrassment but still queasy from the waves of pain. Still holding himself hunched forward he shouted angrily, "You can tell us the truth about what happened to our grandfather!"

At that Old Mr Murchison appeared to shrink. His face contorted with strong emotion but Andrew could not tell if it was anger or fear. Muriel now drew back and stood next to him, obviously puzzled. "Grandpa, what is going on?" she asked.

"The chart," Old Mr Murchison cried, pointing to it. "They mustn't get the chart." His face then twisted with what was obviously pain and he bent forward and appeared to crumple. Muriel cried out in alarm and rushed to hold him up.

Carmen now stepped in front of Andrew and pushed him. "Go and get in the boat Andrew," she ordered. That irritated Andrew and embarrassed him but he realized he was in no condition to either run or fight. The queasiness was making his head spin and he thought he was going to vomit. Reluctantly he turned and staggered off down the driveway.

Looking back over his shoulder Andrew now saw Grandma Murchison appear. As Carmen backed away Muriel glared at them and shook her fist. "You'll regret this!" she shouted.

That shook Andrew too. All his hopes of reconciliation were now dashed for sure. Feeling battered and dazed he tottered on down the driveway past the boatshed and onto the beach. Carmen came along behind him, disdaining to hurry.

As she caught up with Andrew she said, "Well, it is all out in the open now. That old bugger will have some explaining to do I reckon."

Hearing his sister swear like that told Andrew just how angry and determined Carmen now was. It saddened him even more to think of the hurt and anxiety that Grandma Murchison and Muriel must be experiencing. 'Unless they know the truth,' he reasoned. Then he shook his head. He did not believe they did. It was all very distressing. To add to his embarrassment he still shuddered from time to time and had to suppress the urge to hold his testicles in front of his sister. Shame at the tears did not help either.

Once they were on the beach and out of sight of the house Carmen called on him to stop. "Sit down for a minute," she said.

With a sigh of relief Andrew lowered himself onto a convenient rock. Very mixed emotions still boiled in him, along with residual waves of pain. Partly he was angry at himself for getting caught. "That didn't go very well," he muttered.

"No. You'd better not plan a career as a burglar," Carmen replied, giving a wry but sympathetic smile. Then she asked, "Did you find anything?"

Andrew nodded. "I found a chart. I think it was the right one. I've marked this one with the location shown on it."

He held the chart up for Carmen to see. While she looked at it he had another thought and quickly extracted his pencil and wrote on the chart the magnetic compass bearing and magnetic variation. "Before I forget," he said. Then he shuddered as another wave of nauseating pain swept through him. "I got photos too," he added.

Carmen looked at him anxiously. "Are you alright Andrew? Do you want me to get the cat and sail her around to here?"

"I'll be alright," Andrew replied. The thought of being left there alone, possibly to face the wrath of Muriel or her family, did not appeal. In answer he pushed himself to his feet and told Carmen to put the map in his haversack. Swinging that onto his back he set off walking stiffly along the beach. "I guess we don't need to rub out our footprints now," he said ruefully.

At that Carmen gave a soft laugh. "They won't follow us," she said.

"I wasn't thinking of that. I'm worried about them calling the police," Andrew replied.

"I don't think they will," Carmen answered. "Not if Old Murchison has anything to hide. It could lead to some very awkward questions."

But worry over the police stayed as a concern all the way back, and over the next few hours. Andrew half expected to find them waiting at the Yacht Club when they sailed the cat in. However it was all a normal Sunday afternoon. Next Andrew fretted that the police would be waiting at their home, but again the fear was wasted emotion. He and Carmen arrived home to find their father having an afternoon nap and their mother quietly reading.

"How's the boat?" she asked.

"Fine," Andrew replied. He had trouble standing upright still and from time to time experienced sharp pains. 'I hope Muriel hasn't bust something down there,' he thought anxiously.

Carmen at once got him to go to his room so they could lay the chart on the study desk. She went and got a protractor and a notebook and quickly calculated the magnetic back bearing and converted it to a grid bearing. Andrew watched in silent admiration. He half understood but it was a skill that was really only taught on the Leading Seamans Course or Coxswains Course.

Next Carmen placed the centre of the protractor on the tip of Cape Upstart. A few seconds work by her dexterous fingers produced a pencil line that ran out to the Great Barrier Reef. Andrew studied it and nodded. It went within a millimetre of the dot his pencil point had made.

"That's the place," he said. "Echo Reef."

Carmen studied the chart and gave a soft whistle. "Holy Mackerel! That's a long way from where Old Murchison said they were." She quickly measured the approximate distance from the reefs east of Hayman Island to Echo Reef. "Nearly a hundred nautical miles. Two hundred kilometres! No wonder nobody ever found anything. They were all looking in the wrong place."

Andrew was also busy calculating. He placed a ruler on the map and measured the distance out to Echo Reef from Bowen. "About eighty kilometres," he said, then added, "Bowen is the closest port."

They both scanned the map to check but Carmen agreed. She then pointed to all the reefs. "Look where the wreck is. It is right in among this jumble of reefs. The *Merinda* must have been miles off course."

"If she was trying to head into the seas whipped up by a cyclone she probably didn't have much choice," Andrew suggested. "No radar on coastal ships in those days," he added.

Carmen grinned. "Well, we have some idea of where to look. Now let's arrange for the boat."

"Hang on Car. What if this is all wrong? What if this chart just shows a likely spot for diving for pearl shell or something?" Andrew said, anxious not to make more mistakes.

Carmen shook her head. "I don't think so. Just think about how Old Mr Murchison reacted. He was beside himself about you having that chart. No, this is the place. And even if it isn't, we've got to check it out anyway. I am going to phone Mr Tapau right away."

She did. While she spoke Andrew sat and unhappily considered the recent past and gloomily contemplated the possible future. 'It means I will have to go diving again,' he sighed.

Carmen came back looking annoyed and said, "Mr Tapau wants to speak to Dad. He says we can only come if we have parent's permission."

"You wake him then," Andrew said, adding, "And use your sweet-lit-tle-daughter-eyelash-fluttering trick." Then he mimicked- "Please Daddy!"

Carmen snorted but laughed and left the room. A few minutes later their sleepy eyed father joined them. He called in their mother and the story of the chart had to be told, with both of Andrew and Carmen glossing over how they actually came by the information. "It was just on an old chart I saw over at the Murchison's," Andrew explained lamely.

Luckily neither parent pressed the issue and the discussion shifted to the probability of the place shown being the location of the wreck of the

Merinda. Their father arrived at the same conclusion. "We have to check it out, if only for lack of any other specific clues."

The talk then moved to the logistics and administration of a search expedition. As they discussed this Andrew noted that his father had decided the plan could go ahead. 'He wants to know too,' he realized. Suddenly his spirits soared, dampened only by his hurt over Muriel's rejection and her assault on him.

After that it was their father who did the telephoning to Mackay. He spoke to Mr Tapau for about ten minutes before saying, "I see. I will find out and call you back. Thank you."

That didn't sound very hopeful to Andrew and he braced himself for bad news. It was, but not what he expected. His father came back to where he and Carmen were sitting and said, "Mr Tapau has pointed out a significant possible legal snag. The Great Barrier Reef is a World Heritage Marine Park. Large parts of it are closed to anyone without a permit. There are 'green' zones for example, where all fishing is banned. He doesn't want to take his boat into any of them in case he gets into trouble with the authorities. He says he needs to know the location of this reef- its latitude and longitude."

Andrew was aghast. "But.. but that will let our secret out. How do we know we can trust him?"

His father made a face and replied, "We don't. But without his boat it is no go. I can't afford to hire a launch for days on end just on this sort of hunch. Besides, I think he has a right to know. After all, he is putting his launch and his livelihood at risk."

Put like that Andrew had to agree but he felt very uneasy about it. Reluctantly he and Carmen calculated, as near as they could, the latitude and longitude of Echo Reef. These were written on a note pad which he handed to his father. Mr Collins then went back to the telephone.

Carmen put a sympathetic hand on Andrew's arm. "Cheer up 'Grumps'. After all, our enemies already know the location too."

Andrew didn't like Muriel being called an enemy but he said nothing, just nodded.

Ten minutes later their father called to them, "It's Ok kids. The place is in a zone where recreational fishing and diving is allowed. I will just get a few other things organized."

He went back to the telephone conversation. From that emerged a number of key points, some good and others not so good. Among the good points were Mr Tapau saying he would arrange for the hire or loan of diving equipment and spare air cylinders. Among the not-so-good was learning that the *Moa Mermaid* had no air compressor and that she could only manage 8 or 9 knots, depending on the weather.

There was also the problem of when. By now Andrew was almost fidgeting with impatience, wanting to be on the way to Bowen the next day so he was dismayed to learn that it would not be till Wednesday, and that no diving could take place until Thursday at the earliest.

"But by then the holidays will be almost over! That only leaves four or five days for the search," he cried.

"Three," his mother commented. "You must come back on Saturday so as to be rested and ready for when school begins."

Andrew felt like saying piffle to school but managed to hold his tongue. Secretly he was in the mood to keep searching until the riddle was solved.

His father confirmed what their mother had said. "I can only take a few days off work. I need to be back at work next Monday too."

That told Andrew that his father was definitely coming. He turned to his mother. "Are you coming too Mum?"

"I'd like to," she replied, "But I can't leave the shop that long."

Secretly Andrew was pleased by that, suspecting that an anxious mother might be a dampener on the diving operations. The conversation next moved to the minor questions of what to take and how to pack and move it. Transport wasn't a problem as they would go in their father's car but there were a host of minor things to decide. Carmen set to work making a list.

The remainder of the day and evening passed in a flurry of excited preparations, Andrew feeling an itchy irritation of impatience. He was also being gnawed at by yet another worry- the weather. Knowing that bad weather could wreck the whole expedition he made a point of listening to the radio news and then watching the TV late news to see the weather chart. That wasn't so hopeful. The forecast for the Bowen area was for winds of 12 to 15 knots.

'That's not good,' he mused, remembering that winds of that strength would cause waves of up to 1.5 metres- right on the limit for safe diving. That night he did not sleep well. Once again he dreamt he was at sea on a sail boat which kept shrinking but then he found he was on deck and had lost his clothes and Muriel was coming (Or someone called Muriel as the face was all blurry). He tried to hide and to cover himself but he was too late and before he realized what was going to happen she kneed him in the testicles and pushed him backwards over the railings. He went deep into murky green water full of flitting shadows, unable to straighten up or swim.

Monday was a long day. As soon as he woke up Andrew turned on his radio to listen to the weather. That wasn't hopeful, with winds of up to 15 knots still predicted.

'Oh well, still a couple of days to go,' he told himself.

During the morning Andrew finished packing as much as he could, then sat around impatiently, unable to settle to anything requiring concentration. That led to a deal of brooding about Muriel and his dashed romantic hopes. The only bright spots were when some of Carmen's friends came over and the girls had quite a cheerful chatter session, with himself on the fringes. Among the girls were Jennifer, Shona, Tina and young Kylie Kirk and her friend Margaret, Graham's admirer.

"How did Graham go on the army cadet camp?" Andrew asked, genuinely interested.

"Really well so I heard," Kylie answered. "Apparently he helped save some kid who had been bitten by a snake."

"Being a hero again eh?" Andrew commented, his reply almost tinged with jealousy. To keep the conversation going he said, "Wasn't Graham bitten by a snake once?"

Kylie nodded. "Mmm. Yes. Two years ago. Some sort of brown sake."

"Ugh!" shuddered Jennifer. "I hate snakes."

"There aren't any snakes in England are there?" Margaret asked her.

"Only tiny little vipers and I can't wait to get back there," Jennifer replied.

There was then a general discussion about whether Jennifer liked Australia (She admitted she loved it and the people) and if she would be happy back in England when her dad finished his exchange posting with the Royal Australian Navy.

Kylie then asked, "What are we doing for the rest of the holidays?"

"We can go shopping," Shona suggested.

"What about the movies?" Tina asked, meeting Andrew's eye as she did.

"What about sailing, or a trip somewhere?" Margaret suggested.

"I want to go on a dive trip," Shona said. "It has been weeks and weeks and I have asked my Mum to take us out to one of the islands for a day. Who would like to come diving?" She looked at Carmen with raised eyebrows.

"I'd love to," Carmen replied, "But we are going to be away on a dive trip for a few days."

"Oh lucky you!" Shona cried. "Where to?"

"Off Bowen," Carmen answered.

Even as she did Andrew saw her frown slightly and he knew she was annoyed with herself. He had been alarmed at the trend in the conversation but did not know how to remind her to watch what she said without causing even more damage.

Shona looked surprised. "Bowen! That's a long way. Why Bowen?"

By this time Andrew was tense with anxiety. He looked hard at Carmen and she glanced at him, her eyes telling him that she knew she had made a mistake and was angry with herself. She shrugged and said, "Some friends down there invited us to join them. They have a boat and diving gear," she replied.

"Oh, you lucky things! Can I come?" Shona asked.

Carmen shook her head. "No, sorry. It is a family thing."

"When are you going?" Jennifer asked.

"Wednesday morning," Carmen answered.

"How about shopping tomorrow morning and then movies in the afternoon or evening?" Jennifer suggested.

Carmen seized on this to change the subject and shifted the talk to movies and which ones might be worth watching. Andrew was asked by Shona if he wanted to join them. "I'll get Blake to come," she added.

Andrew shrugged and declined the shopping but agreed to the movies. The conversation then drifted onto subjects Andrew wasn't interested in so he left the room and went to study his chart and to read once again about the loss of the *Merinda*. Later in the afternoon he drifted off to sleep while reading. Two hours of afternoon nap made him feel drained and he realized that the cadet camp and travel had probably taken more out of him than he realized.

The Weather Report on the TV news at 7:30 pm was reassuring. Winds had dropped to 12 knots and the announcer said they might drop even more the next day, with a further easing forecast for the day after.

A quiet night in front of the TV and then a good night's sleep with no dreams helped to revitalize Andrew. On Tuesday morning he slept in, then pottered around the house doing chores and fretting with impatience. The weather forecast stayed good, cheering him up even more. For a while he sat and looked at the chart and again reread the accounts of the loss of both vessels. To help with trying to work out what might have happened he redid his calculations and made up a timetable of possible events. Not satisfied with his answers he got Carmen to help when he worked out how long it would take to row a small dinghy from Cape Upstart to Hayman Island.

He worked out that it was 11 days after the cyclone that sank the *Merinda* before the *Deeral* sailed from Cairns. It was then another 15 days before Old Mr Murchison reached Hayman Island. Five days before that, on the 13th of February according to Old Mr Murchison, the *Deeral* had sunk.

Now mathematics cast doubts on that story. Andrew showed his note-book with its calculations to Carmen. "The *Deeral* could have been at Echo Reef by the fifth or sixth of February. They might have discovered the wreck of the *Merinda* anytime after that. That gives about six days to find the wreck and salvage the gold. So Murchison could have had anywhere between five days and eleven days in which to sink the ship and row him-self to Hayman Island."

"Or sail himself if the dinghy didn't have an outboard motor," Carmen added.

Andrew pointed to his figures. "Rowing at three knots he could have covered the seventy five nautical miles in twenty five hours."

Carmen shook her head. "Nobody could row non-stop that long. Eight or ten hours a day would be the maximum. I'd say it took him three days at least."

"That still left him six or seven days which we can't account for," Andrew commented. "It would have only taken four or five hours for the *Deeral* to travel from Echo Reef to Cape Upstart."

Carmen agreed. "Well, we might find something, but I'm going shop-ping. See you at two."

Andrew was left to mull over the facts. Leaving his notes and the chart spread out on his study desk he went and had lunch. Afterwards he got out his bike and rode over to Blake's. The two boys talked for a while, Andrew fending off answers to what he was doing for the remainder of the holidays and quietly turning down suggestions by Blake for sailing or swimming trips.

By 2pm the boys were outside the cinema. The girls arrived a few min-utes later: Carmen, Jennifer, Shona and Tina. When they all went inside and sat down Andrew found himself seated between Shona and Tina. That made him feel distinctly uncomfortable because he thought that Tina was making eyes at him and he still wanted to try to win with Muriel.

'Tina's alright,' he decided, eyeing her ample bosom out of the corner of his eye, 'but I'm being disloyal to Muriel.'

Resolving to be strong he concentrated on the movie and ignored any of the small accidental touches or looks that otherwise he might have con-strued as hints. His emotions weren't helped by having Blake and Shona 'pashing' right beside him. Jealousy and the stirrings of lust made him moody and irritable.

He found it a relief when the movie ended and they could all move outside. Blake and Shona then wandered off arm in arm and Tina was picked up by her mother. As she left she looked straight at Andrew, her eyes apparently full of wistful longing, and said, "Have a good holiday in Bowen Andrew."

Andrew nodded and waved her goodbye, then sighed with relief as the car drove off. Jennifer and Carmen stayed to be picked up by Jennifer's mother and Andrew unlocked his bike and rode home.

At home he parked his bike, unlocked the front door and went inside. After a visit to the toilet and a cold drink he went to his room. The first thing he did was stop and look down at the chart. As he did all thoughts of shipwrecks drained from his mind.

"That's funny," he muttered. "I thought I left my notebook on top of the chart?"

Even as he said this there was an odd clicking noise out in the courtyard. The sound caused Andrew to freeze. 'What was that noise?' he wondered. 'Is there a burglar in the house?'

Chapter 30

Bowen

What sounded like the faint screech of two metallic objects scraping on each other caused Andrew's hair to stand on end. His heart rate shot up and he looked anxiously towards his bedroom door. 'Was that the back gate?' he wondered. A steel gate closed off the breezeway connecting the courtyard to the back yard.

Stories he had heard of people coming home and finding burglars in their house rushed to the forefront of his consciousness. In many cases the intruders assaulted the person who discovered them. Andrew hesitated, anxious lest he become the victim of a bashing. Then shame drove him to act. 'Have a look, you great coward!' he chided himself.

Very cautiously he peeked out into the hallway. Nothing. No sounds either. As silently as he could he padded along the corridor to the back sliding door. At the door of each room along the way he paused, listened, then looked in, ready to counter any sudden attack. Nothing happened but at the back sliding door he got another shock and bit his lip in anxiety. The door was not locked and was not slid completely closed.

'Did Mum leave that unlocked?' he wondered. Sometimes when they were in a hurry they did not lock up as carefully as they might. Still unsure, and disgusted with himself for feeling so scared, Andrew carefully slid the door open, then the screen door outside it. This took a full minute as he did not want to make any noise which might alert a burglar to his presence.

That accomplished he stepped out and peeked around the corner of the brick wall and along the breezeway. Then he got another shock. The back gate was open!

The steel gate was partly ajar, but what really caused a chill wave of goose bumps was seeing the padlock that usually held it shut hanging undone in the bolt- and the padlock was swinging slightly! As there wasn't enough breeze to cause the padlock to swing Andrew could only deduce that someone had just opened the gate.

A glance assured him there was no-one hiding in the laundry and the storeroom door was closed. 'They are getting away!' he thought.

Fear gave way to anger and a concern to catch whoever it was. In ten steps Andrew was at the back entrance. Again he paused for a few seconds out of caution. There was no-one in the back yard but the timber board back fence had what appeared to be scuff marks on it. As neither he nor Carmen had climbed on it for years that got his attention. He hurried across the back yard and peered through the gaps between the planks.

A movement at the corner of the house to his left caught his eye. He stared hard but could see nothing. 'Did someone just go around that corner?' he wondered.

But what to do next? Andrew stood in indecision. He put his hands up, preparatory to climbing the fence, but then hesitated. Could he catch them? And if he did, could he prove they had been in the house? And what if there was more than one of them?

At that moment the sound of a car driving into the front carport came to him. 'Mum. I'd better warn her,' he decided. He hurried through to the front of the house, wondering along the way if anything had been taken. But the big attractive items like video recorders and computers and so on were all still in place. Meeting his mother at the door he asked her if she had closed the back door and back gate. She assured him she had made a particular point of it.

"Unless you opened them later?"

Andrew was sure neither he, nor Carmen had. That got them both searching the house to see if anything was missing or broken. A thorough search revealed nothing. While they were doing this Carmen came home and the story had to be told again. They all looked at the back gate and then searched the house again.

As they did Andrew had a worrying idea nagging at him like a sore tooth. However he said nothing about it to his mother and only when she was out of earshot did he put it to Carmen. He pointed to the notes and chart on his desk.

"I reckon this was what the person wanted. Someone was looking at this," he said.

"Muriel," Carmen at once added.

Andrew nodded and felt sick inside. "That's what I suspect. I think she has snuck in to see what we are up to; to try to find out what we know."

"Is anything missing?"

"No, but my notes have definitely been moved aside. I reckon she, or whoever it was, took a photo, like I did. If they had taken anything we would know for sure that someone had been," Andrew answered.

"But why? What is her motive?" Carmen asked.

Andrew shrugged. "To try to protect her grandfather?" he suggested.

The conversation was interrupted at that moment by their father arriving home. They did not tell him their theory either, but he had to be told about the intruder. Another check of valuables was conducted; and with the same result- nothing missing.

Their father scratched his head, "Beats me," he said. "But as nothing is missing we will just make sure we lock up properly next time. Now, let's get this expedition organized."

That helped, and at once got Andrew both excited and anxious. The fear of having to dive began to slowly grow, like a mental cancer in the pit of his stomach. But he was determined to go ahead with the search so pretended he was keen and helped with the packing and planning. There were more phone calls to Mr Tapau. He confirmed that they were ready and would be sailing from Mackay early next morning at about 0400 hrs. That would put them in Bowen by about 1800 hrs the next day, weather permitting.

The rendezvous was arranged and other details settled. That done Mr Collins reminded Mr Tapau that it might all be for nothing and that they could still say no and pull out if they wished. During supper he said the same thing to Andrew and Carmen.

"Even if we find this wreck I may forbid you to dive on it," he said. "If it is in water deeper than the thirty metres you are trained for- and I mean the seabed, not the top of the wreck, or if there are strong currents or whatever, we will call it off and get professional divers to do it for us. Is that clear?"

Both teenagers nodded and Andrew even felt a spasm of relief. 'If it is too dangerous I won't have to dive,' he thought.

There was also the weather. The TV map showed a large High Pressure cell moving slowly across the Great Australian Bight, with the comment that it might strengthen the winds along the east coast when it moved into the Tasman Sea in a couple of days time. Once again Andrew became both hopeful and anxious- wanting to dive but fearing it and telling himself that bad weather might save him from the ordeal. But that just made him despise himself for his weakness and he knew in his heart that he had to see this thing through or it would bother him for the rest of his days.

More packing followed. Mr Collins then urged brother and sister to bed. "You will be having a long day tomorrow and we don't want you tired out," he said.

So Andrew was in bed by 10:00pm, half an hour earlier than his usual time. But then he could not sleep. Fear of diving, anxiety over Muriel, excitement over the expedition, and a nagging worry that the intruder might return in the night to do something to him, all conspired to keep him restless until well after midnight.

Even then he did not sleep well, with several bad dreams that kept him tossing and turning and surfacing to semi-wakefulness. The bad dreams, or what he could remember of them, all involved being down in the sea, or under it, with big waves, darkness setting in, strong currents, dead bodies and the flitting shapes of sharks and other terrors of the deep.

Andrew woke feeling tired and sick, wondering if he could somehow call the thing off, to avoid the diving. There was also another worry which had grown during the night- should they leave their mother alone in the house if there was an intruder who had somehow gained access to their house?

Andrew put this concern to Carmen when he came out of the bathroom after his morning shower and shave. "Do you think Mum will be safe here on her own?"

Carmen nodded. "I think so. I've been thinking about that and I heard Mum and Dad talking about it. Dad is sure that whoever it was used the spare key to get in the font door. They certainly didn't break in."

That made sense to Andrew but raised another worry- who knew where the spare key was kept? It was really well hidden and not at all obvious. He wracked his brains to try to remember who might have seen him get it and came up with a list of his friends: Blake, Simmo and maybe Graham. There was no-one else he could think of.

'Is one of my friends the person?' he wondered.

The ugly thought that it might be Blake came to nag at him. 'Shona is also Muriel's friend,' he mused. Reluctantly he voiced these suspicions to Carmen.

Carmen nodded. "It will have been Muriel for sure."

Andrew gloomily agreed. "Now she will know where we are going."

"So what? She can't just suddenly up and organize an expedition. It's taken us nearly a week," Carmen said.

"I suppose so. I'm still worried about Mum though."

Carmen put his mind at rest by saying, "Mum is going to have the locks changed this morning. She will be alright. Now, have your breakfast and let's get going. We want to be on the road in an hour."

They were. Just after 0800 the car set off, with Mr Collins and Andrew in the front and Carmen in the back with the extra gear. With him in a folder Andrew had all his papers, notes and the chart. He also had a couple of books. That gave him plenty to read and think about when he wasn't talking to his father or looking out at the scenery. The view did not hold his interest very much, other than to note the milestones of their progress: Babinda, Innisfail, Tully, Cardwell.

There was a short stop in Cardwell for refreshments. While there Andrew looked out across the sea at the distant bulk of Endeavour Island and was gripped and aroused by the many scorching memories of the holiday in April. Carmen and he exchanged a few reminiscences but Andrew was very aware that the island holiday had been something of a traumatic ordeal for her. Tactfully he kept the conversation on the positives, making no mention of the murderous smugglers and the fiery finale.

At 1100 the journey was resumed, south along the Bruce Highway at 100kph through the dry forest and across the swampy coastal plain for 30km to the Cardwell Range. After crossing it they travelled on through the sugar town of Ingham and into the drier country towards Townsville.

By 1pm they were in Townsville. This meant a call on Aunty Bev (Their father's sister) and Uncle Mel. Lunch was eaten in the familiar dining room of the house where they had stayed for six weeks the previous December and January. Once again Andrew was assailed by vivid memories and the strong emotions they evoked of the dramas and adventures along Ross River at that time. He would have liked to drop in on the Schipholls and to see Mark, Jill and Anne but there was obviously no time. Nor did Carmen want any news about their expedition to leak out, feeling sure the Navy Cadet gossip grapevine would soon carry it back to Cairns and Muriel.

Just after 2:30pm they were on the road again. As they drove south out of Townsville Andrew was in the grip of conflicting emotions: nostalgic and erotic memories; a strong desire to solve the mystery; and growing anxiety about having to dive. What was particularly bothering him about this time was that it was such a small, ad-hoc expedition. He was uncomfortably aware that every other time he had been diving he had been surrounded not only by friends but by a team of highly skilled professional divers with all the right equipment for safety. This was altogether different and he admitted to himself that he was really scared.

As they drove, the car radio was kept on and Andrew listened anxiously to every weather forecast, torn by conflicting hopes. The predicted wind speeds were still just too strong for comfort but a least had not increased. The 'High' in the Bight was still moving slowly east but so far had not strengthened. It was the first time in his life that he had been so deeply conscious of the importance of the weather and gave him a new insight into how life might be.

Andrew had only ever been south of Townsville along the Bruce Highway a few times before and he had not paid much attention. Once again he was struck by how flat and how dry much of the country was. An hour's drive had them in the sugar town of Ayr. Then it was 20km more of flat open sugar cane farms to the Burdekin River and its huge road-rail bridge and the town of Home Hill. Then past more farms before the country became dry coastal lowlands of grass and savannah woodlands.

The main feature of interest from Home Hill onwards was being able to see the isolated, but very rugged outcrop of mountains on the left that was Cape Upstart. The sea was never visible as the highway was too far inland, but the mountains were visible in the distance for much of the drive. Just looking at them brought a flood of detailed memories of diving on the wreck of the *Deeral.* With the memories went the emotions of fear, mystery and determination to uncover the truth.

They passed through the small township of Merinda with its railway junction and derelict meatworks just before 5pm. Andrew had seen the name on the map and was interested to see the place. The reality was disappointing, although his father did point out that it had once been a much larger settlement and more important. However he did not know which came first - the town or the ship. To Andrew it just looked a sad, dry little place.

Don River was reached and they stopped at the roadhouse to refuel and for a feed. Half an hour later, and feeling quite worn out, they continued on. It was only a few kilometres more to Bowen. On arrival their father turned the car off the main highway and drove in through the town to the seafront. Andrew received a mixture of impressions- an old town with lots of timber 'Old Queenslanders'; wide streets with not much traffic; some quaint buildings and a general charm of being different from touristy Cairns.

The island studded bay Andrew found fascinating. Staring out over the broad waters of Edgecumbe Bay he said to Carmen, "Oh, this looks great! It would be fun sailing here. Lots of islands to explore."

Carmen nodded. "It certainly looks very pretty. A sailing holiday here would be a good idea."

Their father, who had been stretching himself beside the car, laughed and said, "Next year kids! Let's get this business out of the way first. Anyway, I fancy that small launch coming in across the harbour is the *Moa Mermaid.* Let's go and look."

As he climbed back into the car Andrew studied the launch in question. It was at least a kilometre out and did not look very big, but he felt sure it was the one they were waiting for. From that distance it looked tiny. It also looked old, being quite a dated design. 'I hope it is seaworthy!' Andrew thought, experiencing a distinct qualm.

His father took out his mobile phone and rang Mr Tapau. The answer confirmed that the launch they could see was indeed the *Moa Mermaid.*

Mr Collins put the phone away and started the car. Three minutes of driving had them at the end of the very long main wharf in the old part of Port Denison.

The main town wharf was a very long jetty poking out into the bay. By the time they had walked out along it the *Moa Mermaid* was nosing in to tie up. Andrew hurried on ahead to help with the mooring lines. These were heaved by Jordan, who stood on the focsle, his face one huge grin. Moses Tapau conned her in, his head and half his body leaning out of the half cabin so he could see better.

Close up Andrew was even less impressed by the *Moa Mermaid*. She looked small and old. He knew her to be 15 metres long, with a beam of 4 and a normal draught of 1.7m. She had a raised focsle which ended a third of her length aft. There was then a cabin. The cabin was almost open at the rear and a stern deck took up the last quarter of her length. The stern deck was just above the waterline and only the wooden bulwarks gave her a respectable freeboard aft. But what really bothered Andrew was the signs of age and the peeling paint. The launch had once been painted white above the waterline and bright red below but now it looked mangy and the red had faded to a scungy rust brown. A green fuzz coated the underwater. The sail lashed to a boom above the cabin looked yellowed and the ropes had a grey appearance that made Andrew wonder about rot. A battered plywood dinghy was lashed upside down on the aft hatch cover.

But if the vessel looked poor the greetings were not. The two Torres Strait Islanders clambered onto the jetty and vigorously shook hands, their faces wreathed in cheerful smiles.

"Good to be here eh?" Moses said. "Now we settle this business."

As they talked Andrew studied the two T.Is. Both wore only baggy old shorts. Their black skins gleamed in the sunset. Moses, Andrew noted, looked very fat without his shirt on. Jordan on the other hand, seemed to be all rippling muscles on his torso and arms. They were certainly likeable men and they radiated a sense of both fun and dependability that Andrew found reassuring. When he looked at the launch again he tried to tell himself it must be seaworthy.

'After all, they are professional fishermen. They go out on the ocean all the time in her.'

Despite that he still felt a bit uneasy at the prospect of going out of sight of land in such a tiny vessel. But there seemed to be no escape from that. He could not imagine what he could now say to back out. Knowing that he had talked himself into the situation made him annoyed with himself, even as he gulped with anxiety.

Work now began, lugging gear along the jetty and loading it aboard. It was dusk by then and the wind off the water seemed to drop to a chill quite quickly. It also felt quite strong, making Andrew worry that the weather might be worsening. Having moved the gear to the jetty beside the launch it was then stowed on board. To do this Andrew had to step aboard and then help pass things down onto the stern deck. It was then carried through into the cabin. During all of this the launch moved very noticeably as their weight shifted around it. It did not bode well for how she would cope with waves on the open sea.

Andrew made his way into the small cabin through the open rear section. Inside it was surprisingly homely, but also very smelly. The odours of diesel, oil, fish, paint and salt all assailed his nostrils. The cabin had a bench seat on either side and a table down the middle between them. The benches also doubled as bunks and under them were lockers. At the forward end were the steering wheel and controls and two short sets of steps. One set led up through a small doorway to the focsle. The other went down into the berth deck. On the port side at the forward end of the cabin was a chart table and radio equipment. On the starboard side opposite was the galley- a stove, refrigerator and larder.

Making his way forward and down into the berth deck Andrew found it stuffy and noted that it smelt even worse. There were four bunks, two on each side one above the other. A tiny shower cubicle was to the right of the companionway and the toilet on the left. But most obvious of all was the stump of the mast. The shiny, polished wood went straight down through the middle of the compartment. As he made his way past the mast to the bunk Jordan was indicating to him Andrew caught the whiff of linseed oil and he paused to sniff and then touch the polished wood. It felt lovely and smooth to the touch and he felt a bit better about the safety of the boat.

His gear he placed on the top bunk above Carmen. This gave him a view through a tiny, salt-encrusted porthole whose brass fittings were green with verdigris and salt corrosion. Their father placed his gear on the bottom bunk opposite and then told them both to go back up on deck.

Here Moses said, "We goin' ashore for dinner. I don't fancy Big Jordan's cookin', an' I don' feel like doin' it meself."

"What we gunna have?" Jordan asked.

"Fish and chips man, what else?" Moses replied with a laugh.

So the two T.Is slipped on loose cotton shirts and the whole group walked back along the jetty in the gathering darkness, leaving the launch snubbing at her moorings on the rising tide.

Chapter 31

Into the Night

As they walked away from the launch Andrew looked anxiously back at it. "Should one of us stay to look after the boat?" he asked.

Moses looked surprised and shook his head. "Nah. Why? The old girl sits at the wharf in the Pioneer River for days on end and we have no trouble."

Andrew had no answer to that but he still felt vaguely uneasy. All he could do to ease the worry was to note that the jetty was entirely deserted. There was not even a fisherman in sight and theirs was the only boat berthed there.

During the next hour and a half they went into town and found a cafe, ate fish and chips and then Mr Collins parked his car at a motel where he paid a fee for it to be looked after. That done they all took a taxi back to the wharf. It was 8:45 pm when they climbed out of the taxi at the end of the long jetty. In the darkness it looked much longer and quite spooky, just a few dim lights illuminating it.

As they walked out along the jetty in the darkness Andrew felt his vague sense of apprehension returning. There were now a few fishermen seated at long intervals but still no other boats. The whole scene was peaceful and quite pretty. The lights of the town danced on the rippling wave tops and the moon was just rising to throw a shimmering blanket of silver across the whole bay. The only obvious factor that might cause disquiet was the wind. It seemed to be stronger and felt quite chilly. That got Andrew worrying about the weather again.

Back on board he was able to relax. The boat appeared to be exactly as they had left it. But Moses now introduced another source of stress. He and Jordan unlashed the dinghy and lifted it off the aft hatchway, then raised the hatch cover. Then he gestured inside and said, "You kids had better look at this diving gear we borrowed and check it out. It looked OK to us, but, as I said, we ain't divers. The fella who loaned it, he say it good, but you make sure eh? If it ain't we have to arrange for some more tomorrow, if we can."

That really set Andrew's heart a-flutter. In front of his father and two relative strangers he had to demonstrate that he really did know what he was doing!

Jordan climbed into the hatchway. "This is our fish freezer normally," he explained as he passed up an air cylinder. Andrew gulped and took the cylinder, then carried it aft and laid it flat on the deck. Carmen took another and did likewise. Moses rigged a light on an extension lead from the end of the boom and their father helped lift things out.

Moses pointed to the wet suits and fins now spread on the deck. "These are the sizes you gave me. My mate Andy, he say you better take a few other sizes just in case, because gear that don't fit, leaks or really hurts to wear."

"You can say that again!" Andrew commented, remembering the fins he had worn during his pool training. He was feeling slightly better now because the gear was all so familiar and he had Carmen to help. To his own surprise he actually knew what to do to check it all. There were 10 air tanks and three regulator sets ('In case one goes bung,' Jordan commented). With very little hesitation Andrew screwed a regulator onto the tank valves, made sure the pressure gauge was face down for safety, then unscrewed the valve. Compressed air hissed gently in. On turning the gauge over Andrew saw that the air pressure showed 250psi, which was satisfactory.

Andrew next tested the smell of the air and then the actual regulator. It seemed to give air freely and the alternate worked as well. So did the inflator hose. While he did this Carmen tested a second regulator and air tank. Having checked the regulators Andrew and Carmen then tested each of the tanks and found them all to be satisfactory, all above 200psi at least.

Next Andrew tried on a BCD. Once having adjusted it, he partially inflated it and then deflated it. There did not seem to be any problems there but he was pleased to note a spare BCD on a clothes hanger. Carmen found hers to be satisfactory as well. Brother and sister then set to work making up their weight belts. Andrew knew what weights he needed and he threaded them on to the belt and then stood up and tried the belt for fit and for the working of the quick release catch.

That done he began the more mundane checks of face masks, fins and wet suits. As Andrew zipped a wet suit on his father nodded and said, "I am feeling a lot happier now. Watching you two has at least reassured me that you learnt something on those dive courses. You seem to know what you are doing."

Moses nodded. "Like professionals," he commented.

Andrew certainly did not feel like that. Now he felt scared. With the wet suit on and the face mask on his face and the water lapping alongside the fear of diving hit him with redoubled force. 'I'll be alright in the daylight,' he tried to reassure himself. But he was pleased to have been able to show he was competent with the equipment. That was something.

Once everything was checked they hung the wet suits and BCDs up on coat hangers and then carefully re-stowed the other gear back in the fish freezer. The hatch cover was secured and the dinghy lifted back on top and lashed firmly in place. Jordan grunted with approval at the seamanlike way both Andrew and Carmen tightened the lashings and then tied them with the correct knots.

By then it was 9:50 pm and Andrew felt very tired. As he and Carmen followed the others into the brightly lit cabin their father held out the mobile phone.

"Your mother. Tell her the news and then come and have some supper."

Andrew was glad to hear his mother's voice. It was more comforting than he wanted to admit. He assured her that he was alright and that the diving gear was good. Then he gave the phone to Carmen and went and sat down. A cup of hot cocoa was placed in front of him, along with some powdered milk and a tin of sugar.

"There's condensed milk there if you prefer," Jordan said.

Not having real milk was a bit of a shock to Andrew. Only once before that he could remember had he had powdered milk. Aunt Phoebe used it in her tea, claiming she liked it. Andrew remembered it as having an odd, 'squeaky' feel to it in his mouth when eaten dry with a spoon. Now, rather than admit there was a problem, he cautiously scooped a spoonful into his cocoa and then tried to stir it in. In this he was only partly successful and he hoped that none of the adults noticed the lumps. Sugar was easier and he did some more vigorous stirring, hoping the lumps of powdered milk would dissolve.

They didn't but he drank the cocoa anyway. Carmen joined them and handed the mobile phone to her father. She then set to work to make up her milk. Andrew watched enviously as she quickly whipped it into a cream which then dissolved completely in her drink. Seeing his interested look she said, "Guides. I learnt how to make powdered milk at guide camps."

Moses took a big slurp of hot cocoa and then put his mug down. "Well, we ready I reckon," he said. "We got the boat and a week's provisions. And we got the chart showing us where."

"We hope," Jordan interjected.

Moses grinned and went on, "And we got the divers and their gear. So we get under way now and we be out on the reef by sunrise eh?"

Mr Collins agreed and Andrew felt his stomach turn over with apprehension. Once the launch left the wharf he was irrevocably committed. Now is the time, he told himself, to admit he could not do it. But his tongue would not function and when told to go and cast off the stern mooring he just meekly did so. There was even a moment's temptation to stay up on the jetty but he told himself that would be even more humiliating as they would misunderstand and just come back in again.

So, without betraying any obvious signs of nervousness, Andrew tossed the stern line to Carmen, then ran forward and unhooked the bow line and threw it to Jordan. In three strides he was at the edge of the wharf and with one more he was on the foredeck. It was done- he was committed, whether he liked it or not.

His stomach churning with fear Andrew mechanically obeyed Jordan's instructions to coil the line and then stow it neatly. That done he made his way aft and down the tiny companionway into the cabin, pulling the door shut behind him. By then the launch was already twenty metres from the wharf and under way. The cabin lights had been dimmed and the only light visible inside was a shaded lamp over the chart table and a dim light inside the compass housing.

Moses grinned as he spun the wheel and then pushed the throttle. "No fancy radar and stuff like that on this old tub," he said.

"Only a GPS," Carmen commented, pointing to the Global Position System Indicator resting on the shelf in front of the compass.

"And a sonar set," Andrew added.

Moses laughed so loudly that his big belly quivered. "Yeah, well. That our fish finder. A man's gotta move with the times eh?"

Mr Collins now said, "You children had better get to bed. It is well after ten."

That was the last thing Andrew wanted to do, even though he felt quite exhausted. "Please Dad, not till we are out of harbour."

"Oh, alright. But then no arguments. You need to be rested before you start diving. I know that much."

Andrew promised he would. Carmen then asked if they were to share the watch during the night. Their father did not like that idea, shaking his head and insisting they sleep. "I can do that," he replied.

By this time the launch was several hundred metres from the wharf and was puttering quite rapidly across the small waves. Andrew walked over to the chart table and looked around. To port were the lights of the town, then another cluster that marked the yacht marina. After that there was an area of darkness that the chart marked as a mangrove swamp. Next the bulk of Flagstaff Hill stood up boldly. Lights twinkled from a building on top and there was a small cluster of lights indicating more buildings along the lower slopes leading out to Dalrymple Point.

For ten minutes the launch headed South East, almost directly towards a fairly large island. Andrew bent over the chart to check its name and noted several other islands as well. 'That big one is Stone Island,' he told himself. It had lights on it as well. 'There should be a smaller island off to port, with a lighthouse on it,' he noted.

Even as he turned to look Moses spun the wheel, bringing the launch around to port. Stone Island appeared to slide across the silvery sea and the small, rocky islet appeared. North Head he thought it was called, noting a South Head on the closest part Stone Island. The flash of a revolving light showed that there was indeed a lighthouse on the smaller island. 'We are going out through the North Entrance,' Andrew noted.

As the launch came out from the lee of Flagstaff Hill the size of the waves increased considerably. The bow began to pitch and punch. The first splatters of spray came rattling back onto the front windows. The movement became so pronounced that Andrew felt twinges of real alarm. Glances at Moses and Jordan, showing both chatting unconcernedly, helped to ease his worst fears but he still remained worried that the boat was much too small to go out on the open sea. But that was exactly where they were going and Andrew could only gulp and grip the bench as cold waves of fear swept through him.

The launch was turned even more to pass between Stone Island and North Head. It was then heading North East and the motion changed to a sickening and equally frightening rolling. Andrew watched the horizon slide up out of view, then roll quickly back down again. The waves appeared to be an endless succession of black crinkles sweeping towards them. Andrew felt sure that the launch was going to roll right over and he badly wanted to ask where the lifejackets were. But everyone else looked so calm he did not dare, for fear of looking foolish.

'This thing is going to capsize any minute,' he thought anxiously. For fear of being trapped in the cabin he walked aft onto the fish deck and pretended to be looking at the land. That did hold his interest well enough to dull the edge of the fear. He noted with some surprise that the small island with the lighthouse was actually quite a large island. Then, as the island slid past abeam, the launch altered course further to port and the motion again changed. Now they were taking the waves on the starboard quarter. That was very much easier, with only an occasional sickening yaw and sliding feeling as she went quickly down the face of a particularly big wave.

Carmen joined him and pointed back to starboard, indicating the long stretch of Kings Beach and then the rocky mass of Cape Edgecumbe. More lights twinkled there. "It looks nice even at night," she commented. "I've heard it is a lovely place to visit."

"We will," Andrew said, as much for something to say. "We will bring the catamaran and sail to all those islands back there."

"There are a lot, aren't there?" Carmen replied. "I counted five or six on the chart."

While they were discussing this their father came out. "Right you kids, into bed. It is after eleven."

"Aye aye sir," Andrew replied, thinking that was suitably nautical.

He and Carmen made their way forward, saying goodnight to Moses and Jordan as they passed through the cabin. Jordan was busy arranging bedding on the bench seat beside the galley. Down in the sleeping quarters Andrew was again assailed by anxiety. He almost had a bout of nausea at the smell. However there was nothing for it but to spread his unzipped sleeping bag and pillow and climb into the bunk. He did not change into pyjamas, instead staying in his shorts and shirt. Carmen did likewise so there was no embarrassment.

"Goodnight Sis. See you tomorrow," he said.

"And the wreck of the *Merinda*," Carmen answered.

At the mention of the wreck Andrew experienced a mix of emotions: strong desire to find it; anxiety about diving. He smiled at his sister and then rolled over. Carmen flicked off the light and Andrew stretched out and pretended he was asleep. But sleep was far away. Close to his face on the other hand was the grimy little porthole and he could see the moonlight glistening on the wave tops. From down near the waterline the waves looked enormous and spray continually flew past. Occasionally the launch rolled so that the porthole went under water. That was a mild source of anxiety as well but already Andrew was becoming used to the motion of the vessel and was less worried.

He did drift off into short snatches of broken sleep. The thing that brought him back to wakefulness was thinking about the course the launch was now on. She was now heading almost due north. A picture of the chart formed in Andrew's mind and on it was his memory of the pencil line drawn by Moses. When Andrew had studied it earlier he had noted that the planned course ran relatively close to both Nares Rock and Holbourne Island. Now, lying in the darkness and knowing that the launch was pushing its way across the dark sea close to a place with such a tragic history, he conjured up images he had read in accounts of the wreck of the *Gothenburg*.

His imagination now took over and he wondered if they were on course. 'If we aren't careful we might hit that rock too,' he told himself. So anxious did he become that he started to perspire. Unable to either sleep or set his mind at rest he rolled out of his bunk. For a few moments he studied Carmen in the darkness. She appeared to be sound asleep. So was his father. Tiptoeing so as not to disturb them Andrew made his way up the companionway to the cabin.

As Andrew came up Moses, who was at the wheel, smiled and said, "Can't sleep eh?"

Andrew shook his head. "Strange bed, and unfamiliar noises," he replied, by way of excuses. Moses just nodded to that and kept looking out through the cabin windows, steering easily and standing in a very relaxed stance.

On looking out the first thing Andrew saw was a distant flicker of light out to starboard. He stared for a minute or so, then pointed and said, "Is that a lighthouse?"

"Yep. Holbourne Island," Moses answered.

That gave Andrew and idea of where they were. For a few more minutes he looked out, scanning the sea in all directions. Because the moon had moved higher in the sky the sea now looked much darker, the waves larger and more forbidding. His mind told him they were no larger than before, were only one or two metres, but his emotions made them seem much bigger. To help calm himself he went to the chart table and stared at the chart, then out of the starboard side. All he could see were seemingly endless wave tops.

"Nares Rock is somewhere around here isn't it?" he asked, trying to sound casual.

Moses nodded and pointed off to the starboard bow. "Over that way a few miles. We won't go anywhere near it."

"Will we see it?"

"Nah! It's always below the water. That's why it's such a bloody danger to shipping. You know it ripped the bottom out of a big passenger ship way back in the Nineteenth Century?"

Andrew nodded. "Yes. The *Gothenburg*. In 1875. I read about it in a book."

"Yeah. I read an account of the diver's finding her that fairly gave me the creeps," Moses replied.

At that Andrew shuddered and images from the book he had read filled his anxious mind. Moses went on, "Yeah, I read that one of the divers who went down opened the door of a cabin and found two young girls who were drowned. He said they were holding each other and that their long hair was drifting backwards and forwards in the water. Fair gave me the shivers reading that."

It was just such images that were tormenting Andrew. He felt a spasm of horror which made him swallow. "I read that," he mumbled.

"Yeah," Moses continued, obviously relishing the ghoulish details, "And in another cabin he found a woman lying on her bunk like she was asleep, and in another was a woman standing up, her arms waving up and down as the current moved her, and her hair all floating around her head like seaweed."

For a few moments Andrew pictured these scenes and then experienced an attack of panic as he wondered if he would meet such ghastly things if the found the *Merinda*. Then he shook his head and told himself not to be silly. 'It was more than fifty years ago. There won't be any remains left.'

He voiced this to Moses, who nodded and replied, "Too right. The fishes and the crabs would have long since eaten up anything that hadn't rotted, other than a few bones maybe."

That was an equally disturbing idea to Andrew and he cast around for a way to change the topic of conversation. The only one he could think of was the weather but it worked. Moses told him that the midnight radio forecast for the next day was winds easing to 10 to 12 knots. "Anyway, if we can tuck into the lee of the reef the waves shouldn't be too bad," he added.

Soon after they passed Holbourne Island Andrew took himself back to his bunk, sure that he would never sleep with his mind filled with ghastly images of drowned people. However exhaustion took over and he slipped into a deep, dreamless sleep. He was woken from it at 0530 by Carmen.

"Come on deck," she said. "We are approaching the reef and there is another boat there."

Chapter 32

Underwater Search

Andrew swallowed with anxiety and immediately rolled out of bed. Still rubbing the sleep out of his eyes he made his way up to the cabin. Jordan was at the wheel and Andrew's father sat nearby, staring forward through binoculars. Moses lay asleep on the port side bench seat.

Carmen went back to the small stove where she was busy heating water. "Do you want some coffee or hot chocolate Andrew?" she asked.

"Hot chocolate," Andrew answered then immediately transferred his attention to the view through the forward windows. It was just light enough to see, a hazy grey, with the waves looking like moving wrinkles of lead. They seemed smaller than when he had gone to bed and he hoped the forecast had been right. Right ahead of them, just visible on the rippling horizon was a tiny grey dot which also moved. The horrible thought that someone else had beaten them to the wreck made Andrew squirm inside.

"Are they divers?" he asked as his father lowered the glasses.

"Fair go! Wait till we get a bit closer," his father answered.

Jordan took the binoculars and steadied them, at the same time bracing himself to keep the steering. "Looks like a pleasure launch, or a game fishing boat," he said. He then handed the binoculars to Andrew.

Andrew braced himself and struggled to hold the binoculars on the distant vessel. The motion of the launch was much livelier than when he had done his training off Mackay the previous week but now he was grateful for that experience as it allowed him to finally focus and hold the vessel in his sights. It was just a small launch he decided.

"Definitely not a trawler or anything like that," he commented, handing the binoculars back.

Carmen asked the question, "Do you think they are diving on the wreck?"

Jordan shook his head and laughed. "Doubt it. After all, this is the Great Barrier Reef. We have to expect to have a few other boats around. I'd say they are just recreational fishermen."

There was nothing more to be done so they drank hot coffee and discussed the weather. As 0600 came up Jordan woke Moses. The radio was switched on and they listened to the news and the weather forecast. This still predicted winds of 10 to 12 knots and waves to 1.2 metres.

Moses now took over the con. He switched on the echo sounding sonar. "Not looking for fish," he explained. "This is in case of uncharted reefs. This whole area has not been charted accurately. We don't want to join the *Merinda* on the bottom of the sea. Now, would you all go on deck and help Jordan keep an eye out for rocks and reefs."

They made their way up onto the foredeck. Jordan nimbly climbed the mast and settled himself at the small cross trees, clinging firmly against the rapid swinging of the mast as the launch rolled. Andrew would have liked to join him but Jordan said that was too much weight too high up so instead he stood holding the starboard shroud.

Having just looked at the chart Andrew felt a distinct wave of uneasiness as he looked out over the tumbling waves. In every direction, as far as the eye could see, there was nothing but water. Nor was there any sign of the reef, yet he knew there were several small ones in the area. To reinforce the sense of danger Moses now eased the throttle back so that the launch was only just making way through the water. The chart had indicated depths of about 60 metres but he well knew that any coral reef would be only a few metres below the surface and even awash at low tide. The sea bed could rise abruptly with vertical or near vertical sides.

It was cold out in the wind and his eyes watered but he stuck to the task, determined to do his bit and anxious lest they come to grief like so many other vessels had over the years. The sun slowly rose and a few clouds took more distinct shape. As so often happened what appeared to be a dark line of threatening clouds on the eastern horizon seemed to melt away and leave just a few thin layers. As the launch got closer to it the other boat became more and more distinct and Andrew became convinced it was anchored.

Moses steered straight towards it, reasoning that if it was anchored then it was in the lee of the reef, or in a lagoon. By 0630 it was only about a mile away. Another ten minutes of slow chugging brought it even closer so that Moses was able to study it through his binoculars and call out that it was just a pleasure launch with a couple of men on it.

When it was only about half a mile away Jordan suddenly shouted and they all looked where he was pointing. Andrew distinctly saw the line of distant ripples that could only be where waves were breaking on the windward side of a reef. On their side was an obvious area of calmer water.

After a last few really big waves that sent it rolling and pitching the launch suddenly slid into quieter water.

Jordan again pointed and called down, "I can see the reef. It is a few hundred metres to starboard."

Andrew shaded his eyes and stared, finally detecting the darker colouration of the water that indicated a coral reef just below the surface. He knew from the chart that Echo Reef was only about half a kilometre across- a mere speck in the ocean compared to many reefs but similar to Wheeler Reef where he and Carmen had done their advanced diving course. It seemed to be similar also in the fact that the water everywhere else appeared to be deep.

While looking towards the anchored pleasure launch another uneasy thought crossed Andrew's mind and he said, "Should we go near them? We don't want them to know we are looking for a wreck."

Moses nodded through the windows and spun the wheel so that the launch turned to starboard and headed directly for the reef. Jordan shouted down that he could clearly see the end of the reef off to their right. That made sense to Andrew as well because the chart showed it as an oval shape. The engine vibration slowed even more as Moses allowed the launch to creep in close to the lee of the reef.

"Bottom!" Jordan shouted. "I can see bottom: white sand."

"Got that on the sonar," Moses called back. "Shelving quickly up from about fifty metres. We anchor soon as we spot coral right ahead."

Jordan slid to the deck and went forward to where the anchor was lashed to the railings. He cast off the lashings and released the lock on the anchor chain. Then he lugged the anchor right up to the bow and made sure the chain was free to run. He then stood out on the tiny bowsprit, staring down into the sea, his arm above his head. Andrew kept looking anxiously into the water, afraid they would bump into an isolated coral head. Suddenly Jordan waved and then bent down and seized the anchor. His muscles rippled and he flung it overboard. The motor died away and the sound of the chain roaring out took its place.

A few minutes later the launch was safely at anchor and only about 50 metres from the dark shape of the coral. Close up in the lee of the reef the waves were quite small and the motion of the launch was just a gentle rocking. Andrew noted that both wind and current were running from the reef towards them, so that if the anchor dragged the launch would just drift off into deeper water.

'But so will we when we are diving,' he thought anxiously. That got him worrying about how strong that current might be. It was certainly tugging at the hull and rippling around the taut anchor chain. Another searching look around made him even more anxious. There wasn't a sight of land in any direction. 'This is worse than Wheeler Reef,' he thought. 'At least it has that little sand cay at low tide.' The feeling that they were very isolated and long way from any help made his anxiety about diving increase.

Moses come up onto the foredeck and studied the other launch through the binoculars. "Two blokes, an' they lookin' at us," he said.

That other launch was about 300 metres away, but still too close for Andrew's liking. He wished they had the place to themselves. He took his turn at studying it and saw a white painted pleasure launch of about 15 metres in length. It looked like hundreds of others he had seen- a slightly raised focsle, cabin and small fishing deck aft. The cabin had a steering position on top and there was the usual collection of radar and radio antennae and fishing rods. He saw one of the men clearly, a fit looking man with black hair and tanned body, wearing only shorts. The man was studying them with binoculars and that gave Andrew a real sense of unease. There was a second man working in the cabin and just visible from time to time.

"I hope they don't bother us," he said.

"We will leave them alone and hopefully they will leave us alone," his father answered. "Now, let's have breakfast and plan the day."

Jordan was the cook, and a good one. Breakfast was bacon and fried eggs on toast. When breakfast was finished and the washing up done (by Andrew and Carmen), they seated themselves around the table again. Moses came in from studying the anchor and weather.

"Not dragging," he said. "Low water now and the ebb just starting. We got to watch that so we don't get swung round and onto the reef."

Andrew wanted to ask if they really were at Echo Reef but knew it would insult the men's navigation. 'Besides,' he thought, 'they have a GPS to check with.' As a roundabout way of checking he voiced another of his fears. "I know this is Echo Reef, but what if Murchison got it wrong? He wouldn't have had a GPS. His navigation wouldn't have been that good."

His father answered that. "My Dad would have navigated here and he would have got it right I reckon, even just using the old-fashioned methods of sextant and chronometer. There is no other reef marked within at least ten miles. I think this is the place."

"Even if it isn't," Moses added. "We still have to check it, just to be sure. Now, how you kids gunna do that eh?"

Carmen answered that. She drew a sketch map of the reef as a rough oval aligned NE- SW. "I think we should just swim along the outside edge of the reef to begin with. While we do that you might take your dinghy and go back and forth across the top, if there is enough water, just in case the *Merinda* ran right up on the reef."

"Good idea," Moses agreed.

Mr Collins shook his head. "Don't forget that the dinghy is also the safety boat in case one of the divers gets into trouble."

Moses nodded. "So we don't go far each time."

Carmen stood up. "Right, it is nearly eight O'clock. Let's get moving."

At that Andrew's stomach turned over and he felt sick with fear. But, berating himself as a real coward, he did not tell anyone but meekly went off to get changed into his bathers and then to suit up. Twenty minutes later he stood on the fish deck testing his gear and checking Carmen's, all the while feeling so scared he thought he might throw up.

The next challenge was entering the water. By then the dinghy had been launched and Jordan and Mr Collins were both seated in it. By agreement Andrew and Carmen decided to go into the water on the side away from the other boat, so as not to make it obvious they were diving. But that meant that when Andrew looked out all he could see was deep blue sea and rippling waves stretching to the horizon. The ocean looked fearfully big and his imagination infested it with all manner of ferocious marine creatures.

But Carmen was in and signalling she was alright! And there was his father watching. Not wanting to make his dad ashamed helped. With a gulp of anxiety Andrew put his regulator into his mouth, steadied his breathing and then gripped his face mask and regulator and took the giant stride.

Splash! He was in. It was cold, it was deep, and it was terrifying. With an effort of willpower Andrew got control of himself. After inflating his BCD he spat in his face mask and adjusted it, all the while finning against the current to remain hidden from the other launch behind their own boat's hull. While he did this his body twitched with almost phobic reaction, cringing in anticipation of the jaws rending his body.

Carmen swam into his field of vision and signalled to dive. With a sob and the awful knowledge that he was a weakling and a coward Andrew signalled back and began deflating his BCD. Water came up half over his face mask, then he was back in the air again, then half under, then above the surface, then fully under. His heart rate shot right up and he knew he was gasping for air as though he had run a race.

Through eyes made blurry by growing panic Andrew glimpsed the bottom of the launch. That helped steady him. Using it as a reference point he focused, noting the weed growth. Nearby was the bottom of the dinghy, clear on the rippling silver surface. And there was the anchor chain descending in a tight curve down to the bottom. Looking around under the water actually steadied him. There was a familiarity to it and he realized he could see the edge of the reef only a short distance from where the anchor was embedded in the sand.

Looking behind him didn't help. Away from the reef the water quickly grew deeper and shaded into deep blue or spooky looking purply-grey. 'Just like Shark Alley at Wheeler Reef,' Andrew thought. That got his heart rate up again and he quickly swam over to the anchor chain and then went down it and away from that awful nothingness.

Carmen helped. She was beside him and kept giving him encouraging nods and smiling. A check of his depth gauge told Andrew he was at 12 metres when he reached the anchor. 'That is nothing much,' he thought. Feeling slightly better he followed Carmen away from the security of the chain and towards the dark mass of the reef.

The dinghy went churning overhead, the whirring of its propeller sounding unnaturally loud in the water. Seeing it go on ahead got Andrew all anxious again and he hurried to catch up with Carmen. She waited for him and together they swam past the first isolated outcrops of coral until they reached the edge of the main reef. Here it was only ten metres deep and Andrew felt much safer. Now the scary deep water was only on his right and he had the comforting barrier of the reef on his left to protect him from any large predators in that direction.

Even so he kept looking anxiously back over his shoulder and peering into the gloom ahead for the first tell-tale sign of a shark or whatever. For a while he quite forgot he was actually looking for a shipwreck and instead just swam along beside Carmen, keeping her on the outside.

Slowly his fears eased back. Partly it was familiarity with the environment. It was just like Green Island and Wheeler Reef. And the diving was now almost mechanical. Without even really thinking about it Andrew cleared water that had trickled into his face mask. He also remembered to keep a careful check on the time, on the amount of air left, and on the direction they were swimming.

By agreement they had begun searching counter-clockwise. This was partly on the theory that that side of the reef was more likely to have been the one struck by the *Merinda*, but also because it took them well away from the other boat. So they swam South West, then South as they followed the edge of the reef around. It soon became obvious that the current was stronger on the south side of the reef.

'Because the prevailing wind is pushing it that way,' Andrew reasoned. He went back to scanning the bottom, particularly out in the deeper water, hoping for any sign of a ship wreck.

After twenty minutes of steady swimming they had covered about 400 or 500 metres but were now pushing against a really strong current as they came around onto the curve of the south eastern side of the reef. Carmen attracted Andrew's attention and pointed to her watch, then indicated she had only about 100 psi of air pressure left in her tank. Andrew had even less, only 80. He knew that was because of his gasping breathing at the start and felt ashamed of himself.

It was a big relief to turn back though, even if they had not discovered the wreck. Going back was much easier. Most of the time they just finned along, helped by the current. It only took them ten minutes to return to their start point, the swim only notable for the sudden appearance of a large wrasse which darted into a crevasse and vanished. To his own surprise and relief Andrew recognized the coral formations where they had first reached the reef. He was even more relieved to see the anchor and chain and the dim shadow that was the launch.

He and Carmen slowly rose up the anchor chain, holding on against the current while they kept their rate of descent within safe limits. Five more minutes had them clinging to a couple of old car tyres slung over the starboard side of the launch as fenders. As the *Moa Mermaid* wasn't a dive boat there was no platform or ladder so getting back aboard was a lot more difficult. Moses reached down and took their fins and masks and then helped heave them up one by one. Andrew went last, using the tyre as a step.

Once back on board Andrew sat down immediately, every muscle trembling. Moses helped Carmen off with her gear and then moved to assist him. "Cold eh?" he asked.

Andrew nodded, then added, "And I'm not very fit. That current is stronger than it looks."

While they de-suited and packed their gear the dinghy returned. It was obvious from the faces and body language that they also had discovered nothing. "Very shallow, and no big gullies or swim throughs at this end," Jordan explained.

Hot drinks were provided and the explorers sat around the cabin table to discuss their next move. Carmen pointed on her sketch map to show where she thought she and Andrew had explored to. "About a quarter of the reef," she commented.

Her father shook his head. "No. The reef is at least seven hundred metres across. That would give an approximate circumference of at least two thousand metres. You say you only swam about four hundred."

Carmen shrugged. "So a fifth. That's not too bad for a first go. Next time we will go the other way and I think we will get further because it is more in the lee of the reef."

"That takes us towards that other boat," Andrew cautioned.

"So what? They won't see us. We have to search that area, and the safety boat can just pretend to be fishing," Carmen said.

That was agreed to. Having decided on their next move both Andrew and Carmen sat together to calculate their residual nitrogen and safe dive times and depths. They then went below to change. Andrew had a quick fresh water shower to wash off the dried salt from his skin, then lay down on his bunk to think. As a two hour break was planned Andrew closed his eyes to rest. To his annoyance he found his mind replaying the underwater images he had just seen. That got him anxious about the next dive but also stirred his determination to find the wreck.

He didn't sleep but he did doze and the rest freshened him up considerably. Another big drink of hot chocolate helped even more. By then it was 1030 so he and Carmen again suited up and prepared to dive. This time Andrew wasn't quite as anxious but it still took an effort of willpower to make himself jump into that sea. Both Moses and Jordan went in the dinghy- as a plan to hide the fact that divers were at work. The two T.Is set off to act as innocent fishermen near the other launch.

Once underwater Andrew and Carmen again went down the anchor chain and finned in to the edge of the reef. Here they turned left and headed North West. The tide was now rising but the current in close to the reef was negligible and they were able to swim along easily. There was a lot more marine life in this more sheltered area and the coral growths were more spectacular and fragile- lots of layered and branching coral. Swarms of multi-hued fish provided interest and nothing too large appeared to alarm Andrew.

For ten minutes brother and sister swam steadily along. It was plainly obvious that there was no shipwreck in this area as the coral ended abruptly and with no canyons or gullies in it. To their left the sandy sea bed sloped off as before but at an ever decreasing angle so that it became a very gentle slope dotted with small coral outcrops. Looking at that got Andrew anxious again.

'I hope we don't have to swim way out there away from the reef,' he thought, deciding that any shipwreck in this area would be hundreds of metres out from the coral.

Quite abruptly the pattern changed. They began to encounter strong currents which stirred up the silt and lowered visibility. The currents were coming from their right and the main reef curved that way into a very obvious and deep gully.

'This might be it!' Andrew thought hopefully as he followed Carmen into the gully. It had a sandy bottom and was bigger than he at first suspected, with large outcrops of coral in it. The depth to the bottom was at least another ten or fifteen metres below the ten they were swimming at. Larger fish appeared, including a school of coral trout so big that Andrew became alarmed in case one bit him.

The pair swam South East along the deep gutter for five minutes before Carmen shook her head and signalled to turn back. Andrew understood why. The current was being funnelled through the narrower sections and was just too strong. 'We need to explore this at slack water or on the ebb,' he reasoned.

Carmen crossed to the far side of the gully, a good fifty metres away and continued on North East. They again encountered large outcrops and several times they scared stingrays or large fish. As the pair swam slowly along Carmen angled up towards the surface. When they neared the top she made porpoising motions with her hands, by which Andrew thought she meant she was going to surface but only briefly, then dive again.

That was indeed her intention. As they broke surface Andrew looked around. About a hundred metres off to his left front he saw the white launch riding at anchor. What looked a very long way to his left was the *Moa Mermaid*, rolling at anchor. Of the dinghy there was no sign. Before Andrew could remove his face mask Carmen pulled out her regulator and called, "Dive! We don't want those people to see us."

He was ready for that and immediately began to deflate his BCD. As he slipped back under he looked towards the white launch, his anxiety level going unreasonably up. This time he sank to the bottom with barely a thought for the things in the sea. Carmen made him check his air and the time. They had been in the water for nearly half an hour by then and this time his air was only down to 150psi so she signalled OK and started off swimming to the North East.

They kept on for another five minutes, rounding the northern tip of the reef and starting to swim south along the outside. By then the nature of the reef had changed again. Now it was steep-sided coral in layers which went down deeply to a barely visible, steep, rocky bottom.

As he strained his eyes to see down into the gloom Andrew shook his head. 'If the *Merinda* is down there we will never be able to dive on her.'

There was no sign of any wreck and the water became so deep they could not even see the bottom. The current also grew stronger and the waves overhead could be seen breaking on the edge of the reef above their heads. Even at ten metres depth Andrew felt the suck and surge of the waves so he moved further away from the coral so as not to get accidentally dragged onto it. Carmen shook her head, pointed to her watch, and turned back.

At that moment Andrew saw the shark.

Chapter 33

Where?

Andrew felt his heart stand still. Fear surged and he seemed to freeze up. There it was- his worst nightmare- and heading directly towards him! He wanted to warn Carmen, to cry out, to flee- but all he could do was stare as though paralysed. The shark had appeared from out in the open ocean, swimming directly towards the reef. To Andrew it looked huge and he stared at the grey-white shape as though mesmerized.

Abruptly, when about 25 metres away, the shark changed direction and headed the same way that Carmen was now swimming. Andrew clearly saw its left eye- a black, evil looking eye, he thought. He was sure it was measuring him up for a meal. With his heart rate and breathing both rapidly increasing he managed to turn to face it.

He thought it was a grey nurse, but wasn't sure. 'They are man-eaters,' his anxious mind told him. As it swam closer Andrew could clearly see its gills and the fins which were the blood-chilling trademark of the creatures. Bracing himself to fend it off he wished that he had some sort of weapon, even a knife. He also wished he had not swum out so far from the protecting edge of the coral.

A glance behind to see just how far he was from the coral did not reassure him. It was at least 10 metres and he was sure the shark could cover that in a flash. Hastily he looked back, to be astonished again. The thing was nowhere in sight!

Now he did panic, swivelling his head in all directions to try to detect where it had gone, all the while cringing in anticipation of its bone and gristle-tearing rush. A flicker in the blue off to his left caught his eye and he turned to look that way.

It was the shark. To Andrew's intense relief and surprise he saw that it was swimming away, following the edge of the reef around. 'That is the way we want to go,' he thought with dismay. A moment's consideration told him that they could not possibly swim right around the other side of the reef to get back to their boat. Nor could they safely swim across the top of the reef.

Only now did he look at Carmen to see if she was aware of the shark. She was and was pointing and appeared to be smiling. Smiling! Andrew shook with relief and amazement. But the thing was gone, vanished from view around the curve of the reef. Carmen resumed swimming in that direction and Andrew had no option but to follow. Now, more than ever, he kept moving his head continually to look back over his shoulder, to look beneath him and to look ahead.

He found it a real relief to swim back around the northern corner of the reef into shallower water. At least he didn't now have that gloomy blue abyss beneath him! Of the shark there was no sign, but Andrew kept a very sharp lookout. Even when they entered the area studded with big coral outcrops in the northern end of the large gully he kept anxious watch.

Thus it was that he spotted the movement. For a second he stared, thinking it was the shark. Then he saw that there were two dark things moving and realized they were divers.

'Divers! What are they doing?' he wondered. For no reason he could have articulated he knew he did not want those divers to see him or Carmen. Luckily he was close to her and was able to reach across and tap her. As she looked at him he pointed at the divers, then tugged at her BCD and pointed down.

Carmen understood at once. Both began to descend. Andrew led the way, finning down behind a large coral outcrop which had a series of wide, flat overhangs. After a quick check that nothing with teeth, claws or sharp spines was lurking in under the coral overhang he moved right into its shadow. Carmen joined him. Hoping they had not been spotted Andrew peered out at the other divers.

They were about 50 metres off and were swimming side on to them. They appeared to be heading south along the deep gully that he and Carmen had explored earlier.

'They must have come from the white launch,' Andrew surmised. But were they just recreational divers or spearfishermen- or were they also searching for the wreck?

Andrew was very conscious of the stream of bubbles that swirled up every time he or Carmen breathed out but there was nothing much he could do about it, other than hope that the other divers did not notice them. He could clearly see their bubbles, even at that distance. But the two divers kept on swimming and did not appear to look in his direction.

To his relief they vanished into the silty gloom of the deep gully. As soon as they were no longer visible Carmen tapped him, pointed to her air pressure gauge and then resumed swimming. Andrew looked at his own gauge and was shocked. It was down to 70 psi and he remembered being warned on the course not to let it get below about 80, so as to have a margin for safety.

'We can always surface and inflate out BCDs by mouth,' he told himself as he finned out of cover in Carmen's wake.

He did not need to do that but was down to 50 psi by the time he and Carmen surfaced beside the *Moa Mermaid*. The dinghy was back and they were able to pass up heavy items into it before being helped up over the side of the launch.

A very anxious father met them. "I was gettin' really worried about you kids. What took you so long?" he asked.

Carmen described their dive while Andrew slumped down and towelled himself vigorously. The men listened with interest, especially to the story of the shark and to the incident with the two divers.

Moses nodded. "Yeah, we seen them getting' ready. So I take it you didn't find anythin'?"

Carmen and Andrew both shook their heads. "Did you?"

"Nah!" Moses replied disgustedly. "We went right up that big gully till it got too rough near the far side. Then we come back and went driftin' past that white launch. *Silver Stingray* she's called. Registered in Sydney."

"Did you speak to them?" Andrew asked.

"Nah. Just waved to a guy as we drifted by. He waved back and went on fishin' too. We went right out to the North West for a few hundred metres. Shallow for a long way that way. All white sand with a few outcrops of coral. But no big shipwreck."

"So where is it?" asked Andrew in exasperation. "We've looked all along this side of the reef and around both ends."

Carmen made a face and added, "Which means that it must be in the deep water on the other side of the reef."

Andrew felt quite depressed at that idea, remembering the gloomy dark blue depths and strong currents. "If it is we may never find it, and even if we do it will probably be too deep for us to dive on," he commented.

"We still have to look though," Carmen answered.

"We need to search off to the North West too, to the edge of this shallow flat area," Jordan put in.

"It is more likely to be there isn't it," Mr Collins asked. "I mean, that is the sheltered side of the reef and a ship in trouble would head for shelter."

That jogged something in Andrew's brain and he shook his head. "Not necessarily," he replied. "If it was taking shelter from a cyclone it would depend on the wind direction at the time. That wouldn't be the normal prevailing wind direction."

"By jelly beans! You might be right," Moses cried.

Andrew thought for a moment, dredging up knowledge of cyclones from Geography lessons he now wished he had paid closer attention to. Then he said, "If the cyclone passed to the south of here then the wind would have mostly have come from the south and even the west. If the cyclone went by to the north of here then the main strength of the wind would have changed from southerly to easterly, then to northerly after the eye had passed onto land."

Carmen suddenly clicked her fingers. "It went to the north. I read that in one of the old newspaper accounts. The cyclone's eye crossed the coast near the mouth of the Burdekin."

"So by then the *Merinda* might have been sheltering around on the south side of the reef," Andrew suggested. "That might explain how those survivors got blown past Holbourne Island."

"Maybe," Moses agreed, adding, "But I doubt if those fellas on the ship had any idea where they was. Not back in them days, not after a day or so of really bad weather."

Jordan chuckled and said, "I know fellas what don't have much idea where they are even now, even with satellite navigation stuff."

Moses laughed out loud and replied, "You better not be talkin' about me brother, or you'se gunna have a long swim home."

"Just thinkin' of that time off Carson Reef," Jordan answered with an innocent smile. "Weren't even a cyclone," he added, winking at Andrew and Carmen as he did.

Andrew tensed with anxiety lest the two T.Is be about to have an unpleasant argument. To his relief Moses laughed too and then said, "We was only a little bit off course. But them fellas in the *Merinda,* they were certainly a long way off course, like fifty nautical miles off course."

"If a cyclone went on for a day or two, like they do, that is only a few miles off course each hour," Jordan said. "They would have been changing course as the wind direction veered, to try to keep her head into the wind."

"Sure," Moses agreed. "But it might give us an indication of the ship's heading when she struck. I don't think them fellas was sheltering in the lee of the reef. I bet they didn' even know it was here till they hit it."

Andrew felt a surge of excitement. "I think you are right," he said. "Which means that the most likely location is on the south side of the reef. That is where we should look next."

"OK, we will," Moses agreed. "But you kids is gunna have lunch and then a good rest for two or three hours before you go divin' again. An' this time you stay close to the dinghy. It ain't gunna be no picnic around there."

"Could you search with your 'Fishfinder' echo sounder?" Carmen asked.

At that Moses looked both thoughtful and worried. "Could, but I don' wanna. If we stack this boat on the reef we lose our business eh?"

Carmen nodded. "Sorry. Don't take any risks with the launch just to satisfy our curiosity. Now come on Andrew. Let's work out our residual nitrogen and plan the next dive," she said.

For the next fifteen minutes brother and sister did their calculations. They then joined the adults for lunch. Andrew was feeling quite worn out and had no appetite but his father insisted that he eat to get his energy up. Hot, sweet Milo helped. For half an hour they sat and studied the plans of the *Merinda.* Then he and Carmen went below to lie down and rest.

Andrew did not sleep but he dozed. While he lay on his bunk staring out of the porthole at the tossing wave tops he agonized over whether he would be brave enough to go back into the water. The shark incident had frightened him more than he was game to admit to the others and now he kept replaying the scene in his mind. Each time he pictured the speed at which the sleek, grey shape had approached; how suddenly it had appeared, he broke into a cold sweat.

'It could have attacked before I even knew it was there,' he told himself.

But stubbornly his sense of curiosity got him thinking about where the wreck might be. He tried to picture what it might be like to be on a ship in a cyclone and could only shudder as he imagined the sick feelings of despair and helplessness the people must have felt during those terrifying minutes when it must have been obvious that the ship was in dire peril.

'I hope I'm never in a cyclone at sea,' he thought. Other images crowded in, mostly from an account he had read of American warships in World War 2. As a result of some blunders in the Chain of Command a fleet (The 3rd he thought?) had steamed into a typhoon. Ships as large and powerful as fleet destroyers had been overwhelmed and capsized by the storm. For a few minutes Andrew pictured himself as one of the crew members, locked below and scared stiff. Thinking of what it must have been like as the ship's deck rose and fell beneath his feet caused him to shudder. The effort of imagining what it might have been like after the destroyer rolled over and went under brought him out in a cold sweat. The idea of being trapped inside a sinking ship, knowing that even if no water made its way into the compartment he was in he was doomed, was more than he could face.

'Maybe I shouldn't be a sailor?' he wondered. 'Or maybe not in the navy?' He knew that in warships they closed all the watertight doors when at 'Action Stations'. Now he fretted about whether he was good enough to cope with such a claustrophobic situation. 'I would hate to be locked in and trapped, knowing I was going to die and having time to think about it,' he thought.

He found it a relief to be called on deck to help weigh anchor. Moses explained. "The wind is veering more to the north. It is blowing almost from the east now. That suits us as we can now anchor closer to where you want to explore, except the bottom slopes away more steeply from the reef and the anchor may not hold."

"Is the weather getting worse?" Andrew asked, worried that they might have to give up the search.

Moses nodded his head. "Yep. Sorry, but the radio reckons the wind is going to increase a lot more and swing round to more of a northerly."

Now that he looked Andrew noted that the launch was rolling more and had swung round to lie parallel to the reef. The launch was now much closer to the reef and if the wind veered even more northerly she would be in danger of being pushed onto the coral.

It took them half an hour to up anchor and motor very slowly around to the south side of the reef. As Moses had feared the seabed dropped away much more steeply but by nosing in close to the edge of the coral they were able to get the anchor down and holding, without snagging or damaging any of the coral. That left them again riding safely in the lee of the reef, with the launch being blown away from the danger.

It was a more precarious anchorage though and Moses stayed up on the foredeck watching anxiously for any sign of the wind changing direction again. As they studied the situation Jordan grunted and pointed. "That white launch, she movin' too."

"Sensible," Moses commented. "She be feelin' it worse than us over there."

Andrew resented the presence of that other vessel and he wished it would go away but had to admit it was prudent seamanship to move to a more sheltered anchorage as the wind shifted. Feeling vaguely annoyed and anxious he watched the white launch motor slowly towards them, heaving to and anchoring only about a hundred metres to port.

Jordan shook his head. "She should have come closer to us. She is barely in the lee even now."

"That's close enough for me," Moses replied. "If the wind gets up and either of us starts draggin' our anchor we don' want to be too close."

Carmen looked at her watch. "It's nearly three. Come on Andrew, let's suit up and get on with the search."

Andrew felt his stomach turn over again, all his fears of sharks and the deep blue sea swirling in his churning insides. But to his own self contempt all he could do was nod and walk back to where his wet suit hung swaying on a coat hanger. Despising himself as a coward and a fool he slowly tugged on the suit and zipped it up, then reluctantly set about checking and fitting the remainder of his equipment. This time he insisted on taking a knife, sliding it onto his weight belt.

After doing the pre-dive checks with Carmen he forced himself to make his way to the railing ahead of her and to jump in. Once again the shock of the cold and of fear gripped him and he had to force them out of his thoughts. The close presence of the dinghy with his father and Jordan in it helped. So did the need to fin strongly to stay hidden from the other launch. The current was much stronger here, but the wave pattern was confused and had not yet settled to the new wind direction.

Carmen joined him. Both bobbed there, finning strongly and held up by their BCDs while they spat in their facemasks, and adjusted them. During this Andrew incautiously left his snorkel out and got a mouth full of salt water. This made him feel even sicker and he hastily rinsed his mask and slipped it on. He found it almost a relief to slip under into the quieter water below the surface zone.

It was scary though. Below and behind loomed the deep water and he had to force himself to keep on releasing air from his BCD to make himself attain negative buoyancy. Then he found he had to fin hard to stay near the launch. Knowing that to a shark beneath him he must be clearly silhouetted helped. To get away from a perceived danger zone Andrew made his way down along the anchor chain as quickly as he could safely equalize.

The anchor was wedged in coral rock and silt only a few metres from the living coral and seeing that made Andrew worry about them possibly causing damage to the reef. He knew it was against the law but he also cared. Satisfied that neither the anchor nor its chain would cause any damage while the wind blew from that direction he turned his attention back to the search.

He recognized the general area where they were and was glad it was close to where he and Carmen had turned back on their first dive. Again he led the way, finning along at a depth of 10 metres, while keeping about 5 metres out from the wall of living coral. 'Far enough so that no sea snake or moray eel can just lunge out and get me,' he thought, knowing that such fears were largely irrational, but quite unable to suppress them.

As before he swam with his head continually swivelling, scanning in all directions for any signs of danger (That shark!), and keeping an eye on

Carmen as she followed close behind. After only about fifty metres he recognized a particularly brilliant set of huge, overlapping coral 'plates'. He caught Carmen's eye and pointed. She nodded and smiled. Soon after that they rounded the curve where they had turned back on their first dive and Andrew again pointed and then waited to check that she was alright.

Above and behind them was the dinghy. It was following their bubbles and could be clearly seen bobbing about on the surface. Feeling happier because of that Andrew swam on. The current was strong but he could not decide if it was stronger than before or not. The tide, he knew, was now on the ebb, but he wasn't sure what effect that might have on the reef waters. What mattered was that they were able to make steady progress against the current, although it took a continual effort.

Andrew noted a particularly large outcrop of brown coral ahead and hoped it did not harbour any lurking nasties. Just in case there were any he kept a close eye on the crevices in it as he swam around it. Then he looked ahead and the shock caused him to stop finning.

There it was!

The wreck!

Chapter 34

Coral Growths and Seaweed

Andrew stared at the weed and coral encrusted shape and felt an intense glow of satisfaction. There could be absolutely no doubt it was the wreck of a large steel ship. There was also no doubt in Andrew's mind that it was the wreck of the *Merinda*. 'No other large ship has ever been reported as missing along this section of the Queensland coast,' he told himself.

The wreck was lying almost beam on to the reef. The stern was towards Andrew. Only a few metres below him were the rusted remains of what he was sure was the boat deck. Now all that detailed study of the ship's plans paid off. He saw that the timber planking had all rotted, leaving only the steel framework. This was now so thickly encrusted with coral growths and seaweed that the living matt almost replaced the original decking.

Carmen appeared beside him, obviously grinning. Feeling elated at the success of the search Andrew smiled back and gave her an OK. Then he swam a few metres further out from the wreck to get a clearer view. So absorbed was he that he temporarily forgot to be wary of the gloomy, blue depths to his right. What he could not ignore though was the need to keep finning strongly against the current.

He now saw that the wreck was resting on the edge of a very steep slope. It appeared to be so precarious that he wondered why it had not been dislodged by storms and slipped down into much deeper water. Only when he swam forward to where the bows were hidden in a mass of brown coral did he see that they were deeply embedded in a large crevasse.

'Smashed into the reef and then broached port side to on the reef,' he decided.

There was just enough sunlight to see quite clearly for about 20 metres. After that it all got murky and blurred. To get a clearer picture of just how the ship was wedged in the coral Andrew swam slowly forward, keeping about five metres up and out from the starboard size. The wreck swarmed with small fish but he ignored them and even forgot to worry about larger marine creatures. It was the most exciting and fascinating discovery of his whole life and he stared at it in wonder.

The whole of the boat deck had been swept clean by storms. All that remained was the coral and weed encrusted framework. Of the funnel and masts there was no sign. The only signs of the wheelhouse were a few nobbly looking stanchions and what might have once been the pedestal of the binnacle. There was then a sharp drop down to the forward well deck. Here a gaping black rectangle marked where the hatch covers had once been on the cargo hold. That looked quite forbidding although Andrew did note that along this section of the lower hull there were plates missing and a series of jagged gaps showed.

'She must have been battered a bit by the reef before she swung round to stick the way she now is,' he thought.

The aft end of the focsle was plain to see. Clearly outlined in it was a doorway. The steel door stood ajar and both it and a companionway beside it were thickly covered with coral and weed growths. Beyond that was a big lump of coral that he thought might hide the remains of a winch or capstan. Forward of that everything was hidden by the reef. This had grown out over the focsle and accounted for the wreck remaining upright and held in place.

Feeling absolutely thrilled, Andrew decided that he should have a look inside. There was only one part of the ship he was really interested in- the strong room. From studying the ship's plans he knew that was one deck below the main deck and on the starboard side. 'That should be easy to reach,' he decided. What he really wanted to know was whether the door to the strongroom was open.

'If it is then Grandad and Old Mr Murchison did find the wreck and dived on her,' Andrew told himself. 'And if the gold is gone, then Murchison took it.'

To do this Andrew allowed the current to take him back along the length of the ship. As he approached the end of the cabins, their locations plainly obvious from the circular portholes, he swam down to the level of the main deck. As he made his way aft he peered briefly into the cabins as he went past each porthole. On reaching the sheltered main deck aft of the cabins he reached out to grasp a stanchion which must have once held the boat deck up. Just in time he refrained from grasping the coral, remembering that coral could cause nasty cuts which often became infected.

Finning to maintain his position against the current, he looked in under the remains of the boat deck. What he saw caused him a spurt of satisfaction. Directly in front of him and right at the bottom end of the steps leading down from the boat deck, was an open doorway. This led in to the cabins and the passenger's dining room and saloon.

'The companionway leading down to the strong room is just to the right inside that door,' he thought. Impelled by an intense desire to know, he began to swim forward. Suddenly Carmen tapped at his arm. Alarmed that something like the shark might have appeared he looked at her. He saw she was vigorously shaking her head and pointing up. That was the last thing Andrew wanted to do but when he made to resume swimming Carmen actually grabbed his BCD and again shook her head, gesturing even more emphatically to go up.

Fearing that she might be in difficulties, Andrew reluctantly abandoned his exploration and began to inflate his BCD. Carmen did the same and they rose slowly upwards. As they had only been down at 15 metres they were soon on the surface.

Here Andrew fully inflated his BCD to keep his head well clear of the water and quickly swapped his regulator for his snorkel. The size of the waves came as an unpleasant surprise. After removing his face mask and getting a face full of salt water he hastily placed it back on his face. After he had blinked his eyes clear of the stinging salt he looked around. Carmen was floating a couple of metres away and the dinghy was only about 25 metres off and heading towards them.

The dinghy came to a bobbing halt a few metres off. Jordan shook his head and shouted when they went to swim over to it. "Keep clear unless you are in trouble and need to get aboard. I have to keep the prop running to hold her bows on to these waves," he explained.

Carmen stopped swimming and waved to show she understood and was alright. She took out her snorkel and shouted, "We found her!"

"What?" their father called, cupping his hand behind his ear.

"We found her. She is just down here in about fifteen metres of water. That's to the main deck."

"What are you going to do next?" their father queried.

Andrew answered that. "Have a look inside. Can you pass us the water-proof torches please."

His father looked dubious so Andrew explained further. "The ship is upright. She is lying port side against the reef. The whole thing is covered in coral growths and weeds but she looked safe enough. The door we want is open."

"I don't like it," his father replied.

It was now Carmen who began to argue. "Oh Dad! Fair go! That is the whole reason we came this far. We have to look inside to see if the gold has been taken from the strong room."

"That is only one deck down and just inside the door," Andrew supplemented. He was now afraid that they might be thwarted. 'I just have to know,' he thought.

Carmen obviously thought so too as she said, "Oh Dad, please! I will lie awake for the rest of my life wondering if we don't go in and look."

"We will be very careful," Andrew added.

"I don't like it," his father replied, but that told Andrew that he was weakening. 'He is torn between giving way to us and the fear of having to explain to Mum how he let us get drowned,' he deduced.

"Please Dad!" Carmen pleaded. A wave then slopped into her face and caused her to cough and splutter.

Andrew took over. "It is just down there. We can tie the dinghy to the wreck and take a rope in with us to use as a guide in case our torches go out. We will only be ten minutes."

"Do you have enough air left?" his father asked.

At that Andrew knew they had won. He looked at his gauge and saw it read 150psi. Giving a vigorous nod he said, "Enough for at least twenty minutes."

"Oh alright, but only for ten minutes," his father replied. "Now tie us on."

A rope was passed to Carmen. Each was handed a bright yellow waterproof torch. Andrew replaced his regulator and put his head under. That was a shock. While they had been talking the current had carried them right back around the corner of the reef. He explained the problem and Jordan suggested towing them back into position. Carmen agreed that this was a good idea. Brother and sister then clung to the line while the dinghy slowly butted into the waves.

It was harder to hold on to the line than Andrew had expected but he managed it. The water was so clear that they had no trouble locating the wreck again. After a signal to the boat both put their regulators back in and deflated their BCDs. Carmen took the end of the line and swam down to fasten it to the stanchion near the door. She did this in a way that left about ten metres of loose end. The line up to the surface at once went taut as the dinghy took the strain.

Andrew was now very excited. The idea of diving on a real wreck quite gripped him. Partly this was the ghoulish images of drowned bodies and so on that the accounts that he had read conjured up. There was also the sheer drama and pathos of it all- the tragedy at sea, the lure of sunken treasure.

But at the doorway he paused. Inside looked very dark and gloomy and fears began to seep back in. 'What if I get snagged and Carmen can't get me free?' he thought. Ghastly images of drowning filled his mind. Having nearly drowned twice in Ross River the previous January, and having watched several people drown, he had a deep fear of dying that way.

Then other fears assailed him: of sea snakes, moray eels, of being grabbed by a giant octopus, of sharks and barracuda. It was all enough to make him pause.

While he did Carmen swam past him, taking the end of the rope with her. With a look to check he was following she swam in through the doorway. After that there was nothing for it but to follow. There was no way he would let his sister get into a situation of danger if he could help it. Taking care to avoid the growths festooning the edges of the doorway he swam in.

Once through the door Andrew found it was not nearly as dark as it had looked. So much sunlight came in through the gaps in the rotted boat deck that he could clearly see they were in a corridor at the top of the steps leading down to the lower deck. Down there looked considerably darker and both paused. Close on their left was a doorway in a long bulkhead which extended right across the ship. The door had been wood and was completely gone. A quick look inside confirmed that the large cabin inside had once been the passengers dining room and saloon.

The place was alive with hundreds of small, brilliantly coloured fish. Andrew watched them dart for cover as he and Carmen swam in. There was nothing much to see so they swam back out again, both bumping their air tanks against the doorway as they did.

In line with the top of the steps was another corridor. This ran forward through the superstructure. It was well lit along its whole length by the sunlight streaming in from above through the remains of the boat deck. The handrail shielding the companionway was still in position and Andrew grabbed it to hold himself while he directed the beam of his torch down the hole. It was an action he instantly regretted as the handrail was covered with slimy weed and dozens of small barnacles. Several small cuts resulted.

As the current was much weaker inside the wreck Andrew let go and used his hands and fins to keep away from the walls. Carmen pointed along the corridor toward a door and swam that way. Andrew wanted to go down to the strong room but she had the rope so he followed. The door was also of wood and looked very rotten. From memory Andrew knew it led into the cabin he had briefly glanced into from outside, one of the First Class cabins. There was a door knob, greenish and slimy looking, and Carmen reached down and tugged at it.

For a moment Andrew experienced a horrible feeling of dread, engendered by the diver's accounts of the wreck of the *Gothenburg*. Into his mind came ghastly images of drowned girls in long white dresses, their long hair drifting in the wave motion and their arms rising and falling. The image was so powerful he shivered and almost reached out to stop Carmen.

The door disintegrated under Carmen's pressure. A swirl of rotten wood, slime and other particles engulfed them both for a few seconds, before the current swept it away. Brother and sister peered around the door posts. There were no drowned maidens, just some alarmed tropical fish whose secure home had been destroyed. The small fish flitted off up through the gaps in the overhead stringers or out through the broken porthole.

It had once been a passenger's cabin but now it was just a mush of silt and growths of coral and weed. Quite a strong current flowed in. Carmen looked around then shook her head and turned to make her way back to the top of the steps. Still haunted by the thoughts of drowned girls Andrew was glad to follow her.

As he did a coil of the rope entangled him and he had to stop and remove it. The thought that the rope might be more dangerous than helpful crossed his mind and he made sure he pushed it well clear as he swam back to the companionway.

Once again they paused. Andrew again clicked on his torch and shone it down. In the beam he saw the outline of the strong room door. To his sharp disappointment he saw that it was closed. That motivated him to go down. This time he led the way. In his haste he misjudged the clearance and his J-valve and air tank whacked sharply against the coaming of the hatchway.

He swam down head first and then had to do a contortionist act to turn himself right way up at the bottom. As he did several powerful emotions gripped him. The strongest was fear. It was much darker and the torch beam looked quite feeble. There was also a vivid picture of what it might have been like for an old-fashioned helmet diver to come down those stairs. The mental image of the diver trailing his vulnerable air hose and safety line, and of how restricted his vision must have been, made Andrew shudder with apprehension, even as he was struck with admiration for the courage it must have required.

'If he got caught somehow, his boots or hose snagged on something, he would have been done for,' he thought.

Which instantly led to the thought that possibly his Grandfather had been caught and might even now be lying nearby. A sharp stab of something close to terror shot through Andrew, sending his already rapid breathing up even higher. He swung his torch around and saw that he was in another transverse corridor. As he moved the torch beam something large moved further along the gloomy passageway. The shape flitted into the shadows and out of sight at an open doorway which he thought led down to the engine room.

Once again his heart hammered rapidly. 'Octopus,' was his first thought, instantly discarded and replaced by shark, then with a shake of the head by the word groper. But there was nothing to see but a swirl of sediment. He shone the torch beam around, noting with interest how the air bubbles accumulated in tiny silver clusters in the nooks overhead.

As Carmen lowered herself cautiously down Andrew leaned over and directed his torch beam at the deck. The first thing he noted was that there was no coral and only a small amount of slimy moss-like weed. Instead there was mud and sand. This made its presence felt in a very irritating way as his fins stirred it up and it swirled up to transform the water into a cloudy soup.

The visibility dropped so quickly and so badly that Andrew was both astonished and alarmed. He found he could barely discern Carmen's torch beam and she was only a dim blur, even though she was only a metre away. Suddenly he was very glad of that rope. Thoughts of the groper or octopus sneaking up in the gloom to grab him sent surges of fear, almost panic, through him. It was only Carmen's presence close beside him that held him there.

With an effort of willpower Andrew calmed himself. Then he shone his torch upwards, checking the escape route. That dimly lit square of sunlight at the top of the steps now looked very inviting! Claustrophobia and fears of drowning held him close to panic and he had to struggle to keep calm. His breathing sounded very loud and he was acutely aware that he was dependent on the breathing apparatus to keep him from drowning. He also noted again all the clusters of bubbles collected along the low ceiling. As he breathed out he watched another stream of shiny, silvery froth rise up to join them.

Carmen was directing the beam of her torch onto the strong room door so Andrew turned to face it and did likewise. He saw that the door was made of steel and was of the 'Strongback' type with a raised sill and semi-circular top and bottom. A long steel handle held it in place. Then he noted something that made him gasp in excited surprise- the heavy padlock on a latch to one side was unlocked.

Andrew reached forward and touched the padlock, then turned to look at Carmen. He saw her give a nod and was sure she was thinking the same thing. 'Someone has opened this. Was it Grandad?'

But was the gold still inside? That thought made him reach down and grasp the handle. The thing was slimy with marine growth but he rubbed this off and took a firm grip. As he did he told himself to remember to wear gloves in future. Bracing his feet and knees against the deck and bulkhead he pulled. For a moment he felt the handle move, but then it stopped. After releasing the pressure he swam closer and studied the handle. The thing was not really rusted in place and there were no coral growths jamming it. That made him try again.

Still no movement. To try to work the handle loose Andrew pushed the other way and was rewarded by a definite but slight movement. Encouraged by that he began to push and pull at the lever, working it up and down. Then he found he was gasping for breath and feeling dizzy and light-headed.

Carmen touched his arm and shook her head, then pointed to her pressure gauge. In the swirling sediment Andrew had trouble reading it but he thought it said 75 psi. His own read only 65 and he knew he should go up. But stubborn curiosity got him to try once more. Using all his strength he heaved. The handle suddenly scraped up.

It did not go all the way but that got Carmen to have a go. She worked it loose several more times, then also heaved. The Andrew's intense satisfaction the handle finally slid to the upright position, unlocking the door.

'Now, let's see what is inside,' he thought, taking a firm hold and pulling.

Chapter 35

An Ill Wind

Andrew strained at the strong room door, hauling with all his strength. It was to no avail. The door did not budge. Again he tried, straining till he felt his heart and lungs might burst. But it was no good. He swam down to peer at close range at the sides and hinges. There was no indication that the door had moved at all.

'This door hasn't been opened in a very long time,' he thought. 'In fact, probably not since Grandad and Old Mr Murchison came here.' Then he felt guilty at making such an accusation without real proof and added, 'If they did.'

Tugging at his BCD attracted his attention. It was Carmen and she was making emphatic gestures to surface. Andrew realized with a shock that he was feeling very dizzy and knew he was being silly. He turned and took the rope that Carmen placed in his free hand. She quickly tied the other end to the door handle, then pushed at him to get going.

The rope snagged him several times and kept looping around his right leg as he kicked but he was very glad of it because the water was now so full of swirling sediment that visibility was less than a metre. As he touched the handrails of the steps Andrew experienced another spasm of terror. 'What if the thing that is lurking in the engine room is coming to get me?'

Driven by that thought more than by fear of his air running out Andrew went up the steps and through the hatchway into the relatively bright light of the saloon companionway. Here he again became entangled in the rope and had to stop and free himself. Carmen came up through the opening in a burst of bubbles and kept gesturing to go on up.

Now Andrew needed no second invitation but he was still conscious enough to be aware that they had both been down to 18 metres so he stopped when he reached open water. Here he clung on against the current and waited for Carmen. With a shock he saw that his air pressure was down to 45 and he shook his head. But he was no longer really worried because he could see the surface only ten metres up. The dark silhouette of the dinghy was clearly visible. He was confident he could swim up, even if he had no air left at all.

Carmen joined him and they both rose slowly up the line, staying below their bubbles all the way, even though the normal fears of diving in the deep ocean now began to assail Andrew. He found it a huge relief to break surface but the thought of a shark racing in to rip at his dangling legs got him anxious to get aboard.

But even though he badly wanted to get into that dinghy he was not allowed to. Jordan shook his head and said that the waves were too big and the dinghy too small. Instead Jordan followed Carmen's instructions and secured one of the bright orange fishing floats to the end of the rope and tossed it over as a buoy. Then the dinghy got under way and set off back towards the launch. The waves were now so big that it threw up sheets of spray and the hull was often lost to Andrew's sight as it went into the troughs.

Fear of sharks now took hold of Andrew as he bobbed on the tossing waves. These seemed to be much larger than they had been when he had dived. To avoid getting salt in his eyes he had to leave his facemask on and breathe through his snorkel. With Carmen swimming beside him he set off for the launch, using the current as much as possible.

It was a 200 metre swim and, even with the help of the current, by the time he reached the launch he was exhausted. All he could do was cling to the side of the dinghy as it bobbed in the waves. The wave pattern was very confused, thrown out of any ordered pattern by the change of wind direction and the effect of the current. It was all Andrew could manage to take off and pass to Jordan his torch, fins and weight belt. The weight belt he almost lost as a wave took him under and he let slip one end. Luckily it was the buckle end otherwise all the lead weights would have slid off into the deep water. Grunting and gasping with the effort he held it up for Jordan to take.

Climbing up the side of the launch over the old tyres was a feat almost beyond Andrew. The weight of the air cylinder seemed enormous. The effort was complicated by the way the launch was rolling and tossing. It was going up and down a metre or so and several times the hull slammed against him with almost numbing force. It was a sharp reminder of just how dangerous it might be and how weather dependant diving was. Moses helped by leaning over and grasping his air cylinder, then hoisting him up by that.

Once on the launch Andrew took off his BCD and air tank, then slumped down on a seat and shivered. His father tossed him a towel and told him to rub himself vigorously. As he dried himself Andrew looked out anxiously across the tossing waves and saw the white launch bobbing at anchor only a hundred metres away. That surprised him as somehow he had thought it would have left, to be in port by sundown.

Carmen was helped aboard and her gear eased off. She looked pale and even blue around the lips but was smiling. "We got right down inside to the strong room door," she said, "But we couldn't get it open. We need some tools."

"What sort of tools?" her father asked as he helped hoist off her air tank. The launch was bobbing so much he could only use one hand as he needed the other to hang on with.

Carmen shrugged and looked at Andrew. He bit his lip, then replied, "A crowbar maybe? And a chisel and a hammer; something to wedge in the side of the door anyway."

Moses shook his head. "We ain't got no crowbar. The hammer and a chisel we can manage, and maybe a shifter or such like. We'll have a look in the tool box."

Jordan then shocked Andrew by saying, "Don't forget there's laws about wrecks. I ain't sure what they say but if you start doing things to one or taking things you might be in trouble."

"I have to know what is in that strong room," Andrew answered. Now that he was so close he was determined, lurking octopuses and other creepy creatures notwithstanding.

Then Carmen shocked him even more by saying, "We should be able to find out without doing any damage. Anyway, we have all night to think about it and to find out."

"All night?" Andrew echoed. "Why don't we go down right away?"

Carmen shook her head emphatically. "Because we have done three long dives today and it will take a couple of hours for our residual nitrogen to go down to a safe level. By then it will be dusk."

"I agree," their father added. "You are not diving at dusk or at night. And you are certainly not going back in the water while the waves are this big. Anyway, you both look worn out and I say you have a good rest."

"But it is so close!" Andrew cried. He realized with dismay that he was shaking and was on the edge of tears.

"Piffle! The wreck has been there for more than fifty years. One more night isn't going to change anything," his father replied.

"But... but Dad," Andrew expostulated, gesturing to the white launch. "Someone else might beat us to it."

"Rubbish!" his father replied. "They are just tourists from Sydney. Now go and get out of that wet suit and into some dry clothes. And those hands look like they need some first aid. I will make some hot Milo."

There was nothing for it but to obey. Andrew went to the shower and wished it had hot water. Dry and clean of salt and dressed in warm, dry clothes he felt much better. The hot drink lifted him even more. Carmen joined him and applied antiseptic lotion to the cuts in his left hand.

"We need gloves next time," Andrew said.

Carmen agreed but could only shrug. Meanwhile Moses and Jordan had hoisted the dinghy aboard and lashed it tightly over the hatch cover. That done they all sat around the table in the cabin and Andrew and Carmen described what they had seen. They used the ship plans and a sketch pad to make clear what they were talking about. Andrew was very glad he had sent away for those plans as they made it all easy to understand. There was no doubt that the door they had been trying to open was the strong room door.

As the sun began to set the wind increased and swung even more to the north. The wave pattern became even more erratic and the pitching and rolling of the launch became quite uncomfortable. Several times Moses went up on the foredeck and studied the situation. He came back looking very thoughtful, which made Andrew even more apprehensive that the weather might ruin his plans.

Andrew had always prided himself on being a good sailor and his stomach was quite untroubled but he had a few qualms about the seaworthiness of the launch after a few waves burst into the aft deck. Only the sill across the aft end of the cabin kept it from being awash.

As the launch rolled Jordan pointed to the white launch. "I'm glad I ain't in that thing. Look how she rolls."

Andrew did. The white launch seemed to be moving with a twisting motion. The roll was very marked and rapid and each roll exposed part of her deck. "All that top hamper," he commented, trying to sound nautical and knowledgeable.

As he spoke a man came out onto the aft deck of the white launch. He stared at them for a minute, then moved to the stern and reached down. Andrew saw him help a black clad figure up over the transom.

"They have been diving!" he cried in dismay.

They all looked and Moses levelled binoculars. "Two divers," he said as a second one came aboard. It was obvious even at that distance that it had been difficult getting those divers safely back into their launch. Even as Andrew watched he saw the second diver and the man both stagger and fall out of sight.

"She's got a special dive platform at the stern," Jordan added. "Much easier for a diver to get aboard her than into this old lugger."

Feeling very anxious Andrew watched the second diver get up and then look towards them, still with facemask on. "I wonder if they have been diving on the wreck?" he speculated.

"Not likely. They wouldn't even know it existed and normal divers wouldn't swim around into that strong current and deep water," Carmen answered.

The two divers vanished into the cabin of the white launch and Moses then said, "Never mind them. I think we should up anchor and get out of here."

A wave of disappointment bordering on dismay swept through Andrew. "But we are so close!" he cried. "If we don't dive now it might be months before we can get back here."

Moses looked worried and ran his fingers through his crinkly grey hair. "The weather forecast on the radio, she say the winds along this part of the coast might increase tomorrow to twenty five knots, maybe even with squalls of thirty knots. That means waves up to two or three metres. That is serious weather."

"That other boat is still here," Andrew argued. He was scared, but he was also determined.

Moses was obviously not happy about it but he finally nodded and said, "Alright. We stay and see what it is like tomorrow morning. The wind is usually easier then. One dive as soon as the sun is up, then we are out of here. But if the anchor drags, we go."

Jordan chipped in by reminding them that they only had two more air cylinders each and that they would have to go back to Bowen to refill them anyway.

That was the best deal Andrew knew he was going to get and he was vaguely guilty at arguing to place the others and the launch a risk. He nodded and said OK.

Moses then nodded and said, "Alright, now, what will we have for tea?"

Andrew did not feel like food, was in fact feeling quite nauseous from overexertion, so he said nothing. Instead he took himself below and lay down to think. For a while he lay and fretted, badly wanting to get it all over with. Then he shivered with reaction and fell into a restless doze. He was roused from this to come up and have dinner.

The smell of the food restored his appetite and reminded him of how hungry it was. Despite the motion of the launch Moses had cooked a steak and kidney pie and it tasted delicious. The effect was somewhat spoiled though, by the effects of several sharp gusts of wind which made the launch heel over and veer away southwards. Each time Moses took bearings by eye on the other launch and again carefully studied the sea. To Andrew it already seemed that the wind had picked up and the launch continued to roll with unpredictable jerks as odd waves took it unexpectedly.

The sun set with a nice glow of pink and orange on the undersides of the clouds but the wind felt cold and the waves appeared even more choppy. The white launch still lay at her anchor and appeared to be rolling with a quite alarming motion. As darkness set in the rapid, jerky movement of her lights emphasized this.

The food picked Andrew up physically and he was able to listen to the radio news with interest. Moses than radioed his home, his wife having a radio set there. As he went to talk Carmen touched his arm. "Please Moses, if that is just a normal radio, please don't mention the wreck. Anyone could hear."

Moses nodded and smiled. "It be OK," he assured her. So when he spoke to his wife he just gave the launch's call sign (her registration letters and numbers) and told his wife they had found 'it' and asked her to telephone Mrs Collins to reassure her that the little ones were not drowned yet. Andrew wasn't very happy at the way Moses talked about needing some tools to get inside but there was no direct mention of either the word wreck or the name *Merinda*.

The group then settled back to the table to discuss their plans for tomorrow. Suddenly the movement of the other launch's lights registered in Andrew's consciousness. He pointed and cried out, "Look! That other boat is moving."

They all made their way out onto the fish deck and stared across the tossing black waste. The other launch was obviously leaving as its wildly bobbing lights moved rapidly off in a North Westerly direction. After a few minutes it changed course and headed to the south in the direction of Bowen.

Jordan grunted and said, "Must have heard the weather forecast and decided to get going while he could."

Moses answered him. "If he had any sense he would have gone in daylight, and so should we have."

"We can if you really think we should," Carmen said.

Moses shrugged. "We will see. We are here now and I'd like to know the truth too."

"But not at the expense of another shipwreck and us all getting drowned," Carmen replied.

Again Moses shrugged and he said, "We been at sea in worse."

That made Andrew feel both anxious and guilty but he said nothing, hoping the weather would not get worse. They sat back down again and talked for another half hour or so and then Mr Collins insisted that Andrew and Carmen lie down and rest. He and the two T.Is arranged to keep an anchor watch. Even though it was only 9pm Andrew felt tired enough to go to bed. He took himself below, cleaned his teeth and went to the toilet, then lay down. Carmen came in a few minutes later and touched his arm.

"It will be alright Andrew. We have found the wreck. Now we will get to the bottom of things."

"Bottom of the bloody ocean," he replied with a grin, even though his stomach turned over anxiously as the launch gave another sharp roll.

Carmen laughed and said, "Moses knows what he is doing." She went and lay down and Andrew closed his eyes and tried to sleep. For a while he could not, his mind dredging up all the events of the day. Several times he shuddered with fear at the memories. 'Only one more dive,' he told himself. 'Then I can give it up for good.'

After a while exhaustion helped him to drift into a restless sleep. The need for his muscles to brace themselves against the motion of the launch was annoying and kept him on the edge of wakefulness and several times sharp thumps or crashing noises made him open his eyes in alarm. Each time he hoped fervently that the wind would not get stronger.

'We have to start back to Cairns on Saturday morning to be back in time for school,' he thought gloomily. As tomorrow was Friday the chance of coming back out to the reef looked quite unlikely. Feeling tired, anxious and depressed he slipped back into a fitful doze.

The sound of shouting voices roused him back to anxious wakefulness. This turned to instant alarm when the engine suddenly rumbled into life. He sat up and looked across at Carmen. She was sitting up and pulling on a spray jacket. Andrew did not wait. He rolled out of his bunk and scuttled up the steps to the cabin.

Moses was there, standing at the wheel. The front hatchway was open and a cold wind was blowing in, mixed with flying spray. The launch was rolling with a vicious, jerky roll which made Andrew's heart shoot up to his throat. "What's happening?" he asked.

Moses gestured out, even as he spun the wheel and pushed the throttle forward. "Anchor's dragged. We gotta get outa here fast. Gotta get away from that reef."

The engine was engaged and Andrew realized it was in reverse. He and Carmen stared out into the darkness and what he saw made his breath catch in his throat from fear. All around were the dark, waves. In the faint shimmer of the moon's path was a rippling, tossing mass of waves tops. But what he could not discern was the actual reef. In the darkness there was no sign of it.

"Where is the reef?" he called anxiously.

"Not sure," Moses called back. In the faint light of the binnacle his face looked drawn and he stared astern as the launch began to make way. Then he faced the bows and yelled, "Hurry up and get that anchor up! If we snag that on a coral outcrop it could swing us beam on against the reef."

Andrew now realized just what danger they were in. Out on the foredeck he saw his father and Jordan busily winding the anchor up. "Can we help?" he asked.

Moses shook his head. "No. Stay here and keep your eyes peeled for any sign of surf."

That was a sickening thought too. Andrew moved to the port side and looked out. "I can't see the reef," he said again.

"It's the top of the tide," Moses replied. "We could go right up on it."

The stern of the launch was now butting into the waves. Spray and foam flew up but most was taken away by the force of the wind. Out on the sharply pitching foredeck the two men wrestled with the anchor as it was hoisted aboard. The launch began to buck so dramatically that Andrew swallowed in alarm and felt his skin go cold with fear.

Mr Collins came struggling aft, moving from handhold to handhold. He made his way down the short flight of steps and said, "Anchor is on board. Jordan is lashing it in place now."

Moses grunted and immediately spun the wheel hard to starboard. Then he thrust the control lever forward, changing the gears from reverse to forward. The launch came to a wallowing standstill, then slowly began forging ahead, slamming into the waves as she did. Andrew stared anxiously through the front windows and feared that Jordan would be washed off as spray and waves burst on board and deluged aft. A flood of water poured in through the open hatchway and Moses gestured to close it. Mr Collins pulled it shut and then stayed there ready to open it again.

The launch swung round, beam on to the waves. It then began obviously moving forward. The motion changed to savage rolling for a minute. This was so severe Andrew felt sure they were going to capsize. Then Moses steadied the launch on a course to the south. This brought the wind and waves onto the port quarter. At once the motion eased and the boat began to swoop along, twisting and rolling but in a manner which felt much safer.

Jordan struggled aft and opened the hatch. "Anchor's secure. I give us a bit of staysail eh? Take some of the roll off her."

Moses nodded. "Good idea, but you put a lifejacket and lifeline on first. Mr Collins, could you help him please."

Jordan and Mr Collins both began donning lifejackets. Andrew asked if he could help but Moses shook his head emphatically. "No. You kids stay here in the cabin. If you go overboard I don' like our chances of findin' you, not in this."

One glance at 'this', the madly tumbling waves and dark sea, convinced Andrew he was right. With some anxiety he watched his father and Jordan go back up onto the foredeck. They hoisted a small part of the jib, Jordan lashing the remainder firmly down so that only a tiny triangle was exposed. Then they moved to the cabin roof and raised the mainsail slightly. At once the motion of the launch steadied, becoming a swooping pitch that was almost pleasant. Andrew understood the steadying effect of a sail and felt much happier.

Ten minutes later both men returned to the cabin. Both were soaked and shivering. Jordan pointed up. "One reef," he said, referring to the sail.

Moses nodded. Carmen busied herself at the stove. Andrew kept peering out for any sign of the reef but he felt sure they must be now well clear of it. Just to be sure he glanced at the chart. As they were now heading south and as no other reef was shown within miles he began to relax a little.

After another ten minutes Moses relaxed and took the cup of hot coffee Carmen offered him. "Ok. We safe now I reckon."

"What do we do now?" Mr Collins asked.

"Head for Bowen before the weather gets even worse," Moses replied.

Mr Collins nodded. Andrew felt as surge of bitter defeat and stared out at the sea. To be so close! And to be beaten by a change in the weather!

Chapter 36

Anxiety

Andrew stared astern at the rippling darkness and felt a surge of deep frustration. 'To be so close!' he thought. All he could hope was that the weather reports would turn out to be correct, that the winds might ease on Saturday. 'But we will get only one shot at it,' he mused. Memories of touching that rusty, slime-covered door filled his mind and he gritted his teeth in annoyance and determination. 'I will get back one day, somehow,' he vowed.

So sharp was his disappointment that he was close to tears. He even forgot to be afraid as the launch gave a sickening roll. Water came on board and soaked his legs but he ignored it.

Carmen did not. She came and touched his arm. "You are cold Andrew. Come inside and have a hot drink."

"In a minute."

"No, now! I know you are upset. I'm not happy either but it isn't the end of the world. We will be back. Come on!" Carmen insisted.

Andrew allowed himself to be led back into the cabin. Only then did he realize he was soaked and shivering. His father tut-tutted with concern and made him put on a pullover while Carmen made more hot Milo. Jordan came back wearing dry clothes and took over the wheel from Moses who slumped down on the bench seat.

"Getting' too old for this bobbin' around the bloody ocean stuff," he grumbled, rubbing at his sore legs and back.

Hearing that, and thinking back over the recent crisis made Andrew feel quite guilty. 'If I hadn't argued about staying to dive we would have been back safe in Bowen by now,' he thought. He noted it was already after 2am. Suddenly he felt tired. Having drunk the warm drink he was quite ready to obey his father when he said to go back to bed.

Andrew made his way below and changed into dry clothes then climbed back into his bunk. On the course the launch was now on the motion was quite regular and not nearly as frightening as before. There was just the occasional slithering yaw to make him feel prickles of alarm. So worn out by exertion and nervous excitement was he that he slipped into a deep sleep within minutes.

Hours later Andrew struggled to the surface of consciousness in a lather of perspiration, the lingering ethereal remnants of a bad dream still flickering in his mind. It had been another of those nightmares to do with diving or sailing. This time he had been at sea on a sail boat which had turned into a surfboard. This kept slipping down the front of steep waves. The sky had darkened and mysterious shadowy shapes had flitted about under the water. Suddenly he had slithered off the board and into deep water. There were big waves and a fast current and the shore suddenly seemed a long way off. A girl with long black hair streaming in the water had reached for his hand and he grabbed at it, but instead of pulling him to the surface she had dragged him under!

For a few minutes Andrew lay awake in the darkness, calming his breathing and gathering his thoughts. His mind told him that the waves were even bigger and that the motion of the launch was more violent. He had to brace himself to stay in his bunk. Anxiety drove him to get up but after a glance up the companionway revealed Jordan calmly steering Andrew instead went to the toilet. His watch told him it was nearly 4am.

"Only two or three hours more," Andrew told himself, thinking but not saying, 'if we don't sink first!' But rather than admit his fear or look anxious to Jordan he went back to his bunk. Carmen and his father appeared to be sound asleep in theirs so he rolled over and made himself as comfortable as he could. For a while he lay brooding, sure he would not sleep.

But he did. Carmen shook him awake at 5:30. "Moses wants us up top. So get up, sleepy head," she said.

Rubbing bleary eyes Andrew sat up. It was instantly apparent that the weather was even worse, the motion of the launch even rougher. He sat up and yawned, then made his way to the toilet. After washing his face and smoothing rumpled hair he made his way up to the cabin.

It was just getting light. Moses now had the wheel and he grinned a cheery good morning but from a drawn and anxious looking face. To Andrew's surprise he wore a lifejacket. So did Jordan and a very tired looking father. Moses gestured to the locker. "You kids put lifejackets on please, then stay up top here."

That really got Andrew anxious. As he staggered aft he glanced outside and was appalled at how big the waves were. What appeared to be an endless array of huge tumbling walls of water were hurrying in from the port quarter. 'If Moses is that worried then it must really be dangerous,' he thought. As he pulled the lifejacket on and secured it Andrew began to have frightening images of a huge wave rolling the launch over. For a few seconds he considered what that might be like and how he might manage to get clear of the cabin and the ensnaring rigging.

Having secured the lifejacket Andrew made his way forward to the chart table. A glance at the compass told him that they were still heading for Bowen. Wondering how far it might be he looked through the windows. To his relief he saw the shapes of mountains looming above the haze of sea spray. These were in a long line off to starboard and the chart revealed them to have names like Mt Roundback and Mt Pring. Ahead the bold shapes of Cape Edgecumbe and Flagstaff Hill showed faintly in the mist. Seeing them made him feel even more relieved. There was safety- if they could reach it!

Moses followed his gaze and, divining his thoughts, said, "Another hour or so. You can lie on the bench if you like."

"No, he can't," Carmen put in. "He can help me tidy up and get break-fast ready."

Andrew was given the job of washing up the previous night's dishes. He then sat at the table with his father. Carmen placed a bowl of cereal in front of him and then a plate of toast. Andrew swallowed and felt his stomach turn over. That shamed him as he did not want to admit to seasickness. But, to his own disgust, he knew it was really fear that was upsetting him. This was the roughest sea he had ever been out on and looking at it made him so anxious he became very tense. With an effort of will he acted cool and began to force food down.

Sitting there, trying to overcome the constrictions in his throat and stomach, he found he could not stop continually looking out at those monstrous waves. They seemed to curl up behind. The launch was moving faster than them and kept sliding down their rapidly moving faces but it still looked frightening. Remembering things he had read about vessels being 'pooped' by following seas did not help.

It was the horrifying images of the launch capsizing and of him being trapped inside which drove Andrew to get up and make his way aft to the open rear of the cabin. He was forbidden to go out onto the fish deck which was sloshing with water. Instead he leaned out and looked at the forbidding sight of mile after mile of surging 'white horses'.

As he did Andrew tried to picture famous nautical and naval events he had read about. The cold wind suggested convoys to Russia in World War 2 but he had trouble imagining the little *Moa Mermaid* as even a small

British corvette. His romantic imagination wandered to the age of sail and he began to picture himself as the captain of a storm tossed naval cutter chasing (or was being chased more exciting?) a powerful French sailing frigate. His daydreams served their purpose. He actually began to half enjoy himself and his dinted personal image of being a hardy sea dog received a bit of repair.

Even so it was a very anxious hour. The hills marking the end of the bay seemed to be get closer much slower than he wished and it was a relief to realize that the sun had come up and that he could distinguish individual boulders and even single trees. The sight of the waves dashing themselves against the foot of the headlands did not help to ease the anxiety though. Each wave burst on the rocks with huge showers of spray.

'If we have to swim ashore we will be dashed to pulp,' Andrew thought.

The real moment of crisis came when they had to change course to go into the North Channel. The wind was blowing hard from the North East and they had to run directly before it after they rounded the rocky island called North Head. This was enveloped by a welter of foam and Moses gave it a wide berth. Jordan and Mr Collins went up to furl the mainsail. This was a precaution against an accidental gybe. From numerous sailing embarrassments Andrew understood the need for that. The small jib staysail was left up, to help keep the launch's head downwind.

They seemed to shoot through the gap between Stone Island and North Head. Moses then altered course again to bring the wind onto the starboard quarter. At once the uneasy yawing motion ceased and a slithering, twisting pitching replaced it. A few more anxious minutes on this course and they were level with the end of Flagstaff Hill. Then Moses turned the wheel and the launch came round to starboard again, curving around the end of the point and into the lee of the hill. The effect was immediate. The waves decreased in size and the wind died away to flurries of much less intensity.

Moses turned to them with a grin. "OK, youse can take off them lifejackets now. We'se safe."

Andrew gasped with relief and took the lifejacket off. This was stowed back in the locker and he then straightened up to look about. By then Moses had removed his jacket and was steering with one hand and talking on a mobile phone with the other. Andrew saw that they were not heading for the main jetty but were keeping the land close to starboard.

"Too rough at the main wharf," Moses explained. "We will go in to the marina. We need fuel anyway."

They chugged slowly in to the marina. This was built behind a breakwater on the eastern curve of the bay on the edge of a mangrove swamp. It was a nice modern facility with floating piers to accommodate the tide. At the piers a dozen other vessels of various sizes were already berthed. At least fifty more: trawlers, yachts, old ketches, fishing launches, were moored in lines between tall pilings. The size of the place came as quite a surprise to Andrew.

As they motored in through the narrow entrance an attendant came out and indicated where to refuel. There was nothing for Andrew or Carmen to do except keep out of the way and relax. Andrew felt quite drained and also a bit ashamed at his earlier fears. However he said nothing of this to Carmen and instead discussed what an interesting bay it was. After refuelling was finished the attendant directed them to one of the berths at the floating pier behind the Yacht Club. "Just in front of that white cruiser, the game fishing boat," he said.

Andrew looked at it and heard Carmen say, "That is the boat that was out at Echo Reef."

It was. The name *Silver Stingray* showed up on her transom in silver letters. For a moment he experienced a qualm of doubt but then shrugged. It was perfectly natural that the white launch should have come here to get out of the weather. Even so he felt a peculiar sense of unease as they puttered slowly past. As they did a fit young man in his twenties came out onto the white launch's aft deck and looked at them. He had dark curly hair and wore only a pair of grubby shorts. As they passed he gave a friendly wave.

"Bit rough out there?" he called.

"Just a bit," Carmen answered.

"Want a hand?"

"Yes thanks," Jordan answered.

The young man clambered onto the pier and went along to take the lines as they were tossed to him. The spliced eyes on the ends were looped over bollards and the man then stood and smiled up at them. "Catch much?" he asked Carmen.

"No," Carmen answered.

"Great place for diving Echo Reef, don't you think?" the young man said.

"Yes," Carmen replied.

"Been there before?"

Carmen shook her head. "No. Have you?" she asked.

The young man shook his head. "Never. We are working our way north. I hear there are some great dive sites further up the coast."

"There are. Try Wheeler Reef off Townsville."

During this exchange Andrew remained silent. For some reason he did not feel like talking to the young man. The young man gave a friendly nod and strolled back to his own boat. By then the *Moa Mermaid* was berthed port side to and the engine switched off. Under the direction of Moses they set to work to make her tidy and ship-shape. Lines were neatly coiled, the mainsail re-stowed, the jib furled, the anchor re-secured.

With that done Jordan got them to unship and launch the dinghy. The hatch cover was then removed and the diving gear extracted and laid out. The marina had facilities for refilling air tanks so Andrew was sent to get a small trolley and on this they transported the air tanks to the compressor shed. The attendant set to work filling them, all ten at once.

The wet suits were washed with fresh water and then hung up to dry and the other equipment all rinsed. The refilled air tanks were then collected and stowed. By the time that was done Moses called them in for morning tea. Andrew was astonished to see that it was already 10:30 am. While they sat in the cabin and ate biscuits and drank tea he looked out at the part of the bay that was visible from their berth. The wind was still howling in, ruffling the whole surface of the bay into sudsy whitecaps.

Moses then asked for a detailed description of the door and they discussed exactly what type of tools they might require to open it. Dirty clothing was then bundled up and the whole party went out onto the pier and along it to the shore. At the marina shop they bought a softdrink each, then Mr Collins telephoned home. Andrew and Carmen both spoke to their mother, describing what they had found and asking if they could stay one more day so they could dive on the wreck. She was obviously reluctant and reminded them they had school on Monday.

"Oh Mum!" Andrew cried. "Please! I won't be able to concentrate on school work for wondering what is in there! And I don't know how long we will be able to keep the secret before one of us lets something slip."

What he was thinking about was the possibility of the gold still being there. To his enormous relief his mother sighed and said, "Oh alright! Put your father back on."

Andrew did so and then went over to where Carmen stood. She was studying items for sale in the glass counter. As Andrew arrived she pointed and said, "That's what we need."

'That' was an underwater camera. "What a great idea!" Andrew enthused. "That way we will have some proof."

"It will give us something to show our friends too," Carmen added.

So, when their father returned with the news that their mother would let them say another day- if the weather improved, Carmen asked him to buy the camera. He did this, then told them to take the washing to the coin laundry in town.

"Moses, Jordan and I are going to see about tools," he added.

The whole group then walked into town and had lunch at a cafe. After that Andrew and Carmen went and did the laundry. This took an hour. They then walked back to the marina. As they walked along the foreshore Andrew kept glancing out at the bay. Seeing its whole surface a seething mass of small waves did nothing to calm his anxiety.

"I hope the wind does die down by tomorrow morning," he commented.

"So do I," Carmen answered. "It is nearly twelve. The radio news will be on soon. That will give us a clue."

Brother and sister hurried back to the launch. They were the first ones back so the clothing was dumped on the bench and the radio turned on. The weather forecast after the news was more heartening. It said that the high pressure area was still moving east and was now in the Tasman Sea. It was predicted to weaken and to continue moving in an easterly direction. That meant that the winds along the Queensland coast should ease- to 15 to 20 knots it said. That made Andrew all anxious as he thought that winds of 20 knots would make it too rough to dive at Echo Reef. But that was the best they could hope for so he had to accept it.

Moses and Jordan came walking back along the pier with shopping bags and the tools. As they approached Moses held up a short steel crowbar with a curved end. "This a jemmy. Is it any good for opening that door?" he called.

Andrew went and took the jemmy from Moses as he stopped on the jetty. It certainly looked like the sort of tool that would do the job. Jordan had a chisel and a small sledge hammer which he held up for inspection. "I bought a bag to carry them," he said, showing a canvas haversack. "And I'll drill holes in their handles and thread rope through them so you can tie them on."

The two men climbed aboard and the tools were laid on the table. Carmen showed them her new underwater camera and this was admired and then placed there as well. She then said, "What are you going to do now?"

"Have an afternoon nap," Moses replied. "You kids should too."

It seemed such a good idea that both Andrew and Carmen went below. When their father arrived back a few minutes later he came down and joined them. As soon as Andrew lay down he realized just how worn out he was. Within minutes of closing his eyes he was sound asleep.

Three hours later Andrew opened his eyes, wondering where he was. It took his sleep fuddled mind a few seconds to recollect and then he looked around. On the other bunks lay Carmen and his father, both apparently still asleep. The need to use the toilet forced Andrew to get up. Not wishing to wake the others he was as quiet as he could be but the toilet door did not fit properly and its lock was stiff. The result was that when he came back out again he saw Carmen open her eyes and look at him.

She looked at her watch and sat up, then stood. On seeing that their father was still asleep she put her fingers to her lips and made her way to the toilet. Needing a drink, Andrew made his way up to the cabin. He expected to find Moses and Jordan there but the place was deserted. Carmen joined him and they had a drink, then looked out. Unable to see the bay clearly from where they were irritated Andrew so he climbed down onto the jetty.

"Where are you going?" Carmen asked.

"Just to check on the sea. I want to see if the wind has died down any," Andrew replied.

"I'll come with you."

Brother and sister walked side by side along the jetty and out onto the breakwater. A road ran along this to the entrance to the marina. They turned onto the road and strolled along. Andrew was surprised at how stiff his muscles were and at how worn out he still felt. As they walked along he pointed up to the open, grassy slopes of Flagstaff Hill.

"We would get a good view from up there," he said.

Carmen shook her head. "We would, but it is too far. It must be a couple of kilometres each way. I don't feel like walking that distance."

"This is an interesting place," Andrew commented. "We really must try to come here for a holiday."

"We will," Carmen agreed.

Still talking about exploring the islands which they could see littering the huge bay they walked to the end of the breakwater. The view was not really encouraging. The wind still blew strongly and the whole bay was flecked with the white of small waves. The waves had stirred up the shallow water so that the sea had a grimy appearance.

"Like muddy pea soup," Carmen suggested.

"Yes," Andrew agreed. He felt even more anxious now that the weather forecast might be wrong and that the wind would not lose any of its strength in time for them to go and dive once more on the wreck.

Feeling quite depressed and more tired than he wanted to admit Andrew turned and started walking back. The wind was cool enough to make him shiver. "Let's go and listen to the radio," he suggested.

Ten minutes slow walking had them back at the marina. They strolled slowly out along the pier, studying the other boats with interest. There was no-one in sight on any of them and the only person in view was a lone fisherman over at the end of another pier. As they approached the launch the young man with the dark curly hair climbed down onto the jetty from the white motor launch. Just as Andrew was about to climb back aboard the *Moa Mermaid* he saw the young man hold up his hand in a signal to stop.

"What does he want?" Andrew said to Carmen. The young man hurried along the pier towards them. While he did Andrew glanced on board but saw that there was no-one on deck or in the cabin. Apparently Moses, Jordan and their father were still asleep.

The young man stopped a few paces away and also looked into the cabin of the launch, then pointed back towards his own boat. "Excuse me," he said, "But your friend wants to show you something interesting. Would you mind coming along to my boat for a minute?"

"Friend?" Carmen asked.

"She says she knows you," the young man replied. He began walking back towards his own launch.

Mystified, Andrew started walking. Carmen followed. "Who are you talking about?" she asked.

"In there," the young man replied, pointing to the cabin of the white launch. "It will only take a minute and she thinks you will want to see this." The young man then climbed aboard and held the aft cabin door open.

Now feeling even more curious Andrew climbed aboard and looked around. The white launch was as he expected it to be- modern, well kept and with a lot of plastic, chrome and aluminium. Carmen joined him but she had a puzzled frown on her face.

"What is it?" she asked.

"Something we found at Echo Reef. It is on the cabin table," the young man answered.

That really sparked Andrew's curiosity, and also his anxiety. What had the man found at Echo Reef? Was it from the wreck? Impelled by a strong desire to know what the man had found he walked into the cabin, then stopped in stunned surprise. Carmen, who had followed him in, bumped into him and then let out an exclamation.

"Muriel!"

Chapter 37

Davy Jones's Locker

Andrew stared in shocked amazement.

Muriel!

"What... what are you doing here?" he stammered.

Muriel was seated on a bench seat on the port side of the cabin. She wore a suit of white overalls and looked very tired. In answer she asked, "What did you find in the wreck?"

Carmen, who had come into the cabin, answered, "What wreck?"

Muriel made a wry face, almost a sneer and said, "We know you found the wreck. We heard that Torres Strait Island man talking to his wife."

Hearing that made Andrew mentally groan and he flailed himself for not asking Moses to be more careful. "We haven't found anything," he said.

"Yes you have!" Muriel snapped. "Why else you need special tools?"

Carmen was obviously thinking along the same lines as Andrew as she retorted, "Very clever! So that's why your launch up-anchored and sailed away straight after the radio message."

At that Muriel gave a thin smile, so close to a smirk that Andrew felt a spurt of humiliated anger. "You knew we were there the whole time. You were watching us," he said accusingly.

"Not before you arrived. We were minding our own business searching for the wreck," Muriel answered.

"You only knew where to look because you snuck into our house and looked at my chart," Andrew cried.

At that Muriel gave a harsh laugh. "Let's not talk about sneaking into people's houses shall we? People who live in glass houses...."

A wave of hot shame silenced Andrew. Carmen took up the questioning. "How did you get there before us? Where did you get this boat?" she asked.

"From my friends," Muriel answered.

Andrew looked around at the grinning young man who stood behind them in the doorway. Then he got an even bigger shock as another young man came up through a companionway that led down to another cabin in the focsle. It was Doug. Then a more worrying shock registered. Doug was carrying a loaded speargun, which he aimed at Carmen.

"Hi, trouble makers," Doug said cheerfully. "Nice of you to find the wreck for us."

Only then did it dawn on Andrew that he and Carmen had been lured into a trap. He turned and opened his mouth to warn Carmen to get out but was too late. The first young man, Trevor he was called by Muriel, slammed the cabin door shut and drew a wicked looking diving knife from the back of his waistband.

Trevor shook his head and waved the shiny steel blade warningly. "Now don't do anything silly, like calling out."

"Wha... what are you doing? What's going on?" Andrew stammered, his anxious mind racing to sort out the implication of the situation.

"You are going to show us where the wreck is," Trevor said.

"And if we won't?" Carmen snapped.

"Then we will feed you to the fishes and then find it ourselves. It must be somewhere near where you did your last dive," Trevor replied. His voice was soft but the words had a chilling quality that froze Andrew. Only then did he notice that Trevor's eyes were a peculiar hazel-grey and had a flat, opaque look to them.

'Shark's eyes,' Andrew thought. 'He is a killer alright.'

Carmen was outraged. "This is ridiculous! You can't kidnap us."

Trevor laughed. "We can and we have," he replied in a soft, friendly sounding voice. All the while he had a smile on his face as though he was enjoying the experience immensely.

"I will scream," Carmen threatened.

The smile on Trevor's face widened. "I wouldn't advise that," he answered. "You help us and we will let you go. Cause trouble and we will really hurt you." He then raked his eyes over Carmen's body and nodded with approval. "But only after I have had some real enjoyment," he added.

The threat of rape so shocked Andrew that he felt sick. He turned to Muriel and cried, "Muriel! This is madness! Let us go. We will tell you where the wreck is. It isn't that hard to find. You don't need us."

Muriel sat stony faced and just stared back. She shook her head. It was Trevor who answered, "Too late now kiddies. We've got you. So, co-operate and we will let you go once we have found the wreck."

Andrew did not know what to do. He had been measuring distances with his eye and trying to judge his chances of tackling Doug before he could fire the speargun. Sadly he knew he hadn't a hope. Doug's finger was on the trigger and it was a compressed air speargun. It would take only a split second for Doug to fire. By then Trevor would have attacked him from behind with the knife. Andrew did not think that Doug would actually shoot Carmen but he knew he could not take that risk.

Carmen tried one more appeal to reason. "People will come looking for us soon," she said.

Trevor's smile became thinner. "And we will be all concerned and will help them look," he replied. Then he snapped, "Put your hands behind your back, both of you. Muriel, pass me that tape."

Andrew was very reluctant to do that, fearing that once he did he and Carmen would both be helpless and completely in the power of these people. But the only other option appeared to be to fight and he did not think he had any chance against the two older and stronger young men. Very slowly he did as he was told. By now waves of mounting apprehension, even terror, were starting to make him nauseous.

Trevor was quick. In a few seconds he had bound Andrew's wrists with electrical tape. Next he did the same to a furiously angry and defiant Carmen. Then he wrapped tape around Carmen's mouth so she could not scream. Andrew then suffered the same treatment. Both were then prodded below at knife point. They were pushed into two bunks down in a berth deck. Trevor and Doug produced lengths of rope and securely lashed them to the fittings, legs as well as arms. Muriel and Doug then sat on the bunk opposite and watched them.

To Andrew's intense jealousy Doug put his arm around Muriel's shoulders and she snuggled into him. Seeing that, and thinking that she had been on this launch for several nights, apparently without her parents being around, got him imagining the worst. That fuelled his jealousy and fired an intense feeling of rage and sick impotence.

But fear of dying was a stronger motive and Andrew kept looking up the short companionway at the closed cabin door, fervently hoping that someone had seen them come on board the launch. But nobody came. Time ticked slowly by. Fear and discomfort warred in him to produce extreme reactions of rage and apprehension.

Hours went by. Darkness set in outside the curtained windows. The three villains took turns at guarding them and at going up to eat and drink. From snatches of overheard conversation Andrew understood that his father had asked if they had seen him or Carmen and had been told no. Picturing the anxiety his father must now be undergoing, and the sick feelings he would experience as the night went on, made Andrew feel even worse.

An urgent need to do a pee drove Andrew to gesture with his head towards the small toilet at the bottom of the steps. It took him a while to attract Doug's attention but to his relief Doug finally came over and peeled back the gag, though none too gently. When Andrew made his request he laughed but did untie him and hoist him to his feet, his hands and legs still securely lashed. At the toilet that raised a problem which set Trevor cackling with mirth.

"Hold it for him Dougy Boy!" he jeered.

"No chance!" Doug retorted. His solution was to untie Andrew's hands. That was a huge but painful relief. Andrew had been hoping he could somehow escape or at least yell for help from the toilet but Doug had obviously thought of that and stood in there with him, a knife blade pressed into Andrew's spine.

Afterwards he was tied back down but the tape was not put around his wrists. The gag was replaced, but not as roughly. Carmen was also taken to the toilet by Muriel and then retied. More time dragged by. Andrew tried looking at the villain's watches but was unable to work it out as they wore diver's watches with half a dozen dials and were too far away and were moved too quickly for his eyes to focus.

Finally, after agonising and terrifying hours of waiting, Trevor came back down into the cabin. "Midnight. Time to go. Come up and cast off for me Doug," he ordered.

"What's the weather?" Doug asked as he stood up.

"Radio says the wind is dropping, only twenty knots and likely to drop even more by daybreak," Trevor answered.

That was a relief to Andrew, but only of a secondary kind. Fear of what his fate might be was now so strong he was on the edge of a complete breakdown. Only by an effort of will did he manage to keep himself in check. He lay back and tried to appear calm. But through his mind swirled and squirmed all the ghastly and ghoulish terrors of dying, mingled with bitter and sincere regrets at not having lived, at never having loved a woman, of not achieving his life's ambitions.

The engine rumbled into life, an obviously bigger and more powerful engine than the one that powered the old *Moa Mermaid*. Faintly heard calls and a rocking, sliding sensation told Andrew they were under way, had left the jetty.

'Dad will never find us now,' Andrew thought bitterly.

With that he began to mentally prepare himself for the worst. He did not believe that the two men would let them live. But even then his mind kept searching desperately for some way to escape. Surreptitiously he struggled with his bonds, having to be very careful as one of the villains, usually Muriel, was always there watching them.

The launch began to increase speed and to pitch. Waves began to thump against the hull, telling Andrew that they were now out of the marina and in the bay. Soon after that the launch began to roll as well as pitch and he was able to picture the dark shape of Flagstaff Hill close to port. When the launch began to drive headfirst into large waves he knew they had rounded Dalrymple Point and were out in the North Channel, heading out to sea.

Another fear now came to grip him with fingers of cold sweat- that of drowning. The launch began to pitch and yaw so much he felt sure that, if he had not been tied in, he would be tossed out of the bunk. It was no good now imagining heroic ways to escape from a capsized launch. Trussed up as he was, and lashed to the bunk, there would be no possible hope of escape before he had to take that fateful breath of water.

The fear, and the hammering, went on for hour after hour. It was so relentless that Andrew became exhausted and sick. Mental images of dying, of his body rotting, or of it being torn to shreds and nibbled by fish, made him so ill he began to pant in terror. His mind began to close down and he dropped into short periods of exhausted sleep.

To add to his distress Muriel lay down on the bunk opposite and Doug came and lay with her. They did not actually do anything but just seeing it made Andrew imagine what they might have done. It caused more spurts of impotent rage and jealousy. The only heartening thing was that Muriel did not seem happy and was obviously not enjoying the situation either.

Dawn came at last. The launch slowed and the pitching eased. That got Andrew trying to think clearly again. 'We must be back at Echo Reef,' he decided. 'But what happens now?' He could not imagine what they were to do, nor how the villains could possibly let them go.

The launch slowed even more and the motion eased so much that Andrew felt sure that they were now in the lee of the reef. That raised another quandary- should he help the villains to find the wreck?

Trevor appeared and called Doug and Muriel up on deck. They were gone for about twenty minutes and there was obviously some sort of heated discussion about their next course of action. Muriel and Doug both came back down and produced knives. Doug held his under Andrew's nose and said, "No stupid tricks. Any trouble and I'll mutilate your sister. Just go up to the cabin."

To Andrew's surprise Doug undid all the ropes. For a time Andrew could not move. The muscles were too cramped and the pain of returning circulation too intense. Carmen was the same. It was fifteen minutes before they could crawl up the companionway to the cabin. The three villains were waiting for them. Trevor stood in the aft doorway and had a sawn off, double-barrelled shotgun in his hands. Muriel and Doug sat on one side of the table and Doug indicated that the pair should sit opposite them.

Doug then said, "You are going to show us where the wreck is."

"We will, if you promise to let us go," Andrew answered.

"That's a deal," Doug answered, his eyes flicking briefly to Trevor.

Andrew glanced at Carmen and she nodded. She looked pale and exhausted, with dark shadows under her eyes. He said, "We left a small buoy, an orange fishing float. It is on the south side of the reef."

"That's where we are now," Trevor answered. "The wind is still coming from the North East." He pointed first at Andrew and then forward. "You go out on the foredeck and show me the way. Doug, you keep the girl covered. Muriel Baby, you go and start getting that diving gear ready. We want to get this done and be out of here as quick as we can."

Not seeing any other practical option Andrew made his way up through a small door onto the foredeck. This had a small rubber boat secured on it. Up behind him in the steering position appeared Trevor, still holding the shotgun. Andrew moved to the bows and gripped the stainless steel railings there. Shielding his eyes against the glare of the rising sun he looked around. What he saw dismayed him.

The area where they were was relatively calm water but beyond that was a boiling waste of foam. That, he decided, was the sea breaking on the reef in opposition to the normal currents. Further off he could just detect a curving line of surf which he thought must be the far side of the reef. Out to either side was a vast area of big waves, grey to the eye and all rolling south westwards. But how far around the reef were they? Without the fixed reference point of the anchored launches Andrew was not sure. Anxious to appear co-operative he looked carefully in all directions. Then, just by chance, he glimpsed the orange float. It was only a fleeting glimpse as the launch rose on a wave at the same time as the float, but it was enough. He pointed and yelled.

Ten cold minutes later the launch was holding its position with its bows only a few metres from the float. A problem of seamanship then presented itself to Trevor:- how to anchor in water that was too deep. The dark shadow of the coral was visible only about 30 metres ahead off the port bow and the current was obviously running across it. Andrew stood and watched unsympathetically.

'If he gets this wrong we will end up on the reef and that will be the end of us,' he thought. To his eyes the small rubber boat had no chance of surviving long in those seas.

In the end Trevor shook his head and looked baffled. Then he leaned over and yelled, "Tell Doug to take your sister out on to the aft deck. You go there as well."

Andrew did as he was told. He had briefly contemplated tossing the rubber boat over the side but common sense stopped any attempt. By the time he unlashed it Trevor would have shot him, or Doug arrived. And he did not think he would live long in the churning maelstrom that foamed on the reef. 'And I couldn't leave Carmen,' he thought unhappily.

On the aft deck the two groups faced each other. An angry Trevor stood above them at the rear of the steering position. He looked down and faced Andrew and Carmen, the shotgun still held ready. "How deep is the water on this side of the reef?" he asked.

"At least thirty or forty metres," Andrew answered. "The edge of the reef drops almost sheer. The front half of the wreck is stuck in a gully and the stern is resting on a sort of ledge. After that it drops out of sight."

"Yeah, it looks deep," Trevor said. He turned and juggled the throttles to keep the launch in position clear of the reef, then turned back to Doug. "We can't risk anchoring. I will have to keep the boat under way while you go down for the gold."

"Gold! What gold?" Carmen cried in astonishment.

"The gold that was on the ship when it went down," Trevor answered.

Andrew had heard this with equal surprise. Now he gave a harsh laugh and said, "There won't be any gold. Muriel's grandad took it all when he murdered our grandfather."

Muriel looked shocked and Andrew thought she was going to faint. Then she snarled and spat back, "He did not! You are just making that up and being horrible!"

Trevor gave her an angry and calculating look and then said to Doug, "Your little girlfriend hasn't been telling us the whole truth Dougy Boy. There had better be some gold or you can start looking for another girl-friend."

It took a moment for the implication of that to sink in. Andrew was shocked by the sheer callousness of it and he saw Muriel blanch and lick her lips. She shook her head. "There is gold. It is in a strong room."

"Trevor turned to Andrew. "Did you find any gold?"

"No. But there is a strong room. We couldn't get into it. That's why we needed tools."

Trevor nodded. "We heard that. And we saw the tools those blacks got. We went and got a set." He pointed to a canvas satchel on the deck near a line-up of diving gear. He then said, "Describe this strong room to me, and what we need to do to break in."

Andrew did, mentioning the steps, companionways and the appearance of the steel door. When he finished Trevor surprised him even more by saying, "Right then, you lot get down there and break in, and start hoisting the gold up."

"Us?" Carmen asked in surprise.

"Yes, you. The more of you at work the quicker the job should be done. I don't want to hang around here too long. Now get into those diving suits and get over the side."

There followed twenty minutes of preparation. As though in a kind of numb trance Andrew pulled on a wet suit and found fins and face mask to fit, then made up a weight belt. As he fitted a BCD he whispered to Carmen, "That guy is going to leave us in the sea."

Carmen nodded. "I think so too," she said.

Doug glanced at them and snapped, "Stop talking and get ready. Use those regulators."

Andrew did as he was told. He noted that the satchel of tools was secured to a long rope and that both Muriel and Doug strapped on knives. "Do we get a torch?" Andrew asked.

"Yes. I gather it is dark inside the wreck," Doug answered.

"It is, and there is a lot of fine sediment," Carmen cautioned. "Visibility quickly drops to nothing when it gets stirred up."

During all this Trevor had been keeping the boat near the orange float by using the engine and rudder. He also spent a lot of time scanning the sea and sky to the south. That gave Andrew a faint glimmer of hope. 'He is worried that Dad might guess where we are and follow,' he thought.

But that was no help, more a source of anxiety. It did not stop Trevor from snarling at them to get a move on. Doug picked up his speargun and gestured over the stern. A door in the transom was unbolted and lowered to make a very convenient dive platform.

Doug pointed at the sea and gestured with the speargun. "In you go. You two lead the way, and no funny business. Any trouble and I use this."

Andrew's mind had already been busy plotting possible escapes when they were down in the wreck. Now he just nodded, did a final check of his gear, picked up the satchel of tools, and then stepped over the stern. Only as he splashed in did he think of sharks and such like but he was already so terrified that he just pushed any thought of them aside.

The usual shocks followed:- the cold water, the strength of the current, the weight of the tools, the scary depth of the water. Andrew struggled to maintain a position near the orange float while he took off his facemask to spit in it and rinse it. By then Carmen was beside him and Muriel had jumped in. Doug followed.

Having no other plan and no option, and actually driven by intense curiosity to look in the strong room himself, Andrew dived. Using one hand to slide down the buoy rope and the other to release air from his BCD, he slowly descended. For the first couple of metres the surface turbulence interrupted his vision but then he clearly saw the wreck. The rope led straight down to it. The wreck looked exactly like it had on the previous dive and that gave him some reassurance.

Within half a minute he was down at the level of the door to the saloon companionway. Here he paused and looked up. Carmen was almost down and Muriel and Doug were following. The black silhouette of the launch was tossing about on the rippling surface. The second rope hung in a wide curve. For a few seconds Andrew was almost paralysed by fear, thinking that he would never get back onto that launch.

'Trevor said he would feed us to the fishes,' he told himself. 'He is going to kill us, or leave us here to die.'

Then Carmen settled beside him and gestured to go in. Andrew swallowed and thought he was going to be sick in his regulator. With an effort he controlled his stomach and propelled himself into the doorway. The second rope and the satchel both snagged but he hauled them free and swam around the steps inside. Once he had pulled in more slack on the second rope he looked down into the gloomy interior. That chilled him even more. He suspected that Doug might have orders to kill both him and Carmen there and leave their bodies but he could think of no sensible plan to avert that.

After several deep breaths Andrew swam down the companionway to the passageway outside the strong room door. Anxiously he swung the beam of his torch along the passageway, wondering if he could hide in the purser's cabin, or in the engine room. But the thought of Doug hunting him down with the speargun, or fighting him with the knife, was too much. Instead Andrew turned his attention back to the strong room door.

It looked exactly the same. As the others slid down beside him he knelt to carefully examine it. While he did this he noted that Doug had stayed up on the steps, the speargun at the ready. Already their finning was stirring up clouds of fine silt but it was being moved away by a current. Andrew noted a small area of dark discolouration at the side of the door and decided that was the place to attack.

Using a small but heavy hammer from the satchel he first banged the handle and worked it up and down to get it loose and moving freely. Carmen then took over working the lever of the handle back and forth to ease it even more. Andrew then inserted the blade of a chisel between the edge of the door and the steel bulkhead. His first blow was almost comical. He was so surprised at the amount of resistance in the water that he barely tapped the head of the chisel. But he quickly learned that short, fast taps were the way to do it. The point of the chisel began to work its way in.

Five minutes work right along that edge had the door open a few milli-metres. By then Andrew was panting heavily. He stopped to get his breath back and checked his air pressure. 150 psi. Plenty left. He went back to work. Keeping the chisel point just in he got Carmen to push the door closed, then hammered again. This time the chisel went in enough to open the door almost a centimetre.

'The hinges must have been well greased and there hasn't been much rust down here in the darkness and colder water,' he surmised. There was certainly almost no coral and only a bit of slime. Now he placed the chisel and hammer back in the satchel and took out a short crowbar with a slightly curved end. The narrow end he slid into the gap. Then he braced his feet against the bulkhead and heaved.

At first nothing happed but then the door suddenly moved a few centi-metres. Rather than keep heaving he pushed the door shut again. Carmen saw what he intended and helped him to work the door back and forth. Each time it became easier to move and opened a few more centimetres. Andrew had feared that the job might be beyond their tools but now saw that a bit more work would soon have the door open.

Once again Andrew slid the crowbar in and braced his feet against the bulkhead. Carmen helped and they both strained together. The door sud-denly gave way, pulling right out to half open. This made it possible to enter the compartment and Andrew paused to place the tools down in the satchel. With his heart hammering with excitement and his breath coming in rasping gasps he shone his torch inside.

At first he could see nothing but blurred outlines. Then, as he moved his torch beam back and forth, the shape of the compartment became apparent. It was about 3 metres by 4, the bulkhead to the left angling in as the underwater form of the hull narrowed towards the stern. A swirl of sediment made it hard to see so Andrew carefully eased himself inside the strong room. Muriel slid down and edged in behind him, causing him to move even further into the room. A third torch beam shone in: Carmen's. She leaned in through the doorway.

Andrew now noted that the whole deck was a mass of fine silt and his finning was stirring it up. He also saw that the room was almost empty, with just a peculiar spherical object against the far bulkhead and a few sharp angles which might once have been a trunk or box showing in the lower corner. But then his torch beam picked up a long, thin shape near him. Bending down he picked it up and discovered it was a badly perished rubber hose. The thing had gone almost petrified over time and was stiff and rigid. One end was near him and Muriel shone her torch on it, revealing a straight cut.

By then a ghastly suspicion had been forming in Andrew's mind. He followed the hose along with his torch beam, then gasped in shock at what it revealed. As he pulled the hose up it stirred up a fine mist of silt but it led straight to the spherical shape lying against the far bulkhead. Andrew now recognized the large, round object to be an old-fashioned, brass diver's helmet. Then he noted that it was attached to a flat looking canvas suit all covered in sediment. The suit had mostly rotted but showing through a hole was a whitish, stick like thing.

Andrew stared in horror and gasped in shock. 'Grandad!' he thought, appalled at the realization that the white thing was a leg bone.

Gasping with emotion he turned to look at Muriel. He saw Muriel's face register shock and stunned horror before she turned to meet his eyes. Anger and grim satisfaction at being so ghoulishly vindicated made him point accusingly. Muriel eyes seemed to blaze.

Suddenly Muriel lashed at him with a knife. Instinctively Andrew put up his hand to protect himself. It was the hand that held his torch and her blade slashed across the back of his fingers. He flinched and pulled away, dropping his torch as he did. Blinded by the water and darkness he tried to move away but before he realized what she intended Muriel reached out and tore his facemask off, then snatched the regulator from his mouth.

Chapter 38

Worst Nightmare

Andrew reeled back in terror. In his shock he opened his mouth and gasped. Water gushed into his throat and up his nose, even as his stunned mind screamed that this could not be true. 'This is my worst nightmare!' he told himself. 'I will wake up soon.' But the spasm of coughing and retching that shook him told him it was all too true.

In his panic-stricken and blurry vision Andrew saw dark shapes tumbling and struggling and the beams of two torches showed as dim bands in the swirling cloud of sediment that was engulfing them. Someone bumped hard against him as he struggled to regain his footing. That sent him tumbling down into the silt. His air tank struck the steel deck hard. More water went up his nose, telling him that he was upside down. Frantic with fear he gripped his nose with one hand and groped behind him with his other arm in a desperate attempt to find his regulator.

'Don't panic! Don't panic!' he screamed mentally at himself.

His searching arm scooped the regulator hose into the crook of its elbow just as he had been trained to do. Driven by an urgent need to breathe Andrew swung it forward. But by then he had fallen sideways on the muddy deck. He felt slime and mud and then crackling and snapping sensations, as though he was rolling on dry sticks. His appalled mind told him it was his dead grandfather's bones he was crushing and he whimpered and coughed at the same time.

Desperately struggling to hold his breath and to keep control of his thoughts he fumbled the regulator into his mouth and purged it. Then it took an effort of willpower to use it to breathe, fearing he would suck in water instead of air. But it was air, blessed air.

For a couple of seconds he just lay there, half floundering, while he gasped and coughed. His eyes watered and he feared he was going to vomit into the regulator. But he kept his wits about him sufficiently to take a deep breath and to snatch it out just before his stomach heaved. Sour bile choked at the back of his throat and he tasted mud and seawater, but it was done. He quickly replaced the regulator, purged again and took another breath.

Through all of this his eyes had been frantically trying to work out what the rapidly moving shadows meant. Fearing to be knifed or shot by the speargun he was desperate to be able to see. But without a face mask it was all just a muddy blur. He could make out the dim shape of the doorway with people fighting in it. Then there was an explosion of compressed air bubbles which sent his heart hammering into the top of his sour tasting throat.

'Someone has lost their air!' he thought. But who?

Frantically Andrew groped around the deck for his facemask. As he did his hands encountered slime, mud, rotten timber and other, harder objects. The thought of what these might be made his flesh crawl with horror. The only thing he really recognized feeling was a big, lead soled diver's boot.

Suddenly things got a whole lot worse. The light went completely. For a few seconds Andrew did not understand what had happened. Then the terrifying truth dawned on him- the door had been closed. Now the panic did surge. Frantic to escape he swam towards where he thought the door was. He was wrong and learned it by slamming hard and painfully against a steel bulkhead.

The pain from the blow helped steady him and he realized he was sobbing and panting for air, his heart hammering like thunder in his skull. 'Trapped!' his mind screamed.

With an intense effort of willpower he stopped moving and tried to calm his breathing. But terror and panic kept breaking through as he realized he not only did not know which way the door was, but he could not even tell which way was up. At least not until he got water up his nose. Then he had to cough and blow and grip his nostrils with his fingers.

'Slow down! Stop panicking! Get control! Do what you have been taught,' he told himself.

Summoning up all his remaining reserves of willpower he forced himself to stop moving and to slow his breathing. That was the hardest because the sound and the bile gave him an intense urge to rip the regulator out and to swim for the surface. But what surface? He was trapped, and in total, absolute darkness such as he had never before experienced.

But freezing into a trembling, almost rigid pose worked. Andrew settled on the deck and was able to get his breathing under control properly. Then his mind began to grapple with the other problems. 'I need my face mask, and I need my torch,' he thought. 'Then I might be able to locate the door and find a way out.'

To his intense relief his hands encountered his face mask. That was so comforting that he just lay and shivered for a few seconds before fumbling with it to work out which way it had to go. Then he made himself remember all those training sessions he had hated. He pulled the facemask on and adjusted the fit. Then he lay back and pointed his face in the direction he thought was up and expelled the water. Because he could not see he wasn't sure if it worked or not but he thought it did as his eyes felt easier.

For a few more seconds, maybe a minute, Andrew just lay there and trembled with reaction. He also wondered if he was alone. 'Is Carmen in here with me?' he thought. Somehow he was sure that Muriel and Doug were not. 'They have killed Carmen with the speargun and locked me in to drown,' he thought.

That was such a terrifying idea that it all but paralysed him for the next few minutes. It was the dark that forced him to move. It became so claustrophobic and depressing that it was unendurable. Just in time Andrew realized that he was on the edge of hysteria and real panic, experiencing a frantic urge to rip off his equipment. Only by biting on the rubber mouth piece could he stop himself screaming. He found he was gasping again and that his heart was thumping as though he had just run up a mountain.

Once again he calmed himself by an effort of sheer willpower. 'Find your torch,' he told himself. It was such an obvious and sensible idea that he wondered why he hadn't thought of it earlier. But it was easier said than done. It meant crawling slowly across the bottom, feeling with his hands. Knowing what lay near him in the darkness caused him to shudder with revulsion but he made himself do it.

His hands again encountered the heavy diver's boot so he shied away from that in the direction he thought the door was. Several squelchy objects caused him some concern, wondering if it was his grandfather's remains or just rotting packing cases. Then his hands encountered a solid object in the ooze. It was a small rectangular prism about 15 cm long by 7 cm wide. When he tried to pick it up Andrew gasped in surprise. Even though it was only the size of a blackboard duster he could hardly lift it.

'A gold ingot!' he thought. For a few seconds his spirits lifted with delight at such a discovery. Then he realized with grim irony that he was trapped and the gold, how ever much it was worth, was worthless to him. The idea caused him to give a short grunt of bitter laughter. 'What use is all the gold in the world if I can't get out? I need that torch!'

So he went back to his unpleasant search. More mud and soggy, unidentifiable objects were touched. Then his hands encountered what they sought. The feel of the torch caused him a surge of hope and he sobbed in near hysteria. He had been fearing that the fall might have broken the bulb or somehow damaged the torch but as he picked it up he saw that it was still turned on. The light had not been visible because the torch had sunk into the thick layer of ooze.

But as Andrew shone the beam around he gave another short, ironic laugh. His movements had stirred up so much sediment that visibility was reduced to less than arms length, and even that was vague and blurry. Through his mind flitted the dive instructor's story of the divers who went into the torpedo compartment of the sunken submarine and died when their air ran out before they could find their way back out!

'That will be me, unless I am very careful,' he thought. With that horrifying thought in mind he remembered to check how much air he had left. By lifting the gauge up as close as he could with the torch beam shining on it he was just able to read it. That gave him another shock. '75psi! Already way below the safe level.' Again the dive instructor's warning came to him, this time with chilling force.

Knowing that he had perhaps twenty minutes of air left at most, and then only if he did not squander it in panicky gulps, Andrew began feeling his way across the deck. He was sure it was the deck because he could at least see the direction his air bubbles were rising in. It also gave him a queer satisfaction to note that he had replaced his mask and cleared it almost completely. 'The training really works!' he marvelled.

Once he found a bulkhead Andrew followed it around to the left. 'I must come to the door,' he reasoned. He did. It was on the next bulkhead. Seeing the door caused him to sigh with relief and a shiver of released tension rippled through him. The back of the door was set against the rim of the coaming, the raised sill and edges that gave it its strength. These helped by giving him something to hang on to. His questing torch beam and fingers then found what he so eagerly sought- the handle.

It was one of the long lever type, the same as on the outside. Grasping it firmly and bracing himself he pulled. Nothing happened and a chill of apprehension went through him. He tried again, harder this time. Still no movement! A real spasm of worry checked him and he realized he was panting again.

'Don't get anxious! Conserve the air,' he told himself. Then he shook his head. 'No, no point. If I can't open this I am done for.'

So he heaved with all his might- to no avail. The door was obviously locked or jammed on the outside. For a few seconds he was stunned into immobility by the dread implications of that. Then panic began to surge and he tried again, pulling and pushing with all his might.

Nothing moved. Andrew stopped to get his breath and to allow his hammering heart to ease. He realized he was dizzy. Nausea from apprehension made him think he was going to be sick again.

'Trapped!' he thought with disbelief. 'It can't be true! I am just dreaming this!' But he knew with a terrifying, sickening certainty that he was not. A check of his air shocked him even more. 60 psi! Only ten or fifteen minutes left.

That got him trying again. Frantically he pulled, pushed and scrabbled at the door. It did not budge. A close-up search around the rim revealed no sign of any crack or weakness. Trembling with terror at the knowledge of his own approaching death he clung to the handle and whimpered.

After a couple of minutes his breathing slowed and he began to contemplate his fate. Prayer helped but it was so utterly terrifying and apparently inevitable that he could hardly think straight. In desperation he hammered against the door with the heel of his fists. This was futile as the water cushioned his blows and he lost his grip and slid down.

'I need some tools,' he thought desperately. That got him down scrabbling in the slime again but he knew he had left the tool satchel outside and his tingling fingers found none. They did however encounter the ossified air hose of his grandfather. That was a ghoulish shock and a reminder of his own probable fate. For a few seconds he tried to imagine what it must have been like for his grandfather.

'His air hose cut by his best friend! What treachery! And trapped, locked in here till he ran out of air.' It was a truly horrific image. But then it got worse. 'No, he didn't have long to die. As soon as his air hose was cut the water would have started to flood in. He must have just had time to realize that he had been betrayed. Then the water would have flooded his helmet and drowned him.'

Appalled at the grim and bitter thoughts his grandfather must have had in those last minutes Andrew sobbed and trembled. Awareness of his own rapidly approaching end - 55 psi- seven or eight minutes?- caused him to almost dissolve into a gibbering mess. But then another thought came to him. 'Grandad was down here working. Maybe he had some tools with him?'

Andrew did not want to go near that 'thing' in the decayed canvas and rubber suit but he forced himself. 'He was my grandad. His ghost won't mind,' he told himself, all the while shaking so badly he could hardly keep the rubber mouth piece between his lips.

Steeling himself for the ghoulish ordeal Andrew followed the air hose across the compartment to the big brass helmet. Bending right down so he could see in the murk he made himself look through the glass front window. Slimy, greenish-white showed and Andrew gibbered at himself knowing that he was looking at his grandfather's skull- and that his own would look like that after his dissolution!

Then his hands encountered the suit and what could only be bones. With gasps of nauseous breathing he made himself look. There were no tools. But there was a small, circular, silver object. He picked this up, rubbed the slime off it and brought it close to his facemask. It was a wrist watch. The wrist band had obviously rotted away. Andrew slid the watch into the side pocket of his BCD and resumed his frantic search.

Another air check. 40 psi. Only minutes to go! Now it was getting hard to breathe, to suck enough in with each gasping breath. And then the beam of his torch flickered, dimmed, flickered again, and went out!

Absolute, total blackness enfolded Andrew. It was the darkness off the grave and now the panic did surge. A frantic need to escape gripped him, at the same time as irrational urges to rip off the facemask, breathing gear and BCD. His fingers clawed at his equipment and he began to cough and splutter.

But a tiny part of his terrified brain was still working and it calmed him. 'Stop this!' he chided himself. 'Grandad is here and his spirit will be watching! (Could a soul- or a spirit- or whatever- escape through steel bulkheads, or was it doomed to be trapped too?).' The thought that his grandfather's ghost might be with him both terrified and reassured him. 'You are going to die- so at least die like a man!' Andrew told himself.

With another huge effort of willpower Andrew composed himself. He followed the air hose back to the door, groping for it in the dark. Then he settled there and waited. 'Won't be long. I must have only a few more minute's worth of air,' he thought.

Through his mind ran a stream of regrets- sadness when he thought of his parent's grief; regret that he had never really lived, that he was leaving a life he enjoyed so much and was so looking forward too. 'Now I will never get to make love to Letitia- or any other girl,' he reflected. 'I will have no grandchildren of my own.'

Light!

A dim, hazy blur of light!

It was right near him. A second source of light joined it, stabbing into the murk. 'A torch beam!' his dazed mind noted. Then it struck him- the door had been opened!

But by whom? Was it Carmen come to rescue him, or Doug come to make sure he was dead?'

'Doesn't matter! I've got a chance! I will go down fighting! Quick! While you still have a few breaths left!' he told himself. With a frantic urgency Andrew finned towards the oval of murkiness. There was a diver there but Andrew just pushed at the person, desperate to get out. As he did he banged his knee painfully on the door but that only served to spur him on.

'I'm out!' he thought as his eyes glimpsed the dim outlines of the steps.

Then one of the ropes wrapped around his legs and he came to a squirming standstill with a jerk. In the gloomy light he saw the other diver swim towards him- and the faint light flashed on a steel blade.

'He's got a knife! He's going to kill me!' Andrew thought in alarm.

He kicked and struggled to get away but the rope held him. Then the other diver went low and gripped his ankle. Andrew kicked again but the other diver fended him off and he saw that the person wasn't trying to stab him but was cutting at the rope with the knife. 'Perhaps it is Carmen?' he wondered.

It was Muriel. As the rope parted she rose and he saw her face in her torch beam. She signalled to go up. At that moment Andrew found he was sucking at nothing. He sucked with all his strength but nothing came to his lungs.

'I have run out of air!' he thought in dismay. To be so close! But then he remembered his training. There in front of him, clipped to Muriel's BCD, was her alternate air source. He reached out and grabbed it, while at the same time making frantic 'out of air' signals.

To his intense relief she did not fight him off but allowed him to take the alternate regulator. Now seconds counted as he was struggling to hold his breath ("Don't hold you breath- breathe out," the instructor had said. But how!). Fearing he would black out Andrew pulled his own regulator from his mouth and inserted the other. A moment's frantic fumbling and he had pushed the purge button. In desperate need he breathed in.

'Ah! Air!' Relief flooded through him. But now he felt so weak and dizzy his limbs did not seem to want to move. He felt Muriel grip his BCD straps and then he was lifted up the steps and into the saloon companionway.

'Oh blessed light!' Even if it was only a murky, pale green. More waving coils of rope threatened to ensnare them but these were pushed aside and Muriel hauled him out through the doorway into the open sea. 'The open sea!' he thought thankfully. Never mind the deep, scary blue! What was a shark or two now!

They began to rise. Andrew realized that Muriel had her arm around the buoy rope and that she was gripping him tightly. Her face was close to his and he could see her eyes now in her facemask. The eyes were wide with horror and distress. It was all very puzzling. Doubt about her motives and what might happen next- about what had been happening outside the strong room while he was trapped inside- came to grip him with apprehension.

And there was the buoy bobbing just above him on the surface! A few seconds later Andrew's head broke surface and he gasped with such relief he almost choked. Muriel still gripped him tightly and he realized she was inflating his BCD by her own mouth. That was a relief as he knew he lacked the strength to do any such thing. All he could do was float on the surface, so glad to be alive that he just did not care.

Not until a few minutes had passed anyway. Then he began to recover a little and his wits began to gather. He noted that the waves were smaller than when he went down, and that the sun seemed very bright.

'Where is the white launch?' he wondered. After checking that he was in fact floating well in his BCD he took out the alternate air source and looked at Muriel. "What happened? Where is your boat?" he asked.

Muriel had pulled her face mask down and he saw her already distressed face crumple. "Gone," she cried. "He has left us to die."

It took a few moments for the import of that to sink in. Even then Andrew did not want to believe it. 'Gone?' he thought stupidly. But a look in all directions revealed nothing but ocean- just rippling waves as far as he could see in all directions. A sickening new chill of apprehension began to grip him. 'We will never be able to swim to land,' he thought in dismay. The awful story of the two American tourists left accidentally by a dive boat on the Barrier Reef a few years before popped into his mind to torment him.

'Oh my God!' he thought. 'I might still drown yet!'

Chapter 39

By a Thread.

Andrew pushed his facemask up onto his forehead, the better to look around. The words of the dive instructor saying not to do that because it was the sign of a distressed diver then crossed his mind. He reached up to pull it down and then gave a feeble shake of the head.

'I am a distressed diver!' he thought. He felt so weak and wrung out that he doubted if he could swim fifty strokes. In his mind it was a certainty that without the inflated BCD to keep him up he would just sink. His arms and legs felt so weak he could barely move them.

Then a wave slopped into his face and he swallowed salt water. That made his eyes sting and he coughed and wanted to retch. To prevent being hit in the face again he pulled his face mask back on and placed the mouthpiece of the snorkel in his mouth. That did not work however. Not only was he coughing so much but he just could not stand the claustrophobic feeling and the sucking, rasping sounds and sheer effort needed to breathe. Vivid memories of the last dive caused panic to well up and he had to snatch the snorkel out and gasp at the fresh, clean air.

Muriel still had a grip on his BCD straps and he saw that she was clinging to the rope netting attached to the orange buoy. She turned him so that his back was to the prevailing wind and waves. After another look around he asked, "Where are Carmen and Doug?"

"I don't know," Muriel replied.

"Is Carmen still inside the wreck?" Andrew asked.

Muriel shook her head. "No. She swam out," she replied.

A sicking feeling of dread settled like a cold jellyfish in his stomach. Again he anxiously scanned the waves in all directions. "What happened?" he croaked between hacking coughs.

Muriel let out a sob, causing him to look at her. He saw that her face was convulsed with distress. She said, "I..... I... I did it."

"Did what?"

"Cut her air tube," Muriel answered.

Andrew was aghast. Vivid memories of holding the cut air hose to his grandfather's helmet caused him to shudder and cringe. 'Carmen- with her air cut!' he thought in shocked dismay. He turned to look at Muriel as both fear and anger stirred in him. "Why did you do that?" he asked.

Muriel looked back at him with guilty defiance written all over her face. Then she shook her head and tears filled her eyes. Several times she tried to speak but her voice choked up and she sobbed. Finally she managed to say, "When I looked into that empty room and I saw the diver's helmet and suit there I felt stunned. I realized that what you had said, and what I had secretly denied and feared, was true. It hurt so much!"

Her voice tailed off and she stared away across the waves. Then she began to weep again and sobbed, "You have no idea how much it hurt!" she cried. "To find out that the man you had loved all your life, the dear, sweet grandad who had cared for you and been so kind and gentle, might actually be a murderer!"

Andrew felt her pain but his own anger rose even more. Bitter words about how much it hurt to be locked in a room to die, or to have your air hose cut, rose to his lips but with an effort he kept them unsaid. Instead he let her weep for a minute or so before asking, "But why hurt us? Why cut Carmen's air hose?"

Muriel turned red, haunted eyes on him and wailed, "Because it was you two who brought this about! If you hadn't gone nosing about and digging up things none of this would have happened. I was just so angry that I lashed out. I wanted to hurt you."

"Well you've succeeded!" Andrew retorted, bitterly, sick and angry at his sister's probable death.

"I'm sorry," Muriel cried. Her distress was genuine but that only peeved Andrew more.

"Was it you that locked me in?" he asked.

"Yes."

For a few seconds Andrew was speechless with anger and sick memories of his terror and near drowning. "I don't think you have any idea what you did to me," he commented.

Muriel began to weep again. "I do! I'm sorry. I am so ashamed of myself. I just want to die!"

That got Andrew even more worried. The last thing he wanted was someone else to drown. He looked at her and said, "Why did you come back and let me out?"

"Oh why do you think!" Muriel cried, her distress making her voice catch. "I surfaced and that horrible Trevor wouldn't let me get back into his launch. He pointed his gun at me and wanted to know what was going on and where the gold was. When I told him there wasn't any he just opened the throttle and left."

She pointed off towards the north, then said, "By then I had calmed down a little and realized what I had done. I felt so guilty. It came as a terrible shock to me to realize that I was possibly doing exactly the same thing my grandfather may have done, leaving another diver to drown. I.. I .. just... just couldn't... I knew I couldn't live with myself."

Andrew gave a short, sardonic laugh and retorted, "You couldn't live! I was only seconds from drowning."

"Sorry."

Andrew looked at her tear-streaked, face and trembling lips. "Yeah, well, thanks anyway," he said. He was now worried about surviving with her in close proximity; scared she might do something irrational. Then another thought crossed his mind and he asked, "What became of Doug? Did he go on the boat?"

Muriel shook her head. "No. When I cut Carmen's air hose she tried to swim to the surface. I think Doug went with her. I know he dropped the spear gun."

On hearing that a spark of hope leapt in Andrew's heart. "So she might be alive?"

Muriel nodded. "Maybe. But I didn't see any sign of them when I surfaced the first time."

"The current took them away," Andrew said, speaking more to himself and staring off across the jumbled waves along the west side of the reef. Now his hopes sagged again at the thought of Carmen and Doug being swept away from the reef and off into open water. He knew from hard experience that the sea was so big that the chances of them ever being found before they died of exposure were so slim as to be almost non-existent. Harsh memories of his own ordeal in the sea with Graham and Ken the previous year rose to depress him further.

Andrew shivered, then it dawned on him that he and Muriel were in dire peril from the same source. He realized that he was shaking not only from reaction and shock but also from the cold. Even with the wet suit on he felt chilled. 'We will both die of exposure before the day is out,' he told himself.

That was a chilling thought but somehow it was much easier to face out in the open air and bright sunshine. For the third time in a few hours he began to mentally prepare himself to die.

All this while he had been floating, buoyed up by his inflated BCD and held by Muriel. As he bobbed up and down on the waves his eyes automatically scanned the sea. Suddenly his heart skipped a beat. Something black! 'A shark's fins?' he anxiously wondered.

The sick feelings of fear gripped him again as he strained his eyes to study the surging waves a hundred metres away. Then he saw it again and his heart turned over with fear. He was just about to warn Muriel when he saw a thin, black object go up and then down. 'That was a person's arm!' he told himself.

As they rose on the next wave he shielded his eyes and looked more carefully. This time he almost shouted with joy. Two black blobs were visible side by side. He pointed and then yelled, "It is Carmen and Doug! Look! There!"

It was. One of them waved again and Andrew managed to summon up the energy to wave back. But there was no possibility of going to help them. It was all he and Muriel could do to cling to the float. He knew that if they let go the current would wash them away and he would not have the strength to swim back to it. So he had to watch with his heart in his mouth from anxiety as the two divers battled against the current. For a while it seemed they were making no progress at all and Andrew became fearful that Carmen might slip away when so close.

'But close to what? Even if she reaches us we will still all die,' he thought. 'Nobody will ever notice us this far off the beaten track.'

It seemed a bitter irony. So he flexed his aching fingers and reached over to grab the buoy, allowing Muriel a short rest. She was showing signs of exhaustion by then and allowed him to grab her BCD and keep her in position while she rested.

Five long minutes passed before Carmen and Doug finally reached them. By then both were gasping and showing signs of collapse. Muriel reached out as soon as they got close enough and grabbed Doug's gear. Andrew took a firm hold of Carmen's.

"Oh! Thank God!" Carmen gasped. "I thought we would never make it. Thank you Doug."

For some minutes neither could speak. Only after they had recovered their breath could they answer questions. When asked what had happened Carmen glared at Muriel and said, "I would have drowned if Doug hadn't taken me up using his alternate air source."

"Did you lose the rope?" Andrew asked.

Carmen nodded. "Yes we did. There were so many bubbles we were lucky to even get outside. We just went to the surface and then inflated our BCDs. By then the current had swept us right past the side of the reef."

Doug then joined in, saying, "Luckily a back eddy took us in behind the reef in the shallow water."

"I recognized the place as being near where we anchored," Carmen said. "So we started swimming back along the edge of the reef."

"Then we saw the launch leave," Doug added. "We thought you were on it. What happened? Where did Trevor go?"

Muriel answered that, giving the same story as she had told Andrew.

Doug listened then swore and sneered, "The gutless rat has run out on us!"

"So what do we do now?" Muriel asked.

"Not many options," Doug replied.

"Should we try to reach the coast?" Muriel asked.

Doug shook his head and so did Carmen. Andrew answered her. "Hopeless! It is eighty kilometres at the closest point and the current will take us north and make it three times as far. We have no hope of doing that."

Carmen agreed. "The current is about five to seven knots. That means thirty to forty hours in the sea. The cold and exhaustion will get us before we even sight the coast, if we ever do."

It was a terrifying prospect and Andrew's spirits, which had risen with Carmen's arrival, now began to slump again. In desperation he cast around for some plan to survive but could think of none. 'This reef doesn't even have a little sandy cay which is exposed at low tide,' he thought. It all looked very grim. He shivered again and that set his teeth chattering.

Carmen saw this and said, "Are you alright Andrew?"

"Bit cold and worn out," he answered.

"What happened to you two?" Carmen asked, looking from him to Muriel.

Andrew instantly decided not to make the situation worse so he shook his head. "Tell you later. I got stuck in there and Muriel got me out," he replied.

"What did you see?" Carmen asked.

"Not a lot," Andrew answered. "The sediment got so stirred up I couldn't even see the door or even work out which was up. I dropped my torch."

As he said that he remembered the knife slash and glanced at his knuckles. A shallow, raw cut ran across them but only tiny traces of bleeding still showed. 'I hope that doesn't attract the sharks,' he thought.

"Was there any gold?" Carmen persisted.

Andrew thought quickly and shook his head. "No," he answered. "Just some rotten packing cases and mush." The memory of the ordeal made him shudder and he trembled so badly he found it hard to hold on. 'I will only tell Carmen about Grandad if we look like it is really the end,' he decided.

"We must form a huddle to keep warm," Carmen suggested. Andrew saw the sense in that and Doug backed her up so they grouped tightly together, Andrew clinging to Carmen and Muriel. Andrew knew that he was near the end of his strength so he clipped one of his BCD straps around the buoy rope and another through Carmen's straps. That made it much easier and all he had to do was float. For the next hour the four just floated in a group. Andrew became quite sick and could not stop shivering. That made him feel desperately anxious as he recognized the early symptoms of hyperthermia. 'I won't last till sundown,' he thought.

Once again horrible thoughts of his body being ripped into shreds by fish as it rotted came to haunt and terrify. For the fourth time that day he began to pray and consider how he might face death. It made him both sad and angry that he had involved Carmen in the adventure and that she was going to die too. 'What a tragic waste!' he thought, thinking of what a wonderful life she might otherwise have lived.

For something to talk about he asked Muriel how she knew that Echo Reef was the place to come. Muriel made a sour face and said, "I took a digital photo of that chart at your place. Grandad wouldn't let me see that chart of his and that made me sick with horrible suspicions. I just had to know!"

"So you got Doug and his mate to bring you here by cooking up the story about finding the gold," Carmen said accusingly.

Muriel nodded and wept a little. Then she said, "We got here and started diving and it was quiet a shock when another boat turned up. It was even more of a shock to see you and Andrew on board. Where did you get that boat? Who are those two black men?"

"Torres Strait Islanders," Andrew answered. "One of them is the grandson of one of the crewmen on the *Deeral*- Solomon Tapau. His name is Moses Tapua and he is Luke Karaku's uncle."

That caused another grim train of thought. Not only had Muriel's grandfather murdered Bert Collins but he must also have murdered the two T.Is as well! Seeing Muriel looking very unhappy he asked, "How did you get your mum and dad to let you come with Trevor and Doug?"

Muriel shook her head and said, "I didn't. I just ran away." She turned to Doug and said, "I'm not really sixteen Doug. I'm only fourteen."

Andrew saw a look of sick dismay cross Doug's face. Doug shook his head. "Well don't you say anything about us," he said. "I don't want any more trouble."

"If we survive!" Carmen put in.

A wave of sick jealousy boiled in Andrew as the implications of Doug's comments, and earlier ones by Trevor, now hit him. 'She has given Doug sex in return for the use of the boat!' he thought. It made him both nauseous and sad.

Another period of silence ensued. Each bobbed on the waves, wrapped in their own grim thoughts. Time passed slowly and Andrew began to shake continually and feel dizzy. He knew he was very thirsty. Once again he considered trying to swim to the mainland but the mathematics was too compelling. 'Even trying to navigate would be hopeless. We would swim in semi-circles as the sun kept moving and we kept forgetting to adjust our course,' he told himself. He also knew that adrift in that vast area of ocean meant no hope at all. 'At least here a boat might arrive, some fishermen, or even Dad,' he told himself.

He was now shivering and cramping up and his head began to ache. To ease his growing thirst he allowed seawater to wet his mouth. The stories about shipwrecked sailors in boats going mad from drinking salt water he ignored. 'The cold will kill me long before I go mad!' he thought grimly.

The end seemed near. The sun was now high in the sky and Andrew thought they had been in the water for four or five hours. 'Time to tell Carmen about Grandad,' he decided. He had been dreading having to do that, mainly because it might spark a violent and irrational response from Muriel. Now he shrugged. 'So what? I'm going to die soon anyway. I'd better tell her while we are still alert enough to make sense.'

Andrew opened his mouth to speak and then stopped. 'What is that noise?' He struggled to turn his head. Yes, a noise- and not a sea noise of waves and wind, rather a vibrating, tremor. Hope surged and he shielded his eyes from the glare and looked around.

"A helicopter!" he croaked.

Several kilometres away a tiny dark object was visible in the sky. To Andrew's unspeakable relief it grew rapidly larger and seemed to be heading straight for them. But as it got closer he saw that it would pass half a kilometre to the east.

"Wave!" he shouted (or croaked). To be so close and to have salvation pass them by! It was exquisite agony and irony! He began to wave and shout. The others joined in. To his intense disappointment the helicopter actually turned away and went off eastwards. His hopes turning to bitter despair Andrew watched with dismay as it dwindled in size.

With his heart in his mouth he watched the now distant machine. When it was a kilometre or so away it turned north. Then it began to slowly circle.

'It is following the edge of the reef,' he decided. Even so he did not dare hope that it might come back, lest he be disappointed again. But then he had to hope, in spite of trying to steel himself for another crushing blow.

Carmen turned to him, her red-rimmed eyes wild with hope. "It's coming round. It is circling around the reef."

It was. Andrew began to wave again and called on the others to do so. With his heart swelling as though it might burst he saw the helicopter turn and come buzzing towards them. It was flying at a height of only about fifty metres, low enough so that he could see the two people in the little perspex bubble of a cockpit, and to read the name of the company on its side. Frantically he waved, bobbing up and down as he did so and catching a mouthful of water as a consequence. By now he was so excited he barely noticed.

Then the helicopter was past them and he felt his stomach turn over with dread. Panic and despair began to surge but he kept on waving. 'I can see them! Why can't they see us?' he thought angrily, noting the person leaning out of the right hand side.

Suddenly the helicopter turned sharply to the left, away from them. That both puzzled and worried Andrew. But the helicopter kept on turning, losing altitude as it did. Within seconds it was heading back towards them, now only about 25 metres up. 'Have they seen us?' Andrew wondered, scarcely daring to hope.

The helicopter swung low around them in a tight circle and Andrew saw a man lean out and his arm wave. "They've seen us!" he croaked, or sobbed (He wasn't sure which).

The people in the helicopter had. There could be no doubt about it. The machine began to circle, slow and low. One of the men kept leaning out and was aiming what might have been a camera or binoculars at them. This went on for ten minutes.

"Why don't they land, or hover or something?" Doug snarled.

"No floats," Carmen replied.

Andrew could see that it was a small land machine with skids and the thought crossed his mind that he wouldn't like to be flying that far out to sea in such a tiny machine. It obviously did not have room for any passengers and no external winch or similar equipment was visible. 'But it will have a radio,' he thought. 'With luck they are calling for help right now.'

It was the best that could be done. For the next twenty minutes the helicopter circled, sometimes low and sometimes much higher up. But there was no doubt they had been seen and reported. Thus Andrew was not all that concerned when the helicopter came down low and hovered while the man on the right hand side leaned out and waved and pointed to the south and the machine then buzzed off in that direction.

"They must be low on fuel," he said to Carmen.

"Yes," she agreed. "But they saw us and help must be on its way."

But would it be in time? Andrew worried as a bout of severe shivering shook him.

In the end it was more than 2 hours before the rescue vessel appeared. It was a big, yellow-hulled Volunteer Coastguard launch, a catamaran, all bristling with antenna. The thing arrived so fast that Andrew did not see it until it was only a few hundred metres away. As soon as he realized what he was looking at he sighed with relief and just slumped in his gear, held up only by the BCD.

The launch slowed and nosed slowly towards them, obviously wary of the nearby coral reef. As the launch reached them it turned around and Andrew saw a line of at least a dozen faces looking down at them from the shelter deck and the steering position above it. Only after Carmen had cried out with relief did Andrew recognize his father, Moses and Jordan among the faces. Then he knew he was really safe and relaxed.

The launch was designed and equipped for getting survivors aboard from in the water. It had water jet propulsion so could safely turn it stern towards them. At the stern was a diving deck and open transom. Two crew members in wet suits jumped in with ropes and helped haul them to the launch. Andrew was so exhausted and his fingers so swollen and stiff that he could barely unclip the BCD from the buoy, and from Carmen's air tank. The rescue man then towed him to the stern and he was hauled aboard.

Andrew was so weak he could not stand. His diving gear was stripped off him and placed under the bench seat along the port side. He was then helped onto the seat. By then his father and the two T.Is were with him, towelling him dry and offering a hot drink. The wet suit was left on and a thermal blanket wrapped around him. All Andrew could do was sit and shiver violently as reaction and cold gripped him. He noted Carmen being helped to the seat beside him and gave her a weak grin.

All he wanted to do was succumb to his weariness and collapse but he kept himself focused till Muriel and Doug were both safely aboard. Then he got another shock, one which got his heart going and his emotions working. Muriel's parents were both there- and so were Old Mr Murchison and Grandma Murchison!

Chapter 40

Be Sure your Sin Will Find you Out!

Seeing Old Mr Murchison was such a surprise that for a moment Andrew could not take it in. Then a deep sense of grievance and anger began to simmer. He watched coldly while Muriel was fussed over by her anxious (and obviously angry) parents. Then he shifted his gaze back to the old man and met his eyes unflinchingly.

Old Mr Murchison was the first to look away. He turned to join the group worrying about Muriel. Grandma Murchison cast an anxious glance towards Andrew and Carmen then lowered herself to the seat on the other side, beside Muriel. To Andrew the old lady looked very drawn and shrivelled.

'Poor old thing,' he thought. 'She senses something is badly wrong but I don't think she knows the truth.'

Andrew's attention was then drawn to the men helping Doug. Two of these were uniformed police officers and Doug was vehemently shaking his head and pointing off northwards. 'He's trying to wriggle off the hook,' Andrew decided.

But how much to tell, and to whom? Andrew knew that the whole story was going to cause a lot of pain and heartache. That was something he had no wish to do, particularly to Muriel. Even his strong desire to see justice done was tested by that. He also realized that a lot of it would be- could easily be- denied. 'It will be an our-word-against-your-word situation,' he thought. 'I think I will say as little as possible,' he decided.

The small aft deck was quite crowded by then- three Volunteer Coastguards, two policemen, the Murchisons, Andrew and Carmen, their father, plus the two T.Is and Doug. The captain of the launch addressed them all, saying loudly, "You people are amazingly lucky. That helicopter was looking for the white launch. When they didn't see one the pilot was going to turn around and go home but the observer wanted to see if he could spot the wreck of the *Merinda*. If they hadn't done a sweep around the reef looking for it they would not have seen you."

"Then we would have been dead," Andrew answered.

Muriel's mother glared at him from the opposite bench seat and snapped, "If you two hadn't dragged Muriel into this she wouldn't have been in any danger."

Anger at the injustice made Andrew smoulder but he held his tongue. 'She obviously doesn't know what went on,' he told himself.

But Carmen snapped back angrily, "We didn't drag her into anything. She and her friends kidnapped us at gun point and threatened to kill us if we didn't show them the wreck."

"Oh! How dare you say such things!" spluttered Muriel's mother.

Andrew saw Muriel go pale and shake her head in misery. Again he said nothing until his father said, "Well, what did happen? Speak up Andrew."

Andrew didn't want to but he could see that his father was angry. His father went on, "We have been searching for you two all night and I have been worried sick. It was only this morning when a fisherman told us he had seen you two go on board that white launch that we had any clue. So what happened?"

"We were tricked into going aboard and then held at gunpoint," Andrew replied unhappily.

At that Doug cried, "Oh, you were not! I asked you to come and talk to Muriel and you agreed to join us."

Carmen exploded with anger. "That is not true! You tied us up and said you would kill us if we did not help. We spent all night tied to those bunks with you guarding us. I was terrified. I was sure that Trevor was going to do what he said."

"Oh, you liar!" Doug shouted.

At that Carmen, who had been shaking with emotion, burst into tears. The older of the policemen, a senior sergeant, now asked, "Where is the white launch, the *Silver Stingray*?"

Doug pointed north but said nothing. On the sergeant looking at him Andrew said, "He left us in the water."

"Did you see him go? Did he say anything?" the sergeant asked.

Andrew shook his head. "No. That is what Muriel told me. The launch was gone when I got to the surface."

That turned all eyes on Muriel, which was not what Andrew wanted. She nodded and mumbled, "That's right. When I surfaced Trevor asked if we had ... had... had.. er found any gold in the wreck. When I said no he just drove off."

"Is there gold in the wreck?" the sergeant asked.

The questioning was now taking a line Andrew did not like but he realized that he would have to reveal part of the truth. 'Divers are going to find Grandad's body,' he thought.

The sergeant looked from one to the other. It was Carmen who answered him. "I didn't go far into the strong room but Andrew did. He said there wasn't any."

All eyes now switched to Andrew. He was horribly aware of Muriel's wide eyes and pleading look. He was also conscious of the way Old Mr Murchison was staring at him. The old man looked very tired and drawn. 'Haggard,' Andrew told himself. 'His guilty conscience is eating him up.' He said, "There is at least one gold ingot in there," he replied. "I found it when I was trying to find my torch."

Old Mr Murchison gave a sort of croak and said, "So you searched the strong room?"

Andrew nodded and met the old man's eyes. 'He murdered my grandfather,' he thought, his anger again rising as he suffered vivid flashbacks of being trapped in the strong room. "Yes, I did," he replied in a hard voice. "And I found my grandfather's body."

There was a shocked gasp from Carmen, a wail and sob from Muriel, and a muttered prayer from Grandma Murchison. Muriel's father looked puzzled and angry. He asked, "What do you mean? What are you saying? Your grandfather was lost in a shipwreck. How could he be here?"

Andrew met Mr Murchison's angry glare with a level, cool stare and pointed to Old Mr Murchison. "Ask him. He knows what really happened, and it wasn't a shipwreck."

"What are you saying? How dare you imply? What...?" Mr Murchison spluttered.

But Andrew had seen the old man seem to shrink and his eyes flinch. Without taking his eyes off him Andrew bent down and groped in the zip pocket of his BCD and pulled out the wrist watch. As he opened his hand every eye was upon him. He held out his hand with the silver watch on it.

"I'd say it once had a leather wrist strap," Andrew said. Then he turned the watch over and rubbed at the slime on the back. As he did both Carmen and his father leaned over to look. As the engraved letters became visible Carmen let out a shocked gasp and his father released a long hiss of air.

On the back of the watch was engraved:

H. W. Collins
with love
Xmas 44
Lilly

"My father's watch!" Andrew's father cried in shocked amazement as he took it from Andrew's hand and held it up. He then turned a puzzled look at Andrew. "You say his body is there?"

Andrew shuddered as intense images of him crunching the brittle bones and of seeing the slime festooned skull raced through his mind. He nodded and said, "Yes. In his diving suit, big brass helmet and all. I saw his skeleton- touched it."

"But.. but.. but how did he get there?" Mr Collins asked. He turned to Old Mr Murchison and gave him a puzzled look. The old man seemed to hunch even more and a look that Andrew thought could only be called haunted crossed his face. Andrew's father went on, speaking loudly at Old Mr Murchison. "You said you did not find the wreck of the *Merinda*. You said the *Deeral* sank after hitting a reef in a storm. Yet she was found miles from here, scuttled at Cape Upstart. So how did my father come to be here?"

Old Mr Murchison did not answer but Carmen spoke up, looking accusingly at him. "We were right. You killed the others and took the gold. Then you sank the *Deeral*."

Old Mr Murchison made no reply but Mr Murchison did. "How dare you make accusations like that! What proof do you have? Your grandfather could have died in an accident."

That was too much for Andrew. "He didn't," he said coldly. "His air hose was cut and he was left locked inside the strong room."

"Oh, this is outrageous!" Mr Murchison spluttered angrily. He shook his head and looked from his father to the police sergeant, then back at Andrew. Finally he looked down at his father. "Dad, tell them the truth. Say you did not do such a thing."

All eyes turned to Old Mr Murchison. The old man sat, staring into the distance. Then he shook his head sadly and struggled to his feet. "The Bible has a quote, I think, that says, 'Be sure your sin will find you out.' And it has!"

There was a tense silence. Muriel began to sob and Andrew saw that Grandma Murchison was looking up at her husband with an agonized appeal on her face. Then Old Mr Murchison turned to Andrew and croaked, "It is true. I killed him. And I killed the two Torres Strait Islanders as well. And all for greed."

There was another shocked silence and Andrew saw Grandma Murchison look at Old Mr Murchison aghast, confirming his suspicions that she had no idea. It made him feel very sorry for her. Old Mr Murchison took a deep breath, then went on, "We found the wreck easily, on the second day. We just followed a trail of flotsam and there she was with her masts and funnel sticking out of the water. The gold was there and easy to get at so we set to work and soon had it up on deck, all except one box which burst open."

He paused, shuddered and passed his hands over his eyes before going on. "Then the devil of temptation got me. Bert was right inside the strong room, bending to pick up that last ingot and I just pushed him off balance, then cut his air hose and safety line with my sheath knife. Then I closed the door and locked it. I don't know why I locked it- scared he might get out I suppose, even though I knew his helmet would have been full of water within seconds."

The audience looked sick and Andrew shuddered again. Old Mr Murchison then continued. "I tied his hose and line to a stanchion and then had myself hauled up. The two blacks were all excited and wanted to know what the problem was. I told them that Bert was snagged on some sharp steel. They tried to pull him up but couldn't so I sent one down to help him. Francis Sailboat it was. He just dived in- skindiving, you know, not in a suit like I was. I got the other fella, Solomon was his name, to get me out of my helmet and suit. As soon as he had he went to the side to talk to Francis."

Andrew pictured this and felt ill, knowing roughly what was coming. Old Mr Murchison went on, "Solomon went and leaned over the rail and spoke to Francis, who dived again. As soon as Francis was underwater I hit Solomon on the head with the big spanner we used to unscrew the nuts on the helmets. Then I waited till Francis came up and hit him on the head too, before he could get the water out of his eyes. He just sank out of sight and the current took him away."

At that Old Mr Murchison shuddered and staggered. He clutched at his son and the railing, then shook his head and sobbed. "Oh, it has haunted me all these years! None of it was worth it! It was just greed and then nightmares for sixty years! Horrible! But once I had started I had to go on. So I threw Solomon's body overboard and got away from there."

The shaking old man turned to Andrew. "You guessed right. I took the *Deeral* to Cape Upstart, anchored her and ferried all the gold and some supplies ashore, then scuttled her with explosives. Then I hid the gold and rowed the boat to Hayman Island and told that story."

Andrew nodded and said, "And you went back from time to time to get some of the gold, then pretended you had found it gold prospecting up in Cape York Peninsula."

Old Mr Murchison nodded. He then looked down at Grandma Murchison and croaked, "I'm sorry my dear. Forgive me!" Tears began to trickle down his face and he suddenly convulsed and crumpled up.

There followed a fluster of activity as he was carried into the cabin of the rescue launch. After a short consultation between the police sergeant, the captain of the launch, and Andrew's father, Andrew and Carmen were also taken inside. They were placed in a cabin by themselves and the launch got under way.

And that was really the end of it. Andrew only ever saw Muriel once more, when she and her family walked down the gangplank onto the jetty back in Bowen. She gave him one, hurt, resentful look, and then turned away. He was told that her family moved from Cairns soon after.

There was a delay in Bowen for two more days. During these the police, Carmen, their father and the two T.Is, went back out to the wreck. Andrew refused to go. He spent the day in a motel room or walking the streets of the town. Out at the wreck the police divers and Carmen went into the strong room. Carmen went first and took photos. Then they recovered the remains of their grandfather, and his diving suit, plus the gold ingot. Andrew would not have anything to do with that gold either. It was given to Moses and Jordan to pay for the trip expenses.

Nor would Andrew explain how he had come to be trapped in the strong room. Carmen knew but her story was not enough, without his evidence, to bring Muriel to trial for attempted murder. As Carmen wouldn't testify against Doug, he wasn't charged with anything either and soon slipped away to a dive company in the Caribbean.

Trevor and his launch were located but he claimed he did not desert them. He insisted he left them safe at the buoy while he went searching for Doug and Carmen. There just wasn't enough evidence to charge him either, so amid the fog of accusations and denials he managed to slip off the hook too. He sailed away for foreign parts unknown soon after.

Old Mr Murchison did not live to come to trial. He was hospitalised and there made a full confession. Soon after that he suffered a heart attack and died.

So Andrew and Carmen were a week late back to school and had many stories to tell.

There was finally a decent Christian funeral for Bert Collins. During it Andrew wept and gripped his Gran, who was so immensely relieved to get closure. It made Andrew very proud to come from such a good family and he vowed to always try to live up to the family name, and to be brave and honourable. He also made a secret resolution to avoid going diving ever again- unless duty or obligation required it.

Enjoy more C.R. Cummings stories

The Cadet Under~Officer
by C.R. Cummings
The Army Cadet series

DoctorZed Publishing
www.doctorzed.com

ISBN: 978-0-9875975-5-7
2nd edition 2013

Available in print and ebook.

Fifteen-year-old Elizabeth has been handed a briefcase full of incriminating documents by her dying uncle, documents wanted by a gang of crooks. In desperation she flees into the bush, where she encounters seventeen-year-old Cadet Under-Officer Graham Kirk and his platoon of army cadets. Graham decides to hide Elizabeth until he can contact the authorities.

But how? And who can he trust? As the days go by the crooks become ever more desperate.

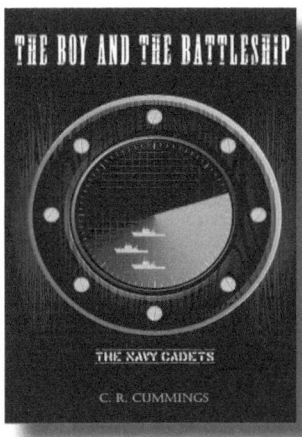

The Boy and the Battleship
by C.R. Cummings
The Navy Cadet series

DoctorZed Publishing
www.doctorzed.com

ISBN: 978-0-9875975-5-7
1st edition 2014

Available in print and ebook

Graham Kirk is nearly thirteen and about to discover the truth about friendship, navy cadetship... and girls. There is Margaret, who is two years his junior and who adores him; Cindy, who is two years older and offers real temptation; and Thelma, the object of his adoration and love.

As he struggles to mature and to achieve love, Graham finds himself torn by emotional conflicts and guilt. Graham struggles with serious moral issues such as sex, honesty and trust.

And there are sinister forces at work. Graham is unwittingly drawn into a desperate and dangerous situation—a US destroyer is due in port and an international terrorist organisation want to give the world a message: death.

The Word of God
by C.R. Cummings
The Army Cadet series

DoctorZed Publishing
www.doctorzed.com

ISBN: 978-0-9942084-4-6
2nd edition 2015

Available in print and ebook

The massive triangular mountain called Walsh Pyramid stands one thousand metres above the floodplain in Far North Queensland. Eight army cadets are hiking towards it, when they encounter a shadowy figure who tells them a tale so bizarre they find it difficult to believe. But not Stephen Bell. He knows it is true and urges the group to act immediately.

As they clamber up the mountain in a desperate race against time, they collide headlong with forces they barely imagined could exist.

Over the ensuing four days they are tested emotionally, spiritually and physically as they seek to vanquish the evil that lurks atop the mysterious pyramid.

An evil that knows no limits.

www.ingramcontent.com/pod-product-compliance
Lightning Source LLC
Chambersburg PA
CBHW051552250626

47157CB00001B/283

* 9 7 8 0 9 9 4 3 3 2 9 6 7 *